G000037559

This book is dedicated to my dad, Jim.
My hero.

The Flower Seller

ELLIE HOLMES

ELLIE HOLMES

The Flower Seller

Published by Ellie Holmes
ellieholmesauthor.co.uk

Print and distribution by IngramSpark
ISBN: 978-0-9934463-0-6
EBOOK ISBN: 978-0-9934463-1-3

JANUARY

Chapter One

Perhaps, if she was lucky, he wouldn't turn up. Jessie Martin looked towards the door of the burger bar as it opened. A gaggle of teenagers entered and her heart rate eased. She went back to nudging the plastic spoon round the cup of tea in front of her, watching the bubbles as they formed and joined before bursting at the cup's rim.

A waitress came to clear the neighbouring table. Jessie felt the weight of her stare, imagining herself through the young girl's eyes: a businesswoman who had wandered into the wrong world.

Jessie was the first to look away. It had been a mistake to choose this place. Her desire for anonymity had won out over common sense. This was a world where the manager was a boy no older than her own daughter and all the customers still had their mistakes ahead of them. Did they even know how lucky they were?

Conscious that the waitress was still watching, Jessie picked up her tea and blew on it, making the bubbles spin. Better to drink and risk being scalded than just sit and stare at it.

Beyond the plate-glass window the Essex market town of Abbeyleigh was in the icy grip of winter. It might have been lunchtime but the snow-filled clouds hung so low that the light was already leaching away. It was not a day to be outside and yet Jessie longed to rejoin the grim-faced people jousting with their umbrellas on the high street. Her desk, a sandwich and her paper had never seemed more inviting. *I'll give him one more minute.*

It had been her daughter Hannah's idea to put an advert in the *Abbeyleigh Gazette*. 'It's time to take yourself out of your comfort zone, Mum. Why don't you get Anne to give you a hand with the ad?'

Sucked into the vortex of her daughter's enthusiasm, Jessie had agreed before she could talk herself out of it.

'So, what have you got so far?' Anne had asked over margaritas in Spike's Bar.

'Newly single brunette, slim, attractive, early forties, non-smoker, good sense of humour, would like to meet man thirties/forties for friendship and maybe more,' Jessie read aloud.

Anne pretended to fall asleep and Jessie slapped her arm.

'Bit dull, sweetie!' Anne said with a smile. 'For starters, you should put early thirties. Everyone knocks a few years off. And do you really want to say slim? It's practically shorthand for flat-chested and you're not. How about "great figure" instead?'

'That's a bit conceited, isn't it?'

Anne threw her a look. 'It's an advert, Jessie. You're meant to be selling yourself.'

'Blimey! I'll just get some fishnets and a red light, shall I?'

'You know what I mean. You should put something in there about being outgoing. That usually leads to some interesting propositions.'

'But I'm not outgoing,' Jessie said.

'For goodness' sake, outgoing just means you're up for a bit of fun. I'm not suggesting for a moment that you put "open-minded". Now that would lead to some replies that would make your hair stand on end. And obviously your WLTM has to be a man in his late twenties or early thirties.'

'Has to be? This is my advert, remember? Not yours!'

Anne smirked. 'So you'd prefer "Recently dumped flat-chested brunette, early forties, lives life with the handbrake on, would like to meet man forties/fifties for visits to the library"?'

'I'd prefer not to be doing it at all.'

Anne squeezed her hand. 'I know, sweetie. And you can stick another pin in your effigy of William when you get home but right now we need to get you back out there before life passes you by.'

The day the advert went live, Anne had texted. *'I see you held on to the word "slim" and eschewed "outgoing", "adventurous" or "fun". You can lead a horse to water . . .'*

'I wanted the ad to have some integrity. I did put late thirties . . .'

'Well, I hope your integrity keeps you warm at night.'

Now, Jessie took another sip of her tea. The notion that a person could find love through an advert was, to her mind, faintly ridiculous. A second-hand car or a nice pine table maybe. But love? Most people went to parties, art galleries or museums. Only desperate people resorted to an advert in the paper.

But I am desperate. Desperately lonely. And my date, if he ever turns up, can't afford to be superior. After all, answering an ad is almost as bad as placing one.

Jessie's heart thumped at the prospect of coming face-to-face with the man she had so far only spoken to over the telephone. Barry Sturridge was a farmer two years her senior.

Would she like him? Would he like her? She tilted her cup and watched the tea pitch back and forth. What if they hit it off and a few weeks down the line they wanted to have sex? What would that first night be like with someone new?

She had been a teenager the last time she'd had first-night sex but the awkward excitement of it all was still terrifyingly real. And she hadn't had cellulite to worry about back then. She pushed the tea away.

Glancing at her wedding ring, Jessie silently berated her husband. *This is all your fault, William! I wouldn't be sitting here if you hadn't betrayed me. 'I'll love you forever,' that's what you said. And I believed you.*

Her anger spiked as she remembered the day William had left.

'What do you mean you won't give me a divorce?' he'd asked, dumbfounded.

They had been standing in the hall of The Lodge, the home they had shared for a lifetime, surrounded by the boxes he'd spent the morning packing.

'I don't want to,' Jessie had told him, watching with satisfaction as his shock had turned to anger.

'But what's the point in hanging on?'

'Because I can. You can have your divorce when I'm ready and not before.'

The burger bar smelt of frying onions and damp clothes. The windows were fogged with condensation and Jessie could feel the heat prickle between her shoulder blades and in the small of her back. Behind her, the teenagers were laughing loudly. Hannah would be proud of her; she was about as far out of her comfort zone as it was possible to get.

Jessie checked her watch. He wasn't coming. Her heart rate increased, but this time with relief. She was pulling on her coat when the door opened and a heavyset man walked in carrying a bouquet of flowers.

'Jessica Martin?'

Jessie hesitated. The teenagers were snickering. 'Yes,' she said.

The man thrust a meaty hand towards her. 'Barry Sturridge,' he said. His grin revealed a chipped front tooth. 'I bet you'd just about given up on me. Blasted traffic in the high street! I've abandoned the pickup in a loading bay.' He had a full head of sandy hair made curly by the snow and a kindly face. 'These are for you.'

Jessie shrugged out of her coat and took the bouquet. Five long-stemmed red roses had been expertly set off by sprays of gypsophila and hand-tied with raffia. Jessie carefully laid the exquisite bouquet on the table. A pool of water immediately formed beneath the stems.

She gave him a smile. 'They're beautiful. Thank you.'

It was a filthy day and, even though he'd been running late, he had paused to choose a bouquet as lovely as this one. Jessie was touched.

In her opinion, when it came to relationships, there were three types of people: the bottom dwellers, the skimmers and the ones who dived for pearls. Jessie was a pearl diver. Was it asking too much to hope that Barry Sturridge would be a pearl diver too?

'Do you want anything to eat, Jessie?'

She thought about the sandwich waiting for her back at the office and shook her head.

'I'll just grab myself a burger, if you don't mind?'

'Of course not.'

A few minutes later, Barry returned to their table. 'I wanted to change but I didn't get the chance,' he said.

He was dressed in a pair of muddy boots and his check shirt, jeans and anorak had all seen better days. Jessie wasn't sure if his reddening face was from the heat of the burger bar or embarrassment at his clothes. In case it was the latter she said, 'I didn't expect you to.' She covered her lie with a smile as she watched him take a large bite out of his burger.

'You look great,' he said as he flicked open a can of Coke. He took a long drink.

'Thank you.' She was wearing her favourite navy dress from Jigsaw.

'Next time we meet, let's make it an evening,' he said.

There was going to be a next time? They both looked away. Her mother had always told her to go to the cinema on a first date. 'That way, if the conversation flags later, you can talk about the film.' Dear old Mum, God rest her soul. What would she have made of her daughter advertising in a lonely hearts column?

'About the ad . . .' Jessie faltered.

'Your first time?'

His gentle smile undid a couple of the knots in her stomach. 'Yes.'

'My second,' he said. 'My sister-in-law, Shelley, is bugging me to try internet dating. It's a bit high-tech for me,' he admitted with a smile. 'You any good with computers?'

'Not bad.'

'You said on the phone that you're a solicitor.'

Jessie nodded. She'd made a joke out of it by saying 'somebody has to be'. The legal profession got such a bad press. She'd discovered long ago that it was better to tell people what she did in a light-hearted way, as if to say, 'Look, we really do have a sense of humour. It's not removed at birth like you thought.'

'I handle the buying and selling of houses and land,' Jessie said, waiting for Barry's eyes to glaze over. She was pleasantly surprised, however, when he smiled.

'I might be able to put some work your way. Arthur Cantor's breaking up Blackcurrant Farm. Dad's buying some of the fields. Once he and Arthur are through haggling, we'll need someone to do the paperwork.' Tomato sauce dripped over Barry's fingers as he spoke. He brought his mouth down to lick the sauce then, catching her eye, searched instead for a paper napkin.

Touched that he was trying to make a good impression and eager to put him out of his misery, Jessie pushed her own napkin towards him.

Barry gave her a grateful smile. 'Thanks. Which firm is it you work for again?'

'Smith Mathers.' Jessie thought about giving him one of her business cards but it seemed pompous, and anyway they were all in her married name of Goode.

Drips of sauce and pieces of fried onion spattered down into the burger carton. Jessie watched as Barry dipped his fries in the sauce. If he was nervous, he certainly wasn't letting it get in the way of a good meal. Jessie heard her stomach growl.

'Been there long?' he asked between mouthfuls.

'Since my daughter started school.'

'How old is she now?'

'Eighteen. She's at Exeter University.'

Jessie remembered how excited Hannah had been in September as they'd packed. There had been no trace of the anxiety that she herself had felt. But then Hannah threw herself body and soul into everything she did; her father's daughter.

'You must miss her.'

'Dreadfully.'

While it was true Hannah would always have her room at The Lodge, it would be unlikely to ever be her home again. Jessie had yet to grow accustomed to the sadness that always accompanied that thought. Part of her hoped she never would.

In her daughter's absence, Jessie had taken over the desk in Hannah's bedroom, preferring to work there, rather than in the study. It was one of the rituals she'd adopted to sidestep her loneliness, like the radio playing softly in the background and the two glasses of wine each evening that helped her to sleep.

'Have you got a picture of her?'

Jessie plucked her favourite photo from her purse. It showed Hannah lying on her stomach on the lower lawn at The Lodge, her dark hair falling around her shoulders, as she laughed up at the camera. 'That was taken just before she went to Exeter.'

Barry carefully wiped his fingers before he took the photograph. 'Pretty girl. Obviously takes after her mum. What's she studying?'

Heat flamed in Jessie's cheeks at the unexpected compliment. 'Law. She's got her heart set on being a criminal lawyer, like her father. Conveyancing isn't glamorous enough for her.'

'Your ad said "newly single" . . .' Barry took a swig of his Coke.

'Yes.' There were cramps in her stomach. Jessie tried in vain to compose herself but tiny daggers pierced her heart as she said, 'My husband met someone he wanted to be with more than me.'

Barry's eyes softened. 'I'm sorry.'

If there was one thing Jessie had come to detest, more than the tart who had stolen her husband, it was sympathy. 'You don't need to be sorry. I'm fine,' she said airily. This wasn't completely true. She was more a work in progress but he didn't need to know that.

It had taken Jessie four months to accept that William would not be coming home. In that time copious bottles of red had been drunk, an ocean of tears wept and the crotch of the remainder of William's trousers removed, the latter two occurring mostly after the wine had been drunk.

By New Year's Day even she was bored with her own self-pity and, drawing strength from Hannah, who had been her rock throughout, Jessie had made the decision to start over. She had thrown away the rest of William's clothes and composed a list of New Year's resolutions: get a divorce, get a promotion, get a life.

'At first, I was going to make him wait for the divorce but then I realised I'd be hurting myself as much as him. I need to move on and the divorce will help me do that.'

'Is your husband at the same firm?' Barry asked.

'Yes.'

'That must be tough.'

Jessie nodded. For months she had stoically endured the hushed conversations and sympathetic smiles of staff and partners alike, their embarrassment equalled only by her own.

'Will you carry on working together?'

Jessie nodded. 'We both have too much to lose to walk away. I'm hoping to be promoted to a salaried partner this summer and William's an equity partner.'

Jessie pictured her younger self splashing champagne into two glasses. 'I propose a toast, to the man who has gone from being an associate, to a partner, to an equity partner, faster than any lawyer in the history of Smith Mathers: my gorgeous husband.'

She pushed the memory aside and took a sip of cold tea.

'What's the difference between a salaried partner and an equity partner?' Barry asked.

'An equity is someone who's invested their own money in the firm and receives a share of the profits. A salaried partner is a member of the partnership who hasn't yet been invited to make that investment.'

The conversation stalled. It had seemed easier when they'd spoken on the telephone. Without a photograph to go on, Jessie had listened to Barry's country accent and coloured in rugged film star good looks. The reality had left her somewhat deflated. She wondered if he felt the same. At least the word 'slim' in her advert should have warned him not to expect a double D cup.

Jessie watched as Barry finished his burger and rolled the paper napkin into a ball before stuffing it into the carton that had contained the fries.

'I like motocross,' he began suddenly. 'Anything with engines really.'

Jessie found herself tuning him out. Of the many reactions she had thought she might encounter today, boredom had not been one of them.

'There's a race over at Penkins' farm on the other side of Stebbingsford on Sunday. Me and my brother Mark'll be going. You're welcome to come along. Shelley will be there.'

'Thank you. But I might have to work this weekend,' she said apologetically.

'Working unsocial hours is one of the things we have in common then.'

'I suppose so.' Jessie forced a smile. *The only thing.* She stared at the table disconsolately. *At least I can stop worrying about first-night sex for a while.*

'My cousin, Jen, is getting married Saturday week. Would you like to be my plus one? Better than standing in a muddy field watching motocross.' He smiled self-deprecatingly. 'The reception will be at the Northey Hotel. It'll give you a chance to talk to Dad about Blackcurrant Farm.'

Jessie swallowed the polite refusal she had been about to utter and reminded herself that Barry's dad, Sam Sturridge, was the president of the Abbeyleigh and Stebbingsford Farmers' Club. Bagging him would be a popular move with the partners. 'Thank you.'

'You're up at The Lodge, aren't you? The fancy house on the hill, out towards Abbey Wood?'

Jessie nodded. She had never thought of The Lodge as a fancy house before. It was just home.

Barry stood. 'I'm sorry but I've got to get back,' he said. 'It was nice meeting you, Jessie.' He held out his hand and she shook it firmly.

'And you.' Pulling on her coat, Jessie swung the bouquet into her arms, a handy barrier in case he had any ideas about kissing her.

The glorious heads of the roses nodded as she hooked her bag over her shoulder. *No man could choose such stunning flowers and not have at least a little beauty in his soul*, Jessie thought and her feelings towards Barry softened. 'Thanks again for the flowers.'

'I'm glad you liked them. I asked the flower seller to pick out something nice.'

Chapter Two

The firm of Smith Mathers solicitors was based in three large converted houses, a ten-minute walk from Abbeyleigh High Street.

The glass-panelled door of Jessie's office rattled as she kicked it shut. Shrugging off her coat, she stood her flowers in the corner of the room. She'd hoped for a spark this lunchtime, even though the idea of it had terrified her. Deflated she sat at her desk and tried to console herself with the thought that Sam Sturridge would be an impressive addition to her client list. It didn't help. Her bottom line had not been her primary concern this lunch hour. Her bottom line couldn't make her laugh like William used to.

Jessie flicked on her desk lamp. Her bottom line was much more likely to make her cry. A tide of panic rose within her as she surveyed the Post-it notes covering her desk: messages from her secretary, Susan.

Unprompted, a memory of a conversation she had shared with William the previous winter floated into her mind.

'Why, after all this time, do you want to be made a partner?' he'd asked, dumbfounded. 'We have a lovely home, a great standard of living. Isn't that enough for you?'

'When we first qualified as lawyers, do you remember how we'd map out our careers: partners within five years, equities within seven? All those things happened for you but they didn't happen for me,' Jessie had responded.

'You wanted to stay at home with Hannah until she started school.'

'Yes, I did. And I was happy to work part-time while she was at school. But Hannah will be off to uni later this year. It's time for me to get on with the next phase of my life and being made a partner is number one on my list.'

'It'll be a hell of a slog. Of twenty-one fee earners you're nineteenth on annual billing. Why should the firm give you a partnership? Where's the incentive? Why don't you save yourself the hassle and forget about it?'

'I'm not afraid of hard work.'

'I'll remind you of that when you're complaining there aren't enough hours in the day.'

He had reminded her. Constantly. And then he'd stopped reminding her and found solace in the tart's arms.

With a sigh, Jessie grabbed a file. She had paid a high price for the pursuit of her promotion. Too high to let it end in failure.

The telephone rang.

'Hello?'

'Your daughter for you.'

'Hello, Mum.'

'Hello, sweetheart.' Jessie's gaze settled on the photograph of Hannah that stood on the shelf above her computer. 'How are you?'

'I'm fine. More importantly, how are you? What was he like?'

That was Hannah. Straight to the point. 'Tall. A little overweight. Blond hair. Blue eyes,' Jessie responded, aping her daughter's style.

'He sounds great. How did it go?'

'He was nice enough but we didn't have anything in common.' Jessie stared at the flowers. Even in shadow, they looked dazzling. At least the flower seller had good taste.

'Did you try?'

'Yes. He asked me to a motocross event on Sunday.'

'Are you going?'

'No.'

'You said you wanted to develop new interests.'

'I don't call standing in a field in the freezing cold developing new interests. The only thing I'm likely to develop there is pneumonia. Anyway, I said I'd go to his cousin's wedding. The family are buying some land. He wants me to do the conveyancing. If nothing else, I'll get a new client out of it.'

'How many men did you go out with before you met Daddy?'

'Three.'

'Another two to go then.'

Jessie looked up as the door opened. 'Damn it, William! You could knock.'

'You expect me to knock when my princess is on the phone?' William sat on the edge of the desk and treated Jessie to his best megawatt smile as she handed over the receiver. 'Hello, princess. How's the prettiest and smartest undergraduate in the country?'

William was wearing his charcoal suit, Jessie noticed. The one she'd bought him. He had christened it his lucky suit because whenever he wore it to court he won. Jessie wondered if he'd been wearing it the night he met the tart.

She tried to be objective as she studied him. His eyes were dark, his skin tanned from the recent winter holiday he had taken with the tart and there was no hint of grey in his thick dark hair. The bastard! So much for being objective.

The lights flickered. Jessie glanced outside. The snow was coming down hard once more. She watched it settle on her blue Renault Clio. The bonnet of William's sporty black Jag was almost as long as her entire car.

Barely two years old, the Jag was William's pride and joy. Jessie well remembered the heated conversations that had led up to its purchase. She had wanted him to go for something more conservative. As usual, he'd listened to what she had to say and then done exactly what he wanted.

She had never been able to stay angry with William for long, she realised. He had always succeeded in talking her round. Except last year, when he'd told her about the tart and hadn't even tried.

In public William could be arrogant but he rarely let it spill over into his private life; the arrogance was simply part of the uniform adopted by a criminal lawyer, like the suit and the briefcase.

'I'm going to be dealing with cons who've been criminals all their lives; how are they going to trust a young buck like me unless I come across as fearless and in control?'

Only Jessie had known how violently ill William had been before his first appearance in court. And only she had been able to appreciate the terrific high he had felt when he'd emerged triumphant.

He had stopped being sick many years before but the highs remained. She didn't share them any longer. She only got the arrogance. The public face. The highs belonged to the tart now, the hugs too.

She turned back from the window as William finished his conversation with Hannah. 'Love you, sweetheart. I'll pass you back to Mummy.'

'I stopped being Mummy when she was eight years old,' Jessie said dryly. 'Bye, darling.'

William waited for her to replace the receiver. 'Did you enjoy yourself on the third of December?' It was his court voice, pleasant but with a hint of steel beneath.

Unperturbed, Jessie began to play back her voicemail. 'I have no idea what you're talking about.'

William stabbed the stop button on the telephone. 'Let me refresh your memory,' he said tersely. 'According to Susan you spent the day in the West End, Christmas shopping.'

Jessie's pen hovered over her notepad. 'You clearly have nothing better to do with your time than check up on me. While I, on the other hand, am extremely busy, so if you don't mind . . .' She indicated the door.

'I do mind.' William folded his arms.

'I'm assuming you have a good reason for checking up on me?'

William stood. 'I've got three thousand five hundred and forty-six good reasons, darling,' he said, his voice heavy with sarcasm. 'You went shopping with our credit card.' He laid the statement on the desk.

'The accused was seen exiting a shop with a large number of bags. Exhibit A, I presume,' Jessie said, amused.

'Joke all you want.' William jabbed at the statement with his finger. 'If you think I'm paying half of this, you've got another thing coming. I'm happy to pay half of Hannah's expenses and half of the bills for The Lodge, but we agreed that card was for essential items only.' William snatched the statement up and leaned across the desk towards her. 'This is taking the piss.'

'So was emptying our joint account to buy a house for you and your tart without speaking to me first, but that didn't stop you.' Jessie sat back, unfazed. 'Besides, Christmas presents are essential items.'

William's expression was stony. 'If you tell me what you bought for yourself, I'll decide whether or not the items were essential. Everything else you can pay for.' He threw the statement into her lap and folded his arms once more.

Jessie could see the impatience shooting from his eyes and took a moment to smooth out a crease in her dress. 'I bought a couple of pairs of shoes, two suits, some sexy underwear and a bottle of perfume. All essential.' She levelled her gaze at him. 'Especially the underwear and the perfume.'

She saw him glance at the flowers in the corner.

'I'll give you seven hundred,' he said tersely. 'But next time you go on a spending spree use your own card.'

Jessie pulled a face. 'It's so much more enjoyable when I know it's partly your money I'm spending.' She waited for the muscle in his cheek to start twitching the way it always did when he was trying to hold his anger at bay. She didn't have to wait long.

'Kicking me in the wallet makes us even, does it?' His north London accent grew stronger. 'Have you any idea how hard it is to keep two households going? You can't throw bills at me like this and expect me to find the money.'

Jessie laid down her pen. 'Finding the money didn't seem to be a problem a few months ago,' she said quietly, her eyes hardening. 'You see, darling –' she invested the word with as much venom as he had – 'I rang the credit card company and asked them for copies of our statements. They made interesting reading. There was the jewellers' bill that came to over two thousand pounds, theatre tickets, hotel bills.' Each statement was imprinted on her mind: dates, places, amounts: the history of her husband's affair. 'I could go on.'

William massaged his forehead. 'Don't.'

'We celebrated our tenth wedding anniversary before I owned the kind of jewellery you lavished on her in the first month. Didn't your conscience tweak just a little at that?' She tossed the statement back at him.

'When we were first together, I wasn't earning the kind of money that allowed me to buy you gifts,' he said evenly. 'Give me a divorce, Jess. Let's have a clean break so we both know where we stand.' He swept up the statement and marched to the door. 'I'll pay half this time. But I want the credit limit lowered.'

'Impossible,' Jessie called after him. 'I can't manage on anything less.'

She allowed herself a brief moment of satisfaction. It wasn't much of a victory but at least she'd put him in a bad mood and these days that was good enough.

With a sigh she went back to listening to her voicemail messages as she wolfed down a cheese sandwich. As she deleted the last message she glanced up to find her senior partner, Walt, standing in the doorway. He was clutching a printout.

'Is this a bad time?'

'No, of course not.' She chased breadcrumbs from her mouth.

'I need a quick chat.'

'No problem.'

She rose, preparing to follow him back to his office.

'Here is fine.' He closed the door and Jessie's heart sank. When the senior partner came to you it meant only one thing: bad news.

She quickly moved a pile of files to free up a chair, cringing inwardly as she went back to her seat. Walt was no doubt taking in the chaos of her office and comparing it to his own, which was always as neat as a pin.

'Do you need another filing cabinet?' Walt asked mildly.

Jessie forced a smile. What she really needed was another pair of hands but sadly that wasn't something you could tick on a stationery list. 'It's been a particularly busy week.'

'Really?'

The hook of his left eyebrow told her all she needed to know. Jessie braced herself for what was coming.

'I like you, Jessie. I always have. But your billing figures are causing the partners some concern. I know you were hoping to be made a partner later this year but on the strength of these figures –' he brandished the printout – 'I'm afraid it's not going to happen.'

Jessie searched for something positive to say. 'I've taken on a lot of new work and I'm busier than ever . . .'

Walt nodded. 'I can see how hard you're working, Jessie. Nobody here is doubting your work ethic. My goodness, you're here most mornings before eight. I often see the light on in your office after seven in the evenings. If anything your hours are causing me as much concern as your figures. No one can sustain hours like that and hope to have anything like a decent work–life balance.'

Jessie's tongue clove to the roof of her mouth with sudden fear. He wasn't here to fire her, was he? 'I'm not sure I understand . . .'

'You've had a lot to cope with this past year. William leaving. Hannah going off to university. I wonder if now is the right time to be putting yourself under this much pressure.'

She saw him glance at the flowers in the corner.

'I think perhaps it would be sensible to put your partnership ambitions on hold for another year and try again when your private life has settled down.'

Jessie took a moment to recalibrate. All right, he wasn't sacking her but the relief she should have been feeling was negated not only by what he was saying but the sympathetic tone he was using to say it.

'My private life doesn't impact on my work,' she said firmly.

He hooked his eyebrow once more. 'I heard you and William arguing a few minutes ago.'

Jessie balled her fists beneath the desk. 'I'm sorry. That was unprofessional. I won't let it happen again.'

'I can have a word with William, if you'd like me to.'

'Thank you but that won't be necessary.'

Walt nodded. 'There is no doubt you have increased your billing. You're on target to rise from nineteenth to sixteenth and that's admirable, Jessie. It really is, particularly given all the upheaval you've faced at home, but it's below where the partners would expect you to be for them to be able to offer you a partnership.'

'Where do you expect me to be?'

'You should be aiming for twelfth.'

'What sort of figure would I need to bill to be twelfth?' she asked, careful not to show her dismay.

He handed over the printout.

The bottom fell out of Jessie's world as she studied the figures. They might as well ask for the moon and the stars. In fact, they were asking for them. Never mind an extra filing cabinet, she'd need to find room for a bed because she would never be going home again.

'You don't reach that figure by working harder,' Walt said as if reading her mind. 'You reach it by working smarter. Yes, you need to increase your client base but crucially you need to increase the quality of your client base. You need to go out and source high-value clients who will give you repeat business. At partner level it's as much about networking as practising law.

'I think you'll make a fine partner one day, Jessie. I'm just not sure you're going to make the grade this summer. Give yourself another year to achieve your goal, that would be my advice.' Walt stood. 'You're a good lawyer, Jessie. Smith Mathers are lucky to have you.'

'Thank you.'

'And if I catch you here before eight in the morning or after seven at night again on anything more than one day a week, I will throw you out of the office! Remember what I said, smarter not harder.'

Jessie nodded. 'I'll try.'

Walt walked to the door. 'In case you were wondering, William wasn't party to the partners' discussions about your billing figures. He took the decision to step out of our meeting at that point.'

'Thank you for letting me know.'

After Walt closed the door, Jessie fashioned the printout into a paper plane and launched it across the room. It landed in the tangled leaves of her spider plant and dangled precariously for a moment before plummeting into the bin.

Well, that just about sums things up.

At least William had had the decency to excuse himself from the discussions about her.

She picked up the business card Anne Jacobs had given her before Christmas. 'His name's Nick Atkins. He's absolutely bloody fantastic. Mild-mannered, diffident even, but actually he's a wolf in Armani. He did my last two divorces.'

Jessie pulled the telephone towards her. Her hopes of a promotion might be in the balance but there was nothing to stop her fulfilling her first New Year's resolution. It was time to get a divorce.

FEBRUARY

Chapter Three

As befitting an equity partner in a major London law firm, Nick Atkins' office contained many personal items of furniture rather than the standard office issue. Jessie scanned the room. It was clearly designed to put clients at their ease, from the comfortable leather chairs to the pot plants on the windowsill, although the box of tissues showed that it didn't always work.

Sleet spat out of the leaden sky and in an attempt to hold the resulting gloom at bay every light in the office blazed. Jessie sipped her tea as Nick read the papers she'd brought with her. Reducing her life with William to a couple of pages of figures had been a painful process.

Jessie diverted her gaze from the paperwork to the bone china cup and saucer she was holding in her lap. The cup was decorated with hand-painted pink peonies. Jessie was in awe of the artist's skill. The china was so fine it was almost translucent. It hardly seemed robust enough to hold scalding liquid and yet clearly it was stronger than it looked. And that's how I must be. Robust.

Nick put the papers aside. 'Tell me about you and William.'

'What do you want to know?' Jessie replaced her cup in the saucer. It went down harder than she'd intended, betraying her own fragility.

'How did you and William meet?'

'We met at university. We were both studying law.'

The cup rattled in her lap. Jessie stood it on the edge of Nick's desk.

'Were you a team?'

'Absolutely.'

'What did you admire about him?'

'His courage and his integrity. If he says he's going to do something, he does it.'

'Would you say he was an honourable man?'

Jessie pulled a face. 'I might have once.'

'And what did he admire in you, do you think?'

She frowned. 'My honesty. My tenacity. My compassion.'

'And why did you make a good team?'

Jessie thought for a moment. 'We balanced one another out. When I got too serious he would joke me out of it. When he got too impetuous, I'd rein him in. My patience countered his impatience, my empathy softened his cynicism and his fearlessness gave me courage.' Jessie took a sip of her tea. 'I thought I was coming here for a divorce not a counselling session.'

Nick laughed. 'Sometimes it amounts to the same thing. I like to get a handle on my opponent and the best way to do that is ask the person who shared their life with them. If one is going to successfully fillet a fish, one first needs to know where the bones are.'

Jessie was taken aback. 'I'm not sure I want to fillet him.'

'That's noble of you.'

'Not what you normally hear?' Jessie asked.

'No.' Nick smiled. 'Most of my clients who find themselves in a position similar to yours wish to seek financial revenge in recompense for the emotional betrayal they've suffered. A more level-headed approach is refreshing.'

Jessie smiled. 'I'm no saint. Believe me I've had my fair share of moments when I wanted to take William to the cleaners. But when all this is over he'll still be Hannah's father and we'll still have to work together. If, with your help, we can bring things to a conclusion fairly and without rancour, William and I have more chance of forging a civil post-divorce relationship.'

'Far be it from me to talk myself out of work, Jessie, but do you even need me? Perhaps a meeting with a trained mediator may be more appropriate.'

'I appreciate your candour but mediation isn't really William's style.'

'He's used to getting his own way?'

Jessie nodded. 'That's why I came to you. I want to cover all the angles.'

Nick smiled. 'Spoken like a lawyer. Have you discussed the divorce with him?'

'We've talked about it in general terms,' Jessie replied. 'To start with, William was full of remorse and eager to soothe his conscience. He's a keen amateur cricketer. He assured me he'd play a "straight bat" with me. Then, in November last year, he practically emptied our joint savings account without speaking to me first. I think he was being put under pressure by the . . . other woman. They were buying a house together.'

'How much did he take?'

'One hundred and twenty K. He justified it by saying we'd even things up when we divorced . . .'

'But you don't trust him to do that?'

Jessie stared at her lap. 'Trust is a little hard to come by lately.'

'I understand,' Nick said gently.

'We've kept our joint credit card going because William wanted to pay half the bills for The Lodge until a final settlement was agreed. I insisted that I must also be allowed to put some personal expenditure on the card as a result of him denuding our savings account and he agreed albeit reluctantly. He is, however, becoming increasingly tetchy about the credit card bills. Now, every time we speak, which admittedly isn't often, we end up rowing.'

Nick nodded. 'People start out with the best of intentions, then when they get down to brass tacks, pride takes over, followed by an unwillingness to give way. Attitudes harden and before you know where you are you are at each other's throats.'

'Sounds familiar,' Jessie admitted ruefully.

Nick unscrewed the cap of his fountain pen. 'Why don't you tell me what you want from this? What constitutes a fair settlement to you?'

'I want to keep The Lodge and I want William to repay half the money he took.'

Nick considered the figures in front of him. 'Taking into account all the other assets you and William hold, that falls some way short of the fifty–fifty split you'd be entitled to after a marriage as long as yours,' he said. 'On what you are proposing it's more like sixty–forty in William's favour,' he added.

'I know.'

Nick sat back in his chair regarding her. 'You're an associate with Smith Mathers. Would it be fair to say if you had worked full-time you might well have achieved equity status as William has?'

'I believe so,' Jessie agreed.

'And if you had worked full-time, as William has, your pension fund would have been commensurate with his. As it is, you took time off to care for your daughter and your pension pot is considerably smaller as a result. I could make a very good case for a pension-sharing order against William's pension in addition to The Lodge being signed over to you. It may not be what you want but it would be remiss of me not to make you aware of the possibility.'

Jessie nodded. 'It's not a road I want to go down. William was devastated when his dad died last year. He started talking about taking early retirement. I don't know if he still intends to do that or not but I don't want to get in his way if he does. Unless . . .'

'Unless?' Nick looked up.

'William has always said that he will pay me back half of what he took from the savings account when The Lodge is sold but I don't want to sell The Lodge and I think that's where the sticking point will be.'

'Which is why you came to me?'

'Yes. I don't see why he can't release some of the equity in the property he purchased in North Street with her.'

Nick made a series of notes before giving Jessie a confident smile. 'Why don't we start with the petition? Did you bring your marriage certificate?'

Jessie nodded and drew it from her briefcase. She and William had been married on a sunny August day, two weeks after her birthday and two weeks before his.

'Jessica Frances Goode versus William Michael Goode and . . .'

'Chelsea Palmer,' Jessie said through gritted teeth. 'I don't know her middle name.'

Insulated from the hustle and bustle of the world outside, the room was very quiet. Jessie watched the ink flow from Nick's fountain pen as he filled in the petition. Every stroke another nail in the coffin of her marriage.

'Do you know the date on which he first committed adultery?'

'It was the second day of June.'

Nick consulted his papers. 'And the adultery is continuing at 24 North Street, Abbeyleigh?'

Jessie nodded. She could have been ordering a kitchen.

'And we want him to pay the costs of the divorce, obviously.'

'Yes.' *A kitchen would have been cheaper*, she mused as she took in the view of the Gherkin from Nick's office window.

Jessie looked down at her wedding ring. She didn't need to twist it off to recall the inscription inside: *Love always*.

Jessie grieved for the idealistic kids she and William had once been. Back then, unimpeded by fear, they had fallen swiftly in love, revelling in the fact that it had been the first time for either of them, living every love song they had ever heard, thinking it would last forever.

Now, a lifetime later, a piece of paper was going to record William's adultery as the reason the marriage had come to an end but had she been as much to blame?

She recalled a time the previous summer when she had been doing too much overtime. The extra hours had left her short-tempered and their sex life had suffered as a result. A month into their drought William had played a particularly hard-fought game of cricket. That evening in bed he'd reached over to stroke her arm.

'Would you give me a back rub?'

So exhausted she could barely keep her eyes open, Jessie had murmured, 'Not tonight. I'm too tired.'

'Please, honey, my back's sore.'

'There's gel in the bathroom cabinet.'

She had felt his body move closer to hers as he'd continued to stroke her arm.

'Jess . . .'

'For God's sake, will you stop pawing at me? You don't want a back rub at all, do you? You want sex. What part of "I'm too tired" didn't you understand?'

She cringed now as she remembered her words and the hurt look on William's face.

'For your information what I wanted was a back rub but as you've got a look on your face that could curdle milk, I'll do without it just like I've done without sex for the last six weeks.'

What he'd actually been craving was intimacy of any kind, she'd later realised. By denying him that, had she pushed him into the tart's arms? Where had her empathy been then?

'It's okay to have second thoughts, Jessie,' Nick said gently. 'You can abandon the petition. Think about it again in eighteen months. Then you could go for a no-fault divorce.'

Jessie shook her head. I may not have been everything William wanted me to be but that didn't give the treacherous bastard the right to absolve himself of our marriage vows. 'I'm prepared to be reasonable over the money but I wouldn't be sitting here at all if he hadn't committed adultery,' she said firmly. 'I want the petition to say he committed adultery.' *Love always – or at least until the decree absolute comes through.*

'Right.' Nick nodded. 'Let's move on to the finances.' He shuffled his papers. 'You and William each hold some shares and small sums in individual savings accounts. William has a higher-value car but you hold some nice pieces of jewellery. So far so even. William's pension pot is substantial as is his stake in Smith Mathers. Your pension pot is small by comparison and you have no stake in Smith Mathers. William has purchased a property in North Street partly funded by your joint savings and in addition you own The Lodge together, which is now mortgage free. Have I overlooked anything?'

'No.'

'And your red line is that you want The Lodge transferred into your sole name.'

'Yes.' A headache began to gnaw at her left temple.

Jessie remembered when she and William had first discovered The Lodge. They hadn't even intended to view it. The house had been outside their price range but William had pestered her into it and Jessie had acquiesced.

The house had won them over from the front steps. Once inside, they had run from room to room, excitedly making plans. It was only when they had stood at the window of the master bedroom that reality had stolen the smile from Jessie's face.

'We can't afford The Lodge.'

William's arms had tightened round her. 'We can raise the majority. It'll be tight but we can manage.'

'And the rest?'

'Why don't we use the money my mum and dad were offering us for the wedding and the honeymoon and put it towards this place instead?'

Now, Jessie's headache worsened. 'There's something you should know,' she said. 'William's parents gave us money towards The Lodge. At least a third.'

'Was it a loan or a gift?'

'It was their wedding gift. I don't want to lose my home,' Jessie said, her stomach quaking at the prospect. She had lost so much in the last few months: William to the tart, Hannah to uni, her self-confidence to self-doubt. She couldn't bear the thought of losing her home as well. Something familiar had to remain, a bulwark against all the uncertainties her new life was throwing at her.

'I understand, Jessie. I'll send the paperwork to the court and then I'll write to William suggesting a round-table meeting. Let me take the lead in that. I'll go in hard and strong, leave William in no doubt that we could make life very difficult for him if we so chose. In comparison, the offer we then put on the table should be attractive. He knows he was in the wrong by taking your joint savings and using them in the way that he did. We can use that to our advantage. Don't look so worried. We may get this wrapped up in record time.'

*

Jessie tried to take comfort from Nick's words on her journey home. But she knew that however much William might want the divorce he'd still fight her on the money. It was in his nature. Goode versus Goode. How had it ever come to this?

The rhythm of the train rocked her gently and Jessie closed her eyes. She pictured the modern kitchen extension at The Lodge: triple aspect with two sets of bifold doors facing on to the garden. It was August. The evening William had sent her world tumbling.

She had just finished watering the garden and had been washing her hands in the utility room when she'd heard William next door in the kitchen.

She walked in to find him sitting at the scrubbed-pine table. She knew he'd met his best friend Jack after work for some batting practice in the nets. Now he was wearing a pair of khaki trousers and a white short-sleeved shirt, his hair still wet from the shower.

'You should look at the agapanthus,' Jessie said. 'They're stunning.' Noticing the glass of scotch in his hand, she asked, 'Have you eaten?'

'I'm not hungry,' he said gruffly. 'Come and sit down, will you?' William held out one of the chairs. 'I need to talk to you.'

Sitting on the padded seat, Jessie was hardly able to contain her excitement. William had been so sweet on her birthday, whisking her from the office to a hotel in Oxfordshire. There had been roses and romantic dinners, early nights and late mornings. How was he going to top that for their anniversary? She watched as he pulled his chair up to hers.

'Jess,' he began, looking pensive, 'I don't know how to say this. I know it's our anniversary next week. This is rotten timing. But there isn't a good time. And I can't stand the thought of pretending that everything's okay when it's not.' He threw back almost all of the scotch.

In his eagerness to get the words out he was speaking so quickly Jessie had to strain to keep up with him, but his general demeanour was enough to set her nerves jangling. She'd read so many dreadful things about men in their prime falling ill and his was such a stressful job.

'I think it's better I come right out with it rather than try to dress it up with excuses,' he continued, his gaze fixed on the glass in his hands.

'What's wrong?' Alarmed, Jessie waited for him to continue. When his gaze finally met hers, she was struck by the aching sadness in his eyes.

He tossed back the rest of his scotch. 'I've met someone else,' he said quietly, bowing his head. 'I'm sorry.'

She had been waiting for him to reveal tearing chest pains and clandestine trips to the doctor. The reality of the situation took several seconds to bite.

'Someone else?'

William stood, massaging his neck. 'I never meant for this to happen.' His tone was defensive. 'I thought I could handle the situation. I thought we'd be okay.'

Jessie looked at him in wonder. *This is not my husband.* 'Just what are you saying?' she asked, bewildered.

His arms fell loosely to his sides as he looked at her, a helpless expression on his face. The empty glass, forgotten now, was still in his hand. 'I've fallen in love with her, Jess. I want to be with her.'

Jessie was certain her heart had stopped beating. The evening air blowing through the doors was fresh now and her bare feet on the slate floor felt suddenly cold. This was still her kitchen with its Welsh dresser, pretty crockery, country-style units and island. Nothing had changed and yet *everything* had changed.

'Our weekend away.' Her voice was a whisper.

'I know.' William's eyes were awash with sympathy. 'I wanted it to be special, to make it up to you. I'd decided to tell her it was over. Then, as I was driving home, God forgive me, Jess, but she was all I could think of. I'm sorry.' He stood the glass down on the table and backed away from her.

The suite had been spectacular. They'd made love in the Jacuzzi and again, after dinner, across the four-poster bed. He'd wanted her quite desperately at times, the intensity of his passion reminding her of their early days. Did guilt do that or had he been thinking of this *tart* as he'd held her?

A thought occurred. The waiter's look of recognition. The glance at her. A smile for William. 'You took her there, didn't you?' Jessie's voice was harsh.

Wincing, William nodded.

Jessie focused on the table. None of this can hurt me because he's not my husband. This is not my life. She traced her fingertip round a knot in the wood.

Then, feeling sick, she went to stand at the sink. Outside, ivy covered the sectional fence that separated the garden from Abbey Wood. Jessie watched the waxy leaves lift in the evening breeze.

'It's Marie, isn't it?' Following his father's death in April, William had insisted the firm hire a junior lawyer to assist him. The lovely Marie Metcalfe had started work three weeks later. She turned to face him. 'Every time I go into your office, the two of you are giggling like children.'

William snorted with derision. 'It's not Marie. Do you really think I'd shit on my own doorstep?'

Slapping her palms down on the table, Jessie said, 'I didn't think you'd shit on anyone's doorstep but that was half an hour ago.' She saw him flinch. 'Do I know her?'

'I don't think so. Her name's Chelsea Palmer. She's a hairdresser in town.'

'A *hairdresser*? What happened? Did you go in for a haircut and end up with a blow job?'

'I met her in Spike's Bar.'

'Let me guess: blonde hair, short skirt, stilettos.' William's silence reinforced the mental picture Jessie was painting. 'What are you? Nineteen again?' she asked disparagingly, remembering the cheap-looking blonde William had dated before her. 'It sounds like case study number one in the midlife crisis handbook.' Jessie gave him a withering look. 'How long's it been going on?'

'Since June.' His face was full of remorse. 'I didn't mean for this –'

'When in June?' Jessie demanded.

William's gaze raked the ceiling. 'It was the first Friday. I'd won that rape trial in Stebbingsford Crown Court.'

Jessie cast her mind back. The client had been acquitted on the fourth day and William had returned to the office elated and bragging about his victory.

'The barrister said he'd never had a better-prepared case.'

'That's nice.'

'What's the matter with you?'

'I've just been given my billing target for the next quarter,' she'd said, handing it to him. 'I've got more chance of winning the lottery.'

William had studied the memo. 'That's not so bad.'

Tears had pricked the back of Jessie's eyes. There she was debating how much sleep she could do without to cram in more time at the office and his reaction was 'Not so bad'.

'When they gave the verdict the girl burst into tears. Her father came after us. He had to be restrained.'

'How awful.'

'There was no real danger. The police –'

'I meant how awful for the girl. She must have been through hell.'

'She lied. My client's the one who's been through hell. Come on, Jess, lighten up! I've just had my biggest win of the year. Let's celebrate.'

'Is he innocent?'

'The jury thought so.'

'Did *you* think so?'

'That's a cheap shot. You know it doesn't matter what I think. My client told me they had consensual sex. It's my job to believe what my client tells me and convince everyone else and today I did my job. Brilliantly.'

'What if your client lied to you?' she'd snapped, William's nonchalance over her billing target con tinuing to grate.

'I still did a brilliant job. Now, are you coming for that drink?'

'I can't. I've got a client first thing and I need to finish this tonight.'

'Damn it, Jessica! Let the clients wait for once.'

'I can't. I'm too busy.'

'You're *always* too busy.' With a sigh of irritation, William had swept his briefcase from her desk, scattering her deeds in the process. 'I remember when you used to be as thrilled as me when I won a case. What happened?'

Now, Jessie found herself wondering: *If I'd gone for that drink with him, would we be having this conversation tonight?*

Both strong personalities, they had fought frequently in the early years of their marriage, compromise not a word that came easily to either one of them. But as they'd grown older, and closer, they had learned when to be confrontational and when to back off, realising that giving way was often a sign of strength not weakness.

In the last few months, however, they had fallen once more to squabbling. Undoubtedly, it had been a difficult time, what with the death of William's father, Michael, and Jessie's increasing workload. But that was no excuse for what he'd done. There was no excuse and her previously unshakeable belief in her husband's integrity only made the truth harder to bear.

'You bastard!' Launching herself at him, Jessie slapped his face. 'How *could* you?'

'I'm sorry.'

'Don't tell me you're sorry,' she said scornfully, shoving him hard in the chest. 'Who made the first move?'

'Don't do this, Jess,' William said. 'What do you want to know that for?'

'Because I do.'

For a moment they faced one another: she defiant, he sorrowful. Then, William clasped his hands behind his head and walked away. 'It was a spur-of-the-moment thing. I'd seen her the week before in Spike's, when Jack and I were having a drink. She flirted. Jack made a joke about it.' William turned to face her. Red marks had risen on his cheek where she'd hit him. 'The following Friday I went back to Spike's on my own. She flirted with me again and this time I flirted back.'

He made it all sound so easy. Perhaps it had been. Jessie's heart shrivelled and she turned away so he couldn't see her tears. It all came back to her then. The calls he'd taken in the study with the door closed, the overnighters in London to attend courses, his happy acquiescence to her ten-day holiday in Florence with Anne.

He'd been irritable too. Like the time when the Jag had been off the road and he had received a call from the police station saying a client was asking for him. He'd blown up at her for the tiny amount of petrol in the Clio. Later, he had returned with a bunch of flowers from the service station, even though it had been three in the morning by the time he had finished with the police. Jessie had filled the basin in the en-suite, too sleepy to hunt out a vase, and he'd kissed her neck and said he was sorry. Now she wondered if he'd even been with the police.

Her husband had been having an affair. She watched him as he began to pace the kitchen. The same breeze that had ruffled the ivy now teased his hair.

'How old is she?'

William paused by the island unit. 'Twenty-four.' His gaze fell to the floor.

'My God! She's a *child*. Only six years older than our daughter. Does Hannah know?'

William shook his head. 'No one knows.' He appeared to be ageing as rapidly as the light was draining from the kitchen.

'You've been having an affair *with a child* . . .' She hated him so much at that moment that she had to look away.

'She's not a child,' he protested hotly.

Heartsick, Jessie asked, 'Is this the first time?'

'Christ, yes. I don't make a habit of it.'

'Then why now?'

'Because I got tired of being treated like a client you didn't have time for,' he said disdainfully.

Jessie recoiled. 'That's not fair! You know how hard I've been working.'

'Christ, yes! Because you never miss an opportunity to tell me.' His tone was contemptuous. 'Head down, work, work, work, no time for anything else. We used to be everything to one another,' he said sadly. 'Now, I don't know what's going on in your head from one day to the next and you certainly don't know what's going on in mine. As for our sex life, well, that's a joke! We hardly ever touch each other. Our kisses are perfunctory and on Friday nights we have sex. We never make love any more.

'I remember one Friday in May. I came out of the en-suite. You were working. You finished dictating the letter you were doing, put your files on the floor and we had sex. Then, afterwards, as I was drifting off to sleep, I heard you start dictating again. At first I thought it was funny; you know, what if you'd left the recording running? Susan would get more than she bargained for when she transcribed it. But then I got angry.' He grabbed Jessie's shoulders. 'You made me feel like I was just another thing on your stuff-to-do list. A tick in a ruddy box. Dictated on completions, yes. Prepared files for Monday, yes. Fucked husband, yes.' He thrust her away from him.

Jessie gasped. 'All I wanted was a bit of support,' she said angrily. 'Going for the partnership is the only thing I have ever done for myself. I needed you to understand. To be patient with me.'

'Patience has never been one of my virtues.'

Stunned, Jessie shook her head. 'You selfish bastard.' She thumped his shoulder. 'You owed me that. All our married life I've had to put up with broken nights, ruined Christmases, spoilt birthdays. You'd get a call from the police station telling you some drunk had been arrested and was asking for you and, at that moment, that drunk was more important to you than me, than Hannah, than anything.'

William put his face close to hers, his fingers squeezing her upper arms. 'That drunk, and the hundreds like him, put food on the table, clothes on your back, sent Hannah to school. You call me selfish?' he shouted. 'I did all that for you, for her. But after Dad died and I needed you, you weren't there for me.' He released her and she staggered slightly.

Stung by the accusation, Jessie reached for him. 'I was.'

William shrugged her off, his face hardening. 'No, Jess. You weren't. After losing Mum a couple of years ago, he was all I had left from the past and he died just like that.' William snapped his fingers. 'No warning, nothing. Living life at a hundred miles an hour one minute, dead from a massive heart attack the next. And do you know what I saw when I looked in the mirror? Him. Chelsea understood. Chelsea listened.'

'Was this before or after you had sex?' Jessie spat.

William's hands twitched into fists and he sent one of the chairs flying. 'You're not going to make me feel guilty,' he roared. 'A few weeks after the funeral, when I booked us a holiday you threw it back in my face. You were too busy, you said. A blind man could see how desperate I was for a break, but not you. You were too busy.'

William had taken the holiday, Jessie recalled. Hannah had gone with him.

Emotionally drained, Jessie sat. 'That's no excuse for what you've done,' she said weakly.

'My world was falling apart and you didn't even notice, or worse you didn't care. There was no excuse for that,' William snapped.

'So you decided to punish me by sleeping with someone else?'

'It wasn't about punishing you. I just wanted you to listen to me. But every time I tried to talk to you there was a call or a meeting or a file that couldn't wait. But it was all right for me to wait. I always had to wait.' William's voice was choked with emotion. 'I ended up hating you for it.'

His face was half in shadow but Jessie could see the tears glistening in his eyes.

'It broke my heart to feel like that, Jess. I wanted to tear down the barriers you kept putting up but I couldn't get through to you.' He cupped her face. 'No matter how hard I tried, I couldn't get through.'

'If it was that important to you, you should have made me listen.' Tears spilled down Jessie's cheeks.

'In the end, it was easier to talk to Chelsea,' William said, withdrawing his hand.

'You're pathetic!'

William shrugged. 'Maybe I am.'

Standing, Jessie said, 'I'm here now.' She pushed him. 'You have my undivided attention now.' She pushed him again. 'Talk to me.'

'And say what? That I was sick with fear that history was going to repeat itself and I was going to end up like him?' William thrust his hands through his hair. 'That I wanted us both to cut back at work, buy a place in Devon and spend our weekends there?' His voice hardened. 'It's too late.'

'It can't be too late,' Jessie whispered.

'It is. You see, I've fallen in love with her, Jess. I shouldn't have and I wish it didn't mean hurting you. But I can't change the way I feel. I don't want to. I'm glad I've met Chelsea.'

Jessie felt the ground shift beneath her feet as everything she had believed in crumbled.

'What does she have that I don't?' she asked, bewildered.

'Time for me, time for a life. She's fun.' William fell silent. 'I should have waited for you to become a partner and talked to you then,' he admitted. 'But I needed someone now, not in six months or a year and I wasn't strong enough to wait. God knows if what I'm doing is the right thing. All I know for sure is that, right now, I need her.'

Each word was a fresh blow. Jessie bent her head. She'd spent her time worrying about interest rates and the housing market. She'd worried about petty office politics and William's chances of becoming senior partner. She'd worried about how Hannah was going to cope in student digs in Exeter. She'd never worried about her husband's fidelity. Her marriage was rock solid, a thing envied by others, but apparently not for much longer.

Anger rising, Jessie exploded. 'Go and have your fun then. If our life together means so little to you, go and be with your whore. I wouldn't want you anywhere near me again, anyway. Who knows what horrible diseases that bitch might have?' She watched with satisfaction as William's face darkened. The muscle in his cheek began to twitch. 'I bet you're not the first married man she's slept with.'

'You know nothing about her,' he snapped.

'I know enough. How many times did you get out of her bed and come to mine?' Jessie covered her face. 'You would still have been warm from being inside her and you would have let me . . .'

'You'd have been too tired,' William said cuttingly.

'But it happened sometimes, you can't deny that,' Jessie shouted. 'How *could* you do that to me?' She raised her hand to hit him again but William caught hold of her wrist. 'You were supposed to be mine,' she sobbed.

'You didn't want me. Our bed saw more action when I was –' He stopped abruptly and let go of her wrist.

'When you were what?'

William looked contrite. 'Nothing. I . . .'

Horror seeped into Jessie's eyes. 'No!' she wailed. 'Please tell me you didn't bring her here.' She gathered his shirt in her hands, tears blinding her as she grappled with him. 'Was nothing sacred to you, you bastard? You had that whore in my home?' Jessie swallowed hard. 'You let her into my bed?'

'It was my bed, too.'

Jessie jumped as a train rattled past the window, breaking her reverie. After he had gone, she had dumped all of the bed linen and the duvet into bin bags and sent them sailing on to the drive. Then, with superhuman strength born out of anger, she had manhandled the mattress downstairs. It, too, had ended up on the drive. She had thought about burning it but, worried it might give off noxious fumes, and not wanting to give William and his whore the satisfaction of poisoning herself, she'd abandoned the idea. Instead, she'd hired a skip and thrown the mattress into it, together with everything else the tart might have touched.

Yes, it was high time to get a divorce Jessie decided as the train pulled into Abbeyleigh Station. *Fight all you want, William. But I won't accept anything less than a fair settlement. You owe me that.*

Chapter Four

Four days later, Jessie sat at a table for two in the balcony area of Spike's Bar. Spike's was Anne Jacobs' kind of place, all chrome and wood and attitude. Jessie much preferred the traditional Northey Hotel but, as it was Anne's turn to pay, she got to choose the venue.

For Jessie, Spike's was synonymous with William and the tart. As she sat watching the Friday lunchtime crowd, she couldn't help but wonder what it had been like that evening in June. Had William been at the bar? Jessie could see him with the top button of his shirt undone, his tie loosened, his jacket in his lap. She wondered if he had kept his wedding ring on, later, while they had sex?

The waitress brought Jessie's order and as she walked away, her boots ringing a tattoo on the wooden floor, Jessie spied Anne by the door and waved.

Her friend was the epitome of winter chic in a red military-style coat with bold brass buttons, teamed with calf-length spike-heeled boots and a black scarf. Her dark hair was tied in a chignon.

Jessie looked down at her own coffee-coloured trouser suit and clumpy boots. *Must do better*, she thought ruefully.

'Sorry I'm late.' A cloud of Chanel No. 5 settled over the table as Anne shed her scarf and coat to reveal black trousers and a red cashmere sweater. 'What's that?'

'Goat's cheese salad,' Jessie said defensively. 'I'm having a fat day.'

Anne grimaced. 'Actually, I meant the wedding ring on your finger. I told you to give it back to him ages ago.'

'I thought I'd give it to Hannah instead,' Jessie said.

'And what's she supposed to do with it?' Anne asked with a laugh as she signalled a waiter and ordered a gin and tonic and a basket of chips. 'Can you believe this weather?'

Jessie shook her head.

It had been snowing heavily since Tuesday and the road to The Lodge had quickly become impassable by car. Jessie had been forced to walk to and from the main road where Walt had been collecting her and dropping her off.

Anne pouted. 'I don't understand why you don't come and stay with me.'

'Because the exercise is doing me good,' Jessie replied as she twirled a strip of lettuce round her fork and made a token effort to dip it in the goat's cheese. 'And because I'm afraid that if William hears I've moved out, he might take it into his head to move in.'

'You really should give the ring back you know. Trust me; it'll get one hell of a reaction. It always has for me.'

Given that Anne had three broken marriages behind her, Jessie could well believe it, but there was one crucial difference between her circumstances and Anne's. 'He left me, remember?' Jessie said and took a sip of her wine.

'So? It'll trigger the guilt. He'll remember how in love with you he was when he bought the ring and what a shit he's being now. I always find that's a good time to cry. He'll feel even more of a shit then.' Anne flashed the waiter a bright smile as he brought her drink. A moment later he returned with her food.

Eyeing Anne's chips enviously, Jessie said, 'I can't cry on demand.'

'Practice makes perfect. But seriously, darling, you have to take the ring off. I don't understand why you're so reluctant. You gave back the engagement ring.'

'That was his grandmother's.'

Jessie drizzled French dressing over her lettuce. It was easy for Anne. She moved seamlessly between relationships, always taking what she wanted, always in control. If Jessie was a pearl diver then Anne was a skimmer.

'Do you miss your exes?'

'Sometimes. But that doesn't mean I'd want any of them back.' Anne's gold bracelet rattled on the table as she squeezed Jessie's hand. 'I know a part of you will always love William, sweetie, but if he was coming home, he'd have done so by now.'

'What makes you think I'd take him back if he did?' Jessie arched her eyebrows. She missed William so much it was like an ache inside her: his boundless enthusiasm, his wisdom, his touch. But she was not about to admit that to Anne. To anyone. 'I gave Nick the go-ahead to lodge the petition.'

Anne's face registered her surprise. 'Fancy not telling me sooner.' She rapped Jessie's knuckles with her fork. 'How do you feel?'

'Like I've failed.'

'Rubbish! It was his midlife crisis. You're blameless.'

'With a marriage as long as ours I don't think either of us could be described as blameless.'

'Has he been served with the papers yet?'

'This morning. He looked a bit shell-shocked, and muttered something about hell freezing over and nobody telling him.'

'So, does this mean you're finally coming out to play?' Anne asked.

Jessie pulled a face. When married, Friday nights had followed the same safe routine: a takeaway, television and sex. It had slipped from Jessie's consciousness that single people went out on Friday nights.

'Don't look like that,' Anne responded. 'I've already told you, if you insist on retiring from the battlefield of life, I'll have no alternative but to buy you a cat.' Anne tapped her manicured nails on the table. 'That's how they start you know, those batty old women who live alone with a hundred cats and ladders in their tights from the cats' claws and jumpers with threads pulled and their hair a fright because they cut it themselves. They've turned their back on life.'

'That'll never happen to me,' Jessie said, laughing, but she knew beneath Anne's banter there lurked a genuine concern. For while Jessie and William had never been ones to live their lives in a social whirl, even the relatively mundane things, like having dinner with friends, had ceased for Jessie when William had left.

Their friends had been embarrassed. Jack and Sue Stanhope were good examples. Their monthly suppers had been a permanent fixture in Jessie and William's calendar. Sue, a slight, immaculate redhead, had been disconsolate on hearing the news of the couple's separation. Not, it had to be said, from the point of view of the separation itself, because she'd always had a bit of a thing for William, but more because of the havoc unintentionally wreaked on her suppers.

'Will you and William be civilised enough to eat together or will I have linguini up the walls?' Sue had asked. 'Surely William won't expect me to invite Chelsea?' Then: 'Would you come if I did?'

Jessie had missed six suppers so far. Undeterred, Sue always rang on the first weekend of the month to ask if she was free for the last weekend. 'There's no pressure.' Which Jessie took to mean, I'm not trying to set you up with anyone. It was nice that Sue made the effort, particularly as her husband, Jack, was William's best friend. Others simply avoided her.

There was little wonder then that Jessie had needed time to heal. To echo Anne's analogy, she liked to think she had merely retired wounded to the field hospital, not been invalided out of the battle altogether.

Jessie could imagine Anne's glee if she were ever to find out about Barry Sturridge, but taking those first shaky steps towards rehabilitation had been something Jessie had needed to do alone. Left to Anne, her reintroduction to the world of dating would no doubt have revolved around tequila slammers and twenty-somethings. The very thought of which made Jessie shudder.

But it wasn't just Anne who was pressuring her. Hannah, too, had been asking questions. To pacify her daughter, Jessie had told her about the coupon she'd clipped for a local dating agency. As soon as things calmed down at work, she had promised Hannah she would register. And then there was the wedding. Perhaps Barry wouldn't seem so bad the second time around or maybe she'd meet someone else.

'How's work?' Anne asked.

Jessie pulled a face. 'Walt told me the chances of me being made a partner this summer are slim to none. He says I should aim for next summer instead. Which is probably sensible but I really wanted to do it this year to prove to William that I wasn't wasting my time.'

'Did Walt say why it was unlikely?'

'I'm not billing enough.'

Anne raised her eyebrows. 'You practically live at that bloody office. What does the man want from you, blood?'

'I need to network more apparently.'

'Well! Why didn't you say?' Anne exclaimed. 'If they gave out medals for networking, I'd have won the lot. I know everyone there is to know, sweetie. What can I do to help?'

'Recommend that all your friends move house or become property developers and that they all come to me for their conveyancing,' Jessie said flippantly.

Anne grinned. 'It's as good as done, darling. Suki is thinking of moving again. Chantelle and Mike have just split up and they're both looking for new houses. Of course the Robertson twins are using Daddy's money to buy and do up flats to let out all over the place. And that group from the Bridge Club all buy and sell property like they're playing Monopoly. And that's just off the top of my head! Have you got any business cards?'

Realising that Anne was serious, Jessie quickly checked her handbag. 'Just a few,' she said, handing them over.

'Not nearly enough, darling! I'll need oodles.'

Jessie smiled. 'Oodles you shall have. Thank you.'

'What are friends for? Of course I shall want something in return.'

'Name it.'

'There's a speed-dating night on Saturday at the splendidly named Cock Inn in Stebbingsford. You simply have to come with me.'

Jessie felt a rush of relief. 'Tempting though that is, I'm going to the Sturridge family wedding reception at the Northey on Saturday. I may be doing some conveyancing work for Sam Sturridge.'

'Never mind. They're always having those things at the Cock. You can come next time. Don't roll your eyes at me like that, Jessica Martin!' Anne exclaimed. 'It's the Cock or a cat, you have been warned.'

They burst out laughing.

'I didn't mean it quite like that,' Anne said, wiping the tears from her eyes. 'Then again, maybe I did!'

'Why are you going to a speed-dating night anyway?' Jessie asked. 'Have you and Stephen split up?'

'No, I just like the vibe. The boys at the Cock are into shots and festivals and having fun. You remember fun?'

Jessie pulled a face.

'Of course Stephen wouldn't be seen dead in a pub. Even Spike's would be a struggle for him. He's a champagne and Mozart type of guy.' Anne tossed back the last of her gin and tonic. 'Did I tell you he's taking me to Paris? We'll be staying at the George V. Poor chap, he'll bankrupt himself. Still, I'm worth it.' Anne motioned for another drink. 'I'll make sure I say thank you nicely.'

Jessie pushed the remains of her salad aside and helped herself to a chip while Anne's back was turned.

'When was it William left?' Anne asked as she reached into her Gucci handbag and drew out her compact and lipstick.

'August.'

The lipstick hovered like a crimson wand in front of lips that were already immaculate. 'My God! You must be desperate. I couldn't go that long without sex.'

'I don't miss it that much,' Jessie lied.

'Tell me William was dreadful in bed and I might just believe you. I suppose you want the whole love thing again?'

Jessie disliked Anne's mocking tone. William had made Jessie feel cherished and in a cold world that was a special thing. Why shouldn't she want that again?

'I want to share my life, not just my bed,' Jessie said. 'I want to matter to someone again.'

Anne nodded sympathetically. 'I'm sure you will.' Her lips twitched into a smile. 'But wouldn't you like to have some fun while you're waiting? A word of advice, though.' Anne shut the compact with a snap. 'Don't tell anyone you're a lawyer.'

'Why not?'

'Because you'll scare them to death; say you work in a shop or something,' Anne replied airily.

'You want me to lie,' Jessie said flatly.

'Of course. All relationships are based on deceit to begin with.'

'They usually end that way too,' Jessie said. 'I suppose I could always say I'm a hairdresser.'

Her sardonic comment was lost on Anne. 'All those months without sex. I don't know how you've managed it.'

'There's more to life than sex,' Jessie said.

Anne's smile was compassionate but fleeting. 'Would you be happy never to make love again?' Anne signalled the waiter and handed him her credit card.

'I didn't say that.'

'We all need other stimuli in our lives, but no sex? I don't want to live in a world like that. No flirting, no grandiose romantic gestures, no orgasms.' Anne gave the waiter a brilliant smile and he grinned back. 'See, sex makes people feel good about themselves.'

Both women stood. 'Have a great time in Paris,' Jessie said as they swapped kisses.

'Don't worry, I will, and I'll give you all the juicy details,' Anne said with a chuckle as she linked her arm through Jessie's. 'If you're not having sex yourself, you might as well enjoy it vicariously.'

Chapter Five

The function room of the Northey Hotel was a modern addition to the original Tudor building. It had no exposed beams or stunning fireplaces, like the other rooms at the Northey, but it did boast a polished wooden floor through which the mobile disco of the Sturridge family wedding reception was now vibrating to the sound of Elvis Presley.

Sam Sturridge had greeted Jessie as soon as she'd arrived. 'I normally deal with Gareth Ellis at Ellis and Son,' he had told her bluntly. 'He's quoted a fair price.' He had given Jessie the figure and waited expectantly.

'I can let you have a ten per cent discount on Gareth's quote,' Jessie had said without hesitation. Her profit margin would take a hit but so long as she had a profit margin she didn't mind. The kudos she would get for introducing Sam Sturridge to the firm would more than make up for it.

To her delight, Sam had accepted.

Now, she turned as Barry nudged her arm. 'The newlyweds will be leaving soon and I promised I'd help with the car.'

'Okay.' Jessie watched him walk away. He looked awkward in a suit, as if it owned him and not the other way round. She turned to stare out of the window.

Barry Sturridge was solid and dependable, with a good heart. He would be unlikely ever to have an affair or hurt her. But they were not for one another and they both knew it.

Nevertheless, wearing a flattering burgundy dress and jacket and with her hair freshly cut and coloured, Jessie was pleased she'd made the effort to come.

It was learning to do things in stages, she realised, being content with the little victories, like dating again, while building up to the bigger things, like fixing a broken heart. If she was not destined to spend the rest of her life with William, it had to be because there was someone else for her. He was out there somewhere. A pearl diver, like herself. *All I have to do is find him.*

'Is it snowing again?'

Jolted from her thoughts, Jessie turned to find a young man in a dark suit standing beside her table. Now that was how to wear a suit. It was all in the shoulders. Confident but relaxed. Jessie couldn't place the man but he looked familiar.

Glancing up at the outside light, she said, 'Yes. It's snowing hard. Have you far to go?'

'No, I'm only in North Street.'

He and William could be neighbours.

'You?' he asked.

'A couple of miles out.' Her jeans, sweatshirt and boots were in Barry's pickup, together with her coat and a torch, ready for the journey home.

'Do you mind if I join you?'

'No, of course not,' Jessie said. She threw him a surreptitious look. Tall and slim, late twenties or early thirties, with straight dark hair that brushed his collar, he definitely looked familiar. She hoped he wasn't a client whose name had escaped her. That would be embarrassing, particularly if he asked her how his transaction was going.

'Owen Phillips,' he said, holding out his hand as he slid on to the banquette seat beside her.

'Jessie Martin.'

'Nice to meet you, Jessie.' His handshake was firm.

'And you,' she said.

Without doubt, he had the most angelic eyes Jessie had ever seen. They were a deep Mediterranean blue and fringed by long dark lashes. Smiling to herself, Jessie sipped her wine. *I bet you're a real heartbreaker with those eyes.*

'I see you every now and then in town,' Owen said. 'You always seem to be in a hurry.'

'That's me,' Jessie admitted ruefully. 'Not enough hours in the day.'

'What do you do?'

Jessie hesitated, remembering Anne's warning. 'I'm a solicitor.' She waited for him to make a disparaging comment or pull a face.

He did neither, simply nodded and said, 'Tough job.'

Jessie smiled appreciatively. People were always talking about the pressure of moving house but imagine being responsible for over a hundred such transactions at one time. Now that was pressure.

'How about you?' Jessie asked.

'I run the flower stall by the churchyard.'

Of course, Jessie could picture him now, in his working clothes, a money belt tied round his waist: the flower seller. 'I thought I recognised you,' Jessie said. 'Did you do the flowers for the wedding?'

'Yes,' Owen said with a hint of pride.

Jessie was impressed. 'I thought the bride's bouquet was exquisite,' she said. 'The lavender and pink roses worked so well with the purple eucalyptus. Perfect colours for a winter wedding.'

'It's very kind of you to say so.'

'Did you study floristry?'

'Not officially. I've worked for several florists though. You pick things up as you go along.'

As someone who struggled to arrange even the simplest of bouquets, Jessie thought Owen was being overly modest.

He sipped from his bottle of beer. 'Valentine's Day next week,' he said. 'Will someone be buying you flowers?'

'I doubt it.'

William had never been one for soppy cards but he'd always given her a single red rose with a note wrapped round the stem. Would he buy the tart a red rose? Did men do that? Take a romantic routine and try it out on every woman in their lives? Probably. Men usually took the easy option.

'Do you need to be a romantic to work on a flower stall?' Jessie asked.

Owen grinned. 'No, but it helps, especially as I spend a lot of my time being a relationship counsellor.'

'Really?'

Owen nodded. 'You can always tell the guys going on a first date. They size up all the bouquets, wishing they knew what her favourite colour was. Then they ask me what they should buy.'

'And what do you recommend?'

'Red roses and white gypsophila. You can't go far wrong with that combination.'

Jessie thought of the bouquet Barry had given her and suppressed a smile.

'Then you've got the regulars: the guys who buy flowers every week and tell you how their lives are going.'

'I thought men like that were a myth,' Jessie said.

Owen smiled. 'No, they really exist. And then you get the others who grade the size of the bouquet on the level of the misdemeanour they're guilty of.' He leaned in closer and Jessie found herself doing likewise. 'I'll put myself out of business by saying this, but if men just thought about the little things, they wouldn't need to come running to me when the big things go wrong.' Owen shrugged. 'Some men don't know how lucky they are.'

'Owen, dear.' Mrs Sturridge laid her hand on Owen's shoulder. 'The flowers are lovely. Thank you so much.'

'My pleasure,' Owen said, standing.

'I don't know how you did it and all on your own too. Barry!' Mrs Sturridge motioned for her son to join them. 'I was just saying what a wonderful job Owen did with the flowers.'

'Very good,' Barry said gruffly. 'It's getting worse out there,' he commented. 'I think once the newlyweds leave we should wind up the party.'

Mrs Sturridge nodded, and then said, 'They were hoping you'd drive them to their hotel; Jen's brother was going to do it but he's had too much to drink.'

'I can't,' Barry protested, 'I'm taking Jessie home.'

Embarrassed, Jessie said, 'I can get a taxi.'

'I'd be happy to run you home,' Owen interjected.

'What a dear boy you are,' Mrs Sturridge said and kissed his cheek as Barry glowered.

'That's very kind of you,' Jessie said, 'but I wouldn't want to put you to any trouble. It's not like you even have to leave town to get home yourself.'

'No trouble at all,' Owen assured her.

'Well, that's sorted then,' Mrs Sturridge said with relief. 'Why don't you get Jessie's things from the pickup? I'll go and give Jen the good news.' Barry looked helplessly at his mother and then at Jessie before heading back outside, a scowl on his face.

Once she'd changed her clothes, Jessie sought Barry out. 'I just wanted to thank you for inviting me. I had a nice time.'

He nodded glumly. 'I'm sorry about not taking you home.'

'Don't worry.'

There was an awkward silence.

'This isn't working, is it?' he said sadly.

'No,' Jessie admitted, relieved that he'd broached the subject, saving her from having to do so.

'Shall we call it a day?'

'I think it'd be best.'

Barry gave her a clumsy kiss on the cheek. 'I hope you find someone.'

'You, too.'

Owen was waiting for Jessie in the foyer. A blue transit van stood at the foot of the hotel steps.

'I've had the engine running so the cab's nice and warm,' he said as he reached for her holdall and swung it on to his shoulder. 'It's hardly the lap of luxury,' he continued, offering her his arm as she climbed inside, 'but it's clean.'

'Thank you.'

He was wearing an old wax jacket over his suit and a scarf tied high round his neck, but he still looked pinched from the cold as he closed her door and ran through the beam of the headlights, his head bowed against the wind. Snow swirled into the cab as he thrust the holdall between them and got behind the wheel.

'It might not be the lap of luxury,' Jessie said as she tugged her seat belt into place, 'but it smells like it.' The scent of roses was all around her, made more powerful still by the heat rattling out of the vents on the dashboard.

The van vibrated noisily as the engine idled. 'Delphi's been good to me,' Owen said, patting the steering wheel with a gloved hand.

'Delphi?' Jessie asked, bemused.

'Delphinium. The van.' He looked at her and grinned. 'Silly habit, naming things. I've done it since I was a kid.' He edged the van out into the traffic. 'Where's home?'

Jessie told him. 'How long have you been in Abbeyleigh?' she asked.

'Since the summer. I moved here from London. Clean start after I broke up with my girlfriend. You?'

'Over twenty years.'

'Have you and Barry Sturridge known each other long?' Owen asked.

'A few weeks,' Jessie replied. She watched the windscreen wipers bat snowflakes aside. 'I'm in the middle of a divorce.' Sitting there in the dark, cocooned from the blizzard raging outside, it seemed the most natural thing in the world to tell him.

'I'm sorry,' Owen responded.

'Don't be. I'm doing the right thing.'

'So it was your decision?'

'My decision to divorce him. His decision to commit adultery.'

'I'm sorry,' Owen said again.

'Unless you were the one who introduced him to her, you have nothing to apologise for.'

Owen laughed. 'Not guilty,' he said.

'Truth is, I'm fed up with people feeling sorry for me,' Jessie confided. 'I did sympathy last year, not any more. I've got a dickhead for a husband not a serious illness.'

Owen laughed again. 'I'm glad you haven't let it dent your sense of humour. So, if you did sympathy last year, what are you doing this year?'

'Rehabilitation.'

'Good luck with that.'

Jessie registered the back note of bitterness that had crept into Owen's tone. He, too, had clearly spent time in the field hospital of life.

'Sounds like you've been there and done it,' she said quietly.

'Been there and still trying to do it would be more accurate,' he said with a grimace.

Jessie gave him a sideways look. 'In the interests of research, mine obviously, would you like to share with the group?'

Owen chuckled. 'Sure, I'm a modern man and if it stops you making the same mistakes I did, I'd be happy to help. Her name was Tessa. I walked in one day and found her with another man.'

'I'm sorry.'

'I did sympathy last year.'

They looked at one another and laughed.

'When you find the next someone special,' Owen said, 'don't hold back, like I did, out of fear of getting hurt. You end up pushing the other person away or, in my case, into someone else's arms and then it's ten times harder to trust the next time, as I'm now discovering.'

They lapsed into silence.

'I noticed you're still wearing your wedding ring,' Owen said.

Jessie blushed. 'Yes, silly really. I should take it off. I don't know what I'm waiting for.'

In her mind's eye she could see William sitting behind the wheel of his Jag. Preparing to drive off to begin his new life with his lover, he had twisted off his wedding ring and stowed it in his pocket. At the time the swiftness of his actions had cut Jessie to the quick. She had moved into the past tense of his life before he had even left the drive. And here she was, months later, still wearing her own ring as if to somehow compensate for William's unseemly haste.

'Do you have any children?' Owen asked.

'A daughter, Hannah. She's at Exeter University studying law.'

They'd left the shelter of Abbeyleigh behind and Delphi was now ambling along the strangely quiet main road, bucking crosswinds that would have knocked a less substantial vehicle off its course. Owen handled the van with confidence despite the tricky conditions and Jessie was not in the least perturbed, even when the snow covered the windscreen almost as fast as the wipers could remove it.

'How long were you and the dickhead married?' Owen asked.

'Twenty-one years. We split up last August.'

Owen whistled. 'That's a lifetime.'

'Indeed.'

'You must have been very young when you married,' he added.

'Gosh, yes. I was practically a child bride,' Jessie said with a grin.

Owen smiled. 'I'm even more impressed that you're ready to put yourself back out there.'

'A friend of mine reckons I want to live my life with the handbrake on. I'm determined to show her she's wrong.'

'I like that phrase. May I borrow it?'

'It's yours to use whenever you wish.'

'It takes courage to start over.'

'So does moving to a new area,' Jessie said.

'Not if I was running away.'

'Were you?'

'Sometimes I feel like I've spent my whole life running.'

Jessie glanced at Owen's face. Wreathed in shadow, it was sombre.

'Why did you choose Abbeyleigh?'

'I didn't want to bump into my past. Have you ever met the woman who . . .'

'Chelsea? No, thank God. I've seen her from a distance though, that was bad enough.' Jessie grimaced. William had driven into the firm's car park one morning and the tart had climbed out of the passenger side: lithe and lovely, blonde and young. They'd kissed as Jessie had looked on from her office, unable to tear her gaze away, even though the sight of them together had ripped what was left of her heart to shreds.

'I still say you're a brave lady, Jessie.'

Jessie ruminated on Owen's words. 'I don't think I'm brave,' she said. 'I could easily lock myself away in my very nice house and never open myself up to pain again but it wouldn't just be the chance of pain I'd be denying myself, would it? For the most part my marriage was a happy one and I miss the shared jokes and routines, someone to laugh with, someone to fight with, someone to give me a hug when I've had a bad day. I want to face the world knowing that there's someone else on my side. Or, as the same friend put it, I suppose you want the whole love thing again. And she's right. I do.'

'Sounds nice,' Owen commented. 'May I ask, is Barry Sturridge your someone special?'

'No. He's a nice guy,' Jessie said quickly. 'But we've decided we're not right for each other.'

'Then I wish you well in your search.'

'Thank you. And you.'

There was something about the warmth of the cab, with the snowstorm raging outside, that engendered intimacy, Jessie realised. If she and Barry had spoken like this she would have been on edge and embarrassed but with Owen it seemed natural and instinctive.

'What you described,' Owen said, breaking the silence, 'do you think that kind of relationship exists?'

'Yes,' Jessie said without hesitation.

'You still have to be willing to take that leap in the dark to find out though, that's the bit I've always struggled with.'

'One day you'll meet someone so special you'll be desperate to take that leap. In fact, it should be your New Year's resolution to find her.' Jessie twisted her wedding ring back and forth. Why was it so much easier to give advice than follow it?

Soon, the buildings dwindled so that just the odd terrace of cottages remained and at the signpost for Abbey Wood Owen said, 'Where to from here?'

'There's a pull-in up here on your left.' Jessie unzipped the holdall and took out her torch. It was going to be a cold and arduous walk up the hill. Her spirits flagged at the thought. 'It was very good of you to do this.'

'No problem,' Owen said cheerfully as the van rocked over the ridge of snow pushed aside by the snowploughs and came to a halt. He peered into the darkness. 'How far is your house from here?'

Jessie pointed across the road. 'Half a mile up the hill.' She tied her scarf round her neck and anchored the ends inside her coat before tugging the zip up as far as it would go. 'Thanks again for the lift.'

'Let me have a go at the hill with Delphi,' Owen offered.

'Please don't,' Jessie said. 'Barry tried it in the pickup this morning and almost got stuck. I've been walking all week; one more trip won't hurt me.' She flicked on the torch and reached for the door handle.

'Wait!' Owen said. 'I'll come with you.' He leaned over to her side of the cab and, ignoring her words of protest, pulled a torch from the glove compartment. 'What sort of man would I be if I let you walk home alone in this?' he asked as he tested the torch.

'Sensible?'

Owen laughed. 'I've got a set of waterproofs in the back. Wait here while I get changed.'

A few minutes later, Owen helped Jessie down from the cab. The wind screamed around them, instantly tearing Jessie's scarf loose and lashing her hair across her face. Undeterred, Jessie repeated her assurance that she would be fine but Owen was having none of it.

'Have you got a hat?' he shouted.

'No.'

'Take mine.' He pulled the woollen hat from his head and settled it on hers, tugging it down firmly over her ears. Then he took the holdall from her hand. The twin beams of their torches danced as they crossed the road.

The act of walking through the deep snow was exhausting and conversation quickly became impossible. Beyond the howling wind, all Jessie could hear was the sound of their laboured breathing and the soft thud of their footsteps as they trudged on.

Her body, clad in so many layers, was relatively warm, but the cold continued to bludgeon her face, her flailing hair making her cheeks sting. It was therefore with considerable relief that Jessie spotted the outside light of The Lodge, shimmering like a beacon through the falling snow.

'This is it.' She threw the words against the raging wind and pointed.

Owen nodded. Once inside, they paused beside the front door, revelling in the warmth and the stillness, glad to be out of the whipping wind.

Jessie pulled the hat from her head and handed it back to Owen. 'Thank you.'

'You looked very nice in it,' he said gallantly.

'Some people have a head for hats,' she said. 'I'm not one of them.'

'A blizzard is no place to make a fashion statement,' he told her as he reached for the latch.

'At least let me make you a hot drink, to say thank you.' Her heart lurched as Owen smiled.

'That'd be nice.'

Leaving their boots by the front door, Jessie led Owen through to the kitchen. It was the newest part of The Lodge, a vast L shape, with the length of the L being the kitchen proper, the tail the dining area and snug. White wooden shutters covered all of the windows and the two sets of bifold doors.

While Jessie fixed two mugs of hot chocolate, Owen peeled off his waterproofs before joining her at the table.

In the harsh electric light, Jessie felt embarrassed by the intimacy of their conversation in the van. What had seemed natural there was out of place now. Owen, too, appeared similarly affected and the silence between them lengthened.

'Is yours the only house up here?' Owen asked finally.

'Yes,' Jessie said. She watched the bubbles on the top of her chocolate spin as she blew on them. 'It started life as the gatehouse to Abbeyleigh Manor but when fire razed the manor, the Coates family decided to rebuild on the other side of town and The Lodge became a private residence.'

Jessie watched Owen lace his fingers round his mug. He had an artisan's hands. To her surprise, she found herself wondering how they would feel against her skin. Suddenly, she was painfully aware of every one of the many weeks that had passed since she and William had last made love.

'When was the fire?'

Jessie forced herself to concentrate. 'Eighteen twenty-six. Before that, the manor was the site of the abbey that gave the town its name.'

'The house the Coates family had built wouldn't be Park Place, by any chance?'

'Yes. I hear it's being converted into a hotel and spa.'

Owen nodded. 'Lydia Coates has asked me to do the flowers for the opening in April.'

They lapsed into silence once more.

'It was nice of you to walk up the hill with me,' Jessie said. 'Mad, but nice.'

'That's me,' Owen said genially. 'Mad but nice. I said I'd take you home. Taking you halfway doesn't count. Besides, I'm used to the cold. Talking of which –' he put his empty mug down – 'I'd better go before I get too comfortable.'

Pausing in front of the hall mirror, Owen took his hat from his pocket and settled it into place. He gave Jessie's reflection a wry smile.

'You look far better in it than I did,' she said.

Grinning, he played the beam of his torch over his palm. 'It was nice meeting you, Jessie. Good luck with the rehabilitation. Remember, be brave.'

'You, too.' She pulled back the door. The air was sharp and the odd flurry of snow was still falling.

'Have you always been a solicitor?' he asked as he stepped outside.

'Yes. Why?'

'I thought maybe you were once a dancer.' His breath clouded around him.

'A dancer?' Jessie laughed. 'Whatever made you think that?' Despite the cold, she was sure she was blushing.

'You have a dancer's legs.' Before she had a chance to respond he bounded down the steps. 'Thanks again for the hot chocolate. Goodnight.'

'Goodnight.'

Jessie closed the door and leaned against it. It had been a long time since a handsome young man had flirted with her. A dancer's legs, indeed. Jessie hugged herself as she checked out her legs in the hall mirror and remembered Owen's smile. Perhaps phase two of her life wouldn't be so bad after all.

Jessie looked down at her wedding ring. She had carried on wearing it to prove to herself and the world that her marriage had mattered to her even if it hadn't to William. It had been part of the grieving process but now it was time to move on.

She gave the ring a tug. It had been on her finger for over twenty years and in all that time she had never taken it off. Now, as if mocking her, it refused to budge. She brought the ring up to her mouth and licked it, hoping to loosen it. Twisting it to and fro, she finally started to work it over her knuckle. When at last she pulled it free she held it up to the light. *Love always.*

'Goodbye, William,' she said, and, walking through to the sitting room, she opened a drawer in the bureau and shut the ring inside.

*

The following Thursday, Valentine's Day, Jessie returned from work to find a red rose on her doorstep. For one disorienting moment she thought it might be from William.

She tore the note from the stem. It read: *For the lady with the dancer's legs.*

MARCH

Chapter Six

Seated in the waiting area of Jessie's solicitors' office, William sipped his coffee.

'Mr Atkins is in conference with his client,' the receptionist had told him. 'They shouldn't keep you waiting too long.'

Not too long, William thought but just long enough to set the nerves jangling. William knew the tricks matrimonial lawyers employed. *You can't kid a kidder*, he thought as he finished his coffee but his eyes still wandered to the clock. He made himself look out of the window. He'd thought he would be immune from the nerves, so accustomed was he to playing the role of an impartial legal adviser. He hadn't anticipated what a difference being a party to the proceedings would make.

He watched the second hand tick round the clock face once more. He'd been pushing for this divorce, eager for a clean break. That was until the petition had arrived and with it a sense of loss that had been as profound as it had been unexpected.

Christ, Atkins, you're good! This is what I'm supposed to do, isn't it? Sit here and brood.

William looked up to find the receptionist smiling at him. She motioned to the coffee pot. William shook his head.

He'd lain awake, night after night, since the petition had been served, planning meetings that would never now take place, rehearsing speeches he would never get to deliver.

'I've made a terrible mistake, Jess. I want to start over. Please, let me come home.'

The words haunted him. Perhaps in another lifetime he would get to utter them, but not in this. Not since Chelsea had caught sight of the petition in his briefcase and dropped her bombshell about the baby.

His initial delight at the news had quickly dissipated. The thought that he would be one of the oldest fathers at the school gates depressed him, as did Chelsea's declared desire for three children, although he'd try to hold the line at two. Feeling disloyal, he pulled out his phone and scrolled through the images of him and Chelsea in the French Alps.

It wasn't that he didn't love Chelsea. She was a sweet girl with a beautiful body and a pretty face but she didn't move him as Jessie did. The petition had brought that home to him. However, he was in it for the long haul with Chelsea now, whether he liked it or not, and the sooner the divorce was finalised the better for all their sakes.

'Mr Atkins is ready for you.'

William tucked his phone away and followed the secretary up to the fifth floor and along a plushly carpeted corridor. The building screamed money. William knew this meeting alone would cost him upwards of five hundred pounds. He didn't want to think about what the final bill would be.

'Mr Goode.' Nick Atkins gripped William's hand firmly. 'Thank you for agreeing to join us.'

'Mr Atkins.'

Jessie was seated by the bookcase. Dressed in a black skirt and a black-and-white hound's-tooth jacket, she looked smart and confident and well she might, William thought ruefully. She held all the aces, although she didn't know it yet, because the one thing he had promised Chelsea was that he'd have the decree absolute before the baby was born.

'Hello, Jess.' She'd stopped wearing his ring a couple of weeks ago he'd noticed. Although not unexpected, its disappearance had still been like a punch to his stomach and now, whenever they met, he studiously avoided looking at her bare left hand.

'William.'

Her smile was brief and tight. He wanted to reassure her, to glibly promise her anything. He didn't want to be mean about the money. He'd give her everything if he could, a salve to his conscience. But how could he?

Babies needed so much *stuff*. It had been bad enough in Hannah's day. William could remember exclaiming, 'This baby isn't even born yet and it owns more than I do!' And Jessie had been conservative in her taste and her spending habits, far more than he feared Chelsea would be.

Nevertheless, he was determined Chelsea and the baby would have the best. It was only fair. But where was the money going to come from? If he could just persuade Jessie to sell The Lodge, but he knew there was about as much chance of that happening as Anne Jacobs joining the WI. He drew out a counsel's notebook from his briefcase and sat down. *Let battle commence.*

'Are you sure you don't want a lawyer present, Mr Goode?'

'I think three lawyers in the room is enough, don't you?'

They all laughed.

'I take it you've got the acknowledgements of service?' William asked.

'I have,' Nick confirmed.

'And is the affidavit ready to be lodged?' William asked.

Atkins settled back in his chair, his fingers slowly working to unwind a paper clip. 'No,' he said.

'No?' William repeated in surprise.

'When my client and I are satisfied that things are going well, then we'll take the step of applying to have the nisi pronounced.'

William smiled. 'I'm going to be a good boy, Mr Atkins. You won't need the carrot and the stick.'

'Glad to hear it.'

'I've made some calculations,' William began. 'The way I see it we have three choices. Transfer The Lodge to Jess, transfer it to me or sell. I think we should sell and split the proceeds seventy–thirty in favour of Jess. In addition, I'll cover all of Hannah's expenses until she finishes uni and we can split our savings down the middle.' William looked at them expectantly, a half-smile on his face. 'It's a fair offer,' he added.

'I don't want to sell The Lodge,' Jessie said.

'We have to be practical about this, Jess. It's the most portable asset we have.' William switched his gaze to Nick. 'If we split the proceeds as I've suggested, it'll make us just about even.'

'Just about even?' Nick repeated. His previously warm tone had dropped a couple of degrees.

William's smile dimmed. 'Yes.'

'What if "just about even" isn't even enough?' Nick asked.

Christ. Here we go. 'I told you I'm prepared to be reasonable.' William held the younger man's gaze. 'Eighty–twenty.'

'Were you being reasonable when you helped yourself to the money in the joint account you held with my client?'

'I've told your client that I'd pay her back when The Lodge was sold.'

'With interest, I hope. I understand you used the funds to purchase the property in North Street. I further understand properties in Abbeyleigh have risen in value even in the four months since the purchase took place. My client would therefore be entitled to a share of the profit you have secured in addition to her original stake.'

'I would dispute the property has risen in value, and anyway the money from the savings account only formed part of the purchase price. Chelsea put in some savings. We took out a mortgage for the rest.'

Nick tapped his fingers on the desk as he reviewed the figures. A full minute passed before he looked up. William knew. He had been counting.

'I'd be grateful if you'd extend us the professional courtesy of not insulting our intelligence, *Mister* Goode. Your offer makes no mention of your pension or your stake in Smith Mathers.' Nick re-formed the paper clip. 'Then there's your car.'

'My car?' William's tone was incredulous. 'Are you telling me you want the Jag?' He directed the question at Jessie. 'You hate that car.'

'We don't want the car, Mr Goode,' Nick interjected. 'Nevertheless, it is an asset that should be taken into account in the final reckoning.'

'These shoes are Italian leather, over two hundred pounds a pair, do they need to be taken into account in the *final reckoning*?' William's voice was heavy with sarcasm.

'It depends,' Nick replied smoothly. 'How many pairs do you have?'

'I don't have time for this.' William curled the notebook in his hand, pointing it at Nick as he stood. 'I came here to reach a settlement, not have a pissing contest.' He settled his angry gaze on Jessie as he stuffed the notebook into his briefcase. 'His hourly rate's a bit high to be playing games, isn't it?'

'I don't mind what his hourly rate is,' Jessie replied coolly. 'You're the one who'll be paying it. If you really came here to reach a settlement, sit down and listen to what my lawyer has to say.' She held his gaze.

Annoyed with himself for losing his temper, William threw Nick an angry look before subsiding into his chair. 'I'm listening.'

'Your wife gave up work when your daughter was born. Then, when Hannah started school, Jessie worked part-time. She only went back to full-time employment when Hannah moved into the sixth form. Jessie's career has been stymied as a result. She has only a small pension pot and is an associate at Smith Mathers rather than an equity partner like yourself.

'We want a fifty–fifty split,' Nick said. 'It is the fair thing to do when a marriage as long as yours comes to an end. The only question is how we split the assets to achieve this result. My client believes the best way forward is for her to remain in The Lodge, which should be transferred into her sole name. We have calculated the value of my client's jewellery, the shares she owns and all of her personal savings. We have also reviewed all of your assets, including the pension fund. Our valuation of your assets is slightly higher than the figures you have produced. On our estimates my client would be entitled to an additional lump sum payment of closer to ninety thousand pounds. Taking a conservative estimate, as my client has asked me to do in the spirit of compromise, she is prepared to accept a lump sum payment of sixty thousand pounds in the hope that this will bring about a speedy settlement.' Nick passed over a sheet of paper. 'It is, of course, up to you where that money comes from.'

Hooking his ankle over his knee, William tried to look nonchalant as he balanced the sheet on his leg and studied it. Swiping the notebook from his briefcase, he turned the pages until he came to the roughly drawn table of figures he'd compiled the previous afternoon. In the corner of the page was an incongruous doodle of a church spire, the view from his office. As he compared the two sets of figures, William felt sick. It was worse than he'd feared.

He took them both in with a sweeping glare. 'Sign over The Lodge and pay an extra sixty thousand?' He gave a bark of laughter and slapped his hand on the notebook. 'I can't put my hands on that kind of cash. Even if I sold the Jag and bought a bike, by the time I pay off the lease agreement I wouldn't realise enough to pay a third of what you're asking. Your client wants The Lodge and sixty thousand? I want a month in the Bahamas. We're both likely to be disappointed until we lower our expectations. I can't pay it.'

'Can't or won't?' Nick asked. 'Yours was a long marriage, during which my client supported your career and raised your daughter. She did those things at the expense of her own career.'

'You're trying to put a price on motherhood.' William directed the statement at Jessie, his voice bitter.

'I thought we agreed to leave Hannah out of this? What you fail to grasp is the nature of the assets I hold.'

'You have savings,' Nick replied.

'They're tied up in bonds.'

'Then borrow the money against the property in North Street.'

'Be realistic. I'm mortgaged up to the eyeballs.'

'Hardly. You have at least one hundred and twenty K in equity: the money you took without permission from the savings account you held with my client. But if you don't want to increase your mortgage on the property in North Street, why not ask your partners to buy you out and continue at Smith Mathers as a salaried, rather than an equity, partner? You could use some of the cash to pay my client and live quite comfortably on the rest.'

William laughed. 'Give up my partnership? After all the years I've invested in it?'

'What about all the years I invested in you?' Jessie asked bitterly.

'If you won't cash in your partnership, there's always a pension-sharing order,' Atkins said.

'I don't want my pension touched,' William said sharply.

He could already hear the metal door of the cage clanging shut. *A fifty–fifty split?* He could forget about the early retirement he'd envisaged. He'd be that hamster in the wheel he so detested until one day, in his dotage, about to give a client's defence, he'd keel over with a heart attack, just like his father.

'It was a long marriage, Mr Goode, and the reason it failed was your adultery. A judge would give my client a fifty–fifty split and a judge would sanction a pension-sharing order to do it. Now, we don't want to raid your pension fund, but if there's no other way . . .' Atkins shrugged.

'I don't think a judge would give you anything more than sixty–forty,' William replied, recovering himself. 'Jessica could live quite comfortably in a two-bedroomed house. There's absolutely no justification for her to remain at The Lodge.'

'Apart from the fact that it's my home,' Jessie cut in coldly.

'Has your client told you that my parents contributed over a third of the asking price of The Lodge?' William asked, hitting his stride.

'Yes.'

'So, morally, I have a . . .'

'*Morally?*' Jessie repeated, her voice rising in anger. 'My God, you've got a nerve. Next you'll be suggesting I move out so you and your tart can move in.'

'Well, now you come to mention it,' William replied smoothly.

'My client is entitled –' Atkins began.

'With all due respect I think this meeting is over.' William slapped shut the notebook. 'I'm prepared to be reasonable,' he said quietly. 'But I won't be taken for a ride. The Lodge has to go on the market. Pure and simple.'

As William slammed his way out of the office, Jessie pictured The Lodge as she'd left it that morning, the two circular stone steps bathed in warm light from the lantern above, wrapping themselves round the large wooden front door; the bold sash windows; and, behind, light, airy rooms, comfortably and lovingly furnished. Who the hell did William think he was, breezing in here suggesting they sell her home? And if that wasn't bad enough, not even offering her all of the proceeds. *Whatever happens*, Jessie resolved, *I won't let him take my home away from me. I've lost too much already*.

'I thought that went well,' Nick said, giving Jessie a smile.

'Really?'

'Absolutely. He knows what we want and he knows that we're prepared to take him to court to get it. He was particularly jumpy about the pension. It seems he still harbours the idea of taking early retirement. We promise not to blow the pension pot apart and in return he signs over The Lodge and gives you an additional cash payment by way of compensation. That just leaves the small change. Give him a couple of days to cool off and he'll come back to us with an offer. Mark my words.'

*

The sitting room was Jessie's favourite room of The Lodge. She loved the delightfully deep window seats filled with cushions, the duck-egg blue walls and the white squashy sofas, into which you could sink and lose all track of time. It was a room that embraced all seasons but was at its best in the winter, when, with the fire ablaze and the lamps lit, it was at its cosiest.

Jessie gazed around the room fondly. The Lodge would not be going on the market. She simply wouldn't stand for it. William would just have to find another way to raise the cash to pay her off.

Pausing to check her appearance in the mirror over the fire, Jessie ran her fingers through her hair. It had been a hectic day, what with having to make up the time she'd missed at work while at the meeting in London. And now, here she was, ready to go out again. But, dressed in a navy trouser suit and cream camisole top, Jessie concluded that, despite the rush, she looked smart and professional.

The sound of the doorbell caused Jessie to frown. She didn't want to be late for her first foray into the world of networking. She pulled back the front door and the frown became a scowl as she found William kicking his toe against the top step.

'Can I come in?'

'Depends.'

'On what?' he asked, sullenly.

'Whether you still want to sell my home.'

'I've got as much say in what happens to it as you do.' William's tone was terse.

Jessie started to close the door. William slapped his hand against it.

'Play nicely, Jess. I could have used my key but I didn't. I rang the bell. Anyway, I've come to apologise.'

Reluctantly, Jessie let him in.

Leaving his coat in the hall, William followed her into the sitting room. 'I lost my temper today. I'm sorry,' he said. 'But I think Atkins aggravated the situation.'

'Really? I thought he was excellent.'

'I don't want to rip you off, Jess.'

'I'm not about to let you.'

William thrust his hands into his pockets. 'You'll have a fair settlement.'

Beware the lawyer adopting a casual stance.

'Atkins has a reputation as a troublemaker. We'd be better off without him.'

'*We?*' Jessie raised her eyebrows.

The silence lengthened, heavy with what was not being said. It reminded Jessie of the times she'd gone to bed to find an icy divide had settled between them down the duvet, William giving her the silent treatment because he couldn't have his own way.

She watched him bring his hand up to rub his neck. 'Has Hannah said how she feels about the petition?'

'She knew it was inevitable. I've promised her that we won't tear each other apart.'

William frowned. 'I remember how it was after the split when she refused to speak to me.' He shook his head. 'I couldn't bear to go through that again. Why did you go to Atkins?'

'He came recommended.'

William's eyes narrowed. 'By whom?'

'Anne.'

He tutted. 'I might have known. Is she still seducing adolescents?'

'Is that the pot I hear calling the kettle black?'

William pulled a face and moved to stand in front of the fire. 'Anyone new in your life yet?' he asked as he stared down at the fire.

'No.'

He looked up sharply. 'Did you buy yourself those flowers then?'

Ignoring him, Jessie sat down. 'When are you going to shift your desk and chair out of the study? They're getting in my way.'

'Next weekend okay with you?'

'Fine.'

'You look nice.'

'I'm going to a reception at Lewis Shaw's.'

'Walt's had a chat with you about broadening your client base then?'

'I thought you stepped out of the meeting when they discussed me?'

'I did. Doesn't mean I can't read a spreadsheet. What you need are property developers. Several of them.'

'Thanks. I'll bear that in mind.'

'Or you could just jack it in. No one would think any the less of you.'

Jessie looked at her watch. 'I really should be leaving . . .'

'I just need a couple of minutes of your time, Jess. Please.' William paused. 'I noticed that cottage you've always liked between Abbeyleigh and Stebbingsford is on the market. Reasonable price, too.'

Jessie gave him a sour look. 'I don't want to move.'

'You're not making this easy for me.'

'I didn't know I was supposed to.'

'I'm under pressure as it is. I want to be fair. I do.'

'Then don't make me sell my home,' Jessie replied. 'Nick says strictly speaking a fifty–fifty split would need a lump sum payment closer to ninety grand. I'm prepared to accept sixty.'

'Jolly decent of you,' he replied sarcastically.

'It is actually. I'm prepared to take less than I'm entitled to in order to bring things to a conclusion. That way we can both move on with our lives. I thought that's what you wanted?'

'It is.'

'Then why do you want to sell The Lodge? If we split the proceeds in half, or even eighty–twenty as you suggested, you'll end up having to give me a larger amount of cash. Where's the sense in that?'

He couldn't argue with her logic. He'd run through the calculations himself. But she didn't have to go home to Chelsea and explain for the hundredth time why his soon to be ex-wife was living in a big house on her own while he and Chelsea were in a two-up two-down and likely to remain there. He'd seen the kind of houses Chelsea pored over in her glossy magazines. He'd tried to realign her dreams with reality but so far it had been to no avail.

'I'm stuck between a rock and a hard place, Jess. I need the divorce.'

'We both do.'

'No, you don't understand. I *really* need the divorce. Chelsea's pregnant.'

It took Jessie a moment for his words to sink in. Stunned, she said, 'Couldn't you have had the decency to wait?'

William threw himself on to one of the sofas. 'For Christ's sake, Jess, it wasn't planned.'

'Is she going to have it?'

'Yes, of course.'

'Does Hannah know?'

William's face took on a haunted appearance. 'No. The thought of telling her scares the living daylights out of me. I'm not sure how she'll react.'

Although the bond between father and daughter had taken a battering over William's infidelity, it had survived. Jessie had no doubt the news of a baby would hit Hannah hard but she would bounce back. William was Teflon-coated where Hannah was concerned.

'So you see,' he said softly, 'I need the divorce.'

'You want to marry her?' Jessie had only just got her head around the idea of becoming an ex-wife. Now she had to contend with the thought of being the first wife. Somehow, it seemed worse.

William nodded. 'Chelsea wants a Christmas wedding.'

Jessie could see him, handsome as ever, in a suit, and the tart, figure effortlessly regained, squeezed into some designer creation that would show off her splendid post-baby bust. It would snow, of course. How could it do anything but for two of life's golden people?

'Did you give her your grandmother's ring?' Jessie studied the swirls in the oatmeal carpet, suddenly unable to look at him.

'No. Hannah has it.'

Her sense of relief was enormous and left her feeling confused. She looked up to find him standing, once more, in front of the fire. 'How do you feel about becoming a father again?'

He stared into the fire and sighed. 'I guess it's a chance to put right the things I got wrong the first time.'

'I don't remember you getting too much wrong the first time.'

William gave her a smile. 'Thanks for that.'

Memories crowded in on her. Jessie saw herself, seven months pregnant, bursting into tears. 'Look at me! I'm fat and I'm ugly and I can't even reach to cut my toenails.'

'Sweetheart –' William had taken her hand and brought it up to his lips – 'you've never looked more beautiful.' Then, pressing a kiss to her ample belly, he'd fetched a bowl of water and bathed her feet and cut her nails, before massaging in her favourite foot cream. He had even painted her toenails a pillar-box red and, every two weeks, he had repeated the process. He'd made a bit of a hash of the nail painting, Jessie had discovered when she had given birth but, even so, it had been a nice thing for him to have done.

After the birth, he'd taken two weeks off to help her, in the days when that sort of thing was unheard of. And the jealousy she had feared had never materialised. He had been so proud of Hannah and so proud of her for giving him Hannah; the love had shone out of his face.

Now, she watched him stroke one of Hannah's photographs. 'I was never there, was I? Always bloody working,' he said sadly.

'For us,' Jessie said generously. 'You were working for us.'

'Yeah.' William shook his head, letting his hand drop. 'Can I rely on you to expedite the divorce?'

Jessie pulled herself together. 'I'll expedite the divorce as soon as we've thrashed out the finances.'

She saw his shoulders tense.

'Which we could do far quicker if it was just the two of us.'

'I told you, no.'

He raised his palms in a conciliatory fashion. 'You want to keep The Lodge. I want my stake in the partnership and the pension to remain untouched. That's a good starting point, isn't it?'

'And if you give me the sixty thousand you can have the absolute before the baby's born,' Jessie said.

'I don't have sixty thousand.'

'Sell the property in North Street. You have equity in it.'

'And live where?' he demanded angrily.

'Rent a place.'

'Rent? Are you out of your mind? Be reasonable, please. I'll have to work all hours to get myself back to the position I'm in now. How is that reasonable when I've got a baby on the way?'

The words 'bed' and 'lie in it' sprang to Jessie's mind but instead she said, 'You're only in the position you're currently in because you used my money to achieve it and I want that money back. You don't like it? You should have thought about that before you got her pregnant.'

'I already told you, it wasn't planned.'

'Not by you, maybe.'

'What's that supposed to mean?'

She tilted her chin and met his furious gaze. They were on dangerous ground and they both knew it.

'Chelsea's going to need me at home.'

'She's having a baby, William, not open-heart bloody surgery.'

'Yes. My baby, and he or she is going to have the best of everything, like you did, like Hannah did.' William massaged his eyes. 'Please, Jess.'

Jessie turned away, determined not to let her resolve crumble.

They'd revelled in Hannah. Absorbing all of their love, she had returned it tenfold with her smiles. Over time, the longed-for second child had somehow slipped from their conversation. Had it ever slipped from William's mind? It had never slipped from hers. Jessie had often wondered why things hadn't worked out for them and then felt guilty because they had Hannah and that was more than some couples ever had. But men always wanted a son, didn't they? The tart would give William a son, she had no doubt.

'All I want is a fair split,' Jessie said. 'We worked as a team. You earned more but I invested time. That makes us even.'

'I don't disagree,' William said, a helpless look on his face. 'But if I don't push for a sale of The Lodge will you take less than sixty grand?'

'Why should I?'

'Because I'm asking you to.'

'Not good enough.'

William passed his hand over his eyes. 'This is a difficult time for me. I'm juggling a lot of demands.'

'I'm not asking you to support me for the rest of my life. I'm asking for a share of what was already mine.'

Eyes downcast, William said, 'I know that but I can't face cashing in the pension. Please don't ask me to do that. With another child on the way I need the security to –'

'I've already agreed to take thirty grand less than my lawyer says I'm entitled to. I'm not going to drop any further and we both know you shouldn't ask me to.'

William looked contrite.

'I don't care where you get the money from but if you want the freedom to remarry that freedom is going to cost you this place plus sixty thousand.'

Nodding, William swept out.

Freedom? He'd never felt more trapped in his life. Frantically he reviewed his options. He'd have to cash in some bonds and insurances, try to build them up again later. And he'd have to find a way to make Marie redundant and take back the work himself to boost his turnover. Not only that, but Chelsea would have to scale back her plans for the family home she wanted. In fact, they should stay in North Street. Consolidate. He winced. That would be a hard sell particularly when he had to break it to her that Jessie was keeping The Lodge.

He was halfway to the Jag, his collar turned up against the wind when he heard Jessie call his name. Retracing his steps, he was dismayed to see her holding out her wedding ring.

'What are you doing?'

'You bought it. It's only right you should take it back.'

'I don't want it back. It's yours.'

'Not any more.'

His heart stuttered at the look of pain in her eyes. It was her eyes that had sold him on her all those years ago. They were the clearest, softest blue. The most expressive eyes he'd ever seen. And now they were telling him he was a louse and a pig and he'd made her miserable all over again. He took the ring from her fingers.

Like most strong women, there was a vulnerability to Jessie that she went to great lengths to conceal. When at last she'd known him well enough to reveal it, the sight of it had melted William's heart. From that day on he'd wanted to wrap her in his arms and never let the world near her again. And yet the awful truth was the world had never hurt her as much as he had.

'I'm sorry.' Shocked to discover he was on the verge of tears, he quickly strode to the car. There was so much more he wanted to say but he couldn't face those eyes.

*

In the sitting room, Jessie banked up the fire and put the guard in place. Then she went into the study to turn off the computer. It was unquestionably a man's room; the furniture was dark and austere, dominated by the huge oak desk with the sage-green leather inlay that William's parents had bought when he qualified. Jessie let her fingers drift over the inlay. How many times had she come into this room after he'd left, just to stand like this and remember?

As she turned off the lights, preparing to leave, a feeling of crushing despair swept through her. Soon, William would tell the partners and his secretary, Lynn, about the baby, and then, like all the best gossip, it would percolate around the office and, eventually, the town. Everyone would be talking behind her back again, whispering and pointing. She felt herself shrink inside.

Pull yourself together, she commanded, sucking in a deep breath. *So what if William has another baby? He can have a whole football team. It's got nothing to do with me. Not any more. Yes, people will talk. But let them. I lived through it once. I can live through it again.*

Jessie glanced at her bare ring finger. There was a white line where her wedding band had been. Get a divorce, get a promotion, get a life. She grabbed her car keys from the hall table. Walt, William and the rest of the partners might have their doubts but she was damned if she was giving up on her dream of being made a partner just yet.

Chapter Seven

Jessie painted a smile on her face as Lewis Shaw approached. The estate agent had asked Jessie out a week after William's betrayal had become public knowledge with the words, 'If you want to get your own back, I'm your man.' Jessie had politely declined.

'You're looking as gorgeous as ever, Jessie.' Lewis kissed her cheek. 'Isn't it about time you gave in and let me take you to dinner?'

'But I'm having so much fun saying no,' Jessie replied lightly.

Lewis grinned, handing her a glass of wine. 'Treat them mean, keep them keen?' He nodded approvingly. 'You'll say yes one day. After all, how can you resist?'

'How, indeed? If you'll excuse me, I need a quick word with Sam Sturridge.' Jessie made her way across the room. 'Hello, Sam.'

Sam smiled. 'Jessie.'

'Everything's set for completion on the land at Blackcurrant Farm in two weeks. There's a letter on its way to you.'

'That's grand. You've done a great job.'

Jessie smiled.

'I was telling George Norris how pleased I was. He runs Brook Valley Farm on t'other side of Abbey Wood. Shame he's not here, I could have introduced you. But I did give him your card. He's thinking about buying a couple of cottages for holiday lets. I suggested he give you a call.'

'Thank you, Sam.' *Contacts are everything.*

The old man looked abashed. 'Speak as I find. You've been very easy to deal with and a darn sight prettier than Gareth Ellis.' He laughed. 'George is a good chap. You'll get on well with him.'

'I'm sure I shall.'

Moving on, Jessie made small talk with a couple of the younger estate agents before she felt someone nudge her arm. She turned to find Gareth Ellis standing behind her.

In his late forties and with his hair rapidly receding, the first thing anyone noticed about Gareth was his forehead, which was lined and tanned. The next was his ready smile.

'Come to nick some more of my clients, Mrs Goode?'

Jessie mirrored his smile. 'Sorry, Gareth. It's a competitive business, and it's Miss Martin now.'

'Right. I'm sorry you and William weren't able to patch things up.'

'I'm putting all that behind me now.'

'Good for you. Although not necessarily good for me, if you're throwing yourself into your work instead,' he commented dryly.

'I'm in Abbeyleigh. You're in Stebbingsford. There's plenty of room for both of us. So long as you stay in Stebbingsford,' Jessie said jovially.

Gareth's smile became a grin. 'It's good to see you, Jess. You take care of yourself.'

'You, too.'

'Jessie.' Lewis Shaw took her arm and guided her to one side. 'There's someone I'd like you to meet. His name's Phil Blunkett. He's a property developer. I sold the Old Mill to him last year. He's converting it into flats. He used London lawyers for the purchase but there might be a chance to persuade him to use local solicitors once the flats are developed. I mentioned your name to him.'

'Thanks, Lewis.'

His hand drifted to her lower back. 'One good turn deserves another, don't you think? Have dinner with me.' His hand brushed her backside.

'I've told you before, I don't think it's a good idea to mix business with pleasure,' she said firmly.

Lewis pulled a face. 'You drive a hard bargain, Jessie. You want me to give up my business for you?' He gestured to his office. 'I'll think about it. How about that?'

Jessie smiled. 'No means no, Lewis.'

'But does it always? You women are a funny bunch.'

'In this instance? No means no.'

'Well, it was worth a punt!' he said, not in the least perturbed. 'Come on, I'll introduce you to Blunkett anyway. Phil, this is Jessie, the solicitor I was telling you about. Jessie, Phil Blunkett. I'll leave the two of you to get acquainted.'

Phil Blunkett was in his mid-thirties, Jessie guessed, handsome in a boyish way, with blond hair that flopped into his eyes.

'Hello,' she said.

'Pleased to meet you.'

'Lewis tells me you're developing the Old Mill.'

'That's right.'

'It's a beautiful property.'

'Yes, it is. We're retaining as many of the original features as we can. I'm confident it'll be stunning when it's finished.'

'If you want the conveyancing work on the flats done locally, I'd like the opportunity to put in a quote.' Jessie presented him with her business card. 'I'm good and, in comparison to London lawyers, better value for money.'

Phil smiled, turning the card over in his fingers. 'It would make more sense to get the work done locally,' he admitted. 'Lewis tells me you're an assistant with a firm here in Abbeyleigh.'

'That's right.'

'But not a partner?'

'Not yet.'

Phil raised his eyebrows. 'I like a lady with ambition. I'm thinking about buying another couple of properties in the area. If I go ahead, I'll give you a call. If that goes well, you might be able to handle the sale of the flats for me.'

'That's great. I look forward to hearing from you.'

If she could bring Phil Blunkett to the firm, it would be a bigger coup than Sam Sturridge. Along with all the new clients Anne was introducing her to, her client list was definitely moving in the right direction.

A smile exploded over Jessie's face when, later that night, she walked back to Smith Mathers to collect her car. *So what if the tart is pregnant? The divorce is under way and I'm working towards my promotion. That only leaves my third New Year's resolution unresolved and it's only March. Way to go, Jessie!*

'Jessie!'

Jessie turned to find Owen Phillips running towards her, a gym bag bouncing on his back.

'I thought that was you.'

'Owen. I haven't had the chance to thank you for my rose.'

'My pleasure. No woman should be without flowers on Valentine's Day.'

'It was a lovely thought.'

'You look very smart,' he said, falling into step beside her.

'I've been to a work thing. You?'

'The gym.'

'How's the rehabilitation going? Anyone new in your life yet?'

'No. How about you?'

'No, but I've met someone I like and I think she likes me. Trouble is I'm a little rusty. I don't know whether to play it cool or ask her out. What do you think?'

'I think if you like her that much you should tell her.'

'That's good advice.' They stopped by the entrance to the Smith Mathers car park. 'So, would you like to have dinner with me? Park Place opens next weekend.' He smiled. 'This is me taking that leap in the dark we talked about,' he added.

Jessie's eyes widened in surprise. Then, delighted, she replied, 'I'd love to have dinner with you.'

Who said New Year's resolutions were hard to keep?

APRIL

Chapter Eight

Jessie dipped the roller in the butter-coloured paint and let the excess fall into the drip tray before applying it to the study wall. Behind her, Owen was singing along to a pop tune on the radio as he glossed the windowsill.

'It's as though my life was grey before I met him,' she'd told Anne. 'Nothing but work and heartache. Owen's put the fun back and now its technicolour. Like those old Hollywood movies where the brightness is eye-popping. I might just burst into song.'

'Please don't!' Anne had replied dryly. 'I've heard you sing.'

Jessie dipped the roller in the paint once more, a smile spreading across her face as she cast her mind back to dinner at Park Place.

They had been escorted to a prime table beside an impressive floor-to-ceiling window and the waiter had promptly returned with a bottle of champagne in a bucket of ice. 'Courtesy of Lydia Coates,' he said. 'A thank you to Mr Phillips for doing the flowers.'

Each floral display had contained two dozen tiger lilies and they, like Park Place, had been beautiful but Jessie could have been sitting in a roadside cafe for all the notice she took of her surroundings after that.

Her focus of attention was Owen, dashing in a black suit, white shirt and blue silk tie that matched his cerulean eyes. His smile was ready and warm and the nerves that had crippled Jessie all day dissolved as he complimented her on her blue dress. She wasn't making a fool of herself. She wasn't deluded. This handsome young man really did want to have dinner with her.

'How's life on the stall?'

'Busy but rewarding. I had a fantastic lead-in to Mother's Day. I put together some baskets with flowers, chocolates and teddies. They were incredibly popular. I'm going to do the same for Easter but substitute bunnies for teddies. How about you?'

'I'm aiming for a promotion at work so it's all a bit manic. The partners have warned me not to get my hopes up and that maybe I'll hit my target next summer but I'm hoping if I do enough in the first six months of this year it might convince them to take a gamble on me sooner.

'The partners always announce the promotions each June so I've got a mountain to climb but I like a challenge. My friend Anne Jacobs has been amazing. She's introduced three new property developers to me in just the last week.'

'Are you one of those people who, when they are told they can't do something, are absolutely determined to do it just to prove they can?' Owen asked. His eyes were eager and attentive, taking in every detail of Jessie's face as he spoke, and her spirits soared. She had forgotten what it was like to be properly listened to. For so long William's attention had only been half there. Hers too, if she was honest.

Jessie nodded. 'Absolutely.'

Owen laughed. 'Me, too.'

Making small talk with Barry Sturridge had been torturous; the same could not be said of Owen. Their conversation was as free-flowing as it was diverse. And they laughed. A lot. Not the false, polite laughter of near strangers but the full-throated roars of laughter that came from two individuals very much in tune with one another. Jessie couldn't remember the last time she'd enjoyed herself so much and the evening passed by far too quickly.

As the other diners dwindled in number, Jessie and Owen traded histories.

'Tell me about your family,' Jessie asked.

'My mum died when I was young,' Owen said. 'I was brought up by my dad and auntie. Dad's a chef. He runs a restaurant in London. He loves to cook, and so do I, but it's not much fun on your own. Maybe I could cook for you at The Lodge sometime?'

Jessie was thrilled. 'I'd like that. Tell me about your auntie.'

'Stella? She's fun. The kind of woman you can trust. Always there for you. I spent some of the happiest times of my childhood with her. She lives in Gloucestershire now. What about your parents?'

'Mum died just before I went to university. My dad remarried about ten years later and they started a new life together in New Zealand. We see each other every couple of years and Skype regularly.'

Later, after Jessie had given Owen a brief account of her marriage to William and its demise, Owen had spoken about Tessa's betrayal. 'It really sucks when the person who was supposed to be on your side turns out not to give a damn. It's a hard thing to come back from. But you are my inspiration, Jessie,' he said, toasting her with his wine glass. 'It would have been easy for you to become bitter after the way William treated you but you haven't; instead you've embraced the challenge of starting over. I want to attack life with the same vigour you have. To live life with the handbrake off.'

Jessie's heart sang.

They were the last to leave the restaurant. A cab drove them back to The Lodge.

'Give us a minute, mate,' Owen said when they arrived. He took Jessie's hand as she got out. 'I'll wait till you're safely inside,' he said.

Jessie didn't know whether to be grateful or disappointed. She fumbled with her key, sending it to the ground. Owen retrieved it.

'Have you had a good time?' he asked earnestly as he opened the front door for her.

'Wonderful. Thank you.'

Smiling, he caught hold of her hand and brought it up to his lips. 'Are you busy on Monday night? I thought perhaps we could go to the movies.'

'I'd love to.' Two whole days and a night until she saw him again. It seemed like an eternity.

As though the same idea had occurred to Owen he said, 'Or we could meet for lunch tomorrow at the Northey?'

'Let's do both,' Jessie said, beaming.

The breeze lifted her hair across her face and Owen raised his hand to brush it aside. At the touch of his fingers to her cheek, they both became serious. Owen's eyes searched hers and Jessie watched a dozen different emotions, from desire to fear to longing, sail across them. Whatever answers he sought, she had evidently given because a moment later he leaned in to kiss her.

It was a gentle kiss, hesitant even, as if Owen expected her to pull away. Emboldened, Jessie put her arms round his shoulders. It felt so good to be wanted again and, encouraged, Owen became a little more daring. One arm encircled her waist, the other her shoulder, his hand stealing up into her hair. Jessie could feel the pressure of his fingers tighten as their kiss became more passionate and her heart soared.

When had she and William last kissed like that? Pecks on the cheek and a quick kiss before sex didn't count. This was proper kissing for kissing's sake and Owen was very good at it.

Jessie could sense Owen's reluctance as he broke away, but despite the exquisite feelings he had evoked in her, Jessie knew she wasn't ready for anything more and, instinctively, Owen seemed to know that too.

His hand slipped through hers until just their fingertips were touching. 'Until tomorrow,' he whispered with a smile.

Now, as Jessie anchored the roller in the drip tray and glanced over her shoulder, her smile widened. Owen was a nice man. For who else would walk half a mile in the snow just to make sure she got home safely? And nice was so underrated. He shared her passion for books and the theatre. And, while he had the ability to make her think, crucially, he wasn't afraid of silence. The walk they had taken one Sunday afternoon on a windswept Essex beach had been testament to that.

Wherever they were, whatever they were doing, he made her feel good about herself, dispelling the months of crushing self-doubt she'd endured.

Like a teenager, she had giggled with delight as she'd spoken of him to Anne. 'He's always sending me emails or texts. Fun stuff about our last date or the next one. He always ends them with a kiss. I print them out,' she'd admitted sheepishly. 'He's sweet, too. He'd been looking forward to seeing the latest John Cusack film but at the last minute I had to cancel. I thought Owen would go to the film on his own; I urged him to. Instead, he turned up at The Lodge and cooked spaghetti bolognese. From scratch. "Don't worry," he said. "I'm not here to distract you, just to feed you." William would have given me grief for days for putting work first. Owen just dealt with it. We saw the film the next night. He said he'd rather wait and share it with me.'

Anne had rolled her eyes. 'He sounds perfect for you. You're clearly as soppy as one another. Have you done it yet?'

'No.'

'Why ever not?'

'I'm not ready.'

'Darling, you're never going to be ready. Take my advice: screw up your courage and go for it before love's young dream finds someone else who will.'

Despite her practised cynicism, Jessie knew Anne was thrilled for her. Hannah, too, had lapped up every detail, seemingly unfazed at Owen's age, which Jessie had guessed to be early thirties because she hadn't yet found the courage to ask him.

'Fancy a cup of tea?' Owen asked as he anchored his paintbrush in the drip tray.

'Please.'

'Why have you got a picture of a cat with a no-entry sign drawn across it stuck to your fridge door?' he asked on his return.

'Anne was always threatening to buy me a cat because I refused to socialise after William left,' Jessie said.

'You seem to have made up for it now,' Owen remarked as he stood two mugs of tea on the dust sheet.

Nodding, Jessie remembered Anne's quip about the Cock or a cat and smiled to herself. The last few weeks with Owen had passed swiftly in a blissful blur. They had been to the theatre twice, the cinema three times and had dined in a host of restaurants in Stebbingsford and Abbeyleigh.

On the Wednesday before Easter, Owen had collected her from work and taken her bowling and, on the Thursday, they'd been to see a local rock band, the A12, perform in Spike's. The bank holiday atmosphere had been infectious and Jessie had drunk beer from a bottle and looked forward to the heady prospect of four days in Owen's company.

Admittedly, they'd earmarked the break to decorate the study, but Jessie was excited nonetheless. Owen had arranged for a friend, Danny, to cover the stall and even the thought of William's visit on Saturday to sort out the contents of The Lodge hadn't been enough to dampen her spirits.

Kissing Jessie's neck, Owen threaded his arms round her waist. Above the radio, Jessie could hear the swish of rain on the gravel. The sound of the downpour and the warmth of Owen's arms gave her a cosy feeling. *How I've missed this*, she thought with a sigh.

'What's this?' Owen asked, picking up a yellowing newspaper cutting.

'I found it this morning. It's a report from the *Abbeyleigh Gazette* on one of William's cases.' Jessie looked once more at the grainy picture of William. His clothes looked old-fashioned, his hair longer than she could remember him wearing it. It was dated the year before Hannah's birth, a lifetime ago.

'So this is the dickhead?' Owen said, studying the picture before handing the cutting to Jessie who stowed it in her pocket. 'When's he due?'

Jessie checked her watch. 'In an hour.' Her mobile sang out and she retrieved it from the hall. 'Hello?'

'Jessie Martin?'

'Yes?'

'It's Phil Blunkett. We met at Lewis Shaw's.'

'I remember.'

'I've decided to go ahead with the purchase of those two properties I mentioned. I know it's short notice but I wonder if you could meet me in Massey Road, number fifty-six.'

'Now?'

'Yes.'

'Okay. I'll be there as soon as I can.' Jessie put down the phone. 'You remember that developer I told you about, Phil Blunkett? He wants me to meet him in town now.'

Owen grinned. 'I told you he'd call. How could he resist? I'll finish up here. You go and get ready.'

*

As Jessie reversed into a parking space in Massey Road, she saw Gareth Ellis exit number fifty-six.

He gave Jessie a cheery wave. 'Hello, Jessie.'

'Hi, Gareth. What are you doing here?'

Gareth smiled. 'I'll let Phil explain, if you don't mind. He's waiting for you inside. Good luck,' he called after her.

Puzzled, Jessie crossed the road and pushed at the open front door. 'Phil?'

'In here.'

She followed his voice into the first of the reception rooms.

'What do you think of the place?'

The majority of properties in Massey Road were Victorian villas, well built and imposing. Jessie took in the peeling wallpaper and bare floorboards of the interior of number fifty-six. 'It gives a whole new meaning to the phrase shabby chic.'

Phil laughed. 'It needs work but that's why I'm interested. This property and number fifty-four next door have fallen into disrepair but they're prime real estate. They just need a little TLC.'

Jessie nodded. Done up, the house would look lovely. She'd acted in the purchase of number fifty-two, which had undergone a similar transformation the previous year. The deal had never actually been finalised, she recalled. There had been something odd about it. She'd have to get the old file out and take a look. That was if the job was hers. 'I saw Gareth Ellis leaving.'

'You did.' Phil rubbed his chin. 'No offence, Jessie, but I only have your word and that of Lewis Shaw to say you're good. You're not a partner at Smith Mathers and I can't afford to play amateur hour.'

'Are you telling me I'm dumped rather than hired?' Jessie asked, trying hard to hide her disappointment.

'On the contrary. I'm going to give you an opportunity to prove yourself. I'm buying both these houses to sell to the higher end of the market. Gareth Ellis is going to handle the purchase of fifty-four. You're going to handle fifty-six. It's a contract race with a difference. But I want a good job done.' Phil held up his hand. 'No shortcuts. Whoever I'm most impressed with gets the Old Mill flats and more besides. I have big plans for this area and I'm keen to forge a link with a local solicitor. The question is which one? Are you up for the challenge?'

'Absolutely,' she said firmly.

'Good.' Phil shook her hand. 'That's what I wanted to hear. I'll get Lewis to forward you the particulars on the property and you can get to work.'

Jessie nodded. 'I won't let you down.'

They shook hands again on the front steps of the property before Phil got into his Porsche 911. Jessie watched him roar away. Taking out her phone, she checked her messages. There were two.

'Hi, honey.' Owen. 'I've tidied up and I'm going to grab some lunch in town and check in with Danny while you and the dickhead are at The Lodge. Ring me when he's gone and I'll come back.'

'*Where* are you?' William. 'We agreed one thirty. I'm here. Where the hell are you? I'm going to give you another ten minutes then I'm going to start without you.'

How could you divide the contents of a house by agreement when only one of you was present? Exasperated, Jessie ran to her car.

'Jessie!'

Gareth Ellis was leaning against the driver's door of his Mercedes SLK. 'I know Phil's just fired a starting pistol but you don't literally have to run.'

Jessie smiled. 'I'm late for another meeting.'

'What did you think of his proposal?' Gareth asked, clearly not ready to let her go.

'It's an interesting way to audition solicitors,' Jessie said, fishing out her car keys.

'Are you going for it?'

'Absolutely.'

'Cool.' Gareth turned to get into his car. 'Don't take it personally when I beat you, will you? I'd hate for us to have a falling out over this.'

Stung, Jessie said, 'Who said you were going to beat me?'

Gareth smiled. 'Taking Sam Sturridge away from me is one thing. This is quite another. There's a reason why I'm a partner and you're not. Just don't get your hopes up, that's all I'm saying. I like you, Jessie, I always have, but not enough to let you win.'

With her temper rising, Jessie struggled to keep her tone even. 'You might not have any choice.'

Gareth laughed. 'That's the spirit, Jessie.'

Chapter Nine

William, dressed in black jeans and a T-shirt, was wrapping wine glasses in newspaper when Jessie arrived.

From one arrogant bastard to another. 'How could you start without me?'

'I have other things to do this afternoon. I can't sit around here on the off chance you might turn up. The list is over there.' He pointed to the coffee table. 'Where were you anyway?'

'I had a meeting with a property developer. It overran. I'm sorry.'

'On a bank holiday Saturday?' William was incredulous. 'I came second best to work during our marriage. I suppose it shouldn't surprise me that I come second best to it during the divorce.'

Jessie tutted. 'Don't be so melodramatic. I've got something for you.' She pulled the newspaper cutting from her purse.

William smiled as he studied it. 'I must show this to Hannah.'

Jessie recalled the long conversation she'd had with her daughter, following William's visit to Devon the previous week.

'Do you think I'll still see Daddy as much once the baby comes?'

'Darling, of course. Your father adores you.'

'What if I decide not to work with him after I leave uni?'

'It still won't change anything.'

'But for as long as I can remember he's talked about us working together. He'll be disappointed, won't he?'

'Perhaps, but he'll get over it. Is this something you're seriously considering?'

'I know it's a long way off and I'm incredibly lucky to have a training contract waiting for me at Smith Mathers. But it's there because of you and Daddy, not because of what I've achieved. My friends are all talking about applying to firms in London or Birmingham or Leeds. No one else is going to a provincial market town. I'm not knocking Abbeyleigh. It's my home and I love it and one day I want to practise law there with you and Daddy, just not straight away. Do you think I'm mad?'

'No. You want to make your own way in the world. That's commendable.'

'I just hope Daddy sees it like that. I don't want it handed to me on a plate because, if it is, how will I ever know if I was good enough to have it on merit? It's one thing doing summer work with Daddy while I'm at uni but once I'm finished there I want to stand on my own two feet. I want to apply with all the other hundreds of applicants to the top law firms and stand or fall on my CV, my results and my interview. I want to get a training contract because I earned it.'

'If you explain it to your dad like you've just explained it to me, how could he fail to understand? You want to prove yourself. It's only natural. And, in the long run, experience at a top law firm will be of benefit to Smith Mathers if you ever did decide to come and work there.'

'I think Daddy might hear me say "Not now" and think I mean "Not ever".'

'Then it's up to you to explain yourself properly. Honestly, darling, I don't think your dad will mind. This is a tough business to get started in and if you want to make that start without a helping hand from us, well, I think that will just make him prouder still.'

Jessie watched as William carefully folded the article and tucked it away. 'How was Hannah?' she asked, eager to find out how William thought their meeting had gone.

'She's got it into her head that the new baby might usurp her in my affections. Hopefully I managed to convince her that that would never happen.'

'By buying her and David an Easter break to the Canary Islands?' Jessie asked tartly. She'd been looking forward to seeing Hannah during the holidays and possibly introducing her to Owen, but Hannah's rushed call explaining her last-minute change of plans had scuppered that.

'She's working hard. She deserves a break.'

'I thought you had no money?'

'The holiday didn't cost sixty thousand.'

Jessie decided to let it go. She didn't want to see Hannah upset any more than William did. If the holiday helped to reassure her, fine. Hannah and her boyfriend would benefit from a week in the sun. She wouldn't mind one herself.

So far as her own reaction to the baby was concerned, Jessie had actually started to pity William a little.

'He says it wasn't planned,' Jessie had told Anne.

'Not by him maybe.'

'I said that. He went ballistic.'

Anne had given a throaty laugh. 'They hate to feel they're not in control. If only the poor buggers were to realise they're only ever in control when we feel like letting them be. Chelsea's going to get all fat and moody and then, when the baby's born, she'll go off sex. Poetic justice, I'd say.'

'Doing some decorating?' William asked, bringing Jessie back to the present. 'I smelt paint when I came in.'

'The study.'

William nodded. 'Making a fresh start?'

'Something like that.'

'So how are you?'

Jessie looked at him in surprise. 'You see me almost every day. You know how I am,' she said warily.

In the early days of their split, he'd often asked how she was; she'd assumed he had been hoping she would tell him she was fine, when he had known full well she was anything but. Back then, she had played down her pain for the sake of Hannah and to make it easier on the partners and staff at Smith Mathers. But Jessie had been determined not to trivialise the upset where William himself was concerned. The loss of a husband was not something you got over by taking an aspirin and going to bed for a few days. She'd decided he would have to come to terms with the guilt by himself.

Now, she wondered if someone had told him about Owen and that William was fishing, hoping she'd confirm the existence of a new man in her life. But why should he care? Unless he equated her starting over with someone new as permission for him to stop feeling guilty altogether. *And if that's the case, you're on your own, pal. Why should I make it easy for you? Nothing about our break-up has been easy for me.*

She studied William's list. 'How do you want to handle this?'

'Contrary to what your lawyer may say, I'm not trying to be difficult. I don't want to go through The Lodge room by room and argue over every little thing. I've deliberately kept the list small. Those are the only things I want. Everything else you can keep.'

Jessie scanned the list. It seemed reasonable. They began to sort through the items together. William produced two boxes from the car and, when those were full, Jessie hunted out some carrier bags.

'I hope I'm going to get some credit for letting you keep ninety per cent of the contents,' William said eagerly. 'Eighteen thousand plus The Lodge is a reasonable offer. What do you want me to do, Jessie, open my veins and let the blood out?' His tone was light but there was steel in his eyes.

'I want you to open your wallet, it'll make less mess. And while we're on the subject of what I want, I'd like your key back.'

'No.'

His vehemence surprised her. 'But there's no need for you to have a key.'

'What's the matter, Jessica? Do you think I'm going to come back later, when you're not here, and clear the place out?'

That particular thought hadn't occurred to Jessie. She'd been more concerned about him walking in on her and Owen. 'Would you?' she asked coolly.

'Of course I bloody wouldn't.' William scowled. 'But while my name's on the deeds, I have a right to a key. And I wouldn't expect that key back any time soon. The way your lawyer's carrying on, my kid'll be at university before we get a settlement. The *younger* one.' He folded his arms. 'Right.' His tone was businesslike. 'That just leaves the figurine.'

'What?' Jessie thought they'd covered everything.

'It was on the list. Hannah's figurine.'

Jessie's heart sank as she snatched up the list once more. It was the only item on the reverse. 'Why don't you take a couple of the paintings instead?'

'Because I want the ballet dancer.'

They had purchased it years ago, when Hannah was having ballet lessons. It bore a remarkable likeness to their daughter and had pride of place on the mantelpiece.

'You can have anything else, but not that.'

'Now who's being unreasonable? I'm letting you keep almost everything and you won't give me the figurine.'

'You know how special she is to me,' Jessie said.

'Every bit as special as she is to me and I want her.'

'Well, you can't have her.'

'You can have your key back.'

Jessie was stunned. 'I shouldn't have to negotiate to get back the key to my own house.' Her voice rose in line with her temper.

William shrugged. 'You seem to want it quite badly for some reason.'

Jessie hated his sneer. Someone had told him about Owen. She just knew it.

'Not that badly,' she replied.

'What makes you think you can refuse me the figurine anyway?' William asked. 'As I recall, I was the one who paid for her.'

'I was the one who saw her first.'

They squared off; two adults taunting one another like petulant children. Too late Jessie saw William dart for the mantelpiece. Agile, from so many years of playing cricket, he scooped up the figurine before Jessie had even moved. His smile was vicious as he held her aloft like a trophy.

'Give her back,' Jessie demanded.

'Make it worth my while.'

The figurine was tantalisingly close to her fingertips. Jessie clawed the air as she jumped. 'William, please!'

'Take the eighteen thousand, Jessie. It's a fair offer.'

'No.'

'Take the eighteen thousand and you can have her back.' William waved the figurine enticingly above her head.

'William.'

'Take the eighteen thousand, Jessie. If you do, you can have the figurine and I'll throw in your key as well. After all, you wouldn't want me barging in when you and your barrow boy are trying to have a quiet night in, would you?' he said, smirking.

Jessie shoved him in the chest. 'You son of a bitch!'

William seemed to lose his balance in slow motion. His arms circled like crazy windmills as he toppled backwards. The figurine sailed from his grasp and smashed on the hearth. He had always been more adept at batting than fielding.

'That's a no then, is it?' he asked.

'Look what you've done!' Jessie cried as she knelt to pick up the pieces.

'Look what *I've* done? *You* pushed *me*.'

Jessie let the pieces fall on to the carpet. It was hopeless. The pieces could never be glued back together. Her eyes swam. 'You did it on purpose.'

'Yeah, now we can have half each.'

Chapter Ten

'What happened?' Owen demanded as soon as he saw Jessie's face.

His hand was on her cheek, brushing aside her tears, as she told him in stammering sentences.

Losing his coat, Owen followed her into the sitting room. He knelt to examine the broken pieces.

'It's hopeless; they won't fit back together,' Jessie said.

Standing, Owen put his arms round her. 'Don't cry, honey. He's a dickhead, remember? He's not worth it.'

Jessie nodded. Owen was right. She'd cried enough for William. But the sight of the shattered ballerina caused her lip to quiver again nonetheless.

It was strange the things a person invested so much emotional energy into. The ballerina wasn't particularly expensive but to Jessie it had been priceless because she equated it to Hannah when she was eight years old: her spindly legs sticking out from beneath a pink tutu, her hair pulled into a severe chignon, a look of fierce determination on her face. How ridiculous. She still had her memories of Hannah as a ballerina. William couldn't break those.

Owen pulled her near.

Wrapping her arms round him, Jessie breathed in the scent of him as she rested her head against his shoulder. 'Thank you,' she said.

'For what?'

'Being here. Holding me.'

With a smile, Owen stroked her cheek. His kiss was easy and gentle. It demanded nothing in return and yet she yearned to give him everything.

His hair was wet from the rain and his eyes seemed bluer than ever. With their faces just inches apart, Jessie felt an almost overwhelming desire to kiss him and, as the thought sped through her mind, her lips were reacting.

At the feel of Owen's mouth on hers her anger melted away. The kiss came to an end but before Jessie could recover her equilibrium, Owen was sweeping more kisses against her cheeks and her chin, before seeking out her mouth once more and possessing it.

'Have you any idea how much I want to touch you?' he whispered as he kissed the soft skin behind her ear. 'To love you?' He found her lips once more.

They had kissed before but never like this. The kisses then had been events in themselves. This time, they both knew their kisses were a prelude to something more.

Owen's breath was hot on her skin and Jessie quivered with excitement as he kissed his way to her collarbone, finding the hollow of her throat.

Breathlessly, Jessie embraced him, winding her fingers into his hair, pressing him to her, rejoicing as she urged him on.

In another part of her brain, Jessie registered how strange it felt to be this close to someone who wasn't William. Owen didn't hold her as William had or kiss her the same way. It wasn't better or worse, it was just different.

She and William had enjoyed a great sex life in the early days, but Jessie doubted it was exceptional. They would have broken no records for endurance and they had never been into anything more kinky than the odd silk scarf round her wrists and sometimes his. Was that dull by today's standards? What if she was older than Owen, but not wiser? What if Owen expected more from her than she was able to give? Jessie backed away slightly.

On seeing Jessie's expression, Owen's hands fell awkwardly to his sides. 'I'm sorry,' he said hoarsely. 'I'm rushing you. I promised myself I wouldn't.'

'No. I'm sorry,' Jessie said swiftly. 'It's just . . . it's been a long time since I've been with anyone other than William and . . .' Her voice trailed away.

Owen nodded. 'Letting go of the past is harder than you think.' He cupped her face in his hand. 'I understand that only too well. But for the first time in a long time, you've made me want to.' He breathed the words into her hair and she leaned into him, wanting to be reassured. 'You must know how I feel about you,

Jessie.' Edging back, he searched her eyes. 'I'm in love with you. Let me *make* love to you.'

Jessie's eyes widened in surprise. 'You love me?'

'Surely you realised?'

'No, I . . .' She faltered. *He loves you, stupid. What are you waiting for?* What was that expression Hannah used to describe a choice that was really no choice at all? A no-brainer.

Jessie was torn. Her body ached for him. His kisses had ignited a burning need inside her, made all the more acute by the multitude of nights she'd spent alone. But her head warred with her body. It wanted her to run away and hide, to protect herself from the emotional pain intimacy could bring.

She ran her fingers through Owen's hair. 'How old are you?' she asked.

Owen met her gaze boldly. 'How old do you need me to be?'

It was a good answer to a foolish question. How old did she need him to be? Was thirty-one acceptable but twenty-nine too young? Or was she guilty of using Owen's age merely as an excuse to keep the handbrake on a little longer?

She pulled him towards her and kissed him deeply.

Owen chuckled. 'I guess I'm old enough then,' he said.

'I guess you are,' she agreed. She took him by the hand and led him towards the stairs. Owen put his arm round Jessie's waist and they climbed the stairs together, she in front, he behind, his lips locked to the side of her neck. At the top of the landing she faltered as she stared at her closed bedroom door. Reclaiming the study was one thing, repossessing the bedroom was something else.

'We can use one of the guest bedrooms if you want,' Owen said gently.

She loved that he'd sensed her discomfort and was trying to minimise it. 'You're not a guest,' she pointed out.

He nuzzled her neck. 'I don't mind.'

'I do! I can't let myself get hung up about this.' She didn't even know why she was getting in such a state about it. It wasn't as though the bed was the same bed she'd shared with William. She'd thrown that out the moment she had discovered he'd slept with Chelsea in it.

Now, the thought of William and Chelsea together in the bedroom she and William had shared for so many years spurred Jessie on. He'd had no such qualms. Why should she? She stepped forward, tugging Owen behind her.

'If you're sure,' he said.

'I'm sure.'

She threw open the door of the bedroom as if challenging it to somehow repel her. The rose colour scheme had given way to simple greens and creams but cosmetic changes only took her so far. It would only really cease to be the room she had shared with William when she took another man into it and he took her.

The rain was tumbling down outside, the afternoon dreary and grey. The bed with its white cotton bedding, patchwork quilt and colourful cushions looked inviting.

Jessie felt her heart rate ramp up as she wondered what it would be like with someone new. They always said it was like riding a bike, you never forgot. She giggled.

'What's funny?'

'I'm not sure how to be with someone new,' she confessed.

Owen turned her to face him. 'I just want you to be yourself. It's all I'll ever want from you, Jessie. But are you sure you're ready? I'd be happy to wait . . .'

'Happy?' she queried. She had felt his need for her as they'd reached the landing and he had pressed himself against her. The insistent bulge in his trousers had not suggested a man who would be happy to wait.

'I can always take a cold shower,' he said with a smile.

'I don't want you to do that.'

He kissed her lips. 'If you change your mind . . .'

'I won't,' she said firmly.

'But if you do . . .'

'Christ, Owen! Are we going to make love or not?' she asked, desire, frustration and confusion all peaking within her.

He gave a throaty laugh. 'I'm just saying.' He held up his hands in supplication.

'Well, don't; those hands can be put to far better use.'

With a quick kiss to her lips, he moved to stand behind her. Sweeping her hair to one side, he reached for the zip of her floral-print silk dress. The doubts gnawed once more at Jessie's insides and she was grateful Owen couldn't see the look of indecision on her face.

How old was he? Young enough that he hadn't wanted to tell her and she was old enough to know better. Toy boys were Anne's thing, not hers. He was probably used to nubile young women with pneumatic chests and no cellulite. She might be in great shape but she wasn't foolish enough to think she could compete with the body of a twenty-year-old. She was glad he was standing behind her. At least this way she wouldn't catch any look of disappointment, however fleeting, on his face.

She felt Owen tug on her zip, easing it down slowly and gently. Her dress fell apart, a co-conspirator, bringing them together. His lips were on her shoulders, whisper-soft kisses that barely registered against her skin. He had the zip all the way down now. She felt the material flow down her body like water and pool at her feet. She went to turn so that she could face him but his arms instantly sailed round her waist, anchoring her.

'Stay there. Let me do this. If you still want me to,' he added.

'I do.' Her breath hitched as she felt his fingers work the strap of her bra. She had spent a small fortune on new underwear, provocative sets in siren red, midnight black and candy pink. Even more on frothy confections of creamy lace with push-up and cut-down cups trimmed with impossibly cute bows. She was wearing none of them, of course. Typical! This morning she had chosen plain white cotton.

Christ, it was like losing her virginity all over again. A memory of William stole into her mind: the only man she had ever known. She felt her bra come loose and fall to the floor.

'Touch me,' she begged, leaning into Owen. 'Hold me.' She knew she needed to feel Owen's hands on her breasts to drive William from her mind. He had no place in this room. He had vacated it a long time ago. Now all she had to do was get him out of her head.

Owen obliged, his hands holding her breasts as his lips journeyed from her shoulder to her neck, ending up in the soft hollow behind her ear. She could feel his breath against her skin, hot and ragged now.

'You're so beautiful, Jessie,' he whispered.

Jessie felt bereft when his hands left her breasts as abruptly as they had claimed them. She wanted to grab his hands and put them back but he was stroking his fingers down the sides of her body now. They came to rest at her hips.

Her knickers were the same as her bra, white cotton, nothing much to write home about. Thank God they weren't the bigger knickers she wore on fat days. She giggled again, a handy release for the tension she was feeling.

'What's funny?'

'I bought a lot of sexy underwear,' she confessed. 'I'm not wearing it,' she added needlessly.

'You don't need sexy underwear,' he said as his fingers skimmed the top of her knickers. 'Besides, I've always had a thing for white cotton.'

She laughed. His lips tracked her spine, sinking lower with every kiss. She could feel herself growing tense even as desire licked at her belly and thighs.

She heard Owen sigh. 'What's the matter?' she asked, concern instantly driving out her growing arousal.

'You have the cutest dimples at the base of your spine,' Owen said. As if to underline the point, he kissed them. 'You should know when we're in bed together I'm going to spend an inordinate amount of time touching, stroking and kissing these dimples.'

Jessie laughed again, carefree, happy, her shyness temporarily forgotten, at least until he hooked his fingers into her knickers and lowered them. She felt them glide down her legs with indecent haste, chased by his fingertips. He stroked both hands down the calf muscle of her left leg, circling her ankle, teasing her heel from the floor. She lifted her foot.

'Owen,' she said, frustration leaching into her words.

'Soon,' he said as he repeated the procedure on her right calf, before his hands glided upwards, tenderly stroking her backside.

His touch made her quiver. She felt him stand, his shoulders level with hers now, his lips nudging her neck. She heard him undo his belt. 'Let me,' she said, half turning, growing desperate now.

His arm moved swiftly round her waist, holding her still. 'I've got this,' he said.

She felt his trousers fall. 'Owen, please.' She was crumbling now from her need for him. To think a few minutes ago she'd cared how old he was. She didn't care any more. All that mattered was satisfying the need that was gathering inside her, a memory of how it used to be, the knowledge that it could be that good again.

She gave a cry as he suddenly put his hand between her legs, his fingers gently but insistently nudging inside her.

'I want you to be ready,' he said.

'I'm ready,' she said tersely.

He laughed softly. 'I want you to be so ready you forget to be shy.'

She covered his hand with her own and pressed him deeper inside her. 'Believe me, I'm already there.'

Withdrawing his hand, he clasped the top of her arms and pirouetted her to face him. His gaze never left her face as he kissed her lips. 'You're so beautiful, Jessie.' Only then did he let his gaze fall, wandering everywhere his fingers had moments before.

Uncoupled from the power of his stare, she too was free to look where she wanted. He tugged his shirt over his head. Her gaze took in the muscles of his stomach, so clearly defined. She let her fingers drift over his taut flesh, felt the muscles shiver under her touch.

'I don't need much encouragement,' he said with a smile.

'I can see that.'

He kicked his jeans away and peeled off his pants.

Jessie's body throbbed at the sight of his erection.

'You can still say no,' he said with a smile.

'Shut up and fuck me!'

'Jessica Martin!' he said, pretending to be shocked as he unsheathed a condom. 'I can see you're going to lead me astray.'

She laughed as she pulled him near. 'Over and over again,' she promised.

Owen chuckled. 'That handbrake's well and truly off now, isn't it?'

*

Later, as Jessie rose from the depths of sleep, she could hear the rain pounding against the window and imagined the last of the shoppers struggling home, cold and wet, cars swishing through the puddles, as murky darkness descended. She felt snug and warm, naked beneath the duvet.

During the endless nights following William's betrayal, she'd longed for someone who could make her feel like a woman again. She hadn't held out much hope. How could a pearl diver ever find the courage to dive again, risking everything, after nearly drowning? But she had known she had to try. She had always been a believer in fate. And fate had sent her Owen.

She smiled. Effortlessly, he had soothed her fears with his ardour and she had felt such joy at being caressed again, held and cherished.

The explosion, when it occurred, had been . . . Jessie frowned. She had an expression for how good it got when it couldn't get any better. It was a phrase she and William had coined: a scrape-me-off-the-ceiling orgasm.

Still half asleep, she reached for Owen. The bed was empty. She opened her eyes. For a moment, hurt and surprise collided within her at the possibility that Owen might have dressed and left. As she turned over, however, she realised he had lit one of the bedside lamps, pulled on his jeans and was standing at the bedroom window. Jessie could see his face reflected in the glass. He looked troubled.

'Owen?'

He turned instantly and smiled but the smile never quite reached his eyes.

Hitching her silk robe from the bedpost, she wrapped it round herself and joined him at the window. 'What is it?'

'Earlier, when I said I loved you, you didn't say it back.'

So that was it. Men could feel insecure, too, of course. She thought of William being sick before his early court appearances. They just hid it so well it was sometimes easy to forget.

'It's too soon for me to say it,' Jessie said, choosing her words carefully.

Nodding, Owen stared out over the garden, lost now to the night.

'And I don't want to lie to you,' Jessie added, trying to take the sting from her words.

'I don't want that either,' he said earnestly.

'I just need time.' She squeezed his hand. 'I'm sorry that you're paying the price for someone else's mistakes,' Jessie said. 'It's not fair, I know.'

'When it comes to relationships other people always end up paying for someone else's mistakes,' he replied.

Jessie was struck by the world-weary look in Owen's eyes as he spoke. He was far too young to have been hurt so badly and it made the fact he'd felt able to express his feelings to Jessie all the more remarkable. Her heart ached for him and she wished she could have responded in kind and meant it but it was just too soon.

'Give me time,' she said again.

He stroked her face. 'Take as long as you need.' This time his smile was genuine. 'I just needed to know there was a chance that one day you could feel the same way, too.'

'A good chance,' she said. Gazing into his soulful eyes, Jessie wondered how she'd ever got this lucky. 'Are you going to tell me how old you are?'

'Does it matter?'

'I'd like to know.'

'I'm thirty-two.'

'Ten years between us,' Jessie said quietly. It was a big gap, almost a generation.

'Age is irrelevant,' Owen said briskly. He slipped his hand inside Jessie's robe and placed it over her heart. 'It's what's in here that counts. In here, we're the same age.'

'But . . .' Jessie stopped herself.

Owen had told her he loved her, with his words and with his body. Wasn't that enough? Don't go looking for problems. Be satisfied.

'We're going to be so good together, Jessie,' Owen said softly. He lowered his hand to caress her breast. 'Let me show you how good.' Taking her hand, he led her back to bed.

Suddenly emotional, Jessie followed. All she had wanted, all she had ever wanted, was someone new to dive for pearls with. Now, astonishingly, amazingly, she had found him.

MAY

Chapter Eleven

Jessie laid down her pen and stretched. As she curled her bare toes into the deep oatmeal carpet, her gaze swept over the butter-coloured walls, clean white shelving, gleaming paintwork and white wooden shutters. In the study, it would always be summer, whatever the season, whatever the weather. She turned the rod of the shutter to widen the slats and take a look outside. Gunmetal-grey clouds were gathering in the sky. She smiled as Delphi, Owen's van, appeared on the drive.

'Danny's minding the stall,' Owen explained, a moment later. 'I thought we could have lunch.' He held up a carrier bag. 'Fish and chips.'

They went through to the kitchen and Jessie put the kettle on and made tea while Owen unwrapped the takeaway.

'How's it going?' Owen asked.

'I always find it hard to work on a Saturday,' Jessie confessed.

'It's the thought of everyone else having a day off. I feel the same,' Owen said as he sprinkled salt over his chips.

'William's been ringing. I've been ignoring him.'

'Is that wise?'

'Probably not,' Jessie admitted. 'But I haven't got time for a row.' She picked up a piece of battered cod and bit into it.

'How do you know you'd row?'

'Because we always do and because his latest offer isn't nearly enough and he knows it. I've already told him I'll settle for less than I'm entitled to. I can't be fairer than that. He knows full well that money he helped himself to was as much mine as his. He's trying to get away with paying me as little as possible because his new girlfriend has expensive tastes but I'm not going to give in to him. Why should I?'

Licking his fingers, Owen poured the tea. 'It's good that you're not letting him bully you.'

'Talking of bullying, Gareth Ellis texted me to say that he's ready to exchange contracts on Monday.' Jessie accepted the mug of tea with a smile and took a sip.

'Are you ready?'

'No,' Jessie said gloomily. 'I really wanted to beat him, not just because I want the Blunkett work but because he was so bloody condescending towards me.' She pulled at a piece of batter and started to pick at the white fish beneath.

'And there's no way you could be ready?'

Jessie shook her head. 'Do you remember I told you there was something strange about the purchase of number fifty-two?'

Owen nodded.

'I got the old file out. There was an agreement that the owner of number fifty could cut across the back gardens of the neighbouring properties to reach the river. I was making enquiries to find out whether it was a formal right of way or an informal agreement that we could terminate, when my purchaser lost his finance and the deal collapsed.'

'What's that got to do with what you're doing now?'

'Number fifty-six is the only property in that line of houses with direct access to the river. If there was a right of way and it was laid down so that the owner of number fifty could reach the river, it must run through the gardens of all of the properties from fifty to fifty-six. I've written to the seller's solicitors expressing my concerns and asking for confirmation of the position. They've told me they think it's an informal agreement but they're investigating.'

'Have you told Gareth Ellis?'

'I've tried. He was more interested in gloating about how close to exchange he was. Maybe his seller's solicitors have given him the assurances he needs.'

'But you don't think so?' Owen said.

'He kept saying not to worry about it and then he started teasing me about how I was just trying to stall him so I could exchange first. He's so obsessed with winning that I'm afraid it might be interfering with his judgement.'

'What if it is? It's not your problem.'

Jessie circled her hands round her mug. 'No, but if it turns out to be a formal right of way it will be Phil Blunkett's problem. I can't see the kind of people Phil is looking to sell to being too pleased to discover someone else has a perfect right to walk across their back garden any time they choose.'

'Fair point.'

'I'm considering having a word with Gareth tonight at the Mayor's Ball. What do you think?' she asked.

'Good idea.'

'I'm not sure he'll listen, especially if he thinks I'm just trying to sabotage his chances.'

'You could always speak to Phil instead,' Owen suggested.

Jessie laughed. 'He really would think I was trying to sabotage his chances then!'

'You'd be acting in your client's best interests. Isn't that what you're supposed to do?'

Jessie nodded. 'Yes, but I'm not sure Gareth will see it that way.'

*

The Mayor's May Ball, in aid of local children's charities, had been held in the magnificent wood-panelled function room of the town hall for as long as Jessie could remember.

So grand a room, particularly with a band playing, could hardly be expected to grow quiet on the arrival of two people but, as Jessie and Owen entered, it seemed to Jessie as though every pair of eyes turned in their direction. She was acutely aware that instead of then politely looking away and resuming their conversations, many continued to stare. It was only as the mayor approached, resplendent in his chain, that Jessie saw William at the back of the group, a look of dismay on his face.

'Delighted you could come,' the mayor said in a booming voice. 'You look beautiful, my dear.' He kissed Jessie's cheek before gripping Owen's hand.

'One down, another two hundred to go,' Owen said through his smile as the mayor moved on.

Jessie laughed, then, seeing Anne in a red twenties-style dress, the couple made their way towards her.

'My God!' Anne exclaimed. 'You two certainly know how to bring a party to a standstill.'

Smiling, Owen took two glasses of champagne from a passing waiter and handed one to Jessie. 'That was the plan. Announce to anyone who didn't already know that we're a couple and proud of it.' He kissed Jessie's cheek.

Jessie squeezed his hand. 'Is Stephen here?' she asked, turning to Anne.

'No.' Anne toyed with her necklace of knotted black beads. 'We've split up. He was just so boring in bed.'

'I thought he was taking his socks off now?' Jessie said.

Owen spluttered into his champagne glass.

'His socks were a manifestation of a far greater problem. I wanted it to work, really I did.' Anne laid her hand on her heart. 'But he only ever wanted sex once a night. Can you imagine? One orgasm a night? I have more than that when I'm alone. Sorry, Owen. You don't mind a little girl talk, do you?'

'Not at all,' Owen said with a grin.

'I'm here with an American called Hank. He's here to oversee a merger but, in the meantime, he's doing a spot of merging with me.' Anne grinned.

'Has everyone stopped staring yet?' Jessie asked.

'Not a chance,' Anne replied gleefully. 'Nor will they. You were supposed to be the wronged wife, remember? Heartbroken, after nasty William ran off with a trophy girlfriend. You weren't supposed to show up here looking like a million dollars with a drop-dead gorgeous toy boy on your arm. You've certainly ruined William's night. He's got a face like a smacked arse.'

Later, as Jessie and Owen danced, Jessie caught sight of herself in the ornate filigree mirror. Anne's million-dollar comment was probably overstating things but Jessie's sleeveless floral dress with a cinched-in waist and bias-cut skirt accentuated everything that was good about her figure. She had found the dress the week before when, much to her delight, Owen had taken her shopping.

Yes, the woman in the mirror looked good. Maybe it was the luscious new French face cream she was using but Jessie thought it was Owen. The office had been rife with gossip, everyone commenting on how radiant Jessie looked. She'd been happy to let them speculate. It countered all the chatter about William's baby.

Her gaze moved on to Owen's reflection. He looked devastatingly handsome in his tuxedo, rented for the occasion, but a good enough fit to fool the keenest eye. She smiled as she remembered how, with consummate ease, he had done up his bow tie. It was an art William had never mastered, always relying on Jessie to fix it for him.

Owen's body felt warm against hers, his arms reassuring. She gave a sigh of pleasure as he kissed her bare shoulder.

In response, Owen's lips worked gently against Jessie's neck and, by the time he found her mouth, Jessie had long since forgotten there was anyone else in the room.

Two hours passed in a whirl of dancing, networking and small talk. When Owen went to refresh their champagne glasses, Jessie felt a hand firmly take her elbow and steer her to one side. 'Is the fact I haven't yet heard from your solicitor a good sign?' William asked. 'Does it mean you're considering my revised offer of twenty-five thousand?'

'No,' Jessie said evenly. 'It means my solicitor's on holiday in America.'

William's face darkened.

If his offers were going to go up in increments of a couple of thousand pounds each time, it would take William years to get to sixty thousand, but perhaps that was the plan: a war of attrition. Well, she wouldn't be the first to crack.

Jessie spotted Gareth on the far side of the room. She'd been putting off speaking to him but now seemed as good a time as any. 'I've got to go. I need to talk to Gareth Ellis.'

Gareth Ellis was entertaining a large group of people. When he had delivered his punchline and everyone was laughing, Jessie said, 'Can I have a quick word?'

'Yes, of course.' He draped his arm round her shoulders. 'No hard feelings I hope, Jessie.' His cheeks were pink and he was slurring his words. 'Like I said at the outset, nothing personal but this is big business, a little out of your league, I think, my dear.'

'Did your seller's solicitors give you an assurance that there wasn't a formal right of way? Because mine won't.'

'Jessie, darling.' He leaned heavily against her. 'Don't worry your pretty head about it. The houses have fallen out of use and some clown at number fifty has opportun . . . opportunistic . . .' Gareth frowned.

'Opportunistically?' Jessie supplied.

Gareth grinned. 'That's the word. He's taken advantage of the situation and used the back gardens as a shortcut. We're going to tell him to bugger off. End of.'

'Then you're confident it's not a formal right of way?' Jessie persisted. 'Because if it is, it could cause Phil real problems.'

'If there's one thing I hate it's hearing my name and the word "problem" in the same sentence. What's up?' Phil asked.

'Nothing,' Gareth said smoothly, grabbing another glass of champagne from a passing waiter. 'I'm all set to exchange on Monday. Jessie is trying to stop me.'

Phil looked at Jessie expectantly.

'I think there might be an issue with a right of way,' Jessie said.

'It's not a bloody right of way!' Gareth exploded, before softening his tone and adding, 'It's nothing more than an informal agreement if not trespass.'

'The seller's solicitor has told you that?' Jessie asked.

Gareth rolled his eyes. 'Yes.'

'Which?'

'What?' Gareth blinked rapidly.

'Is it an informal agreement or is he trespassing?'

'There was an informal agreement between the owners of all of the houses from fifty to fifty-six but that was several years ago when fifty-four and fifty-six still had owners in residence.' Gareth spoke very slowly as if explaining the situation to a child. 'The owner of number fifty has carried on crossing the gardens ever since and rather cheekily in my opinion.'

'But we can stop him?' Phil asked, alarmed.

'Yes.'

'So the seller's solicitor has confirmed that it was an informal agreement?' Jessie repeated.

'Yes.'

'In writing?'

Gareth pulled a face. 'They haven't actually confirmed it in writing yet but they will.'

'And you're going to exchange on Monday?' Phil said.

'Yes.'

'But obviously not until that written confirmation comes in.'

Gareth scowled. 'I'll wait if you want me to but really there's no need.'

'I told you both at the outset, I didn't want any corners cut.'

'I haven't cut any corners. She's just being paranoid,' Gareth said, waving his glass at Jessie.

'It sounds to me like Jessie's being cautious, which is something else entirely. I don't want either of you to exchange until the question of the neighbour's access has been resolved. Let's talk about it again next week. In the meantime, Jessie, would you like to dance?'

As Phil swept Jessie into his arms, Gareth glowered. 'What's your gut feeling?' Phil asked when they were out of Gareth's earshot. 'Is this going to cause me trouble?'

'Potentially. My seller's solicitors won't give me a straight answer and that makes me nervous.'

'Which is why you haven't already exchanged?'

'Yes. As much as I want to win our little race, my trying to stop Gareth from exchanging isn't a delaying tactic on my part.'

They continued to dance.

'You could have let Gareth go ahead,' Phil said.

'I could have done.'

Phil nodded thoughtfully. 'If it turns out to be a right of way and he exchanged without realising that, it would have blown up in his face. You'd have been sitting pretty.'

'Yes, but he would have created a headache for you in the process. My duty in those circumstances is to you as the client. Race or no race.'

Phil smiled. 'A lady with ambition and integrity. I'm impressed. May I ask you something?'

Jessie nodded.

'I understand you and Anne Jacobs are close. Do you know if Anne's serious about the American?'

'As serious as Anne ever gets.' Seeing the look of concern that flashed across Phil's face, Jessie instantly regretted her flippancy. 'What I mean is he's not going to be in the country long.'

'Right.'

Over Phil's shoulder, Jessie spotted Chelsea. She was wearing a low-cut gold gown that accentuated her swelling bosom. The baby bump was at the cute stage. Jessie had to admit Chelsea carried it well.

While Jessie looked on, William appeared at Chelsea's side with a glass of water for her. She watched as he put his arm round Chelsea's shoulders and kissed her cheek. He whispered something and she laughed as his free hand moved to rest on her stomach.

Jessie was shocked at the pain she felt at the sight of them together; it was like a kick to her heart. As an antidote, she looked for Owen. He'd moved to stand next to Lydia Coates. Jessie watched as, laughing, Lydia placed her hand on Owen's arm, her eyes devouring his face as her ample bosom strained against the silk of her designer gown.

The stab of jealousy Jessie had felt watching William now doubled and when the music ended she excused herself and, unnerved, stepped on to the balcony that overlooked the high street. She had experienced a multitude of feelings since the start of her relationship with Owen, many of them euphoric. But fear was a new one. Her heart constricted at the possibility of losing him, of being lied to again and in that instant she realised just how much she loved him.

The concrete balustrade had been strung with fairy lights and, as Jessie stood watching them move gently in the warm breeze, her hand drifted to the diamond necklace she wore. It, together with a pair of matching earrings, had been a present from William to mark their twentieth wedding anniversary. How long had his eye been wandering? She only had his word to say the tart was the first.

She pressed her fists against the concrete. Trust was such a fragile thing and deceit a terrible way for a relationship to end. It left you with nothing to believe in. Not even yourself. The fairy lights blurred as tears sprang to her eyes.

*

Seeing Jessie leave the party, William followed her.

'I now know why you wanted the Jag,' he said bluntly. 'It must be a bit of a comedown to be seen climbing in and out of a flower seller's van.'

'I never wanted the Jag,' Jessie said dismissively.

William moved to stand beside her. 'Surely you can do better than a barrow boy?'

'At least he can tie a bow tie. From the look of it, you're wearing one of those ghastly clip-on things.'

Frowning, William tore off the tie and stuffed it into his pocket. 'The tie may have been fake, Jessica, but at least the tux is my own.' He touched one of her earrings. 'Nice to see you wearing the diamonds I gave you.'

Jessie moved away from him. 'Keep the diamonds, lose the husband. That's what Anne says.'

'Anne would.' He sighed. 'We need to draw a line, Jessie. Will you take The Lodge and thirty-five grand?'

'No.'

Her intransigence made him want to scream. He'd already had Chelsea in tears because she couldn't have the dream home she'd set her heart on. Next, he'd have to let Marie go. She was a hard worker, a good lawyer who'd grown under his stewardship and he didn't want to lose her. 'Please, Jessie. I'm trying to find you the money.'

'Try harder.'

'How badly do you want to be a partner?'

Jessie stared at him coldly. 'Why do you ask?'

'I was thinking maybe we could reach an agreement,' he said evenly. 'The Lodge plus thirty-five grand plus my vote for your partnership.'

Jessie's eyes widened. 'If I get my partnership it'll be because I earned it. Not because I did a deal with you,' she said in disgust. 'Anyway, you flatter yourself. Do you honestly think you hold that much sway over the others?'

'Do you want to bet that I don't?' William asked quietly.

'Sixty thousand. Cash.'

'I'll have to make Marie redundant. Is that what you want?'

'Of course not. Sell the property in North Street.'

'Oh yeah and rent,' William said sarcastically. 'With a baby on the way.'

'This is your mess, William. Don't expect any sympathy from me. I'm prepared to take less than I'm entitled to. The least you could do is pay it without arguing.'

Anger rising, William said, 'If you won't strike a deal, take some advice instead. Don't worry, it's free. Kiss the barrow boy goodbye, Jess. Do you think Smith Mathers want to see one of their partners making a fool of herself with a kid off the market?'

Furious, Jessie was about to retaliate when Jack Stanhope appeared. 'Chelsea's asking for you, William.'

'Better run along, dear,' Jessie said sarcastically.

William shot her a contemptuous look. 'Remember what I said.'

'Everything okay?' Jack asked.

Turning from him, Jessie nodded. 'Never better,' she said briskly.

'Whatever he said, he didn't mean it.'

Jessie's fingers circled the balustrade. 'How do you know he didn't say something nice?'

'Because you won't look at me.'

Forcing herself to smile, Jessie turned round. 'I'm fine, really I am.'

With his thick black hair and deep blue eyes set in a square uncompromising face, Jack Stanhope's appearance could best be described as interesting rather than handsome. He enveloped Jessie in a bear hug. 'Sue and I are here for you, you know. As for William, he's under a lot of pressure. Chelsea can be rather demanding.'

'Not my problem,' Jessie said brightly.

'No, it's not,' he agreed.

'So, this is where you're hiding,' Owen said, joining them.

Jack patted Jessie's hand. 'I'd better get back.'

Nodding to Jack as he passed, Owen moved to stand behind Jessie. Wrapping his arms round her, he rested his chin on her bare shoulder. 'Is something wrong?'

'I don't want you to lie to me, Owen,' Jessie said. 'Even if I'm not going to like what you have to say, better that than you lie.'

Owen turned her to face him. 'I won't do to you what William did. I promise. I've been there, remember? I know how much it hurts.'

Jessie hugged him. 'I'm sorry you have to deal with the doubt that he created.'

Owen stroked her shoulders. 'Nobody said rehabilitation would be easy, darling.'

Laughing, she drew back. 'There's something you should know.'

'What's that?'

'I've fallen in love with you.'

Owen's eyes widened in surprise. 'You're not just saying that because you know I want to hear it?' he asked cautiously.

'If I was saying it for that reason, I'd have said it the first night we spent together,' Jessie said.

Sweeping her off the ground, Owen whirled her around in his arms. 'I was beginning to think you'd never feel able to say it.'

Jessie's heart lifted with joy at the delighted look on Owen's face. 'I needed you to be patient with me and you were.'

Owen stroked her cheek. 'Some things are worth waiting for.'

Jessie smiled. Unsure whether she would sink or swim, Jessie was at least glad she'd found the courage to dive into the water.

Chapter Twelve

The following Friday morning, Jessie was trying to decide between a dove-grey jacket or a royal-blue one to wear over her blue dress for her meeting with Phil and Gareth when Owen stuck his head round the bedroom door.

'I thought you'd gone to work,' Jessie said.

'I was just leaving. Have you changed your mind about selling The Lodge?'

'No, of course not. Why?'

'There's a man hammering a for-sale sign in at the bottom of the drive.'

'What?'

Grabbing her grey jacket, Jessie ran out of the house. A man in his twenties wearing an ill-fitting suit was struggling to make the for-sale sign stand up straight.

'What are you doing?' Jessie demanded.

'The boss said to come and put the sign up.'

'Well, you can take it down again.'

The young man looked from Jessie to Owen and then back again. 'Have you decided to take it off the market then?'

'It was never on the market.'

'But it's in the paper today. It's our star buy. We're having an open house here tomorrow.'

'No, you're not!' Jessie said.

'Look, madam,' the young man began officiously, 'there seems to have been a misunderstanding, I can see that, but I can't take the sign down unless the boss tells me to.'

'Fine. Owen, take the sign down.'

'I wouldn't advise you to do that,' the young man said. 'The sign is the property of Lewis Shaw estate agents. If it becomes damaged in any way –'

'Then it'll be your fault for not taking it down yourself. Now get out of the way.' Jessie turned expectantly to Owen.

Taking a firm grip round the post, Owen hefted the sign from the ground. 'What do you want me to do with it now?' he asked, a smile playing on his lips.

'Go and pin it to William's house in North Street.'

Owen's eyes widened.

'Give it back to him.' Jessie gestured to the young man.

Owen obliged.

'The boss said –'

Jessie cut the young man off. 'I don't care what your boss said. Your boss shouldn't go around advertising people's houses for sale when one of the owners knows nothing about it. On second thoughts, give me the sign back.'

Open-mouthed, the young man passed it over. 'Have you changed your mind?' he asked hopefully.

'No, I've decided to deliver it back to Lewis Shaw personally,' Jessie said as she dragged the sign towards Delphi. 'And give him a piece of my mind, while I'm at it.'

Owen gave the young man a smile. 'I'd get off her land now if I were you.'

He nodded. 'It's too late to cancel the open house, you know. She'll have loads of visitors tomorrow. They'll have seen the ad.'

Owen nodded.

'I'll kill him,' Jessie said a few minutes later as she and Owen set off into town.

'Lewis Shaw or William?' Owen asked, amused.

'Both.'

Owen stroked her thigh. 'The dickhead's only done it to wind you up. You don't want to be late for your meeting with Phil and Gareth.'

'It won't take me long to say what I have to say to Lewis.'

Owen pulled up outside the estate agents' and helped Jessie pull the for-sale sign from the back of the van. 'Be gentle with him,' Owen joked.

Jessie flashed him an angry look. 'Do you know what an open house entails? It means I'm going to have an army of people pitching up at The Lodge all day tomorrow thinking they can wander through the house at will. It's going to be hell!'

'We'll sort it,' Owen said, kissing her cheek.

'How? You heard him: the ad's already gone in the paper.'

'We'll fix up a sign at the bottom of the road to say the open day's cancelled.'

Jessie took a deep breath. That would work.

'Good luck with your meeting with Phil and Gareth. Let me know how it goes, okay?' He kissed her lips. 'Your meeting with them is the most important thing you're going to do today, remember that.'

Nodding, Jessie grabbed the sign and strode into the estate agents'.

On seeing her, Lewis put down the mug from which he'd been drinking. It bore the legend: KISS MY ASSETS.

'Jessie, lovely to see you.'

Jessie banged the sign down across his desk. 'How dare you place my house on the market!'

'What's this?'

'Don't play the innocent with me, Lewis. The star buy? An open house tomorrow?'

'Ah!' Lewis grimaced. 'William said he'd squared it with you. Said you'd changed your mind and that you were eager for a sale.'

'Do I look eager for a sale?'

'No, you look angry.' Lewis grinned. 'God, you're sexy when you're angry.'

'Lewis!'

Lewis held up his hands. 'William came in on Monday and said you two had talked over the weekend and there had been a change of plan. I had all the details from when I prepared the valuation for the divorce. William said to go ahead.'

'And you couldn't pick up a phone and check it with me?'

'I didn't think there was any need. I'm sorry. The ad's already running.'

'I know. Your colleague told me. I want you to fix up a sign at the bottom of my road telling everyone the open day is cancelled. I want that sign put up now.'

'I understand.'

'Now, Lewis.'

'It'll be done, Jessie.'

Checking her watch, Jessie realised she had no time to go and find William. Instead, she'd have to head straight to Phil Blunkett's office at the Old Mill.

'I'm going to be late for a very important meeting because of this so you can give me a lift to the Old Mill.'

Lewis grabbed his car keys. 'Happy to drive you anywhere, Jessie.' His hand settled in the small of her back. 'I wouldn't want this little misunderstanding to spoil our friendship. I'm always here for you, you know.'

Jessie edged away from him.

'Although maybe I'm a little old for you.' He slid behind the wheel of his Jag, the same make and model as William's. 'I saw you on Saturday at the Mayor's Ball with our young flower seller. Didn't know you liked them young, Jessie.' Lewis smiled.

*

When Jessie was shown into Phil's office, Gareth was already seated and drinking a cup of coffee.

'I'm sorry I'm late,' she said.

Phil looked at his watch and smiled. 'You've still got a couple of minutes by my reckoning. Coffee?'

'Thanks.'

Phil's secretary returned with a brimming mug and Jessie smiled her thanks, taking a quick sip.

'Thank you both for coming here this morning. Jessie, do you want to bring us up to speed on what you've found out?'

Jessie nodded. 'It turns out that there was an ancient right of way running across all of the gardens. Abbey Heights, the big house at number fifty, used to own all of that land. When the land was first developed, the owner retained a right of way so he could still reach the river. It was quicker to cut across the gardens than go the long way round by road. The present owner of Abbey Heights keeps a boat moored on the river and he's keen to retain the right of way.'

'If the owner of Abbey Heights is adamant he wants to keep the right of way then the properties aren't for me and, with regret, I'll have to pull out of both purchases. Can you guys put the wheels in motion?'

Jessie nodded.

Gareth coughed. 'My seller's solicitors misrepresented the situation. They led me to believe it was nothing more than an informal agreement that we could cancel.'

'I agree you were probably misled,' Phil said, 'but I fear if Jessie hadn't stepped in you would have exchanged purely on that other solicitor's word, with nothing in writing to support it.'

Gareth scowled. 'I didn't exercise the best judgement, I admit.'

'In the circumstances, I've decided to go with Smith Mathers over Ellis and Son. I want Jessie to handle the sale of the flats here at the Old Mill. I'm sorry, Gareth.'

'Let's not be hasty about this,' Gareth said. 'I and my firm have a lot to offer. It would be wrong to judge us, me, on one mistake. If I may say, it could be a missed opportunity for your organisation.'

'I can live with that,' Phil said.

'Ellis and Son act for several developers. We are in a position to give you a discounted service that I doubt Jessie and Smith Mathers could match.'

'I'm not looking to start a price war, Gareth. This was always about quality of service. Jessie delivered. You didn't. Simple as that.'

With a rueful look, Gareth stood and offered Jessie his hand. 'I underestimated you, Jessie. You'll make a fine partner one day. Congratulations.' Turning to Phil, he said, 'I understand why you've reached the decision you have. I'd welcome the chance to try again in the future.'

Phil nodded. 'I'll bear it in mind.'

After Gareth left, Phil asked, 'When do Smith Mathers make their decision about your partnership?'

'June.'

'I'll be sure to put in a good word for you with your senior partner,' he promised. 'When we first met, you said that you were good and that you were cheaper than the opposition,' Phil reminded her. 'What you neglected to mention was that you were also a whole lot smarter. That right of way would have been a nightmare. Thank you, Jessie.'

*

William had his feet up on his desk, flipping through a file when Jessie knocked curtly on the door.

'Can I help you, Jessica?' William asked, smiling.

She folded her arms. 'I don't understand what you hoped to gain by it?'

'Gain by what?'

'Don't play the innocent with me. You know exactly what I'm talking about. You told Lewis Shaw to put The Lodge on the market.'

'Oh, that.'

'Yes, that. I came out of the house this morning to discover a man hammering a for-sale sign in at the bottom of the drive.'

William rocked back in his chair, smirking. 'I wanted to get your attention.' He spread his hands. 'It seems to have worked.'

'My attention?'

'Yes.' His tone hardened as he sat upright. 'You turn up late for our meeting at The Lodge, you and your solicitor don't bother answering my letters or my phone calls. You say he's gone on holiday but it feels more like he's emigrated and when I tried to speak to you on Saturday, you brushed me off. You're so busy chasing after the Blunkett work and prancing around town with that barrow boy of yours, you appear to have lost sight of the fact that we're in the middle of a divorce. I thought putting The Lodge on the market would help refocus your mind. I'm on a deadline. I can't wait forever.'

'Refocus my mind? My focus isn't the problem here. Make a decent offer and I might start taking you seriously.'

'Forty grand,' William said without hesitation.

'I said a decent offer. I've told Lewis The Lodge is not for sale. And if you pull another stunt like that, you can kiss goodbye to your decree absolute. Do I make myself clear?'

William scowled. 'Crystal.'

*

Owen booked a table at the Northey to celebrate Jessie's success with Phil Blunkett.

'With the Blunkett work secured and all the new people Anne has sent your way, the partners won't be able to resist you now,' he said enthusiastically.

'There's that saying about counting your chickens,' she reminded him. Surely William didn't have enough sway with the partners to ruin her chances at the eleventh hour, did he?

'You'll be fine,' Owen said smoothly. 'By the way, I spoke to Walt on the telephone this afternoon. What a nice man. I asked him if you could have a couple of days off and he said yes.'

'Why?'

Owen stroked Jessie's hand across the table. 'I want to take you away.'

'I can't take a holiday just before the partners' meeting. How would it look?'

Silencing her concerns with a kiss, Owen said, 'While I wish I could whisk you away somewhere hot for two weeks, sadly neither time nor finances allow. I'm only proposing a long weekend in Wales. Walt agreed. He thought it was a great idea, so he's hardly likely to hold it against you, is he?

'Phil told you the first of the flats in the Old Mill would be ready to go on the market at the end of next month. You won't be able to get away after that until August at least. I figured this would be the best time.'

Jessie couldn't argue with Owen's logic.

'So, what do you think?' Owen's eyes were eager as he waited for her answer.

Maybe a few days away from the hothouse atmosphere of Smith Mathers, and William, wouldn't be such a bad thing. And Owen was right, she would be unlikely to get away until August, which seemed a long way off. But then another thought occurred to her.

'I'm not sure I should leave the house unattended,' she said. 'I wouldn't put it past William to try something if he knew I was away and there's no way he wouldn't know.'

Owen thought for a moment. 'You could change the locks.'

'I can't. The Lodge is still in joint names.'

'In that case, change the locks before we go away and give him a fresh set of keys when we get back.'

'He'll be furious,' Jessie said.

Owen shrugged. 'How will he know unless he tries to get in while you're away? And if he does, he'll hardly be in a position to make a fuss, will he?'

JUNE

Chapter Thirteen

The late-afternoon sunshine was soft on the facing hillside. The broad covering of trees that ran like a swag round its summit seemed to sway in the honey-coloured air, so rich and golden Jessie could almost taste it. Below the trees, rugged stone walls separated fields of lush grass where sheep grazed untroubled.

Beneath the hills, in the town itself, a huddle of slate rooftops stood strong and resolute, baking in the sun. Jessie imagined them facing down the harshest of weather with impunity, turning a proud face to blizzard and flood alike.

Stark black shadows fell from huge brick chimney pots and, below them, tiny leaded windows gave out on to colourful window boxes planted with geraniums and lobelia.

The view drew Jessie into it, embracing her with its timeless beauty. Fluffy white clouds hung in a sky that seemed so close, in a land where hills had become mountains and English had become Welsh.

In the garden beneath her, the first roses, butter yellow in bud, paler and blowsier in full bloom, adorned a wooden arbour. Jessie watched a black cat stretch and walk haughtily out of the arbour and across the lawn. In one graceful bound, it sprang up to sit in the full sun atop the side wall. In its wake, the bold papery blooms of a clematis quivered against the ancient brickwork. The flowers were exquisite: pink petals with a vivid splash of raspberry ripple at every centre, as if a child had drawn a paintbrush across each one.

Charmed by all she saw, Jessie felt her anguish over the divorce dissipate. William had been a fool, chasing after a dream of what he thought his life should be. While Chelsea was nothing more than an opportunistic young woman in the wrong place at the right time. Had she even known William was married at the start? At home, William was a dickhead and Chelsea a tart. Here, they were an irrelevance.

Jessie turned as Owen emerged from the bathroom, a towel round his waist, another round his shoulders. His fringe was a collection of wet exclamation marks against his forehead. With a smile, he joined her at the window, wrapping his arms round her shoulders.

'You'll never see a finer land than this,' he said, resting his chin on her shoulder. 'I'd play for hours in those hills when I was a child.'

'Really? I thought you grew up in London,' Jessie said, confused.

'I did. We came here a lot on holiday.' He kissed her neck. 'As a book lover you're going to adore Hay-on-Wye.'

With a contented sigh, Jessie leaned back against him. 'I already do,' she told him.

They had journeyed from Essex that morning, Owen at the wheel of the Clio. He'd put the Beach Boys' *Greatest Hits* on the CD player and together they had sung their way to Wales, their mood as sunny as the weather.

Now, Jessie sought Owen's hand. 'Thank you for bringing me here,' she whispered.

Lifting her hair, Owen kissed the back of her neck. 'My pleasure,' he said softly.

Jessie felt a drop of water fall from Owen's hair and begin a slow, pleasant journey down her neck. Breaching her collarbone, it made a swift descent between her breasts, kissing her stomach before finally soaking into the towelling robe she wore.

'I thought we could have dinner here at the hotel,' Owen said as he took the towel from round his neck and began drying his hair. 'What do you think?'

Their earlier lovemaking had left Jessie with a lingering afterglow. She could feel it now, wrapping her muscles in soft cotton, stroking her hair and laying tiny weights upon her eyelashes. Sinking into the plushly upholstered chair that stood beside the window, she said, with a sigh, 'Good idea.'

In the lazy afternoon sunshine, the muscles of Owen's back were taut and strong as he rubbed his hair, making the view inside the room almost as good as the one outside. With a smile, Jessie remembered how Owen had taken her swiftly across the four-poster bed upon their arrival. The snatched kisses and gentle caresses during their journey more than enough foreplay for them both.

Now, suddenly revived, Jessie went to him. Trailing her fingers over his back, she kissed his shoulder. 'On the other hand . . .' she said with a chuckle.

*

After dinner, Owen grabbed Jessie's hand. 'I'll take you down to the Jacobean mansion,' he said. 'You'll love it. It's built within the crumbling walls of the old castle.'

Jessie looked ruefully at the high heels she'd worn for dinner. They enhanced her dancer's legs but didn't easily lend themselves to sightseeing. She toyed with the idea of changing into her Converse trainers but Owen was already pulling her out of the door of the hotel.

'Come on,' he said eagerly. 'I don't want to waste a minute of our time here.'

To Jessie's delight there was an open-air bookshop within the castle grounds. She and Owen browsed happily, a quick touch to the other's hand whenever they passed by. Jessie picked up a conspiracy thriller.

'Where do I pay?' she asked, stroking Owen's shoulder.

'It's a twenty-four-hour honesty bookshop,' Owen said. 'They leave it up to the buyer to put the correct money in a tin left on one of the bookshelves.'

Enchanted, Jessie located the tin and dropped her coins inside. She heard the satisfying clink as her coins hit others.

'All paid up and legal?' Owen asked.

Jessie smiled and nodded.

'Fancy a drink?'

She linked her fingers through his. 'Sounds nice.'

They found a pub with a pretty garden. Jessie settled herself at a picnic table while Owen went inside.

'Welsh white wine. Made just up the road,' he said on his return. 'It came highly recommended.' He filled two glasses and sat beside her, looping his arm round her waist. 'To us,' he said.

'To us,' she echoed, leaning into him.

As they clinked glasses Jessie wondered if she had ever been happier.

*

Back at the hotel, Jessie woke in the early hours and, looking at Owen asleep beside her, she knew she had been right to hold out for love. With every feeling magnified to the point where her heart constantly felt as if it was either breaking from the sadness of being parted from him or bursting with the joy of being reunited, Jessie didn't think she'd ever felt more alive.

Was this how William had felt with Chelsea? If it was, she was beginning to understand his need to break apart everything they had once held dear, even forgive him for it a little. New love, unsullied by disappointment and compromise, was a precious gift to be cherished.

As Jessie watched the stars wink at her, she smiled at the thought of the days that lay ahead, the memories that she and Owen were about to make together. Beside her, Owen stirred. Murmuring something unintelligible, he curled his arms round her and nuzzled her cheek.

Jessie twined her fingers through his. 'I love you,' she whispered.

A sleepy smile lit up Owen's face. 'I love you, too.'

'Being here, away from Abbeyleigh, it's made me realise what's important.'

'And I'm important?' Owen asked.

'Yes.'

'Why?'

Turning into his embrace, Jessie laced her fingers across Owen's chest and rested her chin on them.

'You make me feel special. I told Anne I wanted to matter to someone again. I think I matter to you.'

'You do.' Owen kissed Jessie's nose. 'Tell me what you love about me.'

Jessie smiled. 'Shamelessly fishing for compliments, are you?' she teased.

He grinned. 'Guilty as charged,' he said as his hands stroked the dimples at the base of her spine.

'Well, let me see, I love your sense of fun, your generosity, your kindness. I love that you're so easy-going; you never get angry when I cancel a date because of work. I love how you rub my shoulders when I'm tired.'

She kissed his chest. 'And I love the way you look at me after we've made love.' She smiled. 'Your turn.'

'I love your honesty,' he said. 'There's no artifice with you. You say what you feel. I love your heart, your passion, the way you've worked so hard for your promotion. I love that you find time in your busy day to stop by the stall. I love the way you look naked in the shower.'

Jessie giggled.

'And I love how it feels when I'm inside you.' Hooking a hand into her hair, he steered her lips on to his. 'I never thought I could have this,' he admitted. 'A normal life. I never thought someone as wonderful as you would want to be with someone like me.'

Puzzled, Jessie said, 'You're one of the nicest people I've ever met.'

A shadow dropped across Owen's face. 'When I'm with you I'm the sort of person I've always wanted to be. But there's plenty about me that's not so nice.'

'I haven't seen it.'

He took her face in his hands and kissed her deeply. 'I hope you never do,' he said with feeling.

'What happened, Owen? It wasn't just Tessa's betrayal, was it?'

He shrugged. 'It's in the past.'

'It's not though, is it? You're still living with the consequences.' As Jessie's lashes grew wet, her tears fell on to Owen's chest.

'Why are you crying?' he asked in amazement.

'I hate that life hurt you. I wish I could wipe the hurt away. Give you back your heart the way you've given me back mine,' she said earnestly.

Owen smiled as he gently brushed aside her tears. 'You are. For so long I've lived life without really feeling, without daring to care. I didn't think I'd ever fall in love again. But that first night, in Delphi, you touched something inside me.'

Jessie watched a shadow flicker across Owen's eyes. 'Sometimes it scares me how much I love you, how much I've grown to depend on you.'

Touched by his honesty, Jessie tightened her embrace. 'At least we'll be petrified together,' she said.

Chapter Fourteen

'*The town of Hay-on-Wye, situated on the River Wye, to the north of the Brecon Beacons and skirting the border between England and Wales, is one of the world's foremost centres of second-hand books*,' Jessie read aloud from the tourist information leaflet they had been using as a guide.

Owen looked at her and smiled. 'There can't be many more bookshops to cross off our list.'

Jessie consulted the map. 'One or two.'

'Perhaps we should leave them until next time.'

Jessie laughed. 'Are you flagging?'

'I need a reason to bring you back,' he said, stroking her neck.

'You don't need a reason,' she said lightly as they kissed.

They were sitting on the dusty attic steps of a three-storey bookshop, books piled at crazy angles all around them.

Owen pulled Jessie into his arms as he stood. 'Why don't we put a picnic together and take it to the top of the hill to celebrate our last afternoon? We can enjoy the view while we eat.'

'Good idea.'

At first, the incline was gentle and, as they walked, they could hear the cooling sound of fast-running water. Soon, however, the real ascent began and their easy banter was stilled. With faces flushed and muscles pulling, they crossed fields and roads, passing close to houses and through communities of sheep and horses.

Above their heads, the perfect sky was dotted with hang-gliders launching themselves from the opposite hill and every so often Jessie and Owen would stop to catch their breath and watch them. Then, turning, they would try to pick out the site of the castle, the clock tower, their hotel.

Eventually they climbed so high that no landmark was discernible. Parallel with the treeline, Owen took Jessie's hand and led her away from the well-trodden path, through the undergrowth, to a spot where he laid out their blanket on the sun-dappled ground.

After the exertion of the climb, the shade from the trees and the gentle breeze provided a soothing respite from the balmy heat and soon they were melting into one another, their tiredness forgotten.

Afterwards, they lay together, exchanging kisses until the breeze sharpened. Then Owen carefully buttoned Jessie's dress before reaching for his shirt. Gathering the blanket and the rucksack, they walked back down the track and out into the last field they'd crossed.

The sun kissed their skin and Jessie luxuriated in its rays, enjoying the heady feeling of being aglow inside and out. They picked a spot well away from the path and Owen spread the blanket once more.

Ravenous, they devoured their bacon, lettuce and tomato sandwiches, followed by fresh strawberries and clotted cream. They washed the meal down with Welsh white wine.

Their siesta was lengthy. The happy chatter of walkers faded into a mosaic of other sounds: the distant lowing of cattle, the buzz of insects, the murmur of the breeze through the trees. Jessie drifted in and out of sleep with Owen's hand clasped in hers.

On waking, they drank more wine and watched the white heat of the afternoon slowly mellow. Jessie leaned her head against Owen's shoulder, her hand on his thigh.

'This is paradise,' she said softly.

Owen chuckled. Refilling their glasses, he handed one to Jessie, 'To paradise.'

'To us.'

Owen's kiss tasted of wine and was hungrier than she'd expected. Jessie placed her fingers against his eager lips. 'Don't get too carried away, darling. It's a long way back to the hotel and I don't want to move yet.' She kissed his cheek. It was warm from the sun.

'I've got something to tell you,' Owen said. 'I was going to do it when we got home but it feels right to do it now.'

Jessie stroked his leg. 'What is it?'

'I've decided it's time to stop running. I want to make Abbeyleigh my home. I've found a place called Blackcurrant Farm. It's out on the Stebbingsford road. I want to turn it into a market garden for fruit, veg and flowers.'

'Arthur Cantor's place!' Jessie exclaimed, turning to him.

Owen nodded. 'I've given my landlord notice that I won't be renewing the lease on North Street. Hopefully, the purchase will go through before Christmas.'

'What will you do with the stall?'

'Keep it. Fortunately, Danny is keen to come on board.' Owen kissed Jessie's lips. 'Without you, I would never have had the courage to go for it.'

Jessie touched his face. 'Are you sure you can afford it?'

'I wouldn't be able to, not on my own. But Dad's willing to invest a large sum. His view is that the money will come to me eventually so I might as well have a chunk of it now and put it to good use. Despite his stake though he'll let me make my own decisions, which is crucial.' Owen smiled. 'He's keen to see me settled. My Auntie Stella is chipping in a few thousand as well. While I'm putting up all my savings and just last week the bank approved my business plan and agreed to put up the rest. When we get back, I'll show you the paperwork.'

'If you need me to do the conveyancing, it's on the house, so to speak,' Jessie offered.

'That's sweet of you. But I've already promised the work to a mate of my dad's or rather Dad's promised it to him.' Owen let his hands rest on Jessie's shoulders. 'All I need you to do is believe in me.'

'I do,' Jessie replied without hesitation.

*

They were a few yards from their hotel, debating whether to first have a beer or a bath, when a man stopped in front of them, a smile breaking out across his face. 'Well I never, Mitch Johnson. What are you doing here?'

'I'm sorry?' Owen said sharply.

'It's me, Jerry. I worked with you for a while at The Manor House. I left to work on the cruise ships. Don't you remember?'

'I think you're mistaken, mate. My name's Owen Phillips.'

The man looked confused then apologetic. 'I'm so sorry.'

Jessie watched the man walk away. 'How strange. He seemed certain he knew you.'

'They say everyone has a double,' Owen replied with a shrug. He glanced over his shoulder, then, turning back, his face softened into a smile. 'Now, how about that beer?'

Chapter Fifteen

Standing in the kitchen at The Lodge, Jessie arranged the pink peonies Owen had given her. It had been a sultry day and the evening breeze, through the open doors, felt wonderfully cool as it tugged at the hem of her dress.

The peonies had been a parting gift. The previous evening, after they'd been to the cinema, Owen had told her that he had to go away for a few days.

'Problem?' Jessie had asked.

'No, Dad and Auntie Stella want to see the paperwork from the bank.'

'I wish I could go with you,' Jessie had said, settling her head on Owen's shoulder. 'I'm longing to meet your family.'

'Stella's only in London until Friday, otherwise we could have gone up at the weekend, but with all the Blunkett work you've got on right now it wouldn't be fair of me to pull you away during the week. We'll organise something later in the summer, I promise. Dad can fix us a meal at the restaurant.'

Jessie had bitten her lip. 'Owen?'

'Yes?'

'They do know about me, don't they?' Jessie had lifted her head to look into his eyes.

'Of course they know about you,' he replied. 'Do you honestly think I could keep quiet when I feel the way I do about you?'

His kiss had been passionate and Jessie had chided herself for being foolish but she couldn't quite banish the fear that he was in some way embarrassed about her. Perhaps he was worried that his father or his aunt wouldn't approve of the age gap. Jessie knew her fears would only be dispelled when she finally met them both. She resolved to make it happen soon.

As the doorbell rang, Jessie looked up. Half hoping it might be Owen back early, she was disappointed to find William, in jeans and a T-shirt, waiting on the top step.

'Can I come in?'

Shrugging, Jessie went back to the kitchen.

'They from him?' William gestured to the peonies.

Jessie paused in the cutting of a stem. 'If you mean, are they from Owen –' she snipped the stem – 'yes, they are.'

'Coals to Newcastle, isn't it? Flowers from a flower seller?' He raised his eyebrows. 'How was Scotland?'

Jessie's eyes flashed with irritation. 'We went to Wales and it was lovely.' She jiggled the peonies.

'Where is lover boy?'

'London. He's visiting his family.'

'Without you?' William said pointedly.

Jessie met his gaze. 'Owen had business to discuss with them. I couldn't go. I had to work.'

'It's true about Blackcurrant Farm then?'

Jessie stood back to appraise the flowers. 'Yes.' She tweaked one of the stems.

'He's got that kind of money, has he?'

'I'm not going to discuss Owen's finances with you,' Jessie said curtly.

'Jolly good. Why don't we discuss our own?'

'I would if I thought there was any point.' Jessie wrapped the discarded stems in newspaper and threw them in the bin.

'Forty thousand's a substantial increase on my last offer.'

'When you're starting from such a low threshold that isn't difficult,' Jessie pointed out.

William held up his hands. 'I'm just trying to keep everybody happy, Jess.'

'Well, you're failing.'

Looking apprehensive, William said, 'The reason I'm here, apart from to talk to you about the money, is to tell you the partners' meeting is being put back.'

'What?' Jessie cried, stunned. 'Why?'

'I'm taking Chelsea to Paris.'

Jessie took a moment to let the news sink in. Then, clamping down on her disappointment, she said, 'When will you be back?'

'In time to see Hannah when she visits.'

'And the meeting?' Jessie asked.

'Last Friday of the month. Provisionally. But you know what it's like this time of the year. It's difficult to get everyone together. Walt's talking about postponing until September.'

'September?' Jessie cried, her pretence at nonchalance disintegrating. 'But you were meant to be discussing my possible promotion to partner . . .' She had been building herself up to the decision in June, becoming increasingly nervous, hoping she'd done enough to convince them. The thought of waiting until September was almost unbearable.

'I know.'

'Why are you doing this?' Jessie rounded on him. 'You could go to Paris any time.'

'It's Chelsea's birthday,' William replied. 'She's never been to Paris. She's always wanted to go. I'm sorry, Jess. When Walt talked about postponing until September, I knew you'd kick off like this. But it isn't my fault. Look, if it means that much to you I'll speak to Walt, get him to definitely agree to have the meeting in June. If I did that and I went up to forty-two thousand, could we call it quits?'

Jessie slammed her palms on the table. 'Damn it, William. I'm not going to barter for what is already mine,' she said, disappointment making her tone sharp. Wrenching open a drawer, Jessie took out a set of keys and threw them across the table towards him.

'What are these?'

'Keys to The Lodge.'

'I've already got keys.'

'I changed the locks before I went to Wales.'

'You did what?' William exploded. 'Why?'

'Because I didn't trust you.' Jessie arched her eyebrows. 'I can't think why.'

*

Hannah Goode, tall and willowy, waved to her mother as she stepped off the train. Her shoulder-length dark hair was tied in a French plait and, with her sunglasses on top of her head, her dark eyes, William's eyes, were in full view. She was wearing cut-off denim shorts and a T-shirt that revealed a classic figure: a full bust, a slim waist and tapering sun-kissed legs.

'Hello, Mum.'

'Hello, darling.' Jessie gave her daughter a hug. 'Good journey?'

'Yes.'

'You haven't eaten, have you?'

'A sandwich hours ago,' Hannah said.

'Good. Owen's got a feast planned.' They loaded Hannah's bags into the car. 'It's so good to see you,' Jessie said, touching her daughter's cheek as she drove the Clio out of the station car park.

'It's nice to be home. Is Daddy back yet?'

'Tomorrow, I think.'

'I wanted to thank him for arranging for me to do my work experience with Howard in August. I hope I have friendships from uni that last for as long as Daddy's has with Howard.' Hannah flicked on the radio. 'Are you and Daddy any closer to reaching a settlement?' she asked as she fiddled with the radio. Pop music flooded the car.

'We're negotiating terms.'

'Which we both know is lawyer speak for doing bugger all,' Hannah said.

Jessie winced at Hannah's directness.

'Who's digging their heels in?'

Jessie sighed. 'I think we're both being equally stubborn,' she said truthfully.

'Can't you find a way to compromise? They haven't even picked a date for the wedding yet and Chelsea is already turning into bridezilla. She's giving Daddy such a hard time.'

Jessie felt her daughter's gaze fall on her.

'My heart bleeds for him,' Jessie said lightly.

'It should. You wouldn't believe some of the venues she's talking about booking.'

'Even more reason for me to get my money before she spends it all.'

'She wanted to go to Paris because she wants Daddy to buy her dress there.'

Jessie threw Hannah a look. 'That girl does realise your father is a country solicitor, not a member of the Rothschild family?'

Hannah shrugged.

'Do you get on?' Jessie asked.

'Yes. We're not like best buddies or anything but I try to make it work for Daddy's sake.'

'You're a good girl.'

The conversation lapsed. Hannah tapped her legs in time to the music. 'I'm looking forward to meeting Owen.'

Jessie's heart roared into overdrive. 'Are you?'

'I think it's great you've found someone.'

As Jessie slowed for the traffic lights, she shot her daughter a quick glance. Hannah was staring at the shops. 'Do you . . .' Jessie cleared her throat. 'Do you mind that he's so much younger than me?'

'Of course not.' Hannah turned to her. 'I think it's cool.'

For the first time since waking, Jessie felt herself relax. She'd been a whirlwind all day: dusting, hoovering and scrubbing, and as the hours had passed she'd grown steadily more anxious. What if Hannah disliked Owen? What if Owen disliked Hannah? Now, finally, she let herself believe it would all be okay.

'What's Owen cooking for us?'

'Garlic mushrooms as a starter, roast beef for the main course and some chocolate creation that will probably have a million calories for dessert.'

Hannah chuckled. 'Sounds great. I'm famished.'

When Jessie pulled up outside The Lodge, Owen was waiting with the front door open. He was wearing a red-and-white-check chef's apron over black jeans and a white short-sleeved shirt. With a beaming smile, he held out his hand to Hannah.

'It's wonderful to finally meet you, Hannah. Your mum's told me a lot about you.'

'Just so long as she hasn't got the baby pictures out,' Hannah said with a grimace.

'Not yet.' Owen reached for Hannah's bag and suitcase. 'Let me take those upstairs for you.'

Looking back at her mother, Hannah gave an approving nod of her head.

'Is there anything I can do?' Jessie asked a moment later, when Owen returned to the kitchen.

'No thanks.' He kissed her cheek. Then, taking up a knife, he started chopping herbs. 'It'll be ready in an hour.'

Jessie caught sight of Owen's mug on the drainer. It bore the legend: HORTICULTURALISTS DO IT IN WELLIES. Jessie put it away as Hannah walked in.

'Do you need a hand with anything, Owen?' Hannah asked.

'Ladies, *please*.' Owen laid the knife down and, taking up a bottle of red wine, poured them both a generous glass. 'Why don't you go and sit in the garden, enjoy the last of the sunshine and let a man get on with his work?' He ushered them out of the back door, making a shooing motion with a tea towel.

Giggling, Hannah linked her arm through her mother's. 'I couldn't imagine Daddy ever chasing us out of the kitchen,' she said. 'Now, chasing us into it, that's a different thing.'

They sat in thickly padded sun chairs beside a white cast-iron table. Ahead of them, the garden seemed to sigh in the gentle light of early evening. Jessie could hear Owen in the kitchen humming along to Puccini on the radio.

'I like him,' Hannah said.

Ridiculously, Jessie felt tears spring to her eyes. 'Do you really?'

'What's not to like, Mum? He's gorgeous. And he's doing you the world of good. You look terrific.'

Jessie smiled into her wine. If Hannah had but known it, she felt as if the day had put five years on her.

'Are you and Owen living together?'

'No!' The word came out like the crack of a whip.

'Okay.' Hannah gave her mother an amused look. 'I was only asking because, if he was living here, I didn't want you, or him, to think he had to move out just because I'd come home.'

'Well, he doesn't and he isn't,' Jessie said, gulping her wine.

'That's all right then.' Hannah nudged her mother's foot. 'I wouldn't mind if he stayed over.'

'Please, Hannah.' Jessie held up her hand. 'You may be a thoroughly modern young lady but I, on the other hand, languish several decades behind.'

Hannah giggled. 'How's work? Phil Blunkett keeping you busy?'

'Yes. Damn. I meant to drop into the office on the way back and pick up a file. Phil will be calling from London tomorrow and I haven't had a chance to study the paperwork. Would you be all right here if I popped back into town?'

Hannah tilted her sun chair back and saluted her mother with her wine glass. 'What do you think?'

*

William stared at the papers on his desk without seeing them. He'd made an excuse about an urgent case just to get out of the house. The trip to Paris had been a disaster and the atmosphere, since they'd returned early, frosty. He could still see Chelsea's tear-stained face as she'd ranted at him in their hotel suite.

'The only thing I wanted for my birthday was *your* decree absolute. That bitch is never going to give you a divorce, is she?'

'Don't call her a bitch.'

'That's right,' Chelsea had cried. 'Mustn't criticise Saint bloody Jessica. She's living in that big house all alone while we're stuck in a two-up two-down. I want a nice house, a garden. I want a ring on my finger.'

'I know you do. I want you to have those things, too.'

Sharp-eyed, Chelsea had searched his face. 'Do you, Will? Do you really? Sometimes, I think you'd like to go back to her.'

'Don't be ridiculous. That's your hormones talking. They're driving you crazy. They're driving us both crazy.' He'd put his arm round her. 'I'll get the divorce, I promise.'

'And the house?'

'That may take a little longer,' he'd admitted.

'It's always me that has to compromise, isn't it?' Then she'd sobbed, shrugging away from him. 'If you loved me, you'd buy it for me now.'

'If you loved me, you'd understand,' he'd replied.

Maybe he should make Marie redundant, cash in the pension and let Jessie and Chelsea squabble over the spoils. It wasn't like he was ever going to be able to retire and enjoy the money, was it?

He looked up to find Jessie in the doorway.

'I didn't think you were back until tomorrow.'

'Chelsea wanted to come home,' he said brusquely. 'Is Hannah here?'

'At The Lodge. It was good of you to arrange with Howard for her to do her work experience with him.'

William grunted and looked out of the window. The clock in the church tower was chiming seven.

'Owen's cooking for us; I'd better go.'

William gave her a cold stare. 'That was an incredibly stupid thing you did with the locks.'

'I had my reasons.'

'Did you stop to consider what would have happened if Hannah had needed to come home?' he asked.

'Well, I . . .'

Lips pursed, William sat back. 'What if, heaven forbid, there'd been an emergency? How would I have got in?' He shook his head. 'Honestly, Jess, it was so irresponsible.'

Jessie felt a twinge of guilt. 'If you weren't being so difficult I wouldn't have thought it necessary.'

'You think I'm being difficult? Sweetheart, I haven't begun to be difficult.'

'Why are you being like this?' Jessie asked. 'You have everything you want.'

If only. William stood and splashed scotch into a glass. 'Maybe I can't stand to see the woman I once loved making a fool of herself,' he said quietly.

'Oh my God! You're jealous!'

'Jealous?' William laughed as he resumed his seat. 'You're out of your mind. If anything, I feel sorry for you. You and your bit of rough.' He sneered. 'How long do you think that's going to last?'

'About as long as you and yours,' Jessie replied tartly.

Settling back, William cradled the scotch in his lap. 'You can't see it, can you? The way the barrow boy's getting his feet under the table. He's playing you, Jess. He doesn't care about you. He's just out for what he can get.'

'Are you sure it's not Chelsea you're talking about?' Jessie asked, raising her eyebrows. 'I bet she couldn't believe her luck when you walked into her life.'

William drained his scotch. 'If it makes you feel better to rubbish Chelsea, go ahead. It doesn't change anything.'

'No, you're still a cheating bastard.' Jessie turned on her heel.

'It's so easy for you to blame everything on the affair, isn't it?' William shouted after her. 'It stops you having to wonder if you weren't perhaps a little bit responsible for what happened.'

'I'm not to blame because you couldn't keep it in your trousers.'

'I wouldn't have needed someone else if I hadn't been abandoned by you.'

'You think I abandoned you? Christ, you're pathetic!'

'I'm pathetic?' William stood, hands spread on the desk. 'Have you taken a look at yourself recently? God knows what you've done to your hair and I'm not denying you have great legs but that dress is the kind of thing I'd expect Hannah to wear.'

Smarting, Jessie retaliated, 'You want to know what the real problem was with our marriage, William?' She banged the file she'd been carrying down on the desk. 'Your ego.'

'Were you happy?' William asked.

'Yes.'

'Liar.' William spat the word at her.

Jessie stepped back, staring at him coldly. 'I may have been preoccupied. I may not have realised just how much you needed me after your father died, but that was no reason for you to go and pick up a stranger.'

'You make her sound like a prostitute. Chelsea was fun . . . is fun.'

Jessie laughed. 'Which is it, Will?' she asked. 'Past tense or present tense?' She stalked to the door, smarting as she replayed his comments about her hair and her dress. 'By the way –' she tossed the words over her shoulder – 'I'm glad we split up. Being with Owen has made me realise that you were never as good in bed as you thought you were.'

William waited until Jessie was out of earshot before he sent the papers flying from his desk.

*

The dining room at The Lodge looked out over Abbey Wood. With the light in the room restricted as a result, Jessie had chosen cream for the walls and Chinese jade for the carpet. A beautiful antique mahogany dining table stood in the centre of the room. It had been a wedding present from her father.

As Jessie entered, she found Owen laying out silver cutlery from a red leather case. She traced a finger down the intricately patterned handle of one of the dessert spoons.

Looking up, Owen smiled. 'Hannah suggested we use the family silver. I hope you don't mind?'

'No, of course not. I should use it more.' In the centre of the table was a thin glass vase holding a stunning white orchid spray. 'The table looks lovely.'

Owen grinned. 'I wanted everything to be just right for Hannah. Did you get your file?'

'No. I had a run-in with William and left it behind. I'll pick it up first thing tomorrow.'

Ten minutes later, the delicious aroma of garlic mushrooms and toasted squares of herb bread filled the room. Jessie and Hannah exchanged smiles as Owen poured the wine. He had barely taken his seat when the doorbell rang.

Jessie slapped her napkin down. 'I'll go.'

*

'I've brought your file,' William said. 'You left it on my desk.'

Taking the file, Jessie mumbled her thanks before starting to close the door.

'Wait a minute.' William put his shoulder against the frame. 'I want to see Hannah. I've brought her a present from Paris.'

'Can't you give it to her tomorrow?'

'No, I want to give it to her now.'

'We've just sat down to dinner, William. Why don't you leave it with me and I'll see that she gets it.' Jessie held out her hand.

William's face hardened. 'Are you trying to stop me from seeing my daughter?'

Exasperated, Jessie said, 'Don't be ridiculous. I'm just –'

'Good.' Not waiting for her to finish, William pushed past her.

'William!' Furious, Jessie tried to reach for his arm but he shrugged her off. A moment later, she heard Hannah's delighted cry.

'Daddy!'

'Princess.'

Throwing the file on to the hall table, Jessie marched back to the dining room where she leaned against the door jamb, a look of angry resignation on her face as William and Hannah embraced.

'When did you get back?' Hannah asked.

'A couple of hours ago,' William replied. 'This is for you.'

With a giggle of excitement, Hannah tore at the exquisitely wrapped package to reveal a bottle of designer perfume. 'Daddy, this is my absolute favourite. Thank you.' She gave William another hug.

'Mr Goode.' Owen rose and offered William his hand.

Shake his hand, you bastard, or I will kill you, Jessie thought.

William hesitated for just a moment too long before gripping Owen's hand and shaking it firmly. 'Mr . . .'

'Phillips. Owen Phillips.'

'Mr Phillips, yes.'

Jessie recognised William's court voice: cool and professional.

He quickly returned his attention to Hannah. 'Princess, you look terrific. I thought we could have a spot of dinner. You can bring me up to date on your news.'

Jessie pushed herself away from the door jamb and was about to protest when she caught Owen's glance, the slight shake of his head.

Hannah's face fell. 'Daddy, I can't. Owen has . . .'

'Of course if you don't want to,' William said, looking hurt.

'You must go, Hannah,' Owen said firmly.

'But you've gone to so much trouble,' Hannah said, clearly torn.

'There'll be plenty of other times,' Owen replied, meeting William's gaze.

William inclined his head, acknowledging the challenge implicit in Owen's words.

'Is it really okay, Mum?'

Jessie gave a clipped nod. She had been looking forward to the three of them having dinner together and even the fact that she would now have Owen to herself couldn't completely allay her disappointment.

As William ushered Hannah to the Jag, he turned and waved at Jessie. 'Ciao,' he said.

Wanting to hit him, Jessie gave vent to her feelings by slamming the front door instead. The mirror in the hall shook with the impact.

Owen put his hands on her shoulders. 'Calm down, darling. It really doesn't matter.'

'Yes, it does,' Jessie replied. 'You've gone to so much trouble. That bastard did it on purpose because I told him you were cooking for us,' Jessie berated herself. 'I should have known better.'

'It's only food, Jessie. I can cook for Hannah another time. Besides, it could be a blessing in disguise.' He kissed her neck. 'I get to spend the whole evening alone with you, courtesy of your husband. With a bit of luck, they'll be out for hours.'

Chapter Sixteen

The following afternoon, the heat was so oppressive that it drained every ounce of Jessie's energy. Even the fan, which stood on the floor of Jessie's office, propped at an angle by two law books, refused to oscillate, as if the effort was too much.

'Hello, Mum.'

'Hello, darling.'

'I've brought you a peace offering.' Hannah handed Jessie a choc ice. 'Owen says hi.' She laid a red rose wrapped in cellophane on Jessie's desk.

Cracking the chocolate with her teeth, Jessie savoured the delicious ice cream as it slipped down her throat. 'You've been to see Owen?'

Hannah nodded. 'I apologised to him, too.' She gestured to the choc ice. 'We're going bowling tonight, you, me and Owen.'

'Great.' Jessie chased a piece of chocolate with her tongue as it skated across the block of ice cream.

'Does that mean you're not mad at me any more?' Hannah asked hopefully.

'I was never mad at you.'

'But you are with Daddy?'

'It's a beautiful day. Let's not talk about your father.'

'Don't be like that. Daddy rang Howard last night and he told me all about his plans for my work placement. He's hoping to take me to the Old Bailey. He's got a trial listed there. Isn't that great?' Hannah beamed.

Jessie smiled at her daughter's enthusiasm. 'You do realise you're condemning yourself to weeks of hard work during your summer holidays?'

Hannah nodded. 'I know, but think of all the things I'm going to learn.' Hannah paused to nibble her chocolate. 'By the way, Daddy wants to take me up to the West End on my birthday. Apparently, Howard keeps a flat in town and he said that Daddy and I can stay there, so I'll be catching the train back to Exeter direct from Paddington on Saturday.' Hannah licked a dribble of ice cream from the back of her hand. 'Is that okay?' she asked, looking worried.

Only seeing her daughter for a snatched hour or so on the morning of her birthday, a time of day when Hannah was never at her best. *Christ, William, you've outmanoeuvred me again.*

Realising the silence was stretching uncomfortably, Jessie managed a weak smile. 'I'm disappointed I won't see more of you on your birthday, but if that's what you want to do . . .' *Damn, now I sound churlish.* Jessie could see the disappointment on Hannah's face.

'It sounds fun,' Jessie added. 'I'm sure you'll have a great time.'

'Is it really okay, Mum? I thought maybe you were going to be mad again.'

At you?! 'No,' Jessie said.

Hannah opened up the wrapper of her choc ice and scooped the last of the chocolate on to her finger. 'Daddy really does want to reach a settlement, you know,' she said cautiously. 'Couldn't you and he meet up rather than keep going through your lawyer?'

Jessie's eyes narrowed. 'Did William ask you to speak to me about this?'

'No. The opposite, in fact. But he seemed really down when I asked how things were going. You promised me you wouldn't tear each other apart. Remember? You said it would be a civilised divorce.'

She had said that, hadn't she? She'd meant it too. It seemed a lifetime ago.

Hannah was watching her, a look of apprehension on her face. Divorce was tough on the children, Jessie reminded herself, however old they might be. 'I'll speak to him,' Jessie promised.

Hannah smiled. Screwing up the wrapper of her ice cream, she aimed it at the bin. It flew straight in. 'Did you really have no idea that Daddy was having an affair?'

Surprised at the question, Jessie shook her head. 'None.'

'He took you away, didn't he? To Oxfordshire, for your birthday.'

'Yes.'

'And you had fun, didn't you?'

'Yes.'

Hannah chewed her lip.

'What is it, love?' Jessie asked, concerned.

Hannah sighed. 'David and I had such a brilliant time when we went to the Canary Islands but in the last few weeks –' she shrugged – 'it's not the same. It's like he's somewhere else. A couple of times he's missed dates. He said he was working and lost track of time. But he's never done anything like that before. And I've caught him having furtive phone conversations. You know, where someone is obviously being cagey about what they say because someone else has walked in?'

'Have you asked him if anything's wrong?'

'I've tried.' Hannah picked at her cotton trousers, head bowed. 'He says everything's fine and changes the subject.'

'There could be an innocent explanation for his behaviour,' Jessie said gently. 'Maybe he really is busy. As for the phone calls, perhaps you're imagining it.'

'Or maybe there's someone else,' Hannah said bluntly, her eyes sad. 'I was round at his place last weekend. He was in the bathroom and I picked up his phone. I was so close to checking his messages. Isn't that awful? It's so sneaky. I don't want to be like that.'

'But you didn't check them?'

'No, but that was only because I heard his flatmate in the hall. I would have done otherwise. It wasn't my conscience that stopped me. You and Daddy brought me up to treat people how I'd like to be treated myself. I'd hate someone to check my phone without my permission and yet I would have done that to David.'

'You were upset,' Jessie said gently. 'We all do irrational things when we're upset.' Jessie thought about her own behaviour and William's. The divorce had hardly brought out the best in them, she reflected ruefully.

'We've been together almost a year but I think he's going to break up with me, Mum.'

Jessie came round to Hannah's side of the desk and gave her daughter a hug. Hannah had dated since she was fifteen, much to William's chagrin, but David had been her first serious boyfriend.

'The worst thing is, I don't know why this is happening,' Hannah continued. 'I haven't changed. We haven't had a row. It's like he just got bored with me. Do men do that? Or is it me, am I boring?'

Jessie kissed Hannah's head. 'I've never met a less boring person in my life.'

'You're biased,' Hannah said quickly, drawing back.

'Anyone who knows you would say the same.' Jessie stroked Hannah's cheek. 'There aren't rules to govern who we fall in love with and equally there are no rules to say how we break up. You need to talk to him. Find out exactly where you stand. But, even then, you may not get all the answers you want.'

'Did you get all the answers you wanted?'

Jessie hesitated. 'Eventually. Communication, that's the key. Not just at the end of a relationship when things are already going wrong but all the way through.'

Hannah nodded, tears pooling in her eyes. 'At least the only things we have to argue about are a couple of CDs.' She settled into her mother's arms. 'Don't tell Daddy about this, will you?' The words were muffled against Jessie's shoulder. 'He'll want to punch him or something. It won't help.'

Jessie smoothed Hannah's hair, holding her as she cried. Sometimes daughters needed their mothers even more than their fathers.

*

A week later, like a condemned woman awaiting her hour of execution, Jessie watched the hands of the clock in her office edge slowly round. The partners' meeting had been going on for two hours. There was a lot on the agenda – her promotion just another item for the partners to discuss, a relatively small point to them, everything to her. Thank goodness they had found space in their diaries to have the meeting in June after all. Jessie wasn't certain her heart could have stood the suspense until September.

A good-luck card had arrived in the post that morning from Hannah, and Owen had brought her breakfast in bed, her newspaper tied in pink legal ribbon like a barrister's brief. Even Anne had telephoned, enquiring whether she would be too grand for lunch once she was promoted.

They all thought she would do it. But what if she didn't? What if the hours of hard work turned out to be for nothing? What if Sam Sturridge, Phil Blunkett and all the others weren't enough to convince the partners to give her a chance?

Even if her figures for the first half of the year were replicated in the second half she still wouldn't hit her target of being the twelfth-highest fee earner. Depending on what the others did she was likely to fall short at fourteenth but it was still an impressive increase on where she had been. Surely they would give her credit for that?

But what if William stuck the knife in, angered by her refusal to accept a lesser settlement? The civilised divorce she had promised Hannah hadn't exactly come to pass. William was the second-highest fee earner after Walt. The partners would listen to what he had to say. What if he said no?

By the time the meeting broke up half an hour later, Jessie had given up any pretence at work, too uptight to concentrate. She held her breath as Walt entered her office.

Striding across the room, his face broke into a grin as, hand outstretched, he declared, 'Congratulations, partner!'

Elated, Jessie found herself grinning inanely. 'Thank you.'

As she came out from behind the desk, Walt enveloped her in a hug. 'No one deserves it more. You've done a hell of a job, Jessie. Your figures weren't quite where we wanted them to be but the increase is impressive and no one can argue with the calibre of your clients.'

'Thank you so much,' Jessie repeated, stunned. She could hardly believe it. All those hours. All that heartache. She'd done it. She was a partner.

Walt rubbed his hands together. 'As I am sure you are aware, it's a tradition that the new partner takes the old partners out for a drink.'

'I just need to make two quick calls,' Jessie said.

'Okay. We'll be over at the Northey waiting for you.'

Jessie sat for a moment after Walt had gone, letting the news sink in before telephoning Hannah and leaving a message on her voicemail. Then she rang Owen.

He whooped with delight as she told him. 'That's fantastic, sweetheart. I'll get the champagne on ice. Get away as soon as you can.'

*

William chose not to accompany the other partners to the Northey and when Jessie returned to the office, a little the worse for wear but gloriously happy, she discovered that he'd already gone home.

Several of the partners had told her what a ringing endorsement William had given her. Jessie had been surprised and touched in equal measure. Perhaps twenty-odd years of marriage counted for something after all.

The elegant onyx pen holder that Hannah had bought for William's fortieth birthday held pride of place on his desk. Jessie plucked one of the pens from it and searched for a Post-it note.

Widening her search to the top drawer of the desk, Jessie pushed aside cheque-requisition slips before stopping, transfixed by the sight of what lay beneath: a photograph of her and William taken on Harbour Island in the Bahamas some three years earlier.

They were grinning like maniacs for the camera while a perfect azure sea shimmered in the background. Happiness shouted from the photograph. It seemed impossible to Jessie that they had ever been that happy, but there was the evidence.

She studied the photograph. They looked so relaxed. Their smiles were easy and genuine, embracing their eyes. Their heads were bowed towards one another and William had his arm round her shoulders, gripping her to him, while she had her arm round his waist.

They had been so close in every sense of the word. How could they have travelled so far apart in such a short space of time?

Feeling as though she'd seen something she shouldn't, Jessie stuffed the photograph back. Snatching up a Post-it from the drawer beneath, she scribbled, *Thank you, J* and left.

When she got home, Owen showered her with champagne.

'Congratulations, darling. I knew you could do it.'

They ate dinner in the garden and finished the champagne before Owen swept her into his arms. That evening their lovemaking touched new heights. But, as

Jessie drifted off to sleep in Owen's arms, it was not Owen she thought of, nor even her promotion. It was the photograph in William's top drawer.

JULY

Chapter Seventeen

The sound of a wind chime rose on the breeze as Jessie stepped into the courtyard garden of the Northey Hotel. After walking through the air-conditioned bar, the heat hit her like a hammer blow. In front of her were six tables arranged in a circle on the cobblestones. Cast-iron plant holders ablaze with hot-pink petunias stood beside them.

Jessie scanned the packed tables and saw William raise his hand.

He'd caught her, after post, that morning.

'Are you free for lunch?'

They had barely spoken since the night he'd spirited Hannah away from The Lodge and Jessie was taken aback by his question. 'Why?'

'Because we can't leave things unresolved forever. How about it? Lunch at Sp–'

Jessie had raised her eyebrows.

'The Northey,' William had said quickly. 'The forecast is great. We could eat in the garden.'

'Okay.'

Now, as she approached, William folded his newspaper and stood to greet her. 'Thanks for coming, Jess.' He motioned to a waitress. 'What would you like?'

'I'll have a gin and tonic please,' Jessie said. The umbrella over the table provided a welcome respite from the sun as she studied the menu. 'And a ploughman's.'

'I'll have a ploughman's too,' William said.

The waitress nodded and left.

Jessie fanned herself with the menu. 'What do you want?' she asked.

William pushed his sunglasses into his hair. 'We're unlikely to get the absolute before the baby comes but I'd like the nisi.'

'Then you should be talking to Nick, not me,' Jessie said, putting her sunglasses on the table as the waitress returned.

'I'd rather talk to you. What will it take to get the nisi, Jess?' William asked when they were alone again.

'Nick thinks sixty thousand is reasonable,' she said.

William's gaze didn't waver. 'Is that what *you* think?'

'Yes.' Jessie paused in the buttering of a hunk of French bread.

'It was never my intention to deny you what was rightfully yours,' William said, sipping his beer. 'I just wanted to find some way to do it that wouldn't wipe me out. The way I see it, we didn't split the contents of The Lodge down the middle. You kept ninety per cent. I should get some leeway as a result.'

Although William wore a ready smile, Jessie could see the tension in his jaw. Picking up her gin and tonic, she asked, 'How much leeway did you have in mind?'

'A settlement of forty-five thousand.' William's face was eager, his eyes boring into hers as if sheer willpower alone would be enough to get him what he wanted.

Buckling under the pressure of his gaze, Jessie looked away. A passion flower had been trained against the side wall. Jessie gazed at the white flowers with their elongated petals and the blush of purple at their hearts. The flowers were supposed to signify something about Christ but she couldn't remember what.

'Jess?' William's voice was gentle, cajoling.

Jessie continued to stare at the flowers. She could tell him she would settle for nothing less than sixty and walk away, but she knew he had a point about the contents and she'd promised Hannah she would try to compromise.

'Fifty-five,' she said, turning back.

'Forty-seven and a half.'

'Fifty.'

Relief flooded into William's eyes. 'Deal,' he said.

'Deal,' Jessie echoed.

Their handshake was firm, polite. But as their eyes met and the import of what they'd just done sank in, they drew back their hands swiftly, breaking eye contact. Could those same hands once have expressed passion? It hardly seemed possible to Jessie now.

She sought refuge in her drink as the seconds bled into minutes, punctuated only by the hum of a bee.

Jessie stared at her food. She seemed suddenly to have lost her appetite. *But why? I've won. This is what I've wanted all year. All right, it's substantially less than I'm entitled to but it will mean a clean break, no more bad feelings and I get to keep The Lodge. So why don't I feel triumphant? Why do I only feel numb?*

She watched the thick green foliage of the passion flower lift in the breeze. When they'd first come to the garden, red roses had run riot over the wall and after that it had been a clematis, so dark a shade of violet as to be almost black.

Unbidden, memories presented themselves to her. Their tenth anniversary. The first time, financially, they had been able to celebrate with more than a meal. William had bought her a sapphire art deco brooch and she had given him a pair of gold cufflinks. In addition, their first holiday to the Bahamas had been booked.

William's parents had joined them at the Northey to celebrate and they had sat at a table in the corner of the garden drinking champagne. Rather a lot of champagne, because later that evening William had insisted Jessie dance with him around the garden of The Lodge even though it had been two in the morning but, pleasantly merry herself, she had indulged him.

Was it their fourteenth or fifteenth anniversary when a thunderstorm had driven them out of the garden and into the bar, ruining the meal left abandoned on the table? Shortly afterwards, a lightning strike on a nearby substation had plunged the Northey into darkness and they had been forced to celebrate their anniversary by candlelight with nothing more than crisps and wine.

William had given her a diamond necklace and matching earrings for their twentieth anniversary and coincidentally she had chosen a diamond tiepin for him, eschewing the china that tradition dictated they should have bought. Perhaps they had known, even then, that they would never make it to sixty to celebrate diamonds for real.

The leaves of the passion flower blurred as tears sprang to Jessie's eyes. A lifetime together finalised with the shake of a hand in the place where they'd celebrated so many anniversaries. Jessie wondered if the irony of the venue had occurred to William. But men didn't get sentimental about things like that, did they? He didn't appear to mourn, like she did, the loss of those two young people full of hope and dreams and love.

As if to underline the point, William suddenly asked, 'Will you apply for the nisi now?'

Blinking rapidly, Jessie returned her attention to him. William had resumed his meal with gusto, she noted. 'I'll ring Nick this afternoon,' she said and, mentally stirring herself, added, 'We might as well get the paperwork signed up now so it's ready for when the absolute comes through.'

'Fine.' William held out his beer glass.

Picking up her own glass, Jessie tapped it against his and they drank to the settlement. 'Do you intend to get rid of Marie?'

'No. I cashed in some bonds and released a portion of my pension.'

Jessie was relieved. 'What about costs?'

William looked down at his plate and smiled. 'Ah yes, costs. You didn't need him, you know, your fancy London lawyer.'

'The fact remains I've got him,' Jessie said, finishing her drink. 'And he's going to want paying.'

'Don't worry.' William swigged his beer. 'I'm not going to spoil the ship for a ha'p'orth of tar. Halves do you?'

'Halves will do nicely, thank you.'

'Can I pay twenty-five thousand when the decree absolute comes through and the balancing twenty-five thousand at Christmas?'

'Yes, that's fine.'

She watched him move his plate to one side and, arms folded along the edge of the table, he leaned towards her. 'We've both said and done some things we probably regret,' he said, his keen gaze holding hers. 'But now that we've got a settlement I'd like to think we could put it behind us.' His face lightened. 'Try to be the best of exes, if not for our own sakes then for Hannah's.'

Disappointed, Jessie nodded. She didn't know what she'd expected. Perhaps a fulsome apology for the affair and for his boorish behaviour since or maybe a grand declaration of his undying love for her. But a quick negotiation, followed by a 'let's be friends' speech, did not seem nearly enough for so long a marriage.

She watched him order another beer. In the not too distant future, this man she had known intimately would disappear from her life for three months of paternity leave and when he returned he would be a father again and possibly even married. When that time came they would greet one another as nothing more than business partners. The thought was a surreal one.

'You not hungry?' he asked.

'It's too hot.'

The numbness Jessie had felt was fading now. In its place sadness swirled, mixed with anger at William for having brought them to this. How could he be so businesslike when something that had once been so beautiful was dying? After everything they had been through, he must still have some feelings for her, surely?

Jessie anchored her sunglasses in her hair. She had never felt more awkward. Was this it? Was she just supposed to walk away now?

'Are you okay?' William asked gently.

So foolish, she thought. *This is what I wanted, him out of my life; a fresh start.* Taking herself in hand, Jessie said, 'I'm fine.' William's dark eyes betrayed no emotion as she looked into them. He had his court face on: inscrutable. She hated him for it. 'You?' she asked hopefully.

'Absolutely.'

His response was so enthusiastic, his smile so broad, that new hurt was heaped on old. Jessie was under no illusion this meeting sealed the end of their marriage far more than any piece of paper bearing the title decree absolute could ever do. This was the last chance either of them would have. If things were not said today, they would remain forever unsaid. She wanted to scream at him. *How can you feel nothing? And if you do feel nothing, why is there a photograph of us in your desk drawer?*

Jessie had thought of a number of explanations. Perhaps he'd forgotten the photograph was there. Or, maybe, he had taken it out of his wallet and been unable to throw it away. Or perhaps he was still a little in love with her and wasn't quite ready to let her go. She wanted to ask him before it was too late but, as she stood, her mouth went dry, the words dying in the back of her throat.

William stood too. 'You have to get back?'

Was it her imagination or did he sound disappointed? And just when she thought he had a heart of stone. 'Yes. Don't you?'

'In a while. I thought I'd have another drink and enjoy the sunshine. Then I'll nip home and tell Chelsea the news.'

His words were a kick to her stomach. Out with the old and in with the new. Could he have made it any more plain?

He came round to her side of the table and leaned in to kiss her cheek. 'Thanks, Jess.'

Flustered, Jessie stammered something about seeing him later. He nodded and resumed his seat. She hovered for a moment in limbo, shivering in the baking sun.

At the door of the bar, she looked over her shoulder. Part of her had hoped to find him watching but, instead, his head was bowed as he studied his paper. The wind chime jangled in her ear, jarring her nerves.

Men are different, she thought sadly as she walked away.

Chapter Eighteen

Jessie had just secured one earring when the telephone rang and the second slipped through her fingers.

'Hello?'

'Jessie? It's Walt. I'm at the office. Are you busy?'

She knelt to retrieve the earring. 'I'm due at a reception at Lewis Shaw's. Why? Is something wrong?'

'William's here. He's been drinking.'

'Ring Chelsea.'

'I suggested calling Chelsea. William got upset, aggressive even. I can't leave him, Jessie. If he stays here all night the office will smell like a brewery and God knows what the cleaners will say. Who else shall I call? Jack?'

'Jack's away. Spain, I think.'

Jessie met the reflection of her gaze. Two weeks had passed since her meeting with William. The decree nisi was due to be pronounced on the second of August. She could hear Anne's voice in her head saying, 'This is not your problem,' but the muscles in her stomach had tightened as soon as Walt had started to speak. William drunk at the office? It was inconceivable and yet here was Walt telling her it was true.

'I'll be there as soon as I can.'

*

The smell of alcohol hit Jessie as she climbed the stairs. Like a vapour trail from a plane, she could have tracked William down anywhere by it.

Walt was sitting on the edge of William's desk, a sour expression on his face. William was slumped across the blotter, his head resting on crossed arms, apparently asleep.

'I can't get much sense out of him. But it looks like he's been in a fight.'

'He'd always walk away from a fight,' Jessie said. Even if his ire had been roused, she was sure William's overriding sense of vanity would have stepped in to prevent any threat to his good looks or reputation.

Walt shrugged, his displeasure obvious. 'What he needs is a bed for the night.'

Jessie nodded. 'Will you help me get him to the car?'

'Of course.'

Walt managed to sit William up and, as she looked at him, Jessie's heart split in two. He had indeed been in a fight. There was a cut to his left cheek around which the blood had congealed, a swelling to his left eye and bruising to the left side of his chin.

'Come on, William, time to go.' Walt gave William a rough shake.

Groggily, William came to. 'What?' Unfocused eyes searched Walt's face.

Each grabbing an arm, they lifted William to his feet.

'Don't need any help!' William proclaimed and pulled away from them with such vigour that he staggered backwards. He did a double take at Jessie and touched her face in wonder. 'Jess?'

'I've come to take you to The Lodge.'

'Home?' The word seemed to light a fire in his eyes and he strode out from behind the desk before stopping in the doorway, a puzzled expression on his face. 'But I don't live there any more.' He swayed slightly as he looked at Jessie for confirmation.

'Well, you do tonight,' she said briskly.

*

Parking as close to the front door as she could manage, Jessie set about getting William out of the car.

He was singing a Sinatra song. Badly.

'You're getting the lyrics wrong.'

'What?'

'Never mind.'

'Don't you want to go to the moon?' William asked suddenly. He gripped Jessie's hands tightly, seemingly as determined to pull her into the car as she was to pull him out.

'Not right now,' she responded.

'We'll go next week then,' he said affably.

'Let's go and sit in the kitchen. I'll make you a nice cup of coffee.'

William stared up at the house, frowning. 'We can't go in there.' He grabbed hold of Jessie's arm.

'Why not?'

'It's moving,' he whispered as if the house might hear and object. 'It's not safe.'

'It's perfectly safe,' Jessie said wearily.

'No.' He shook his head. 'We must call someone,' he said and pushed his finger into her shoulder to underline the point. 'An architrave. He'll know what to do.'

'Archi*tect*.'

'Yes, we'll need one of those, too.'

'I'll call them once we're in the kitchen. Come on.'

The steps to the front door seemed to take an age to negotiate as William's weight made Jessie buckle.

William began to sing once more.

He flung his arm wide to emphasise a note and, losing their balance, they careened into the hallway. William sagged against the wall while Jessie got her breath back.

Suddenly, he grabbed the neck of her top. 'I told you this house is not safe.'

'The house is fine. You're the one who's not safe,' she snapped.

Finding this funny, William giggled the rest of the way into the kitchen and then sat, humming to himself.

Jessie made a coffee and put a mug in front of him.

'Never played the flute,' he said suddenly. 'You?' he asked.

Jessie shook her head. 'Drink your coffee,' she said in a tone she hadn't used since Hannah was seven.

'Had piano lessons when I was a kid.'

Jessie sat on the edge of the table. 'What happened, William?'

'Gave them up when the other kids started calling me a sissy.'

'Tonight. What happened tonight?'

He started to sing once more.

'Who did you fight with?'

'She smelt of lavender.'

'Who did?'

'My piano teacher.'

Exasperated, Jessie set about cleaning him up. When she'd finished, she wrapped a towel round a packet of frozen peas and put it against his face. 'Hold this.' William took the bag obediently.

It was then she noticed his knuckles. Both hands were red and cut and the blood had run into his cuffs. So there it was, she thought, he had taken an active part in the fight, not just been the victim of an assault. Methodically, she worked to clean his hands.

'Who did you have a fight with, Will?'

'Fight?' he asked. His eyelids drooped even as he spoke.

As his elbow slipped off the table, she deftly caught the peas. Rewrapping them, she placed the towel on the table and guided his head towards it. William settled on to it with a sigh.

As quickly as she could, Jessie made up a bed in one of the guest rooms. With difficulty, she roused William and, hooking her hand under his left arm, she urged him to his feet.

At the top of the stairs, William turned automatically towards their old room. 'No,' she said, steadying them both against the banister. 'You're sleeping in here.'

'The guest room,' he said.

'That's right.'

'I'm a guest!' he announced loudly as he tumbled through the doorway.

She manoeuvred him to the end of the bed before letting him pitch backwards. 'I could think of plenty of other words,' she commented dryly as she looked down at him.

William caught hold of her arm. 'I love you, Jess. Not supposed to say it but s'true,' he lisped.

Jessie's heart lurched even though she knew it was the drink talking.

Within moments, William was asleep. Jessie pulled off his jacket. Then she unbuttoned his shirt and slipped off his shoes and socks before pulling his trousers down. She decided to leave his boxer shorts on. They were silk, of course, with a suggestive Eiffel Tower design. She suppressed a giggle. They had to be the tart's choice. With a final glance, Jessie picked up the duvet and threw it over him.

Later that evening, after her bath, Jessie checked on him. William hadn't moved, the strength of his snores a testament to how peacefully he slept.

His words came back to her. *I love you, Jess.* Not past tense but present. As in today, at this moment, he loves me. It would explain the photograph in his drawer. Jessie's heart contracted with sadness for him, for them both, if it were true. Why hadn't he said something to her before he'd got Chelsea pregnant, before she'd fallen in love with Owen, before it was too late?

The doorbell jolted her from her thoughts and she cast a nervous look over her shoulder. It had to be Owen. Who else would call at this time of night?

With fingers made clumsy by nerves, Jessie lit the outside light and opened the door on the chain just to be sure. To her surprise she could see the back of a woman. A tubby woman.

'Can I help you?'

The tubby woman turned round and Jessie's surprise turned to shock as she recognised Chelsea. 'Is William here?'

Jessie took a step backwards. No preamble, no apology. Bold as brass, this woman, this *tart*, who had stolen her husband, now stood on her doorstep, demanding to know his whereabouts. Had she no shame?

'No,' Jessie said. She banged the door shut, surprised at how hard she was breathing.

'Mrs Goode, please open the door.'

'Go away!'

'Please, Jessie. I need to know if he's here.'

Jessie closed her eyes. Ever since she'd known William was having an affair she'd imagined this moment. But not like this. In her mind's eye, she had been the one to instigate the confrontation, hurt and anger held at bay while she coolly took her rival apart. Jessie was ashamed to discover that, in reality, such sureness had deserted her.

Gulping in air in a vain attempt to steady her nerves, Jessie released the chain and wrenched open the door with such ferocity Chelsea almost fell across the threshold.

She studied the woman in front of her. She was dressed in dark-blue leggings and a voluminous white shirt with a daisy motif. Jessie recognised it as the logo of a shop that she considered herself to be too old to enter.

The tart's long blonde hair was tousled, her eye make-up smudged. She was, without doubt, one of the golden people. Even in distress, perhaps *especially* in distress, she managed to look beautiful. It was a rough and ready type of beauty. Yes, the woman on the doorstep was a man's fantasy. Like a snapshot, Jessie got some idea of how it had been for William: like being knocked down by a freight train was how she imagined it.

'You knew he was married,' Jessie said, mustering as much authority as she could manage in a silk robe. 'Maybe not at the beginning but eventually you knew and you didn't care. It didn't stop you.'

Tears brimmed in Chelsea's eyes. 'I was already in love with him when he told me he was married. The only thing I cared about by then was making him happy, something you'd stopped doing a long time before I even met him.'

To her alarm, Jessie realised Chelsea was shaking. Confronted by this fragile woman, Jessie felt the smart, sassy comments she had dreamt up for such a moment evaporate. She watched Chelsea's delicate fingers pick at the door frame.

'Just tell me he's okay.'

'What makes you think he'd come here?'

'Because he still loves you,' Chelsea said quietly, her gaze rising to meet Jessie's.

Jessie barely had time to react when she noticed the bruises, like finger marks, on Chelsea's lower arms and the cut to her lip that she had tried to disguise with magenta lipstick.

'What happened?' Jessie asked.

'We had a fight.'

To her own surprise as much as Chelsea's, Jessie reached out and lifted Chelsea's chin. A heady fragrance assailed her nostrils. How like one of the golden ones to douse themselves in perfume at a time of crisis.

'William didn't do that,' Jessie said. She was nevertheless relieved when Chelsea shook her head. 'Who did?'

'Is he here? Please, I have to know. I'm worried about him.'

Chelsea's foot was in the doorway, preceded to a certain extent by her bump. Jessie had steadfastly tried to ignore it but there it was in all its swollen-with-a-new-life potency, right under her nose, in her own house: her husband's unborn child.

'William's here,' Jessie said tersely.

'I need to talk to him.'

'Not tonight,' Jessie said firmly. 'If he wants to speak to you, he'll come to you tomorrow.'

Chelsea hesitated and then nodded. Jessie saw her hand drift to her belly and give it a rub.

'Would you give William a message?'

Jessie nodded numbly.

'Tell him I'm sorry and that I love him.'

Chapter Nineteen

The sun streamed into the kitchen as Jessie buttered toast. Vivaldi poured from the radio and she hummed along as she waited for the kettle to boil.

The music stopped abruptly and she looked up to find William standing in the doorway, one hand raised to shield his eyes from the sun. He was dressed only in his boxer shorts. He walked over to the window and closed the shutter with such force Jessie thought it would end up in the sink.

'Good morning,' she said brightly.

'How did I get here?' He spoke in a gravelly monotone as he pulled back a chair and gingerly sat down.

'Walt found you at the office. He rang me.'

'Where are my clothes?'

Jessie jerked her thumb towards the back door. 'Drying. I did my best to get the stains out.'

'Thanks, Jess.' He held his head in his hands and, from his tone, Jessie could tell gratitude was far from his mind. 'What the hell am I supposed to wear now?'

'I thought I was helping,' she said as she munched her toast.

'If you want to help, you can get me a couple of aspirin.'

Jessie mixed a glass for him. 'Do you want to tell me what happened?'

'No.' He took a sip of the aspirin.

'I have a right to know.'

He looked at her through half-closed eyes, one hangover-induced, the other from the swelling that now had an unhealthy purple tinge to it. 'What time is it?'

'Just after ten.'

William gave a vague nod and began to massage his forehead.

'I rang the office to say I'd be late in. I told them you'd come down with summer flu.'

'They know I'm here?' he said in surprise.

'No, I told them you'd rung me.' Jessie hesitated before continuing. 'Chelsea turned up last night.'

William continued to rub his head.

'She said to tell you that she's sorry and she loves you,' Jessie said, keeping her tone even.

William got to his feet and, splashing cold water into the glass that had held the aspirin, he drank deeply.

'Did you hear me?' Jessie asked.

'I heard you.'

*

When Jessie returned to the kitchen, dressed and ready for work, she found William drinking a mug of black coffee.

'Did you say Walt found me?' he asked, squinting up at her.

'Yes.'

'Was he pissed?'

'Not as pissed as you.'

William laughed. 'You know what I mean.'

'He was angry. What were you thinking, going to the office?'

William stared into his coffee. 'Jack's in Spain. I had nowhere else to go.'

His words tugged at Jessie's heart and she sat down. 'Why don't you go back to bed, give the aspirin a chance to work?'

'You're not throwing me out then?' Humour softened his eyes.

'Not yet.' She smiled. 'I'll get you a few things in town and pop back at lunchtime.'

His hand on hers was hot where he'd been holding the coffee. 'Thanks.' He gave her fingers a squeeze. 'For everything. I assume it was you who cleaned me up?'

'Yep.' Jessie drew her hand away, too many memories colliding within her. 'There wasn't much I could do about your eye, though,' she said, busying herself with her briefcase.

'I'll live.'

'You should ring Chelsea,' Jessie said as she prepared to leave.

'The only person I'm ringing is Walt, to apologise, and then I'm going to take your advice and go back to bed.'

*

As Jessie approached the stall, Owen gave her a wave and kissed her cheek. 'How are you?'

'All the better for seeing you.'

'What have you got there?' Owen pointed to her bulging shoulder bag.

'Files,' she said airily. She decided not to mention the clothes and toiletries for William that she also carried.

Owen leaned in to nibble her ear. 'You work too hard.'

Jessie smiled and let her hand wander through his hair. The busy street seemed to fade away as she looked at him. 'I do love you,' she said.

'I love you too, Miss Martin.' He settled his arms round her waist. 'Let me prove it by buying you dinner tonight.'

'How about a movie and dinner tomorrow night instead?'

'Okay.'

He grabbed her hand and pulled her over to the stall. Plucking a white rose from one of the buckets, he presented it to her with a kiss. 'Until tomorrow.'

And that's how it starts, Jessie thought as she walked away, clutching the bag and the rose. *A deliberate omission is as bad as a lie, even a white one. It risks leading to another and then another and another.*

Why didn't I trust Owen enough to level with him about William?

Looking over her shoulder, she saw Owen press his fingers to his lips and wave. Jessie returned the wave but guilt snatched away her smile.

She hadn't told him because she wasn't sure he would understand her compulsion to help her ex. She wasn't sure she understood it herself. *Or maybe I understand it only too well*, she thought, *and don't want to acknowledge what it means*.

Chapter Twenty

Jessie returned home that evening, hot and tired. She found William working in the sitting room. He was wearing the new beige trousers and white polo shirt she'd dropped off for him earlier. A glass of scotch stood on the table beside him.

'Hello,' she said.

'Hi.'

'Have you started dinner?' she asked, more in hope than expectation.

'I don't think I could face food.'

'It might help if you stopped drinking. Do you want to feel tomorrow morning how you felt this morning?'

'You've no idea how I feel,' he said wearily.

'Why don't you tell me?'

'Why don't you leave me alone?'

'Chelsea knows you're here. She'll be back.'

William contemplated his scotch. 'Did the two of you have a cosy chat last night?'

'Don't be absurd.'

'Did she tell you what happened?'

'No. You have to talk to her.'

'I don't *have* to do anything,' William replied sullenly.

'I don't want her turning up on my doorstep again,' Jessie said.

'Well, you shouldn't have told her I was here, should you?' He tossed the scotch back.

'I tried lying. Unfortunately, unlike you, I'm not very good at it.'

*

Cold water splashed blissfully over Jessie's bare feet as she worked the hose around the tubs of geraniums and fuchsias on the patio. Wearing a pair of cream linen trousers and a matching sleeveless top, she took the steps to the first lawn at a run and padded across the spongy grass; she could already feel the tension of the day beginning to slip from her shoulders.

The crescent bed was a nightmare to mow around but with its majestic collection of agapanthus it was a beautiful sight from the house. The sweet smell of wet earth rose to meet her nostrils as she watered and Jessie closed her eyes, breathing deeply.

Ahead of her, curved borders extended down both sides of the lawn before turning inwards to form a pincer shape either side of the weeping willow. It was a magnificent specimen with a gnarled trunk and branches that dipped so low they brushed the grass with their elongated leaves. A wooden seat had been built round the willow's trunk where, a lifetime ago, she and William had often shared a bottle of wine. It was Jessie's favourite spot in the garden.

Lifting the veil of branches, she walked on to the upper lawn. A second hose was connected to a tap outside the shed and Jessie spun it out. As she let the water play over the clumps of lilac, their blooms now a distant memory of early summer, she sensed William beside her. He gave her a washed-out smile.

'I'm sorry. I shouldn't take my anger out on you.'

'I didn't have to help, you know,' Jessie said. Realising that the soil was turning to a quagmire at her feet, she twitched the hose, moving it on.

'Why did you?' he asked, hands thrust deep into his pockets.

Jessie's gaze met his. 'I feel I owe you.'

'*You* owe *me*?' His incredulity was obvious.

'You accused me of not being there for you when Michael died. Even if, in reality, that's not true, the fact that you perceive it to be true is bad enough. And anyway, you might be right. I probably wasn't as supportive as I could've been.' It had been a weight on her mind for some time and had been compounded by Chelsea's words the previous evening. Jessie shook out the hosepipe, uncomfortable under his gaze. 'But I can't help you if you won't let me in,' she added and walked on up the garden, leaving William where he stood.

'It's over,' William called after her.

Shocked, Jessie halted. 'How can it be over? What about the baby?'

William shrugged. 'The baby's Chelsea's problem now. Why should I care?' His tone was savage. 'I was nothing but a meal ticket to her.'

'What on earth are you talking about?'

'You mean you haven't figured it out yet?' William said, his eyes full of pain. 'The baby isn't mine.' He batted aside the fronds of the willow tree and disappeared.

Letting the hose fall on to the lawn, Jessie ran after him. She found him beneath the willow, one hand resting on the trunk, shoulders hunched.

'Are you sure?'

'Yes.' He sank on to the seat.

Appalled, Jessie sat beside him. 'What happened?'

'I went home to check on Chelsea.' He cleared his throat. 'There was a man there. Pete.' He spat the name out. 'Chelsea was in tears. This Pete was shouting, throwing stuff. Chelsea ran to me, begged me to get rid of him.' William snorted and shook his head. 'Even then she didn't let the act slip.

'She told me he was an old boyfriend from Plymouth who'd come to cause trouble. I told him to get out. The next thing I know, he's grabbing Chelsea by the hair and hitting her. I saw red.' Resting his elbows on his knees, William massaged his forehead.

'I launched myself at him and we got into a fight. The whole time he's screaming at Chelsea to tell me the truth. Then he said it. He said, "Tell him the baby isn't his." I looked at Chelsea and I knew he was telling the truth. She hadn't said anything but I could see it in her eyes.' There was a catch to William's voice. Sitting back, he rested his head against the tree trunk.

'It all came out then. How they got reacquainted when she went to stay with her mother last year. A one-night stand she said, but I don't know.' He shrugged. 'She stayed with her mother for a month in all. It was only supposed to be two weeks but her mother got flu or so she told me, but that could have been a lie as well.' William spoke in a monotone, his face impassive.

But Jessie could see the devastation in his eyes, made more poignant by the bruising and the swelling. 'I'm so sorry,' she whispered.

Her sympathy caused him to frown. 'When she found out she was pregnant she decided to lie about the dates. Come August, she was going to make out the baby had come early. Scheming little bitch obviously thought a lawyer would provide a better future for her and the baby than a sailor.'

'Surely she didn't think she could get away with it?'

'She nearly did. If Chelsea's mother hadn't spoken to this guy's mother down in Plymouth and told her about the pregnancy, she would have done.' He slammed his fist on to the seat. 'I can't believe I've been such a bloody fool.' He stood up. 'I deal with liars and cheats all day. I pride myself on knowing a wrong 'un when I see one and yet I go and fall for the biggest lie of all. What am I going to tell everyone, Jess? What the hell am I going to say to Hannah?'

Jessie knew nothing could be worse for a proud man to bear than humiliation and his pain knifed through her. As he turned away, she realised it was because he didn't want her to see him cry. Hannah's birth, his parents' deaths, the revelation of his affair: they were the only times Jessie could recall William crying. Men were so stingy with their tears.

Watching his shoulders silently begin to shake, Jessie, desperate to do something, anything, to comfort him, reached out and, taking his free hand in hers, gave it a squeeze. William returned the pressure in grateful recognition before marching away.

As Jessie finished the watering and started on dinner, her mind was like a butterfly, barely alighting on one thought before it fluttered on to another. How many nights had she lain in bed, cursing William, wishing to bring down all manner of evils on his head? And yet now that something dreadful had happened she felt only sorrow for him.

William came into the kitchen and gave her a tired smile. 'I've been for a walk in Abbey Wood. Clear my head.'

Jessie had always assumed that falling in love with someone new would cure her of William. Now, as she looked at him, bruised and hurting, she knew there was no remedy for her feelings for him and that, even more confusingly, it was perfectly possible to be in love with two men at the same time.

*

'This business with Chelsea,' Jessie began, resting her fork on the edge of her plate. 'You are positive the baby isn't yours?'

'Yes.'

'What will you do about your things, the house?'

'I'll get my stuff tomorrow. As for the house, it's going on the market. Fancy taking on a bit of conveyancing work?' He smiled, then winced and touched his cheek.

'Is it really over?'

'Yes,' William said firmly. He helped himself to more wine. 'You know what's ironic? It would've been over long ago if she hadn't been pregnant.'

Jessie's heart skipped a beat. 'What do you mean?'

He met her gaze. 'I was going to ask you to take me back. I realised I'd been a fool, that I wanted you, not her, but before I could say anything it was too late.'

'When was this?'

'February. The petition made me realise a divorce was the last thing I wanted.'

Jessie pushed her dinner aside, all appetite gone. He had meant what he'd said when drunk. She almost wished he hadn't spoken. Then or now.

'When I think how mean I was to you over money, and it was all for her, to give her and the baby what they needed. I'm so sorry.' His voice was bitter. 'I suppose I'll be grateful for the way Chelsea behaved, eventually,' William continued. 'A lucky escape. After all, I could never have cut back at work with a baby to look after. But right now I feel stupid. Everyone's going to have a field day, aren't they? Hotshot lawyer suckered by his own vanity.'

Jessie felt her insides melt at the fear in his eyes. She wished she could tell him it wasn't true, but what was the point? He was right. They would have a field day. Everyone liked to see someone else laid low, particularly someone like William. Jessie had longed to see the self-satisfied smile wiped off his face more than most. But not like this. Never like this.

Adopting a businesslike tone, she said, 'If you don't rise to their bait, they'll move on to someone else.'

'Speaking from experience?' William asked softly.

Jessie nodded.

'Christ, Jess. To think I did that to you. And for her.' His eyes were full of remorse. 'Sorry isn't a big enough word.'

She looked away, unnerved by the emotions that were clashing within her.

'I never stopped loving you, you know.'

'We were married a long time,' Jessie said, heat flaming in her cheeks.

'Did you ever stop loving me?' Suddenly his fingers were warm on the back of her hand.

Jessie pulled away, covering the action by pretending to look at her watch. 'It's been a long day,' she said and began to clear the table.

'You forgot your wine.' William stood her glass beside the sink as Jessie filled the bowl.

'Thanks.'

'Dishwasher broken?' he asked.

'No. I've got out of the habit of using it. It's such a waste when it's just me.'

William took a plate from the rack and started to dry it. 'Just like old times,' he remarked with a chuckle.

'What do you want me to say to Hannah when I next speak to her?'

'Don't say anything. I'll drive down to see her. Tell her face-to-face that her old man's a fool.'

'You're not a fool.'

'Why don't you come with me? I could do with the moral support and Hannah would love to see you.'

'I can't get away at the moment.' Jessie grimaced. Was this how supportive I was before? 'I've only just been given my partnership. I don't want to blow it in the first quarter,' she said, seeking to take the sting out of her words.

'Are you sure I can't persuade you?' William slipped his arms round her waist.

'What are you doing?' Jessie asked sharply.

He nuzzled her neck, laying a line of soft kisses from her ear to her shoulder. 'You used to like it when I did this.' His breath tickled her skin.

Involuntarily, she leaned into him as his right hand rose to clasp her breast.

'William, we can't do this.'

'We can do anything we want,' he whispered.

Jessie shook the drops of water from her hands and turned in his arms. He had thrown the tea towel over his shoulder. She had forgotten how he would always do that. Inexplicably, the sight of it made her heart flip over. Such a silly thing, and yet . . .

He held her tightly in his arms, one hand stroking her back while the other moved into her hair. Tentatively, she put her arms round his shoulders.

William frowned. 'That stuff you said about me not being any good in bed. Did you mean it?'

Jessie shook her head. 'I just wanted to hurt you.'

The kiss was everything she thought it would be and the memory of a thousand other kisses leapt into her mind. But had those kisses ever been as passionate, as desperate, as full of love?

As their lips parted, she pressed her face to his shoulder. William. Her William. She was heady with the smell of him, the feel of his body against hers.

'You never answered my question,' he said quietly. 'Did you ever stop loving me?'

Held fast in his embrace, she saw the look of concern flash through his dark eyes. 'You know I didn't,' she said.

She brought her lips back to his and surrendered herself to him, feeling the fire in her belly leap, as their tongues duelled. *I remember this*, she thought. *God, how I remember: his power, his strength, his gentleness. This was how it used to be. In the kitchen, in the dining room, in the hall sometimes, if we'd been out and couldn't wait.*

He was whispering words of love into her hair, just like before, and Jessie felt her knees grow weak. With wet fingers, she fumbled with the buttons of his shirt and, casting the shirt aside, she raked her hand over his chest. Slowly, with the lightest of touches, she tracked her hand down to his taut stomach. William moaned.

Jessie tilted her head back, loving the feel of his lips on her throat. She felt him undo her buttons deftly with one hand while the other stroked the back of her neck. He slipped his hand inside her top and she sighed, her fingers curling into his hair as his fingertips brushed her breast.

They were going to do it here, in the kitchen, just like the old days. The doors were open and the night air, chill now, swept round her ankles and shoulders. As he pressed himself against her, she felt the sink bite into her lower back. Maybe this was not the best place. Maybe they should go upstairs. The bed called to her with its soft mattress and fluffy down-filled pillows.

William had his head to her breast now and she knew only the solidness of the sink at her back was holding her up. How could his caresses be so familiar and yet, at the same time, make her feel so wild and reckless? She thrilled to his touch, every sinew of her body alert, alive. Had it ever been this good? Had she ever wanted him quite so violently as she did at that moment? Or he her?

The telephone cut through her excitement. For a heartbeat, they both became still.

'Leave it,' William hissed as he sought Jessie's mouth.

Jessie manoeuvred herself away from the sink. 'I can't,' she said. 'What if it's Hannah?' Breathless, she picked up the receiver. 'Hello?'

'Is William there? Can I speak to him?'

Jessie closed her eyes and thrust the phone at William. 'Chelsea,' she said tonelessly.

Swearing, William snatched the phone from her. 'Don't ever call me here again,' he thundered and slammed the receiver down just long enough to cut the connection before lifting the handset once more and leaving it to dangle against the wall. 'Sorry, I've been screening the calls to my mobile. I guess she thought she'd try her luck.'

They both knew the moment was gone but still he reached for her hand and leaned in to kiss her neck but Jessie was already moving away. She ran a flustered hand through her hair and shakily began to do up her buttons.

'Jess . . .'

She shook her head. Her William was gone. In his place was a man who had lied and cheated and broken her heart. Chelsea was no longer the mother of his child but she had still been his lover.

Then there was Owen. What on earth was she thinking? How had she let things get so far out of hand? William was the past. She was with Owen now. Owen was the future.

'Jess?'

'No, William.' She pushed him away.

'I want you so much,' he said, grabbing her hand.

'You only want me because you haven't got her.'

'You know that's not true.'

'Leave it, William. Please. I'm going to bed. Alone. And tomorrow you must leave.'

AUGUST

Chapter Twenty-One

Jessie watched the windscreen wipers swish in double time against the downpour as she pulled up outside The Lodge. William's Jag was parked by the double garage.

Jessie pursed her lips. She had agreed to Hannah's request that William be allowed to stay at The Lodge but only on the condition that he was gone before her return from holiday. Trust William not to honour that agreement.

The day after his pass at her, William had left early, stopping off in North Street to collect his belongings before heading for Exeter to see Hannah. There had been no time to talk. Now, the prospect of talking scared her. *Please, let Hannah be with him.*

Jessie didn't want to jeopardise what she had with Owen. It was a simple, delightful romance, unsullied by rows. With William, everything was complicated and always would be. And yet, as she ran through the rain, Jessie's heart beat a little faster at the prospect of seeing him again.

Stowing her suitcase in the hall, Jessie followed the delicious smell of roast lamb into the kitchen.

'Perfect timing, Jess. Another ten minutes and we were sending out a search party.'

She threw him an incredulous look. 'You were supposed to be gone before I got back.'

William nodded. 'Guilty as charged. Hannah and I wanted to make it up to you for missing your birthday.' He gestured to the oven.

'There was no need.'

William splashed wine into a fresh glass. 'Roast is almost done. Be a shame for the three of us not to enjoy it. I promise I'll leave once the dishwasher is stacked.' He offered the wine glass to her with a smile.

Despite her reservations, Jessie smiled back, her heart pitter-pattering around the kitchen. Dressed in jeans and the white polo shirt she'd bought him, William looked relaxed. His cuts and bruises had healed and the tiredness that had pulled at his eyes was gone. There was no denying he was a handsome man. Jessie sipped her wine. But he's not my man. She turned as Hannah entered the kitchen.

'Hi, Mum.'

'Hello, darling.' Jessie kissed Hannah's cheek. 'I'm going to unpack. Why don't you come with me? You can tell me what you've been up to.'

*

'How was Wales?' Hannah asked from the bedroom doorway.

'It was lovely. Owen and I had such a nice time when we were there in May, I couldn't believe it when he said he was taking me back there for a week. It was a wonderful birthday present.' Jessie smiled at the memory.

'He loves you, doesn't he?' Hannah said, moving to sit on the bed.

Jessie detected a note of disappointment in her daughter's voice. 'Yes, he does,' Jessie said. 'And I love him,' she added gently.

Hannah nodded as her eyes filled with tears. 'I hate that bitch for what she's done to Daddy. When I think of all the sacrifices he made for her.' Two fat tears slid down Hannah's cheeks. 'Did you know he didn't even want to be with her any more? That he stayed because he thought the baby was his. If only Chelsea had told him the truth before things got serious between you and Owen, there might have been a . . .'

'It's over between your dad and me, whether he's with Chelsea or not,' Jessie said firmly.

Hannah nodded, struggling to compose herself as her lip quivered. 'He said you were the best thing that ever happened to him.'

'He had a funny way of showing it. You should have warned me he was still here.'

Hannah looked contrite. 'When you told me Owen was staying in Wales to visit friends I didn't think you'd mind. When will he be back?'

Jessie finished unpacking her suitcase and began sorting the clothes into piles for washing. 'About a week, I think. He plans to call in on his aunt and his dad on the way back.'

'Didn't you want to go with him?'

'Yes, of course I did but Phil wants me to see two new properties he has his eye on for development. They go to auction next Thursday so I could hardly put him off. Still, it doesn't matter too much; Owen's aunt Stella and his dad are coming to The Lodge next month. It'll be so lovely to finally meet them.'

Hannah chewed her lip. 'Daddy's putting on a brave face but he's dreading going back to work. He won't stay in North Street either. He said he'd rather sleep at the Northey. I know you wanted him to be gone before you came home but can he stay a little longer, Mum? At least while I'm here.'

'Did he put you up to this?' Jessie asked sternly.

'No. But he needs our support. Please?'

'I'll think about it. How's David?'

Hannah ran her hand over the duvet. 'We've split up.'

'Darling, I'm sorry.'

Hannah shook her head. 'I was the one who finished with him in the end. I couldn't get a straight answer out of him. I've been trying since June but things were just drifting on. I'm pretty sure there was someone else. He didn't seem too fazed when I ended it. Why do people have to be so deceitful, Mum? Why can't people just tell the truth?'

Why, indeed? Jessie gave her daughter a hug.

'I'm all right,' Hannah said firmly. 'If he wants to play silly games, he can go ahead but I'm better than that.'

Jessie smiled. 'Yes, you are.'

*

Throughout dinner William and Hannah regaled Jessie with tales of their time in Exeter. After dinner, Hannah went to visit friends while William stayed to share a pot of tea with Jessie.

'Are you going to work tomorrow?'

William nodded. 'Got to face everyone sometime,' he said with an air of resignation.

It was such a contrast to the man who at dinner had been full of wisecracks and funny stories. With Hannah gone, Jessie realised, William felt able to let the act drop.

'I'm not looking forward to it. Those who know the truth will think I'm a fool; those who don't will think I'm a bastard for running out on her.' He rubbed his thighs. 'What did Walt tell people?'

'He said you and Chelsea had split up and you were going away for a few weeks.' Jessie paused. 'I told the ones that mattered the truth.'

William winced as if in pain and looked away.

'Would you rather they thought you a bastard?'

He laughed sourly. 'Hobson's choice, isn't it? Did Hannah tell you about David?'

'Yes.'

'She thinks the little shit was two-timing her.'

'There seems to be a lot of it about,' Jessie commented dryly.

William looked apologetic. 'She seems okay though. Despite everything.'

Jessie smiled. 'Our daughter is made of tough stuff. Have you heard from Chelsea?'

'She wrote me a letter.'

'What did she say?'

'I haven't opened it yet.'

'That's mature.'

William pulled a face.

'How did you leave things with her?'

'I told her I wanted her out of my house and that it was going on the market as soon as I got back. She said she was going to her mother's.' William's voice was cold.

'Will you see her again?'

'Not if I can help it.'

Could feelings die that quickly?

He gave her a strained smile and, standing, lifted two keys off his key ring. 'Decree nisi's being pronounced tomorrow so I guess you should have these back.' They were the keys to The Lodge.

Jessie took a deep breath. 'Why don't you hold on to them for a few more days? Hannah told me you planned to stay at the Northey tonight. You might as well stay here until you can make other arrangements.' Jessie watched his face brighten. 'But there are ground rules,' she said quickly. 'What happened last month was a mistake. I'm with Owen, now. I want you to respect that.'

William gave a thoughtful nod. 'Thanks, Jess.'

*

The next day, as Jessie turned out of the drive, she noticed William's hands balled into fists, the knuckles like the snow-capped peaks of a mountain range. He was wearing his lucky charcoal suit.

'I think I'm going to need all the luck I can get today,' he had told her earlier when she'd commented on it.

Feeling sorry for him, she'd offered him a lift to work. Now, eager to divert his attention from what lay ahead, Jessie said, 'Hannah's looking forward to working with Howard.'

William nodded. 'It's a good opportunity for her to see how the big firms operate. Although I'm beginning to think this work-experience placement might've been a mistake,' he admitted. 'What if the big city seduces her?'

'Would it be such a bad thing if it did?'

'You think I'm crowding her?'

'Working with you would be a big step. I don't want her to feel she has to say yes for fear of disappointing you.'

As they pulled into the car park, William sighed. 'I didn't feel this nervous the first time I stood up in court.' He threw open the door and, looking back at Jessie, grimaced. 'I don't know how you did it,' he said. There was a new-found respect for her in his eyes.

'I had no choice,' Jessie said. 'And neither do you. Come on, I'll walk in with you.'

*

The following morning, William, dressed for the office, whistled a pop song as he opened the door of Jessie's bedroom. The room was cool, the curtains dancing in the breeze from the open windows.

Jessie lay on her back, one arm thrown over her head. Her hair, longer than she had worn it in years, was spread over the pillow and across one creamy shoulder.

William stood the tray he was carrying on the floor and, with his fingertips, stroked the inside of her forearm. 'Jess.'

Jessie stirred. Her eyes were dreamy as she looked at him. Then, as consciousness descended, she pulled the duvet up to her shoulders. 'What are you doing in here?' she asked sharply.

'I've brought you breakfast,' William said, amused at her reaction. 'To say thank you for yesterday. If things had been the other way round, I'm not sure I could have done what you did.' He smiled. 'But I guess that just means you're a nicer person than I am and we both knew that already.' William hoisted the tray into the air before setting it down on the bed. 'See?' he said. 'No strings attached.'

Jessie smiled. 'Would you pass me my robe?'

William picked up the robe from the nearby wicker chair, handed it to Jessie and gallantly went to look out of the window. Her modesty made him smile. Did she really think he couldn't remember every curve of her body, that if he closed his eyes he couldn't see her lying there, beautifully naked?

His heart pulled for her. He had to somehow win her over. Maybe if he talked to her on their anniversary he could persuade her to finish with Owen and give him a second chance. It was worth a try. 'I spoke to the estate agents. They're sending someone round to value the house in North Street today.'

'That's good. You can turn round now,' Jessie said.

William sat on the end of the bed. 'Breakfast okay?'

Jessie nodded, sipping her tea. 'Great. Did you read Chelsea's letter?'

'Yep.' William helped himself to a slice of toast. 'Baby girl. Seven pounds. Called it Marika.'

'That's it?'

'As far as I'm concerned it is.' He crammed the rest of the toast into his mouth and stood. 'I've got a full list in the magistrates' court so I can't stop.'

He wasn't looking forward to seeing the ushers and the magistrates. It was a small town. They would all know. Still, it couldn't be any worse than it had been at the police station. Jack aside, the rest had been bastards and he'd had to respond to their jokes and snide comments with a painted-on smile, knowing that if he showed any sign of weakness it would only prolong the agony.

Jessie's eyes were tender as she looked at him. 'Today will be better.'

'It can't be any worse,' he replied. Wanting to kiss her and knowing he couldn't, he gave her a smile and left.

Chapter Twenty-Two

'Someone looks happy.'

Jessie glanced up from her phone to find William in the doorway of her office. 'Owen's just texted to say he's coming home tonight. He wants me to meet him at the station.'

William's smile dimmed. 'I guess that means you won't be joining Hannah and me for Chinese then?'

'Sorry, no.'

*

Paying no heed to the commuters who were streaming off the London train, Owen, dressed in baggy shorts and a Greenpeace T-shirt, lifted Jessie from the ground and swung her round.

'God, I've missed you,' he said, kissing her.

Jessie laughed. 'How did everything go with your family?' she asked eagerly as they walked to the car.

'Great.'

'When are they coming to see the farm?'

'Soon.' He threw his bags on to the back seat. 'What do you want to do tonight?'

'I don't mind.'

'Let's stay in,' Owen said with a grin. 'I fancy an early night.'

'Okay.' Jessie pulled into the traffic, her breath coming in shallow bursts. 'Why don't we stay at yours?'

'Mine? What's the matter with The Lodge?'

Jessie could sense him looking at her. 'Hannah's home.'

'Of course, I forgot. How is she?' he asked amiably.

'She's fine. She's having Chinese with William tonight.'

'The dickhead's back, is he?' Owen sounded surprised. 'Have you seen him?'

'Yes.' *He brought me breakfast in bed*. 'The decree nisi was pronounced yesterday.'

'When do you get the absolute?'

'Six weeks.' Jessie swung on to the roundabout and headed for the town centre.

'Not long now then,' Owen said. 'You'll soon be a free woman.' He leaned across and kissed her cheek. 'Christ, you look good,' he said, his hand on her thigh. 'Too good, considering you've been at the office all day.'

Jessie blushed.

There was no residents' parking scheme in North Street. Backing into the first available space, Jessie realised she had parked outside the house William had once shared with the tart. A for-sale sign was in the window.

'He's put it on the market then,' Owen remarked.

Jessie nodded.

'Will he stay, do you think?'

'Stay?' Jessie was confused.

'In Abbeyleigh. Let's face it, he's been made to look a right prat in front of everyone.'

'Abbeyleigh is his home.'

Owen turned his key and threw open the front door. The heat hit them like a furnace. 'In my book, home is wherever you want it to be,' he said, stepping back so Jessie could enter first.

The door opened directly on to the living room; ahead was the galley kitchen. Upstairs there were two bedrooms and a small bathroom.

'I'll get us something to drink,' Owen said.

Jessie had been to Owen's house only a handful of times. He disliked the cramped rooms, sparse furniture and the proximity of the street. Jessie had told him that none of that mattered but she knew he was embarrassed by it all the same.

'Ice and water okay?' Owen called.

'Fine.' Jessie walked into the kitchen. Standing at the back door, she looked out over the tiny yard. It had been concreted over with just a hole left for a rotary washing line. A kitchen chair stood in one corner with a mug on the floor beside it. In her mind, she saw herself painting fences and adding pots. For a flower seller he had surprisingly few flowers.

She cried out in surprise as Owen pressed a cold glass to the back of her neck. 'Have I told you that I missed you?' he asked.

Jessie giggled as he kissed her neck. 'Yes, but you can tell me again.'

Laughing, he leaned against the cabinet and sipped his water. 'So, what have you been doing with yourself?'

'The usual.' Uneasy under Owen's gaze, Jessie drank her water quickly. Then, tipping the ice into the palm of her hand, she pressed it against her throat and neck. 'There's something I should tell you.' She stared down at the chequered lino. 'William's staying at The Lodge.' Nervously, she lifted her gaze.

Owen took a long drink as the silence lengthened. 'Whose idea was that?' he asked finally, his voice as cold as the ice in her hand.

'Hannah's.'

'*Hannah's?*'

'William didn't want to stay in North Street. He was going to book into the Northey but Hannah –'

'And you agreed to this?'

Jessie could hear the disappointment in his voice. 'Yes.' She tipped the ice back into the glass and stood it on the drainer. The sudden tension, coupled with the heat, made her feel weary. 'It took a lot of guts for him to come back and face everybody. It didn't seem fair to make him stay in a hotel.'

Owen's eyes widened in surprise. 'From what you've told me, he didn't care that much when you had to face everybody.'

Jessie didn't like the accusations Owen's eyes were throwing at her. 'It'll only be for a few days. Then he's going to look for somewhere to rent. Honestly, it's no big deal.'

Drops of water splashed the worktop as Owen slammed his glass down. He suddenly looked very young.

'I'm going to have a shower,' he announced.

Jessie heard him take the stairs two at a time. Then the bathroom door slammed. She banged her fist against the drainer. The last thing she'd wanted was to hurt his feelings. Why couldn't he understand that she was trying to do the right thing? Why did he have to make her feel guilty when she'd done nothing wrong?

Kicking off her shoes, Jessie climbed the stairs and opened the bathroom door. Owen's clothes were a heap on the floor. Catching hold of the zip of her dress, Jessie added it to the pile. Her bra and knickers quickly followed.

Pulling the shower curtain back, she stepped into the bath. The water was wonderfully cold against her hot feet. Wrapping her arms round Owen's waist, she laid her cheek against his shoulder.

'I feel as if I owe you an apology,' she said.

Owen turned, water cascading over his tanned skin. 'Are you and William sleeping together?'

'No.'

He searched her eyes and then brought his forehead down to hers. His wet hair soaked her fringe and as they embraced he swung her round, plunging her under the jet of the shower as his mouth closed over hers.

The cool water hit her sweltering skin and instantly she felt invigorated. The suffocating heat had been pushing at her all day, wearing her down. Now, as the water pelted her body, her lethargy disappeared as Owen took her quickly, urgently against the cold tiles of the bathroom wall.

Afterwards, Owen dried Jessie's body before allowing her to do the same for him. Then, wrapped in fresh towels, they laid down together on Owen's bed.

Jessie's skin tingled and, feeling the welcoming depths of contentment steal upon her, she sighed, ready to let sleep take her.

A few minutes passed before Owen laced his fingers through hers. 'I wouldn't have minded if you had,' he said.

Jessie knew instantly what he was talking about. 'I haven't,' she replied sleepily.

'But you wanted to.'

Jessie lifted her head. 'I still find him attractive,' she admitted. 'It doesn't mean I acted on it.' She ruffled Owen's damp hair.

He ducked his head away. 'If you feel that way about him, why are you divorcing him?'

Jessie rolled on to her side. 'Because sometimes the spark isn't enough.'

Accepting the invitation of Owen's open arms, Jessie settled her head against his chest.

'Jessie?'

'Yes?'

'If you wanted to make a go of it with him and I was standing in your way . . .'

Jessie raised herself on one elbow and leaned in low to kiss his lips. 'You're not,' she said softly. She let her hair fall over her face, the ends brushing his neck and shoulder. He had once told her how much he liked to see it like that, all tousled from their being together. 'It's over between William and me,' she said calmly. And she meant it. Love and attraction were all very well but without trust they were meaningless.

With a smile that made her heart contract, Owen settled back, cradling her in his arms.

'You know when I said that I wouldn't have minded?'

'Yes.'

'I was lying.'

*

As the last of the daylight bled from the sky and the shadows deepened into pools of darkness, Owen lit the bedside lamp and went off to the kitchen, a towel slung casually around his slender hips.

Jessie could hear the sizzle of a pan and cupboard doors banging. Happy to let him rustle something up for them, she wriggled her toes. The safe smell of freshly laundered cotton greeted her nostrils as she turned into the pillow.

Soon Owen was back bearing a tray of bacon sandwiches. When they'd eaten, Owen leaned across and planted a lingering kiss on Jessie's lips. 'Time for dessert.'

He cleared away the debris of their dinner and when he returned he brought with him a tub of strawberry ice cream. Clambering over the bed to where Jessie sat, wrapped in her towel, he put the tub down beside her.

'You really are very beautiful,' he whispered and, nudging her lips with his, he undid the loop of her towel, gently pushing her back against the bed.

The evening was sultry, her skin sticky despite their earlier shower but the first drop of ice cream on her belly still made Jessie cry out. The ice cream carved out its own path over her skin and, as it trickled down from her navel, following quickly in its beautifully cool tracks was Owen's tongue.

As the sweet scent of strawberries filled the air William had never seemed so far away.

*

It was just after midnight when Jessie let herself into The Lodge. She had hoped to sneak up to her room, unobserved, but she could hear the television in the sitting room and felt obliged to stick her head round the door. William was watching an old Steve McQueen film.

'Hi, Jess.'

'Hello. Hannah in bed?'

'Yes. Big day tomorrow. Howard's got a case in the Old Bailey and he's taking Hannah along. By the way, he and Diane are happy for her to stay at the flat so at least it saves on the commute.'

Jessie sat on the arm of the sofa. 'Is she okay?'

'A bit apprehensive. I've been thinking about what you said, maybe it would be a good idea to let her spread her wings.'

'At least that way if she comes back to you, you'll know it's what she wants,' Jessie said.

William nodded. 'Wise words.' He gave her an inscrutable look. 'Good evening?'

'Yes. Lovely.' With her unkempt hair and no make-up left she wondered if he could tell, just by looking at her, what she had been doing. Probably. Colour flooded her cheeks and, angry with herself, she said, 'Have you found anywhere to rent yet?' The words came out more sharply than she'd intended.

William looked hurt. 'Give me a chance.'

'It's just that I've had an idea.' It was actually Owen's idea, but she thought it best not to tell him that.

'Oh yes?' William was watching her warily.

'Several of the flats in the Old Mill are finished. I'm sure Phil wouldn't mind renting one of them to you. Would you like me to ask him?'

'Sounds great,' William said without enthusiasm and turned back to the film.

*

Three days later, with Hannah in London and Phil Blunkett proclaiming himself happy to let William move into the Old Mill, Jessie decided to broach the subject again.

'It's not often you get the chance to stay in a penthouse.'

'Makes a change from the doghouse I suppose,' William had replied. 'I'll move out this weekend, okay?'

'Perfect.'

No sooner had he given his assent than notes started to appear. Jessie found them all over the house. The one inside her briefcase said: 'You work too hard. Go and sit in the garden.' The one on her eye cream said: 'You have gorgeous eyes.' The one on her blotter at work said: 'You're looking beautiful today.' The one on her pillow simply said: 'I love you.'

The notes were a reminder of their early years together, when everything had been fresh and new and William would often leave scraps of paper for her to find. Then it had seemed romantic and Jessie had saved them all.

Now, the current crop left her feeling uneasy. Flushed with a ludicrous pride at the sight of one, she would smile as she read it and, as she read it again, her smile would grow. The notes made her feel loved and that was the problem: William wasn't supposed to make her feel like that any more. Owen was.

She decided she had to put a stop to them. William was trading on their past, using something familiar and cherished to manipulate her feelings. The fact that she loved it made her hate it even more. She left a Post-it on his desk. *Stop it, please!*

They had never discussed the notes. Then or now. It had been part of their charm. Consequently, no comment was passed on their demise either and although it was what she wanted Jessie couldn't help but feel life became a little duller without them.

On the afternoon of her wedding anniversary a bouquet arrived. It was a gigantic arrangement of crisp white and sun-drenched yellow lilies, ox-eye daisies and delicate miniature roses. Sprays of gypsophila and mimosa rounded the bouquet out, with lush ferns providing an elegant backdrop. The bouquet was swathed in cellophane and tied with frothy white and yellow ribbons. It was only after Jessie had admired the flowers for some minutes that she noticed the card. It was pinned to the thin paper backing, almost hidden by the ferns.

Jessie had assumed the flowers were from Owen as barely a week went by when he didn't leave a bouquet at reception for her. Now the handwriting told her different. Part of her didn't want to spoil her enjoyment of this magnificent creation by reading the card. Part of her didn't want to feel guilty that she'd received beautiful flowers from a man other than her lover. But part of her wanted to know what William had to say and that part of her won.

The card read: *Have dinner with me tonight.*

Jessie crossed the corridor to William's office.

'I don't think that's a good idea,' she said without preamble.

'My cooking's not that bad, is it?' William asked, looking disappointed.

Jessie smiled and waggled her hand. 'You did once burn scrambled egg.'

'That's not fair. I got distracted. About tonight, I just wanted to say thank you for letting me stay and I've already bought all the stuff,' he said, indicating the shopping bags in the corner. 'Come on, Jess. It's our last night together and it *is* our anniversary. Have dinner with me, please.'

Jessie wavered. He'd obviously gone to a lot of trouble. What harm could it do? After all, he'd be leaving in the morning. 'Okay.'

Chapter Twenty-Three

Jessie put on her favourite yellow dress. It was silk with a flared hem and spaghetti straps. She was just on her way out of the bedroom, when her mobile rang. Owen had texted to say he loved her. Jessie sent back a smiley face with the words: 'I love you, too.'

She hadn't had the guts to tell him she was having dinner with William. Guilt knitted her brows but she forced the feelings into a box and shut the lid. She didn't want to feel guilty tonight. She wanted to enjoy dinner and then wave William off to his flat tomorrow, knowing that if ever there was a debt owed over his father's death it had been fully repaid.

The dining table, with its white cloth and beautiful silverware, looked fresh and inviting. A bottle of champagne stood in an ice bucket with crystal flutes ready beside it. On seeing her, William took the bottle of champagne from the bucket and began to work on the foil. 'I've said before that sorry isn't a big enough word for the hurt I caused.' He spread his hand to indicate the table. 'I thought maybe a gesture like this would help and I wanted to thank you for letting me stay. Most women would have told me to jump in the lake.' The champagne cork popped and he grinned. 'So, enjoy,' he said.

Enjoy, Jessie did. They ate prawn cocktail, followed by spatchcock chicken with new potatoes and steamed vegetables, and for dessert they had raspberry pavlova, although William informed Jessie he would be eating humble pie instead.

'Have you had a nice time?' William asked.

'Lovely, thank you. It was all delicious.'

'I can take very little credit.' His smile was warm, his eyes bright as he refreshed her glass. 'Mr Marks and Mr Spencer did most of the work. I mostly reheated.'

'And there was me thinking you'd sculpted that pavlova with your own fair hands.'

William laughed. 'Probably just as well for us both that I didn't.' He took a sip of his champagne. 'Did I tell you I'm getting my office redecorated?'

Jessie shook her head.

'Yeah, it was time for a change. I'm going for pistachio. What do you think?'

'Very nice.' Jessie hid her smile behind her glass. How like William. Pistachio. Why could he not just say green like everyone else?

'I got you a present,' he said.

'Why?' Jessie asked, surprised.

'For our anniversary.'

Jessie looked at him in astonishment. 'I don't think we're in a position to celebrate, do you?'

Ignoring her, William took a white box, tied with a pink ribbon, from beneath the table. He held it out with a smile.

Jessie undid the bow, conscious that William's gaze was on her. A simple meal. A thank you. That was all she'd expected. Had she been naïve? Or had she been lying to herself? Had she secretly hoped for more? Was this a prelude to being back in his arms again?

She lifted the lid of the box. Inside, on a bed of pink tissue paper, was the porcelain figure of a ballerina, just like the one William had smashed. Jessie's eyes misted over.

'Where did you . . .? How . . .?' She was at a loss for words.

'I'm sorry I broke the original. Why don't you go and put Hannah back where she belongs?'

Jessie stood the figurine on the mantelpiece, moving aside the vase Owen had bought her to make room.

'She looks good, doesn't she?' William said.

Jessie nodded. 'Thank you.' She sat in one of the fireside chairs as William sat in the other and told her the story of his search for the figurine.

When he'd finished, he moved to the edge of his seat. 'I'm sorry for what I put you through, so very sorry,' he said. His dark eyes were pools of sadness. 'Chelsea was a mistake. She was my midlife crisis. Do you know how many times I've used that as a defence for my clients? Personally, I always thought it was bullshit. I never understood why the bench fell for it. Now I've come to the conclusion that they'd experienced a similar thing for themselves. I don't intend to have another.'

'I'd have preferred an affair with the golf course.'

'With my handicap?' William joked. 'It was transitory.'

'You were going to marry her.'

'Only because I thought I'd got her pregnant. Temporary insanity, Jess. Please don't hold me accountable for the rest of my life.'

Jessie shrank back. 'Why are midlife crises a man's prerogative?' she asked. 'It's not that simple, William. You don't get to sit there looking expectant and have me tell you everything's okay. You took my world and you broke it. Your excuse for doing that is you're a man and therefore you're weak and I should pity you. How would you have felt if I'd been the one having the affair?'

'Devastated,' William said flatly. 'Every time anyone told me how well you were looking it would twist the knife. I hadn't put that smile on your face. He had. Don't you see, Jess?' He moved to kneel in front of her. 'We both had affairs.'

'No,' Jessie replied swiftly. 'I had a relationship once you told me our marriage was over. That's a very different thing.'

William covered her hands with his, gripping them tightly. 'Were you justified? Absolutely,' he said. 'Did it hurt like hell to watch you? Yes, it did.'

'If you were as devastated as you claim, how come you were so cool with me when we met to discuss the divorce at the Northey?' Jessie demanded, pulling her hands away.

'Meeting you that day was one of the hardest things I've ever done,' William confessed. 'And letting you walk away afterwards was harder still.' He reached out to stroke her cheek. 'I made myself stare at the newspaper because I knew if I looked up and you were still there I'd make a fool of myself by running after you. What could I do, Jess? I was trapped.'

'You seemed fine.' She hardly registered that his hands had settled over her knees.

'I was making the best of a bad situation. Believe me, I was far from fine. I love you,' he said earnestly. 'I will always love you. That's why I want you back.' He stroked her legs.

Jessie reached down to stop him. 'William, no.'

'You love me too. You can't deny it.'

'I don't know how I feel any more.' Gripping his shoulders, she pushed him away from her before running from the room.

*

Sitting beneath the willow tree, Jessie watched its majestic boughs sweep the lawn, periodically obscuring her view as they whispered back and forth. On the roof of the house two doves sat. The male was bowing and cooing to the female, trying to woo her but, every time he got close, the female edged away.

When Jessie looked down at the lower lawn, she saw William coming towards her, a bottle of wine and two glasses in his hands.

'Peace offering?' he said.

Jessie shrugged. William poured the wine and they drank in silence, each lost in thought, each waiting for the other to speak. Several minutes passed before he touched her hand. His fingers were cold from the wine bottle. He gave her hand a gentle squeeze and released it as suddenly as he'd grasped it.

The next moment, she was in his arms. His kisses were like fire to her cool lips, burning her with the strength of his longing. Like molten flows of lava they poured over her skin, down her throat, over her shoulders, his passion searing her.

Kissing him back, emotions that scared her, which she would never have dared put into words, erupted within her. Her fingers worked at his hair, excitement peaking as he pushed the straps of her dress from her shoulders and brought his lips to the hollow of her throat.

'I want you back,' William said hoarsely.

In the grip of fierce desire, Jessie thought about it. How easy, how wonderful it would be to let William continue, to have him make love to her here beneath the willow tree.

She would have to tell Owen it was over. Jessie pushed the hurt this would cause from her mind. *It's not as if it will come as a surprise to him. He already suspects how I feel.*

How do I feel? Her own words came back to her. 'Sometimes the spark isn't enough.' It was plenty right now. But what happened after they made love? Would it ever be possible to leave the bad memories behind? 'William, no!' Jessie said. She gathered the straps of her dress, the breeze fanning her skin, which, seconds before, had smouldered under his touch.

'What's wrong?'

'I can't do this. I don't want to do this.'

William gave her a searching look and, taking her hands in his, said, 'I'll do whatever you want me to do, just please say you forgive me and that I can come home. Now that I'm free, there's nothing to stop us.'

'I'm not free,' Jessie said quietly.

'Owen?' William was incredulous. 'Come on, Jess! Owen was a sexual itch you had to scratch. Now you've done that, surely you can see there's no future in it. He's just a kid.'

'A kid I'm in love with.'

'I will do anything to get you back. Anything. Name it.'

'There's nothing you can do.'

'But you love me. I know you love me,' William said.

Jessie stood. 'It's not enough,' she said sadly. 'Wanting you, loving you. It's not enough.'

'How can that not be enough?'

'You hurt me and you lied to me. Yes, I love you. But I love Owen, too. The difference is I trust Owen. He knows what it's like to have his heart ripped out. He wouldn't do that to me. My trust in you has gone and I don't see how that will ever change.'

'It was one mistake,' William cried, reaching for her.

'A relationship without trust can't work.'

'And I suppose you know everything there is to know about Owen?'

'I think so.'

William bit back a laugh. 'You haven't even met his family.'

'They're busy people.'

'His dad lives in London, Jess. Not Timbuktu. The reason you haven't met them is either because he doesn't want you to or because he's hiding something.'

Jessie turned away. It was the one thing that had troubled her. Had Owen deliberately not introduced her to his family because she was so much older than him? But, no – the age gap had never been a problem for him. It was just that everyone led such busy lives: his father with the restaurant, Owen with the stall. It was hard to get together.

'Don't be angry with me,' William said quickly. 'I just don't want to see you setting yourself up for a fall. One idiot in the family is enough.'

'Is that what you think I'm doing, setting myself up for a fall?'

'He's a kid,' William repeated. 'Where's the future in that?'

Jessie edged away. 'Maybe I'm not looking for a future any more. Maybe I just want some fun. Like you did.'

William accepted the blow with equanimity. 'We used to have fun,' he said gently. 'We could again.'

'I don't want you back.'

'That's not what your kisses said.'

'Wanting you and wanting you back are two different things. How could I believe in you?'

'I'll make you believe. I'll make it my mission in life to love and protect you. I'll never give you cause to doubt me again. On Hannah's life, that's what I'll do.'

'I'm sorry.'

'Jess, please.'

There were tears in William's eyes and Jessie closed her own eyes, not wanting to witness his pain, not wanting to be swayed by it. William had lied and cheated and she would always remember, however hard she tried to forget.

'It's over,' she whispered.

William swallowed hard. Frown lines bit deep into his forehead as he stood motionless, seeking to compose himself. 'I'll get my stuff. I'll leave tonight,' he said gruffly. The hurt seeped from his eyes, embedding itself into his compressed lips and hunched shoulders. 'If how I feel right now is one tenth of the way I made you feel when I told you about Chelsea, I wouldn't have me back either.'

As he walked away, Jessie sank on to the seat, drained. Her wine glass had been knocked over and, picking it up, she filled it once more. *I did the right thing*, she told herself, her hand shaking as she drank.

A few minutes later she heard the front door slam and William's car rev up. *If how I feel right now is one tenth of the way I made you feel . . .* It had been an eloquent speech but then he was good with words. He made his living from them, that and twisting the truth. Jessie watched twilight slide across the garden. By the time she returned to The Lodge it was pitch-black and she had drunk all the wine.

She crawled into bed. But if she thought sleep would bring her some relief she was mistaken. Exhausted, she flipped the pillow over. The cool cotton felt refreshing against her hot cheek. Something grazed her temple. Raising her hand to brush it away, her fingers closed over a piece of paper.

Easing herself up on one elbow, she flicked on the bedside lamp. The Post-it note said: *I'll find a way to prove to you how much I love you. I'll make you trust me again.*

Jessie wasn't sure what touched her more: the words William had written or the fact that he'd known that sometime in the hot night she would flip the pillow over.

SEPTEMBER

Chapter Twenty-Four

The doors of Spike's Bar had been pinned back and the warm air of an Indian summer floated in, carrying with it the occasional thump of a passing car stereo.

William sat at the bar, his tie in his pocket, his jacket over his knees. Jack Stanhope was beside him dressed in jeans and an England rugby shirt.

'Take those two,' Jack said, nodding towards the end of the bar. 'Businesswomen, I'd say.'

William followed his friend's gaze then sat back toying with his scotch. 'You're married,' he pointed out dryly.

'You're not.'

William smiled. 'I'm not in the market.'

Jack feigned an exaggerated look around. 'A beautiful summer's evening and our hero nurses a scotch in the trendiest bar in town and who's on his arm? A thirteen-stone police sergeant who doesn't find him remotely attractive. Perhaps you should be in the market, son.' Jack sipped his drink. 'How long are you planning to keep this up?'

'Until I get her back.'

'Which could be never.'

'She won't throw away over twenty years for a barrow boy. She's getting her own back and having some fun in the process.' William winced as he recalled Jessie's birthday card from which the word 'husband' had been notably absent. 'Jess and I are having a few difficulties, that's all.'

'The last time Sue spoke to Jessie, you were having a divorce.'

William pulled a face. 'I'm telling you, this thing with Phillips won't last.' He became thoughtful. 'But instead of waiting for it to fall apart on its own maybe I should help it along a bit. Find a way to discredit him. It shouldn't be too difficult. I don't trust the guy as far as I could throw him. I just need to do a bit of digging. Would you do a PNC check for me?'

Jack rolled his eyes. 'I thought you were doing the digging? That's called misuse of the police computer, in case you were wondering.'

'He's hiding something.' William was adamant. 'Take his family. Jess has been pushing to meet them for months. He keeps putting her off.'

'I'd have been quite happy never to meet Sue's family,' Jack said, finishing his scotch. The two friends exchanged grins.

'Same again?'

'Please.'

'They're coming down this weekend.'

'Who are?'

'The barrow boy's dad and aunt. They're coming here. Not the other way round.'

'So?'

'So what's he hiding in London?'

With a sigh Jack said, 'What do you think he's hiding?'

'Another woman, maybe.'

Jack grinned. 'Yeah. Perhaps he's married with three kids.'

'I'm serious, Jack,' William shot back, annoyed.

Jack gave his friend a sympathetic look. 'I admit Owen's always been a little too eager to please in my opinion. But honestly, I think you're clutching at straws.' He clapped William on the shoulder. 'Let the relationship run its course. If you start digging into Owen's affairs, all you're going to do is piss Jessie off.'

'Only if she finds out.'

*

Jessie stood the white jug on the dresser and rearranged the pink and white roses in it. She wanted everything to be perfect for Stella. Standing back, she cast a critical eye around the room.

The rose-pink walls were set off by white woodwork and an extravagantly soft white carpet. The furniture was also white and old-fashioned with a distressed air.

Tweaking one of the pillows, Jessie nodded to herself, satisfied. She'd be happy to stay here; she hoped Stella would be too.

The sound of a vehicle crunching over the gravel sent her to the window. Delphi.

Owen had woken her that morning with breakfast in bed and then he'd made love to her, lingering over her body in such a delicious way that the early start she'd wanted had been lost.

When half-heartedly she had complained he had tenderly brushed her frown away, saying, 'Dad and Stella are coming to meet you and see the farm. They're not going to be carrying out a military-style inspection while they're here.'

You don't know women, Jessie had thought ruefully. 'I want everything to be perfect.'

'The Lodge always looks great. Chill your heels.'

'Chill my heels!'

Owen grinned. 'What can I do to help?'

'Go home.'

Owen's grin had widened. 'Okay. I'll give you a couple of hours and then I'll come back and take you to lunch before we meet their train.'

Jessie was halfway down the stairs when Owen came through the front door. 'You promised me two hours. You've only been gone forty minutes,' she said crossly. Owen looked up at her with dull eyes and a cold hand seized Jessie's heart. 'What's wrong?'

Stumbling forward, Owen sat down heavily on the second stair.

Jessie joined him, her hand seeking his. 'Darling, what is it?'

Owen massaged his eyes. 'Stella's dead.' Shock bled all the emotion from his voice.

'My God! What happened?'

Owen stared at the carpet. 'Car accident. She was on holiday in Wales. Last day before she came home. Police reckon she lost control in the rain.' He relayed the details staccato fashion. 'They don't think there was anyone else involved or that she suffered.' Owen swallowed. 'They've taken the car away for examination.'

Jessie shivered, remembering their own drive through the valleys of Wales and the dizzying views. It had looked beautiful then. She pictured it now, rainswept and desolate. 'What a terrible shock.'

'Can I have a drink?'

'Of course.'

They went through to the sitting room and Jessie poured Owen a scotch. He downed it in one go.

Blinking back tears, he said, 'She was so eager to meet you and see the farm. I can't believe this has happened.' He took the decanter from Jessie's hands and poured himself another drink. 'She always drove like a maniac. We all teased her about it. Dad said the boys are devastated.'

'Stella's sons?'

Owen nodded. 'Mark and Luke.'

'When did the accident happen?'

'Yesterday.' Owen kicked his foot against the hearth. 'She was supposed to be stopping off briefly at home before driving up to London to meet up with Dad to come here.' He shook his head. 'You know I left my mobile at my place?'

Jessie nodded.

'When I got home there was a message from Dad. He rang last night. He didn't want to break the news to me like that so he just said it was urgent and could I ring as soon as I got the message; it didn't matter how late it was. Of course, spending the night here . . .' Owen's voice drifted away. 'I bet he thought I was never going to ring. Dad's distraught.'

Jessie's heart went out to both of them. 'I'm so sorry, darling,' she said, drawing Owen to her.

He clung to her for several minutes. 'I can't take it in,' he said, edging away.

'I wish there was something I could say.'

Owen shook his head. Wiping away his tears with the back of his hand, he gave a ragged sigh before checking his watch. 'I'm going to catch the eleven twenty. Dad needs me.'

Jessie nodded. 'Yes, of course. I'll drive you to the station.'

'I don't know when the funeral will be. Dad said the police have to finish their investigation first. It all seems so unreal.'

Jessie picked up her keys from the hall table, weighing them in her palm before she spoke. 'I know this isn't a good time,' she began gently, 'but your aunt was going to contribute to the purchase of the farm . . .'

'I can't think about that now,' Owen said sharply.

'Sweetheart, you have to,' Jessie persisted. 'Do you have anything in writing?'

'No, but the boys will honour it.'

'You're sure?'

'Of course. They're family.' Owen's face softened as he looked at her. 'Stop being such a lawyer.'

Chapter Twenty-Five

Anne's voice was background noise as Jessie scraped a knob of butter on to the end of her knife and placed it on top of the grated cheese. Then, picking up her fork, she mashed both the butter and the cheese into her jacket potato.

'Can you believe it?' Anne's tone had suddenly become more strident. 'Two hours on balloons alone.'

Jessie tried to imagine a time in her life when she would have two hours to waste on something as frivolous as balloons. Irritated, she mashed the potato harder.

'I swear this party is going to be the death of me,' Anne continued, taking up a forkful of her macaroni cheese. 'After we finish here, I've got to ring Spike's. I got a text to say there's a problem with the menu.' Anne raised her eyes heavenwards. 'How many things can go wrong with one party? I'm beginning to think the whole thing's a ghastly mistake.' She took up her gin and tonic with a heavy sigh.

Jessie knew her friend was waiting for her to disagree. Peevishly, Jessie spun the moment out for as long as she could. Then, feeling mean, she relented. 'Everyone's looking forward to it.'

Anne set her glass down. 'Are they really?'

Jessie nodded. 'Will Hank be there?'

'I finished with Hank a couple of weeks ago,' Anne said nonchalantly. She twisted her fork through the melted cheese that had congealed on the side of her plate. 'Phone sex is no substitute for the real thing and anyway there's someone else.'

'You don't hang around!' Jessie exclaimed.

'Life's for living, Jessie. We're all going to end up like Owen's Stella one day.'

Jessie's gaze dropped to the dark floral carpet. 'The police have released the body,' she said quietly. 'The funeral's next week.'

'Terrible business,' Anne said, motioning for another gin and tonic. 'How's Owen?'

'Quiet,' Jessie replied.

Anne patted Jessie's hand. 'He just needs time. The funeral will help.'

Jessie wasn't so sure. It had been two and a half weeks since Stella's death and they still hadn't resumed their lovemaking. For a couple who had barely gone two days without intimacy, two weeks seemed like an eternity. Especially when all she wanted to do was hold him and ease his pain. But on the couple of occasions when she'd tried to initiate something he'd gently but firmly pushed her away, saying that he wasn't in the mood.

Jessie had only the death of William's mother and then his father to compare the situation to. In both cases, after the initial tearing grief had dissipated, they had each been desperate to gain succour from the other's embrace.

Jessie watched the rain spit against the Northey's leaded windows. Perhaps Stella's death had given Owen pause for thought. Maybe he no longer wanted to be with her but just didn't know how to tell her.

Anne rapped her knuckles on the table. 'Earth to Jessie.'

'Sorry?'

'I said I saw William on my way here. He was looking a bit rough. Sexy though, in a knocked-down, dragged-out kind of way.'

Jessie smiled. 'He spent the night at the police station. There was a robbery at the post office.' Jessie picked up her wine glass. 'So who is he then, your new man?'

Anne pushed away the remains of her pasta. With her gaze firmly fixed on the menu she said matter-of-factly, 'Phil Blunkett. We bumped into each other at a do in Stebbingsford. He drove me home. I invited him in for coffee and let's just say it was strange where he thought I kept the cream.'

The two women exchanged smiles.

Anne ordered a slice of sticky toffee cheesecake. 'I know I could chew him up and spit him out if I wanted. But I don't want to. I love the fact he's warm and caring. I want to cherish those things.' Anne grinned. 'I know, it's enough to make you want to throw up, isn't it?'

Jessie smiled.

'If it's possible, one month before my fiftieth birthday, I feel like a teenager again. He's so wonderful to be around.' Pausing, Anne drew tracks across her cheesecake with the tines of her fork. 'I know he's young.' She glanced up. 'Obviously, not as young as Owen.'

Jessie kicked her under the table.

Laughing, Anne fended off the attack. 'I think I'm in love,' she declared.

'You always think you're in love,' Jessie said dismissively.

'It's different this time. I really am.' Hugging herself, Anne said, 'He is gorgeous, isn't he?'

'Yes, he is.'

'Did you ever think about it, with him I mean?'

'No.'

'It's okay, you can tell me the truth.' A mischievous smile lit up Anne's face.

'I never did,' Jessie said truthfully.

'Not even when you've seen him on site, all hot and sweaty in those ripped jeans and that hard hat?'

'No.'

'Why not?' Anne looked shocked.

'Because I've been with Owen ever since I've known Phil.'

A sly smile crept across Anne's face. 'That doesn't stop you thinking about it.'

'Well, it does me.' Jessie looked down at her lap, shaking her head. 'Am I the only person in the world who believes in monogamy?'

'Yes and we love you for it,' Anne said.

Jessie watched Anne eat. 'Did you ever think about it with William?'

Anne's fork hovered in mid-air. 'Once or twice,' she confessed.

'But you never acted on it?' Jessie managed to squeeze the words past the lump that had suddenly risen in her throat.

'Of course not!'

Feeling ridiculously relieved, Jessie gulped the remains of her wine.

'Why haven't you told Nick to apply for the absolute?' Anne asked.

'There's no hurry.'

Anne tilted her head, licking toffee from her fork. 'You're still in love with him.'

Jessie smiled. 'Suddenly you're an expert.'

Anne chortled. 'It's the new me. Get used to it. Maybe you should give it another go,' she suggested.

'I couldn't trust him,' Jessie said sadly. 'William doesn't love anyone as much as he loves himself. I know that now. Besides, I have Owen.'

*

On Jessie's return to the office, she found William in the kitchen.

'They've let you out then,' she said.

'Finally.' He gave her a tired smile.

His tie was yanked to one side and he had a day's growth of stubble. Anne's words came back to her. *Sexy though, in a knocked-down, dragged-out kind of way.* Jessie fumbled with the tea caddy and the lid bounced off the linoleum floor. Retrieving it, she threw a tea bag into her mug and doused it in milk. 'You need a shave.'

'I need a shave, something to eat and some sleep. Not necessarily in that order. None of which I'm going to get because I'm due back at the cop shop in half an hour.'

'You love it,' Jessie said.

William snapped his fingers. 'I knew there was a reason why I did it.'

The kettle began to rattle as it emitted a cloud of steam, working itself into a frenzy before clicking off. Jessie splashed water into both their mugs. Hers depicted a pastoral scene. His had the words TRUST ME, I'M A LAWYER emblazoned across it.

William roused himself to stir in two sugars and a drop of milk. 'You okay?' he asked.

'Fine,' Jessie replied brightly. 'I've just had lunch with Anne. She's in love.'

'Who's the poor bastard this time?'

'Phil Blunkett.'

William snorted. 'I'd have thought he'd have had more sense.'

'She says it's different this time.'

They met each other's gaze and smiled.

Feeling disloyal, Jessie added, 'It could be true.'

She watched William pick up a packet of custard creams from the worktop and sniff them before helping himself to one. 'Owen got a date for the funeral yet?'

'Next Tuesday morning,' Jessie said guardedly.

'Gloucestershire?'

'No, London.'

'You going?' William crammed another biscuit into his mouth.

'No. I didn't feel it would be the right time to meet the family.'

William nodded. 'You're probably right.'

Chapter Twenty-Six

The sun lit up pale streaks in the milky sky as William slid into the middle carriage of the train and found an unreserved seat by the window. He was dressed in jeans and a blue sweatshirt.

Owen was on the opposite side of the carriage, five seats ahead, with his back to William. It was just after ten o'clock and the train was half full.

Trailing a man to a funeral was a pretty despicable thing to do and yet William had felt compelled to follow his instincts. Was he misguided? Had his desire to find something, *anything*, with which to discredit Owen meant that he'd lost all reason? Jack certainly thought so. He'd denounced William's plan as utter madness, saying, 'It takes years to become a good surveillance officer. People have a sixth sense about being followed and what are you going to say to Jessie if Owen catches you?'

What indeed? William met the reflection of his eyes. *You're not doing this for you. You're doing it for Jess.* Somehow that made it all right. Anything could be justified if it was done in her name and for love. Couldn't it?

A train rattled by on the opposite track, a blast of colour and noise. William watched it disappear. It could be that he was seeing shadows where there were none but what if he was right?

The thought niggled at him. Why had Owen's family never been to visit? Where were his friends? Owen was a gregarious sort of chap by all accounts. The kind of man you would expect to have lots of friends. So, where were they? Something wasn't right and William intended to find out what it was.

As William exited the train an hour later, his eyes frantically raked the tide of humanity that was surging towards the end of the platform, funnelling through the gates and past the guards. There were so many dark heads and dark suits.

Once on the main concourse, the size of the task William had set himself became apparent. What if Owen had gone to buy a coffee or a paper? What if he had already descended to the Tube? Then, with a wave of relief, he spotted his quarry heading for the taxi rank and sprinted after him.

William managed to grab the third taxi.

'Where to, mate?'

'Believe it or not, I want you to follow that cab,' William said, pointing to Owen's taxi.

The impressive façade of the British Museum greeted William's incredulous gaze when Owen eventually disembarked. Careful to keep a safe distance, William shadowed Owen as he headed for the Department of Ancient Egypt and Sudan.

At a leisurely pace, Owen moved through the Egyptian rooms, reading the information cards and studying the displays. In the next hour, he circled three more exhibits, taking as much time and care as he had in the first.

On exiting, he walked briskly for several minutes before disappearing through the revolving door of a foreign bank.

The smoked glass left William in a quandary. Did he risk going in? Abandoning logic, he struck out for the door with his head down. If he timed the revolution of the door correctly, it would give him enough time to survey the lobby and if necessary walk straight back out.

With a dry throat, he set the door in motion. The lobby was sparse, dominated by a giant reception desk. Three leather sofas formed a triangle around a similarly shaped table and a bank of lifts winked at him from the far wall. No one but the receptionist was present.

'Can I help you?'

'Could you tell me about the bank? I've had a recommendation.'

As the receptionist spoke, William leaned casually against the desk, casting a glance at the telephone and the diary beside it. Robert Toms was noted as having just arrived. The name of Owen Phillips was nowhere to be seen.

Easing back, William said, 'May I take a business card?'

Turning the card thoughtfully in his fingers, William exited the bank. What was a flower seller doing in a high-octane place like that?

Thirty minutes later, Owen left the bank, mobile to his ear. He maintained a relaxed amble as he chatted on the telephone. Then, stowing the phone inside his jacket, he paused to look around him.

They had walked into a vibrant area full of shops and bars, the streets packed with office workers in search of their lunch. Owen stopped in front of a cinema. Glancing up at the boards publicising the films, he checked his watch once more and mounted the steps.

William trotted after him. The cinema, with its old-fashioned gilt plasterwork, had seen better days but the lady in the ticket booth was pretty and gave William a welcoming smile. Only one film was due to begin in the next quarter of an hour.

'One for *Lawrence of Arabia*.'

'Where would you like to sit?'

'Where did the last chap choose?'

William met the ticket clerk's gaze full on as if the question was perfectly normal. Unnerved by this bravado, the girl merely pointed to an aisle seat midway down the auditorium.

'I'll sit here.'

William's seat was seven rows back and five seats in. As the house lights dimmed and with Owen safely in sight, William tucked into a slice of pepperoni pizza and settled down to watch Peter O'Toole do his stuff.

*

'Incredible!' Jack declared that evening in Spike's. 'What happened after the film?'

William shovelled a large forkful of shepherd's pie into his mouth, washing it down with a mouthful of beer. 'He went to a wine bar, had a couple of drinks and then caught the train home.'

'He must have seen you,' Jack concluded.

'No.' William was adamant.

'The guy led you a merry dance all over London,' Jack said.

'That's what I thought. But where's the pay-off? He never once acknowledged I was there. If I'd successfully dragged someone behind me all day, I wouldn't be able to resist giving them a sign, letting them know that I'd seen them. Moreover, there was no funeral.'

'I still can't believe you trailed the guy all day and weren't seen,' Jack said.

'I was too good,' William replied.

'You are such an arrogant bastard.'

'I am,' William cheerfully agreed. 'And I'll tell you what else I am.' He stabbed his finger down on the table. 'I'm right about him.'

'I agree he acted suspiciously,' Jack said. 'But where's your proof? I know it's not something you normally worry about. With you defence lawyers, it's all smoke and mirrors but . . .'

'I'll get proof,' William said grimly. 'Now I know I'm right, I'll get proof.'

*

Jessie was on the telephone to Anne when she heard Owen come in. Finishing her call, she said, 'I wasn't expecting you yet.' They were empty words but she felt as though there was a barrier around Owen these days that prevented her from getting too close or saying anything meaningful.

'I caught the five twenty.'

'You should have rung me.'

Jessie was at a loss what to say next. Words had been so easy to find before Stella's death.

'Maybe I should go home,' Owen mumbled.

Spurred into action, Jessie linked her arm through his. 'You shouldn't be alone.' She led him into the kitchen.

The silence descended once more as she opened a bottle of wine. When she turned round, Owen was seated at the table rubbing the heels of his hands into his eyes.

Jessie placed a glass of wine in front of him and kissed his head. 'Was it so very awful?'

'Worse,' Owen said gruffly. He grabbed the glass and drained half its contents. 'I didn't go.'

'I don't understand,' Jessie said. 'What do you mean, you didn't go? Where've you been all day?'

'Everywhere,' Owen said wearily. 'On the journey into London I kept thinking about Mum. It brought it all back. It was early so when I got to Liverpool Street

Station, I took a taxi to the British Museum instead. I know it sounds crazy but I've always liked it there. You can find incredible peace amongst the exhibits.' He sighed and finished the wine. 'Then I called in on a friend who works in a bank. I said I was in London on business. It was the weirdest feeling sitting in his office discussing football. It was as if, while I stayed there, I could pretend the accident had never happened, that there was no funeral, that everything was fine.'

Jessie frowned. 'Have you spoken to your dad?'

'I rang him. I said I was sorry but I couldn't go. He said he understood and that it was okay. But it's not okay, is it?' He rubbed his hands over his face. 'I let him down. I let them all down. Mark and Luke must be furious. And do you know what's worse?'

Jessie shook her head.

'I don't believe I could feel more terrible now than if I'd gone to the bloody thing.'

Owen held his head in his hands as his body convulsed with sobs. Putting her arms round his shoulders, Jessie laid kisses on his taut fingers. 'It's okay, darling,' she whispered.

When, at last, the storm abated, he said hoarsely, 'I'm a shit, Jessie.'

'No, you're not.'

He gripped her wrist with such force that Jessie let out a cry of surprise. 'Do you love me?' His eyes burned into hers.

'You know I do.'

'I need to hear you say it.'

'I love you.'

Pain shot from Owen's eyes and he tore his gaze away. Letting go of her wrist, he stood up, knocking the wine glass to the floor in the process. 'But if you knew me, if you really knew me . . .' he raged.

Shocked, Jessie said, 'I do know you!'

Owen shook his head.

Jessie looked at him in surprise. 'So what is it you're not telling me? What deep, dark secret do you hold that's so terrible?' She smiled, trying to jolly him out of the black mood he was in.

Owen locked his hands behind his head. Shards of glass crunched beneath his feet.

'Owen . . .'

'I wouldn't know where to begin,' he said quietly, lowering his hands. He looked at her with haunted eyes. 'What do you see in me, Jessie?'

'I see a good, kind man.'

He shut his eyes as if her words were too much for him. 'I thought Tessa had cured me of love, but you –' he spat the word at her – 'you made me believe again. It was better when love was dead.'

'No,' Jessie said. 'You're wrong. Shutting people out can never be better.' She reached for him but he backed away. 'You've been like a stranger these past few weeks and I can't bear it,' Jessie cried. 'Why won't you let me in?'

'Because I need you and I hate that I need anyone because love doesn't last and one day we'll cry like we're crying now except then we'll be alone.'

'It doesn't have to be like that,' Jessie said vehemently. She took him in her arms and held him tighter than she'd ever held anyone, fighting his resistance, crushing him with her love until, finally, he held her too.

They stumbled upstairs, neither wanting to relinquish their hold on the other. Their tears had washed their pride away and now there was nothing left but a need for one another that burned with its intensity. They still wore most of their clothes as they had sex across the bed and yet the act was somehow more intimate than it had ever been before.

Later, unable to sleep, Jessie went to the study. There was no trace of William left. And yet he was everywhere. It was as though the hours he'd spent working in the room had somehow embedded his spirit into the walls. She could paint over them but she would never be rid of the echo of him. Was that how it was always going to be?

Jessie turned on the computer with an angry stab of her finger. William was only here in this room, in her mind, because she chose to let him be. It was time to finish things, once and for all. Nick already held the paperwork signed and waiting in his file.

She fired off an email to him. 'Please apply for the decree absolute.'

Chapter Twenty-Seven

Jessie watched from her office window as a battery of brake lights illuminated the monochrome day. Within seconds, the lights were extinguished and the door thrown open. William alighted, glancing up at her window. Jessie shrank back but not before she saw the cold, hard fury in his eyes. So, he knew.

Moments later, he was in her office. It was a thunderclap of an entrance followed by another crack as the door slammed shut.

'How could you?' His voice was cold, his face ugly with anger.

Jessie was, however, transfixed by the reappearance of the wedding ring on his ring finger. He hadn't worn it since he'd left her. Rocked by the sight of it, she murmured, 'How could I what?'

'Don't play games,' William shouted. 'You know what. The fucking decree absolute! How could you do that without discussing it with me?'

'We've discussed everything there is to discuss. There's nothing left to say.'

William thumped the desk before swiping Jessie's pen holder to the floor. 'How could you do it now when I was this close to –'

The door flew open. Walt stood on the threshold. 'Is everything okay?'

'Everything's fine.' William ground the words out, his gaze not leaving Jessie's face.

'An accident.' Jessie scooped the pens up and forced a smile.

'You're sure you're okay?' Walt said, unconvinced.

Jessie nodded. 'Perfectly.'

Nodding, Walt closed the door.

'We can't do this here,' William said tersely.

'We're not going to do this anywhere,' Jessie replied. 'I've made my choice. Now the divorce is final we can both move on.'

'Please God, promise me you're not going to rush into anything with him.'

Her love for Owen was the shield she held up to deflect the words of blame and longing that tumbled from William's lips, the imploring looks, the brief but devastating touch of his hand. And, when she could bear it no longer, she turned and looked out over the car park, down towards his car and remembered the day he'd climbed out of it with the tart.

It was embarrassing to have him come here like this, pleading with her. Where was his pride? But perhaps pride was what drove him on. He did not want to concede defeat to a barrow boy.

Jessie's resolve hardened. Well, he was going to have to get used to the idea. Following their rapprochement on the night of the funeral, she and Owen had become closer than ever and Jessie was excited now at what the future might hold.

'All I needed was time to prove myself,' William said angrily.

'I gave you a lifetime. And what difference would it have made anyway?' Jessie asked, folding her arms. 'There's nothing you can do or say that's going to change my mind.'

'That bastard, Owen –' William began.

'Why is he a bastard?' Jessie demanded. 'Because he has me? All Owen has ever done is love me. He gave me back my smile, my pride. The things you took with you when you left and you'd denigrate him for that?'

'He's not what you think he is.'

'Neither were you.'

'Jess, listen to me –'

'No, William. Even if Owen didn't exist, we'd still be over. How could I ever trust you again?'

The silence stretched painfully between them.

'I'll find a way,' William said quietly, defiantly.

Exasperation sent Jessie's hands balling into fists. 'William, please!'

'We may be divorced –' William's voice cut through hers – 'but this is not over. You and I are not over. I won't let us be.'

OCTOBER

Chapter Twenty-Eight

Balancing a counsel's notebook on his knee, William made quick entries in it before strolling over to the custody sergeant.

'Unless you've got any more punters for me, Ted, I think I'm done.'

'You mean two dealers and an ABH aren't enough for you, you greedy bastard? Jack wants a word before you go.' The sergeant summoned a young PC. 'Go and find Sergeant Stanhope.'

William returned to his seat. He was dressed in an old pair of jeans and a jumper; at the weekends the felons had to take him as they found him.

'We spend all night catching them and locking them up and you spend all morning getting them out again,' Jack said wryly. 'Can I have a word?'

'Certainly, but not here. I have a reputation to protect.'

'He's thought of very highly in low places,' Ted quipped.

'So I've heard,' Jack said, leading William away from the custody area.

'What's up?'

'I did a PNC check on Phillips. Nothing.'

'Worth a try,' William said philosophically.

'Why don't you come to our supper this month? I'll get Sue to set you up with someone nice.'

'No thanks.'

Jack gave his friend a worried look. 'William, Jessie has the absolute. It's over.'

'No,' William growled. 'Something about Phillips isn't right and I'm not going to rest until I find out what it is. If you don't want to help me . . .'

'I never said that.'

'Good. Because there is one way we could get some answers.'

*

'I can't believe we're doing this,' Jack whispered.

'We're not,' William replied. 'I am. You're here as my lookout. Not that I need one,' he added hastily. 'They're at The Lodge. We won't be disturbed.' William pulled on a pair of leather gloves. 'Ready?'

'No,' Jack grumbled, 'but let's get on with it.'

William closed the back door of his house in North Street and crossed the small rear garden. Jack fiddled with his own gloves as William unhooked the gate. It was one thirty on a Sunday morning and the lane behind the group of terraced houses was deserted.

'I want you to stay with me until I'm in,' William whispered, 'then nip round to the front. If you see them coming, knock on the window and walk away.'

'Have you any idea what they'll do to us if they catch us?' Jack asked.

William gazed at the silhouette of his friend in the darkness. 'No one is going to catch us.'

'Damn it, Will! Misuse of the police computer is one thing but this is breaking and entering.'

'Entering maybe,' William conceded, 'but I have no intention of breaking anything.'

He eyed the six-foot gate and fence before optimistically lifting the latch. The gate wouldn't open. 'Looks like our boy's security-conscious.'

'Sensible chap,' Jack replied. 'There are a lot of undesirables about.'

Their strained expressions dissolved into smiles.

'If you want, you can give me a bunk up and then leave,' William said.

Jack tutted. 'And what sort of mate would that make me? Just remember, you owe me. Big time.'

Tucking the torch into his jacket, William put his foot into Jack's cupped hands. Still in good shape, he scaled the wooden panel easily. The fence rattled and shook as he landed on the other side. It sounded unbearably loud to both men as somewhere nearby a dog barked.

A block of light shone out from a property three doors up. Jack pressed himself against the fence, silently reciting a string of swear words. On the opposite side, William crouched, a moment's doubt flickering through his mind.

Then the door closed and the light was gone. Taking a shaky breath, William rose and eased back the bolt. Reluctantly, Jack stepped into the back garden.

'That was close,' he muttered.

'That was nothing. Hold the torch.'

'They'll have me off the force so quick my head'll spin,' Jack said. 'Of course that will be the least of my problems because Sue will kill me.'

'I'll kill you if you don't keep that light still.'

Jack directed the shielded beam at the lock while William set about picking it.

'Jesus Christ!' he cried as the door swung back. 'Where did you learn to do that?'

'You can't spend hours in the company of petty criminals and not pick up a few tricks of the trade,' William said. 'Go and keep watch.'

He searched the kitchen first then moved on to the living room. Opening the folder Owen had left on the table, he made his way through it, flicking past the particulars of Blackcurrant Farm to the pages of calculations beneath. At the back was a group of bank statements from a high-street branch. William scanned them quickly.

Disappointed, he shut the folder. There had been no mention of the London bank.

Punching 1471 into the telephone, he felt a sharp pang when he heard the robotic voice chant back the number of The Lodge. Then, quietly, he went upstairs. The bathroom cabinet held all the things he had expected and none of what he'd hoped to find: scales maybe, needles, drug paraphernalia.

The box room was bare. William hesitated on the threshold of the main bedroom. Taking a deep breath, he edged the door open and switched off the torch. A pale orange glow from the street lamp played over the walls.

Beside the alarm clock William found a solitary photograph of Jess. She looked happy and relaxed, her smile touching her eyes in the way that had always melted his heart. It seemed criminal to leave this beautiful picture of the woman he loved beside another man's bed and yet he had to. Nothing could be out of place. Owen must never know he'd been there.

He checked the bedside cabinet and his heart flip-flopped at the sight of the condoms in the top drawer. Forcing himself to carry on, he looked behind and above the wardrobe and then set about the interior.

The bulk of the wardrobe was made up of casual clothes, at one end hung two suits. William recognised one from the day of the funeral. As he had with all the trousers, William checked the pockets. Nothing. He was about to turn away when he remembered the jackets. With his right glove in his teeth, William felt inside the pockets of the funeral suit. Empty. He tried the second suit. His fingers closed round a small square of paper. Drawing it out, William unfolded it.

By the light of the street lamp, he could see it was a newspaper cutting. Catching his breath, he tilted it to the light to get a better look. It showed a picture of a woman standing outside a florist's shop: JUSTINE'S FLOWERS. Beneath it was a small piece about the new shop. There was no banner. Nothing to show which paper the article had appeared in or on what date.

Was she a friend? A business colleague? She had to mean something to Owen; why else would he have kept the article? And kept it for some time, judging by the condition of the paper. Consigning it to memory, William refolded the cutting and replaced it.

On returning to the living room, it struck him that, beyond the photograph of Jess in the bedroom, there were no other photographs anywhere and certainly none of the unfortunate aunt, either out on display or in albums. There were no paintings or pictures on the walls and no plants. It was as though the person living there was simply stopping over on the way to somewhere else.

Deciding not to push his luck further, William bolted the gate and locked the back door. Then, lifting the catch of the front door, he opened it slowly. The street was quiet. He closed the door gently behind him.

'Anything?' Jack asked gruffly.

'Something. Maybe.'

*

If September had been a gentle month of pleasant temperatures and lengthening shadows, October had been ushered in with all the grace of an ill-tempered person late for an appointment. Torrential rain and gale-force winds had delivered a fractious double whammy. No sooner had the leaves turned russet and ochre, little golden nuggets, in a forgiving September sun than they'd been torn asunder by October's rage.

Jessie, dressed in grey trousers and a cream angora sweater, watched her first fire of the autumn as it devoured twisted newspaper, kindling and coal. There was something special about the first fire of the season: a cosy introduction to long nights and the countdown to Christmas.

Owen should be here, Jessie thought, as she stared into the fire. But he'd left unexpectedly for London. A family conference had been the message on her voicemail.

It was after eleven when she heard Owen's key in the door.

'This looks like my idea of a perfect room on a cold night,' Owen said. 'And you're the perfect woman.' He gathered Jessie to him and kissed her.

His lips were icy. His hair so cold it felt almost wet. 'Please tell me you haven't walked from the station,' she said.

'I haven't walked from the station,' he replied with a smile and moved to stand in front of the fire, flexing his hands in the warm glow.

Jessie denounced him with a laugh. 'Liar. It's Friday night. There must have been cabs about.'

'I fancied the walk.'

Shaking her head, Jessie said, 'I'll get you a brandy. Purely medicinal,' she added as she pressed the glass into his frozen hands a moment later.

'Thanks.' Owen downed the brandy quickly.

'How did the meeting go?'

Frowning, Owen stood the empty glass on the mantelpiece and stared into the fire. 'The boys said I didn't show Stella the respect she deserved. They're right of course.'

'I'm sure Stella would have understood.'

'Maybe. The meeting degenerated into a slanging match. The upshot is I can kiss goodbye to Stella's money.'

'I was afraid this might happen.' Jessie rested her hand on his back. 'What will you do?'

'Dad said he'd see if he could lend me some more but I don't like the idea of it so I'll go back to the bank next week.'

'I thought you were at your limit?'

'We're only talking about twenty thousand. In comparison to the whole deal it's a paltry sum. Don't look so worried.' He stroked Jessie's cheek. 'The bank has been with me all the way so far. It would be stupid to let the deal go sour now.'

'And if they refuse?'

'They won't refuse.' He kissed the tip of her nose.

'But if they do?'

'I'll find a way. I've come too far to let things fall apart now. Anyway, Dad said he'd try and talk the boys round. Who knows? It might work.'

Chapter Twenty-Nine

Only Anne Jacobs could wear a low-cut, micro-skirted red dress on her fiftieth birthday and look fantastic. At an age when most women greeted another birthday like a bout of cystitis, Anne, radiating confidence through every golden pore, had embraced it, turning it into a celebration.

'This place is really jumping,' Owen commented approvingly upon their arrival at Spike's.

Jessie nodded. Happy and relaxed, she stroked the back of Owen's hand. Their spot of rushed lovemaking had made them fashionably late but Jessie didn't care because it had given her cheeks a colour that no blusher could replicate and self-esteem that was off the scale. Enjoying herself tonight would be easy.

'Do you want to dance?'

'We should say hello to Anne first.'

'Righto.' Owen led Jessie through the gyrating crowd to where Anne and Phil were dancing. 'Happy birthday,' Owen shouted over the music.

'Owen, darling. It's lovely to see you.' Anne kissed his cheeks, leaving behind vivid red lipstick marks. 'Jessie, you look stunning,' she said, gripping Jessie's hands and admiring her halter-necked blue dress. 'William's here. Hannah managed to twist his arm. Isn't she gorgeous?'

'Yes, she is. Happy birthday.' Jessie handed over a package. 'Hello, Phil.'

Jessie gave Phil a peck on the cheek as Anne eagerly tore at the paper. Concealed within was a weekend pass to an exclusive health resort.

Anne gave a squeal of delight. 'How fantastic!' she exclaimed. 'Thank you.'

'For the woman who has everything,' Owen said.

Phil chuckled. 'Would the birthday girl like another drink?'

'Another Bloody Mary, please. I'm colour-coordinating with my dress,' she told Jessie and Owen with a giggle.

'Sounds like you've been colour-coordinating quite a lot,' Owen remarked dryly.

Anne roared with laughter. 'May I steal your man for a dance?' she asked Jessie.

'The first dance is Jessie's, I'm afraid,' Owen said.

'So be it.' Anne fanned herself with her present. 'Until later then.' She blew them both a kiss and made her way to the bar.

Laughing, Jessie removed Anne's lipstick marks from Owen's cheeks before settling into his arms.

'She's having a good time,' Owen said.

'So am I.'

'Good.'

Ten minutes later, Jessie caught Anne's pleading look and tapped Owen on the shoulder. 'I think Anne needs rescuing from the mayor. Be an angel and do the honours.'

'Excuse me, sir, but Anne did promise me a dance,' Owen said boldly a moment later.

With reluctance, the mayor relinquished his hold.

'Thank you a thousand times,' Anne said. 'For the last few minutes I actually began to feel my age.' She reached over to squeeze Jessie's arm. 'If you can find Phil in this mêlée, you're welcome to him.'

With Phil nowhere in sight, Jessie made her way to the bar and grabbed a free stool. Scanning the dancers, she spotted William. He was dressed in a black suit and white shirt and was dancing enthusiastically with a slender, dark-haired girl in a black sequined dress. It took a moment before Jessie realised the girl was Hannah. She raised her hand in greeting and her daughter waved back. As the song ended, Hannah joined her mother at the bar.

'Hi, Mum.'

'Hello, darling.'

Jessie kissed her daughter's flushed cheek and frowned as she ordered a vodka and tonic.

'Why didn't you come up to The Lodge earlier?' Jessie asked. She knew it was only right that Hannah stayed with William sometimes, but she had seen so little of her daughter on this visit that it was hard not to be bitter.

'Daddy was at the police station in Stebbingsford. I sat in on the interview.' Hannah sipped her drink. 'Mum, I need to talk to you about Christmas. I want to spend it with Daddy this year.' Her gaze dropped to the glass in her hand. 'Of course, I'll come and see you and Owen on Boxing Day.' She finished her drink slowly before flicking a worried glance at her mother. 'You don't mind too much do you?'

Jessie minded terribly. Aware that an uncomfortable silence was developing and that Hannah was studying her intently, Jessie said, 'I'll miss you but I understand.'

Hannah gave her mother a hug. 'Thank you. I hated the thought of leaving Daddy on his own this year and you do have Owen.' She gave Jessie a beatific smile and kissed her cheek before rejoining the throng on the dance floor. Jessie watched her go. They had never spent Christmas Day apart. Jessie glowered at William's back.

'I've done my duty,' Owen said, returning to Jessie's side.

You do have Owen. Jessie caressed Owen's face.

The DJ was playing a love song. Jessie drifted into Owen's arms. They continued to sway together in companionable silence as one song faded out and another took over. It had been a while since she and Owen had danced and then it had been alone in the sitting room with only Frank Sinatra for company.

'Is it next week you go to the bank?' Jessie asked casually.

'It was today actually.'

'Today!' Jessie exclaimed. 'Why didn't you say? What happened?'

'I'll tell you tomorrow.'

'Tell me now,' Jessie demanded, edging back.

Pulling her near, Owen kissed her. 'The only thing I'm planning to do in the next couple of hours is have fun. The words "bank", "business" and "money" are not going to cross my lips or yours. Do I make myself clear, Miss Martin?'

Reluctantly, Jessie nodded.

*

Anne gave William a hug. 'Isn't this a glorious party? I seem to recall that over an hour ago you promised me a dance.' She slapped his jacket playfully.

'And I'm here to deliver,' William replied. Holding out his hand, he swept her into his arms with a flourish.

Cosying into him, Anne made no pretence of separation for appearances' sake. She had always liked William and copious amounts of pink champagne and several Bloody Marys had left her pleasantly merry. There was no chance of muddying the waters with William. As Jessie's ex he was unattainable but there was nothing in the rule book that said she couldn't flirt.

'Why are you here with Hannah?' She breathed the words into his ear. 'It's a cruel waste.'

'On the contrary, Hannah is the ideal party date. She's beautiful, she laughs at my jokes and she won't tell me when I've had too much to drink.'

'Do you hear that?' Anne asked, cocking her head suddenly as if to listen. 'It's the sound of Abbeyleigh's eligible women sobbing into their cosmopolitans. Why are you wearing your wedding ring?'

'Because I still feel married.'

Anne stroked William's face. 'You're an idiot.'

'I love you, too.'

'You have to move on.'

'So everyone is fond of telling me.'

'You and I would've been great together,' Anne mused. 'We'd have set this town alight.'

'I'm too old for you,' William replied with a smile.

Anne settled her head on William's shoulder. 'Time has a way of catching up with you,' she said with a sigh. 'Take tonight. I can party as hard as ever but it'll take me longer to recover.'

'How much champagne have you had?' William asked, amused.

'Which one of you said that?'

Kissing her forehead, William grabbed her to him and declared, 'Hold on tight to both of us, darling, and we'll show the others how it's done.'

Ten minutes later, a heart-shaped cake was unveiled to a round of applause as Phil Blunkett announced that he was 'whisking this wonderful woman away to Italy for two weeks', and then the DJ turned up the volume and everyone returned to the dance floor. Somewhere in their midst, Owen was dancing with Hannah.

'You're the most dazzling woman here.'

Jessie turned at the sound of William's voice.

'If I got us a taxi, we could be home in ten minutes.'

His hand was hot on her bare arm. Jessie edged away.

'You've had too much to drink.'

'Probably,' he conceded. 'But it doesn't alter the fact that you look amazing.'

Jessie folded her arms. 'Hannah tells me she's spending Christmas with you.'

'I've tried to talk her out of it,' William said. 'What can I do? She's got your stubborn streak.'

'You've as much right to spend Christmas with her as I do.' Jessie sighed. 'I'll miss her, that's all.'

'I miss you,' William said softly.

In annoyance, Jessie caught hold of his right hand and held it out in front of him. 'Is that why you're wearing this?' she asked bluntly.

'Do you think that piece of paper means anything? Do you think it stops me caring?'

'It should.'

'You can trust me,' he said fiercely. 'You can trust me a lot more than you can trust him.'

Angry, Jessie rounded on him. 'You humiliated me in front of everyone,' she whispered furiously. 'You screwed your bimbo behind my back and then you left me for her so the whole town could get a good look at you rubbing my nose in it. I could have gloated when you told me about the baby but I didn't. I offered you the sanctuary of The Lodge and this is how you repay me? By constantly running Owen down, by making things uncomfortable for me at the office, by pushing for a reconciliation that's never going to happen?'

'I'm sorry I let you down,' William said, upset. 'Just give me a chance to make it up to you and everything will be all right again, I promise.'

'You promised to be faithful to me. Look where that got us,' Jessie said bitterly.

As she moved off, William grabbed her arm. 'I'm trying to make amends.'

'It's too late.'

'Don't say that. I need you.' His voice was desperate.

Jessie jabbed her finger at him. 'You should have thought about that when you were banging your bimbo and again when you were packing your bags. You have no one to blame for this but yourself. I've made my choice.' On the verge of tears, she said, 'You have to let me go.'

'You're making a terrible mistake.'

Jessie tossed her head. 'If I am, it's my mistake to make.'

*

As the party wound down, couples paired off. Hannah had found a handsome waiter to dance with. Anne and Phil were draped round one another. William had Sue in his arms but seemed more intent on watching Jessie. Meanwhile, Jessie tried to make herself small in Owen's embrace, her heart in turmoil.

As the door to Spike's burst open everyone, except Anne and Phil, jumped in surprise.

'This is the police,' Jack announced unnecessarily. 'We've had a complaint about the noise. Who's in charge here?'

Anne prised herself away from Phil with a giggle. 'I am.'

'Well, Mrs Jacobs, I have only one thing to say to you. Happy birthday, darling.' Jack kissed her cheeks. 'I trust a fine time was had by all?' he said, surveying the wreckage of party streamers and balloons.

'Perfect,' Anne responded and melted back into Phil's arms.

'You there,' Jack cried, pointing at William who still had his arms round Sue. 'Unhand that woman immediately.' Letting Sue go, William held up his hands in self-defence as Jack approached. 'Honestly, Sue, I can't leave you alone for a minute, can I?' Jack said, giving his wife an affectionate kiss. 'William –'

'I deny everything,' William said jovially.

Jack laughed. 'Wouldn't be the first time, my friend.' He pulled him to one side. 'I need a word.'

The two men went to sit at one of the tables.

'Joe Wilson's been arrested for assault. He's asking for you.'

William rubbed his hands over his face. 'I've had too much to drink. Ring Marie.'

Jack nodded. 'You okay?'

William looked behind him. 'I tracked down Justine's Flowers. I'm going away for a couple of days next week to check it out while Hannah's in London with Howard.' He paused. 'I told Jessie she was making a terrible mistake being with Owen. She said it was her mistake to make.'

'She's right,' Jack said. 'Why don't you let it drop?'

'Because she doesn't have all the facts. How can she choose between us when I'm being honest and he's a lying son of a bitch?'

'You don't know that for sure.'

William rested his head in his hands. 'I keep thinking about that night in here. Why didn't I walk away from her? Why didn't I laugh her off like I did when you were with me?'

Jack knew William was talking about Chelsea. 'She was a pretty girl.'

'That's no excuse,' William said morosely.

Jack looked over William's shoulder. 'Hi, Hannah.'

'Is everything okay?' Hannah asked, looking concerned.

'Everything's fine,' Jack said smoothly, standing up. 'What you need,' he said, directing his words to William, 'is black coffee and plenty of it.' He patted Hannah's shoulder. 'Time to take your dad home, Hannah.'

*

The Lodge looked stately in the starlight. As she climbed the worn stone steps, Jessie thanked God and William that it had remained her home.

She took off her make-up quickly, calling through to Owen as she did so. 'Great party.'

'It certainly was.'

'Anne is so lucky going to Italy. Have you ever been?'

'No.'

'We must go. You'll love it. Anne and I went to Florence for ten days last year. It was sublime.'

When Jessie came out of the en-suite, Owen was already in bed. Jessie settled against his chest with a happy sigh. 'I love you,' she whispered.

'I love you, too,' he murmured sleepily.

'Tell me what happened at the bank.'

'Tomorrow.'

'It is tomorrow,' Jessie protested. 'Owen?'

He was asleep.

*

When Jessie woke in the early hours, Owen was missing. No light shone from the en-suite so Jessie pulled on her robe and went downstairs. Owen was in the kitchen mixing an aspirin.

'Are you okay?'

'Headache. Sorry if I woke you.'

'It's not like you to get a headache,' Jessie said, concerned. 'And you hardly had anything to drink tonight.'

Owen shrugged. 'One of those things.' He sat at the table.

Apprehension knotted Jessie's stomach. 'What did they say at the bank?'

Owen drank the aspirin. 'I don't want to talk about it.'

'But that's silly!' Jessie remonstrated. 'You have to tell me sometime.'

'They turned me down,' he said. Standing, he rinsed his glass and placed it on the drainer. 'A flat no,' he said, turning to face her.

'I'm sorry.'

He shook his head. 'They said if I just had a little more capital they'd consider it. But if I had more capital I wouldn't be going to them in the first place, would I? Still, there are other banks.'

'You're not going to raise the finance that way,' Jessie said gently. 'They work on a points system. If you're at your limit with one, you're at your limit at all of them.'

'Damn it, don't you think I know that? But I have to try.' He squeezed the bridge of his nose. 'Sorry, I didn't mean to bite your head off. Dad says he'll remortgage the restaurant but I don't want him to do that. If I could just get the boys to reconsider, but they won't even speak to me. I wish there was another way but if there is I can't think of it.'

'Your dad doesn't have to remortgage,' Jessie said. 'You can borrow the money from me.'

'No way!'

'Why not? William's just paid me the first instalment of our settlement. The money's just sitting in an account. I'd rather do something useful with it.'

'I couldn't,' Owen said firmly.

'Why not?'

'Because it wouldn't be right.'

'Why not?'

'For one thing, the dickhead would kill you and then he'd kill me.'

'The dickhead doesn't need to know.'

'What if the business fails?'

'I trust you.'

Owen sneered. 'You shouldn't. Just because the stall's successful doesn't mean this venture will be.' He touched her face. 'It was sweet of you to offer.'

Jessie squeezed his hand. 'I'll probably make more from this deal than I would if the money was invested conventionally. I have faith in you even if you don't have faith in yourself.'

'Do you really believe I could take your life savings?'

'Twenty thousand pounds is hardly my life savings,' she said evenly.

'I don't know, Jessie.'

'Why put your dad to the inconvenience of a remortgage when I can transfer the money to your account in time for completion?'

'Just suppose I said yes, we'd have to put everything in writing including the monthly repayments and I'd –'

'Owen!' Jessie stopped him with a kiss.

'But you have to be sure.'

'I know what I'm doing,' Jessie said firmly.

'I wish I did,' Owen replied. He kissed her forehead. 'We'll talk about this again in the morning. You should sleep on it.'

'I won't change my mind,' Jessie said. She stroked Owen's temples. 'I bet that's a tension headache brought on by your visit to the bank. Let's go back to bed. I'll give you a back rub; it might help.'

Chapter Thirty

The rain lashing the window made William look up. It was midweek and Spike's was quiet. Outside, the wind was buffeting office workers on their way home.

This time last year the change in the season had seemed romantic. Lost as he had been in a haze of passion, autumn had meant an opportunity to snuggle up on long, dark nights in front of open fires. The thought of walking hand in hand with Chelsea on snowy days had filled him with a childish delight. What a prat! Autumn was cold and wet. It was a season when things died – in his case, common sense.

As Jack entered the bar, William indicated the scotch he'd bought in anticipation of his friend's arrival.

'Cheers,' Jack said.

'Cheers. I had an interesting trip,' William began.

'Good. You can tell me about it in a minute. I had an interesting visit from Jessie.'

William squinted towards the bar. 'What did she want?'

'For me to persuade you to leave her alone and take off your wedding ring.'

'She's been a busy lady. Walt threatened to sack me.'

'What?!'

'"Review my position with the firm" is what he said.' William shrugged. 'It means the same thing.'

'Was he serious?'

William twisted the glass of scotch in his hands. 'If it became a straight choice between me and Jess, I think he might be serious, yes. I haven't really had my eye on the ball these last few months and, thanks to Blunkett, Jessie's bringing in more money than I am now. They wouldn't want to lose Jess.'

Jack blanched. 'Christ, Will. You've got to stop this.'

'I can't.'

'Look, mate, I know you love her and you're trying to do the right thing by her but –'

'I know why Owen's in Abbeyleigh.'

Jack put down his glass. 'I'm listening.'

'Justine Anderson was away. But I spoke to a friendly and knowledgeable barmaid. About four years ago a man by the name of Matthew Harrison became the manager of a florist's shop owned by Justine Anderson. They became friends. The business flourished. They became lovers. Then Mr Harrison suggested Justine open up a new shop. The deal went through and there was a nice article in the newspaper . . .'

'The clipping you found?'

William nodded. 'By this time Justine trusts Mr Harrison completely. He's a good-looking guy, slim build, dark hair, much younger than Justine herself but he's affable and everyone likes him. That is until he absconds with twenty-five thousand pounds of Justine's money and is never heard of again.'

Jack sat back, regarding William through narrowed eyes. 'You think Matthew Harrison is Owen Phillips?'

'It fits.'

'Where's your proof?'

'The newspaper cutting.'

'That doesn't prove anything.'

'Why would he keep it unless it was a souvenir?'

'Perhaps he and Justine Anderson are old friends.'

Ignoring him, William continued. 'I went to the library and looked up the story. The police said there were similarities between the Anderson case and others.'

'Why Jessie?'

'I think he knew she was separated and that as a couple we were reasonably wealthy. He's not a barrow boy at all. He's a conman.'

'You think the purchase of Blackcurrant Farm is a scam?'

'That's my guess. As I understand it, Phillips's family were going to invest in the farm. Now, say one of the members of the family who was going to invest was dear old auntie –'

'And she died,' Jack said, taking up the theme.

'He'd be short on the purchase monies.'

Jack tapped his fingers on the table. 'It's all supposition. I could contact the local police and –'

'No!'

'If Phillips is the man you think he is we need to arrest him.'

'You said yourself: I have no proof.'

'So let me talk to the locals. They may have photos, samples of handwriting.'

'And how are you going to explain how I connected Owen Phillips to what happened there?' William dropped his voice to a whisper. 'Are you going to tell them we broke in?'

Scowling, Jack drained his scotch. 'What do you want to do?'

'Nothing. I think as soon as Phillips starts to press Jess for money she'll see him for what he really is.'

'And then?'

'The completion of the farm is due to take place on the tenth of November. If he can't persuade Jess to part with her money by then, I think he'll skip town.'

'And I'm just supposed to let him?' Jack growled.

'Yes, because I'm telling you this as a friend not as a copper.'

'You're putting me in an impossible situation.' Jack rubbed his chin. 'If it's the same guy, he should be locked up.'

'Have you any idea what it would do to Jess? It'd be all over Abbeyleigh and beyond. I'm not going to let her be humiliated like that. It happened once because of me. I can't stand by and let it happen again. I'm begging you, Jack. Don't say anything.'

'The guy's clearly got a lot of charm. Are you sure Jess wouldn't fall for it?'

'Positive.'

William watched with apprehension as Jack turned things over in his mind.

'If she refuses to hand over the money and he leaves town, I'll turn a blind eye.'

'You're a mate.'

'But –' Jack held up his hand – 'if we find out she's agreed to give him the cash, we do things my way.'

William sobered. 'You mean bring in the police?'

'Yes. Looking the other way if he leaves town is one thing, looking the other way while he commits a crime is something I can't do and you shouldn't ask me to.'

*

'I've had a bad day,' William announced as he closed the front door. 'What's for tea?'

'Tagliatelle carbonara,' Hannah replied from the kitchen.

She gave him a grin and handed him a glass of red wine.

'I feel better already.'

'Why did you have such a bad day?'

'I don't want to talk shop tonight, honey,' William said. He clawed at his tie and flung it on to the table before sitting down.

'There's something I need to talk to you about,' Hannah began hesitantly. 'Although maybe this isn't the right time.'

'What is it?' William asked, giving her a smile.

Hannah took a deep breath. 'I know I'm incredibly lucky to have a training contract lined up at Smith Mathers but would you mind awfully if I didn't take it up? It's just that I'd like to stand on my own two feet for a bit after I leave uni. I still want to come and work with you eventually, I'd just like to do my training and maybe another couple of years at a city firm. You hate the idea, don't you?' she said flatly.

'No, I don't hate the idea. But do you realise how tough it will be to get a training contract in the city? Everyone will be applying to the same firms and there are only so many trainees they can take on.'

'I know but that's the point. I want to see how my CV and my results stack up against everyone else. If I walk straight into a contract with you, I'll never know.'

'I don't suppose you'll consider a training contract at Howard's firm either?'

'He's already offered me one and I turned it down. It's very kind of him and I told him that, but I want a contract because someone with no particular interest in me thought I was good enough.'

Standing, William kissed Hannah's forehead. 'Good for you. It takes guts to strike out on your own.'

'Are you really okay about this?'

William nodded.

Hannah's face lit up with relief. 'I've been so worried about telling you.'

William put his arm round her shoulders and kissed her temple. 'Even if you decide that the city is where your future lies, that's okay too. So long as you're happy, that's all I care about. Of course I want us to work together but you have to want it as much as I do. You're not choosing an easy path but I'm proud of you.'

Hannah grinned. 'Thank you so much for being all right about it, Daddy.' She flung her arms round him.

Kissing her again, William resumed his seat and, taking up his wine glass, asked, 'How's your mother?'

'She's fine. Daddy, I really wish you'd start dating again. I was talking to Anne at Spike's . . .'

'I deny everything,' William said jovially.

Hannah punched his arm. 'She was saying she could arrange for you to meet some great women.'

'Heaven forbid that Anne should take a hand in my private life.'

'She's just being nice. You need to start over. If you did, you wouldn't be so stuck on Mum.'

William finished his wine and poured another. 'In the first place, I'm not stuck on your mother and, in the second, I'll decide when I start dating again.' He kissed the top of Hannah's head. 'Now, what can I do to help?'

'You can drain the pasta for me,' she said, not bothering to hide her exasperation.

'Okay.'

'I just want you to be happy,' Hannah said.

'I am happy,' William insisted.

'I think it's really sweet that you're still in love with Mum and I'd be thrilled if the two of you got back together but there's no future in it. If there were, Mum wouldn't be investing in Blackcurrant Farm.'

'She's what?' William roared.

'I-investing in the farm,' Hannah stuttered, fearful at her father's sudden wrath. 'I'm not supposed to tell you but I thought it would help you to let go if you knew how serious she was about Owen.'

'How much is she putting in?' William demanded.

'Twenty thousand pounds.'

Ribbons of pasta decorated the sink as the saucepan slipped from William's hand and thudded to the floor.

NOVEMBER

Chapter Thirty-One

The *Dam Busters* theme sang out from William's mobile as he parked the Jag in front of The Lodge. Seeing Jack's name on the display, William let the phone ring.

He could imagine the message Jack would leave. It would be something to do with Jessie and Owen and money. Just as it had been every day since their meeting at Spike's and every day William had told him he'd heard nothing. What else could he say? The last thing he wanted was for the police to be involved.

The throbbing sound of a diesel engine made William look up.

'You're late,' he barked when Owen jumped down from the van. Their meeting had been fixed for twelve forty-five; it was now almost one o'clock.

'I had customers,' Owen said nonchalantly. 'They're more important than you.'

William had to bite down on his anger as he waited for Owen to open the front door of the house he himself had lived in for so many years. When at last they were inside William said, 'I've got a proposition for you.'

'Yeah?' Owen walked into the sitting room, leaving William little option but to follow.

'I want you to leave town.'

Owen laughed. 'I bet you do.'

'I know about the farm, Owen, or should I call you Matthew? I know what a bastard you are and I'm not going to let you do to Jess what you did to Justine.'

'Is this supposed to mean something to me?' Owen asked.

You're good, William thought, impressed in spite of himself at how Owen had retained his composure. *But I'm better*. 'I followed you to London. I know there was no funeral. You probably haven't even got an aunt.'

'You followed me?' Owen was incredulous.

'Yep, all the way,' William confirmed. He didn't want to appear pleased with himself but it was hard not to. 'It's years since I've seen *Lawrence of Arabia*.'

Owen hung his head and then shook it as if he was having trouble assimilating what William was saying. Then, eyes blazing with indignation, he looked up. 'And you call me a bastard?'

William scoffed. 'Don't play the innocent.'

'I didn't go to the funeral because I was too upset.'

'Yeah, you looked pretty cut up in the cinema,' William commented dryly. 'Let's not play games. I'll give you twenty-five grand to leave Abbeyleigh now. You were going to fleece Jess for twenty; fleece me for twenty-five and leave now.'

Owen's eyes widened in surprise. 'Is that what you think I'm doing? Fleecing Jessie? I never asked her to lend me the money. She offered it.'

'We both know you're a conman. You spun her a line and she fell for it.'

'If you're so sure about this, why aren't you talking to Jessie?' Owen challenged. He sat on one of the window seats. 'You won't say anything because you know she won't believe you. No one will.

'If you hate the fact she's lending me money, and I'm not crazy about the idea myself, I'll take what you're offering but only to put towards the farm because I'm not going anywhere.'

'Nice try,' William said curtly. 'You've got a day to pack your bags.'

Owen stood. 'For Jessie's sake, I'll pretend we never had this conversation but if you pull a stunt like this again, I'll speak to Walt and tell him about your over-active imagination. As I understand it, you're already on a formal warning at work.'

William gave a hollow laugh. 'Threaten me all you like. It doesn't change anything.'

'Threaten?' Owen smiled. 'I haven't threatened you, William. I'm simply stating facts. For a man who loves his job, you appear to be playing fast and loose with yours.'

William watched as Owen poured himself a scotch. Was it his imagination or did Owen's hand shake a little?

'I feel sorry for you,' Owen continued, waving his glass at William as he returned to the window seat.

'You leave Jessie for that slapper Chelsea. Then, when it turns out she's slipping a sailor one behind your back and the kid isn't yours, you come running home, expecting to be forgiven. God, how we laughed.' Owen drank his scotch.

His words left William reeling. He looked towards the mantelpiece. The familiar silver-framed images of Hannah greeted his gaze and he took strength from them. At one end, stood the picture of Jessie that Owen kept beside his bed. William felt his stomach turn.

'You've lost her,' Owen said quietly. 'Accept it and walk away while you still have some pride left.'

William's eyes burned with hatred, his hands twitching into fists.

'You want to hit me?' Owen asked. 'Come on then.' He put his glass on the bureau and stood, beckoning William on.

'I want you to leave.'

'I'm not going anywhere. I'm having too much fun with your ex-wife.'

Unable to contain himself any longer, William launched himself at Owen, punching him in the mouth. Owen staggered backwards. Shaking out his hand, William watched with satisfaction as Owen pressed his fingers to his lip. They came away covered in blood.

'You can hit me again if you want,' Owen lisped. 'I'm not going to fight with you. Man of your age, you could have a heart attack. I wouldn't want it on my conscience.'

Grabbing a handful of the younger man's clothes, William brought his face close to Owen's. 'You haven't got a conscience. Take my offer. Leave town.'

'I heard you the first time and the answer is still no. The sad thing is you didn't even want her until I had her. A double bed gets cold at night when you're on your own, doesn't it?'

While Owen might have refused to trade physical blows, his punches were landing verbally. In response, William tightened his grip. Invigorated by anger, he almost lifted Owen from the ground as he said, 'You picked the wrong woman this time. Twenty-five thousand pounds in cash to leave Abbeyleigh. You've got a day to think about it.'

The rattle and slap of car keys hitting the floor made both men start. The only thing William's brain registered when Jessie entered was the fact that she was wearing new shoes: navy with mid-height heels and a white and navy trim round the toe. He could hardly bring himself to look at her face. When he did, he found her eyes were double their normal size.

'Get out.' Her voice was icy.

A hundred words jostled in William's mind but his tongue was stilled by her calm anguish. Shooting a baleful glance at Owen, he strode from the room.

Jessie followed him. 'You complete and utter bastard,' she cried. 'You're trying to buy Owen off? How could you?' She pummelled his chest with her fists, forcing him out of the door. 'You are never to set foot in this house again. Do you hear me? Never!'

'I was only thinking of you,' William said miserably.

'You're biologically incapable of thinking of anyone but yourself,' Jessie shouted.

There were red spots of anger in her cheeks and her eyes brimmed with tears that he knew she was too proud to let spill in front of him. Christ, what had he done?

'Is that what you think I'm worth?' Jessie asked.

'Don't be ridiculous,' he said.

She held on to the Jag's door as William climbed inside.

'That's what you offered him, so doesn't that make it my market value? Forty-something female, good condition, reliable, all her own teeth, one child, one dickhead of an ex-husband who cheated on her, needs a good home.'

'Stop it, Jess. Please.'

'Don't tell me to stop it! Don't speak to me! I hate you!' she shouted and slammed the door with all her might. Stepping back, she aimed a kick at it, swiftly followed by another.

Shaken, William fired the engine.

'You spent more than twenty-five grand on your precious bloody car, you bastaaard!' she yelled as he pulled away.

The anger dissipated as quickly as it had risen and Jessie was left drained, her mind numb before William had left the drive.

'Don't get upset, Jessie,' Owen urged. He put his arm round her shoulders. 'The man's a fool.'

'You weren't tempted then?' Jessie tried to make a joke of it as they returned to the sitting room but her shock at the crassness of William's actions robbed all the humour from her ashen face.

'I wouldn't swap you for a million pounds.'

Jessie managed a smile. 'What's he done to your face?'

'It's nothing. Just a cut.' Owen poured Jessie a scotch, using the same glass he himself had drunk out of a moment before. 'Drink this,' he urged. 'I'll go and wash my face.'

Jessie was seated in one of the fireside chairs, the scotch untouched, when Owen returned. He knelt beside her. Jessie reached out to stroke his chin, tilting his head to get a better look at his lip.

'See,' he said. 'No harm done.'

Her gaze slid away. She drank some of the scotch, coughed and drank some more. 'Why now?' she asked as she searched her memory for anything that could have triggered William to do such an outrageous thing. 'Apart from a few words at the partners' meeting last week, there's been no contact between us. It's been wonderful. What was he even doing here?'

Owen stood, one hand in the back pocket of his jeans. 'That's my fault, I'm afraid,' he said sheepishly. 'He asked to meet me. I was curious. Believe me, I had no idea he was going to do something like that.'

'How could he?' Jessie's voice wavered as it rose.

'Far be it from me to make excuses for the man,' Owen said, 'but he's clearly not himself. Maybe the trauma of finding out the baby wasn't his and then failing to be reconciled with you has been too much for him.'

'You think he's having a breakdown?'

'I'm no expert but no one in their right mind would carry on like this. I think you should stay away from him,' Owen said. 'He's irrational. There's no telling what he might do. And I think you should tell Walt.'

'Owen, I couldn't!' Jessie said, horrified. 'If I say anything there's a good chance they'll throw him out of the partnership. I couldn't do that to him.'

'What he needs is a break,' Owen said. 'Six months, somewhere hot, somewhere he can get his head together.'

Jessie nodded. 'I should talk to him but . . .' Her voice trailed off. 'I don't think I could stand being in the same room as him right now.'

Owen's eyes softened. 'Why not ask Anne to speak to him for you? She's fond of William but at the same time she won't hold back from saying what needs to be said.'

Jessie brought her hand up to Owen's cheek. At least one of them was thinking straight. The sight of the cut on his lip strengthened her resolve. William had gone too far this time. She would make him understand, through Anne, that he must seek a leave of absence for six months or else leave for good.

*

William pulled up outside Anne Jacobs' ivy-covered house on the edge of town. He tried to collect his thoughts as he watched the windscreen wipers clear the film of drizzle that settled between one sweep and the next. A moment later he was standing on the front step, watching through the Flemish glass as Anne approached.

'I got your message. You said you'd spoken to Jess. Is she okay?' William asked.

'It was a strange call. She sounded upset.' Anne showed William through to the kitchen. 'She thinks you're having a breakdown.'

'What? Oh, great! I should have seen that coming.'

'She wants me to tell you that she feels it's in everyone's interests if you take a six-month sabbatical as soon as possible, preferably abroad, certainly away from Abbeyleigh. In the meantime, she doesn't want you to speak to her or communicate with her in any way. She says if you don't comply, she'll go to Walt and say it's impossible for the two of you to work together and the partners will need to decide which one of you they want to retain.' Anne laid her hand on William's arm. 'What the hell is going on?'

'I just wanted to get her away from him.'

'What did you do?' Anne asked, wide-eyed.

'Apparently made things worse instead of better. I took a gamble. It didn't pay off.'

Anne gave William a sympathetic look. 'Perhaps it's time to draw a line under your relationship with Jessie and think about the future. I could ring any one of a dozen women who'd be delighted to have dinner with you tonight.'

'I don't even want to have dinner with myself tonight.'

He could still recall her shoes in perfect detail: the mid-height heel, the navy and white trim round the toe. He thought it absurd but at least it stopped him remembering the devastated look on her face.

Anger suddenly burned within him as he pictured Owen's mocking smile. He hated that Jessie had told Owen about Chelsea's deception. Had he been the subject of pillow talk between them? The anger twisted and spurted like a volcano that had found a new path along which to spew its molten fury. Perhaps he should let whatever was about to unfold play out without his intervention. If Jessie didn't want him back, why should he care what happened to her? But he did care. Who was he kidding? He couldn't stop himself from caring.

'This is about the money she's investing in the farm, isn't it?' Anne said. 'I suppose Jack told you. I asked him not to.'

William looked horrified. 'Jack knows?'

Anne nodded.

'I have to go.'

'But wait, what do I tell Jessie?'

'Tell her I accept her terms.'

Cold needles of rain stabbed at William as he sprinted to his car. Once inside, he rang Jack.

'When were you going to tell me?' Jack asked.

'Please say you haven't called them.'

'I didn't need to. You brought them here yourself, Sherlock! When you were checking out that florist's shop, you paid for your room at the hotel by credit card. The manager told Justine someone had been asking questions. She went to the police and now they want to talk to you. DI Watkins arrived this morning.'

'What? No! Christ! Shit! Fuck!'

'What have you done? On second thoughts, I don't want to know. Just keep my name out of this.'

*

DI Watkins and DS Miller were waiting for William on his return to the office. Watkins was in his late thirties with a slim build, a pinched face and slicked-back brown hair. His blue eyes narrowed as he studied the interior of William's office.

'I'd offer you a drink,' William said as he sat down, 'but you'd both say no. What can I do for you?'

He made no attempt to move the files that cluttered the two adjacent chairs and the officers remained standing.

'We understand you've been asking questions about Justine Anderson. We'd like to know why.'

'I thought Justine Anderson would be able to give me some background information on Owen Phillips.'

'And he is?'

'My ex-wife's boyfriend,' William said.

'What made you think Justine Anderson knew Phillips?'

'He had a newspaper cutting of her. I figured she must be a friend.'

'He showed you this cutting?'

'Not exactly. It fell out of his pocket at the Mayor's Ball. I don't think he even realised he'd dropped it.'

'Do you still have the cutting?'

'No. Owen was talking to Lydia Coates at the time. I didn't want to interrupt so I slipped it back into his pocket and moved on. It was only when I started to have my doubts about him, it came back to me and I decided to follow it up. I didn't speak to Justine Anderson. She wasn't there.'

'You seem to have absorbed a lot of information from a cutting you saw only briefly,' Watkins observed.

'I'm used to digesting a lot of information in a short space of time.' William indicated the piles of paper in his office. 'Do you want to tell me what this is about?'

'Justine Anderson was the victim of a serious crime four years ago. She doesn't like people asking questions about her.'

'So I gather.'

'You say you have doubts about Phillips. Tell me about them,' Watkins pressed.

'Gut instinct, mostly,' William admitted. 'He seemed to come out of nowhere. No friends, no family, none that came here anyway. There was just something about him that set alarm bells ringing. Years in this job maybe – who knows? I didn't want to see my ex get hurt.'

'I know the barmaid told you what happened to Justine. Do you think Owen Phillips is Matthew Harrison?' Watkins asked bluntly.

William shrugged. 'If I had proof, I would have come to you lot.'

'But you suspect he might be?'

'It's possible or he might just be a friend.'

'Thank you, Mr Goode. You've been very helpful. However, I'd appreciate it if you left any future enquiries to us.'

'Yes, of course.'

*

William punched Jack's number.

'They wanted to know what led me to Justine.'

'What did you say?'

'I told them about the cutting.'

'What?!'

'I told them Phillips dropped it at the Mayor's Ball.'

'And they believed you?'

'It doesn't matter. It's all the explanation they're going to get.'

'What else did you tell them?'

'Nothing. They're detectives. Let them figure it out. Ring me as soon as you know anything.'

*

It was the following afternoon before Jack telephoned.

'They know about the farm. They're pretty sure he's their guy. They're making enquiries about Stella now. There were two fatalities in the area. One might be her if Stella was a nickname. If not, he was lying.'

'Is he under surveillance?'

'Yes. Justine Anderson and her brother are coming to Abbeyleigh tomorrow night to carry out a formal identification.'

'I can't let that happen.'

'What choice do you have?'

'Perhaps if he were to disappear . . .'

'Are you listening to yourself?'

'Calm down.'

'Don't tell me to calm down! You're talking about assisting an offender. Jesus Christ, you could go inside for that.'

'Only if I get caught.'

'You have to let justice take its course.'

'Justice? Jessie's going to be devastated when she learns the truth. Then she's going to have to deal with a trial. The whole town are going to be whispering behind her back. I know what that's like. I've been through it with Chelsea. Is that the kind of justice you think Jessie deserves?'

'Of course not but –'

'You're a good friend, Jack. The best. But I have to do this.'

'Will–'

'If it all goes tits up, I'll keep your name out of it, I promise.'

*

Working by the glow of his computer screen, William paused with his fingers hovering over the keys as Walt entered.

'Fancy a drink?' he asked. His eyes looked strained behind rimless spectacles.

'I'll pass if you don't mind.'

Walt waved in acknowledgement. 'You're the last one so set the alarm.'

Opening Joe Wilson's file, William reached for the telephone.

'Joe? It's William. I need to go over a couple of things with you. Are you free tomorrow night? I'll come to you. Okay. I'll see you at eight.'

Thirty minutes later, William shut down his computer and locked up the office. The car park was deserted. He checked his car over then turned up the collar of his coat and walked home.

Chapter Thirty-Two

Back at the office early the next day, William wondered if there would come a time that day when he would lose his nerve. Bottle it, as his clients would say. Is this how they felt before a job? Heart racing, mouth dry, torn between right and wrong? He doubted it. Most of his clients never gave a thought to the consequences of their actions – that was half their problem. William, on the other hand, was painfully aware of what the consequences of his actions might be.

It was an hour later when Walt strolled by William's office and did a double take before pausing in the doorway. 'Did you go home last night?' he asked with a smile.

'Eventually,' William said. 'Car's playing up.'

'Everything okay between you and Jessie?'

'I've barely spoken to her. Why?'

'She told me she wanted to work at home for the rest of the week.'

William shrugged. 'Nothing to do with me.'

*

It was late afternoon when William finished signing his correspondence.

'I've left my notes on Joe Wilson at home,' he told his secretary, Lynn.

The outside light shone across the cracked concrete of the car park. William slid into the driver's seat of the Jag and pretended to turn the key. For appearances' sake, he pretended to give it another go before feigning annoyance and running back up the stairs.

'Sorry, Lynn, my car's playing up. Can I borrow yours?'

She handed him a bunch of keys held together by a green alien with Velcro hands.

'You're an angel,' William said. 'If I run you home later, could I keep the car to drive to Wilson's place? I'll drop it off at yours after. I'll fill the tank, of course.'

*

As William approached Owen's stall he couldn't help wondering where the officers keeping watch were hidden. At a guess, he would say the second-floor storeroom of one of the nearby shops.

A riotous version of 'Jingle Bells' echoed from a fashion outlet across the road as William selected a bunch of mixed blooms.

Owen snatched the flowers from him. 'Come to up your offer?'

'Would you be interested if I had?'

Owen smirked. 'Jessie thinks you're having a breakdown.'

'I wonder who put that idea in her head?'

'It's a pity you're not still married, she could've had you sectioned.'

William bit back the retort that sprang to mind. 'How much for the flowers?'

Owen told him.

William pretended to hunt for change. 'I might not know who you really are but I know what you do and you know I know, so let's cut the bullshit. You're leaving Abbeyleigh tonight.'

'Like hell I am.'

'You're going to take Jessie to the firework display in the park. Just before seven thirty you'll leave. Be careful. You're under surveillance. I'll be waiting for you in Mason Road. I'll be in a blue Ford Fiesta. Make sure you're not followed and that you've got some money on you. Leave everything else.' William tipped the correct change into Owen's hand.

Owen let the money fall into his money belt. When he looked up, his eyes were bright with amusement and something else.

William prayed it was curiosity.

'Give me one good reason why I should.'

Despite the frosty air, William felt the sweat break out on his forehead. 'Justine Anderson's arriving from London tonight to ID you with a view to pressing charges.'

*

William watched as the first of a series of fireworks lit up the night sky. He checked the clock on the dashboard and then glanced behind him. No one was in sight. Two loud explosions made him start. The sky over the park was alight with pink and white flashes. William checked the clock again. He had to give Owen time to get there, he reasoned, but what if the police had sensed something was wrong and moved in? What if Owen told them about the planned rendezvous? Involuntarily, William checked his mirrors again.

Rockets had begun to whizz and bang all around him now, shredding his nerves still further. Surely if Owen thought all hope of the money was gone, he would leave? But what if he didn't? What if his plans to buy the farm were genuine? What if he really did love Jessie?

So deep in thought was William that when Owen finally opened the door and climbed into the passenger seat, he let out a cry of surprise.

'On edge are we, Mr Goode?'

Embarrassed, William fumbled for his key. 'You took your bloody time.'

'Evading surveillance isn't easy,' Owen replied.

'I'd have thought you would have had plenty of practice over the years.' William put the car in gear.

'Not so fast.' Owen laid his hand on the steering wheel. 'How do you know about Justine?'

'We haven't got time for this,' William said tersely.

'Make time.'

'I found a newspaper cutting of a florist's shop. I tracked the shop down and that led me to Justine Anderson.'

'What cutting?'

'The one you keep in your inside jacket pocket,' William said with satisfaction, enjoying the look of astonishment on Owen's face.

'You picked my pocket?'

'Not exactly. I broke into your house while you were at The Lodge and then I picked your pocket.'

Owen stared at William in disbelief.

'Can we go now?'

'I don't understand. You offer me money to leave Abbeyleigh. Then you bring the police in and now you're helping me get away.'

'I didn't bring the police in. Justine Anderson brought them in when she found out I'd been asking questions.'

'Hell of a woman, Justine. You say she's due in tonight?'

'That's right.'

'When?'

'What is this?' William demanded.

Owen leaned closer. 'You were desperate enough to offer me money, so clearly you're desperate enough to lie. When will she be here?'

'She's on the nine twenty from Liverpool Street.' William was grateful he'd had the foresight to check on the times of the trains because he was certain Owen had done the same. 'We're wasting valuable time.'

Owen sank back in his seat and stared out of the window. 'Okay, drive.'

Relieved, William swung out of Mason Road. He was careful to use the back roads that were devoid of traffic cameras. 'What did you tell Jessie?'

'That I was coming down with flu.' They were on the outskirts of town when Owen asked, 'Where are we going?'

'Stebbingsford.'

'Why?'

'Because I say so.'

'Is this yours?'

'My secretary's.'

'Very generous of her to lend you her car. Is she another one of your lovers?'

'No.'

'That was the one thing Jessie was grateful for, you know, that you didn't screw around with someone from the office. Was Chelsea really your first?'

'Yes,' William replied through gritted teeth.

'So what's the plan then, Will? Blacken my name and then be there to provide a shoulder for Jessie to cry on?'

'I thought that was your plan,' William said.

'Jessie deserves better than either of us. Why don't we have a gentleman's agreement to stay away from her?'

'You're not a gentleman,' William said scathingly.

'She'll never have you back. For one thing, you were crap in bed.'

William's hands tightened on the steering wheel.

'Why did you suspect me?'

'Instinct,' William replied.

'But clearly you don't want me arrested.'

'I just want you as far away from here as possible. Abbeyleigh is a small town and when it comes to any kind of scandal it's a *very* small town. I wasn't prepared to stand by and see Jess humiliated.'

'Again,' Owen interposed. 'Humiliated, *again*. You did it the first time, remember?'

'I'm never likely to forget.'

'Neither is Jessie.'

'Like you care,' William responded angrily. 'How many women have you tricked? How many hearts have you broken?'

'I've never put a ring on a woman's finger and promised to remain faithful to her. You broke Jessie's heart, and even if I do say so myself I think I did a damn good job of putting it back together.'

'Yeah, you're a real Boy Scout. And how do you suppose she's going to feel when she realises it was all a charade?'

'It wasn't. I love her.'

'And you lie for a living,' William said.

'Not about this.'

'You're a fraud, Owen. You tricked her into trusting you and you would have tricked her out of twenty grand if I hadn't stopped you. You don't know the meaning of the word "love".'

'Am I supposed to take lectures in morality from a man who slept with his mistress in the marital bed?' Owen asked archly.

William slammed on the brakes and the car skidded to a halt. 'Do you want me to throw you out here in the middle of nowhere?'

Owen raised his hands in mock surrender and they lapsed into silence.

'I'll need the car.'

'I'll drop you at the station. You can catch a train.'

'For a lawyer you're not very smart, are you? They'll be waiting to take me off.'

'I'm sure you'll think of something.'

'You'd better pray I do because if I get caught I'm going to make damn sure I take you down with me.' Owen shot William a sideways glance. 'Have you any idea of the kind of trouble I could get you into?'

'I probably know that better than you,' William admitted candidly.

'Talking of trouble, how's Chelsea? Do you keep in touch?'

William grated the gears as he took a right-hand turn towards the station.

'I imagine it was a bit of a blow to find out the kid wasn't yours when there you were with the nursery painted all ready to play daddy again. You do know you were a laughing stock, don't you? The whole town was pissing themselves at the hotshot lawyer who was so flattered by the attention of a young blonde he fell for the oldest trick in the book . . .'

William pulled into the kerb and brought the car to a halt. Wrenching on the handbrake, he reached across to grab Owen's jacket. 'Which is precisely why I had to stop you. I won't let Jess be made a laughing stock. She doesn't deserve it. You're scum,' William said and shook Owen to emphasise the point. 'And one day, somewhere far away from here, you're going to be a bit too cute and the police are going to be waiting.'

'You'd better hope that day's a long way off,' Owen said, straining against William's grip.

'I don't care what they do to me,' William responded, his tone cavalier.

'You should. The law takes a dim view of assisting an offender.'

William threw Owen against the door. 'The law takes a dimmer view of fraud,' he said. 'Get out.'

*

Easing to a halt in the neighbouring road, William wound down the window and gulped in cold air. Finally, after a lifetime spent dealing with criminals, he had crossed the Rubicon and committed an offence himself.

He knew that breaking into Owen's house had also been a crime but he hadn't thought of it in the same way as no harm had been done and the risks of being found out had been so low. Helping Owen to evade capture was in an entirely different league, however. The risks of slipping up and being arrested were sky-high and he had little doubt that arrest would mean a custodial sentence. He opened the car door and threw up on the verge.

Grabbing the bottle of water he had stowed in the glove compartment, he rinsed his mouth out. Then he poured water into the palm of his hand and splashed it over his face.

He had always known travelling with Owen would be a test of his temper. What he hadn't been prepared for was the resurgence of the emotions he had so carefully buried about Chelsea: the shock, the anguish, the shame.

His blonde goddess leaving unexpectedly, and heavily pregnant at that, was bound to have caused a furore. He had been painfully aware of the sniggers and the jibes, even though he'd steadfastly tried to ignore them. It was the only way to carry on living in Abbeyleigh and survive.

William sighed. At least the same thing wouldn't now happen to Jess. She would be sad at Owen's leaving and rumours would fly. But rumours were rumours and, with nothing to substantiate them, they would eventually die down.

He tilted the rear-view mirror so he could check his appearance. Owen's words rattled in his brain: *The whole town was pissing themselves.* Well, Abbeyleigh had had as much fun as it was going to with the Goode family.

Chapter Thirty-Three

Jessie had just switched on the computer when she saw a car pull up on the drive. She recognised one of the men: the tall, languid figure of DS Sam Miller.

'Hello, Sam,' she said, meeting them at the door before they had a chance to ring the bell.

'Hello, Jessie. This is DI Watkins. Can we come in?'

'Miss Martin.' Watkins held out his ID for her to examine.

Jessie led them through to the sitting room, her heart rate ramping up. 'Is something wrong?'

'Can you tell us where Owen Phillips is?'

'Owen?' Jessie repeated in surprise. 'He's at home. In fact, I've just rung him.'

The two men exchanged glances. 'Did you speak to him?'

'No. He's got the answer machine on. Poor love thought he was coming down with flu last night, that's why he left the fireworks early. What's this about?' she asked.

'Have you spoken to Mr Phillips since?'

'No.'

'I'm sorry to have to say this, Jessie,' Sam began, 'but we believe the man you know as Owen Phillips is someone my colleague here has been seeking in connection with a series of deceptions involving women, each of whom has lost a substantial amount of money.'

A smile twitched on Jessie's lips. 'You're not serious?'

'I'm afraid we are,' Watkins said. 'We understand Mr Phillips intended to purchase a farm later this month. We believe he told you that his aunt would be investing in it and that he later told you she'd been killed in a road accident.'

Jessie's eyes widened. 'That's right.' Feeling her legs grow weak, Jessie sat on the sofa.

'Did he seek the money Stella would have put into the farm from you instead?'

'He didn't seek it. I offered it.'

'I'm sure you thought you did,' Watkins said superciliously.

Jessie bridled at his tone.

'Did you pay the money over early?' Watkins asked.

'No.'

'It's still in your account?'

'Yes.'

'Are you sure?'

'Positive.'

'Did you ever meet Stella or any other member of Mr Phillips's family?'

'No. His father and Stella were due to come to The Lodge the day Owen got the call about the accident.'

'Did he take the call here?'

'No. North Street.'

'Were you present at the time?'

'No. I can't believe what you're telling me. Owen would never do something like this. The very idea is crazy. It's a mistake.' Jessie was adamant.

'Owen Phillips bought a ticket to London at Stebbingsford station last night.'

'What?' Jessie said, bewildered.

'Just after eight o'clock, Phillips was seen on CCTV at Stebbingsford station buying a ticket for the eight fifteen train to London.'

'I don't believe it.'

'I've seen the tape, Jessie,' Sam said. 'It's definitely him.'

'Then he must have got a call from his father.'

'Do you know his father's full name?'

Jessie frowned. 'I don't think he ever told me.'

'His telephone number, perhaps?'

'I'm sorry. I don't have that either.' Jessie saw the look that passed between the two detectives. 'But that doesn't mean anything,' she said, agitated. 'Do you actually have any proof?'

'No one of Stella's approximate age was killed in an accident at the time Phillips said it occurred.'

'You must have got the date wrong.'

'We don't believe Stella ever existed, Miss Martin. We think she was part of a scam designed to relieve you of your money.'

'That's ridiculous! You didn't see him the day he got the news that Stella had died. He was devastated.' Jessie got up and went to the window. 'I held him in my arms. He cried like a baby.' The scene was so vivid in Jessie's mind she could almost hear the sound of Owen sobbing.

'He's very good at what he does,' Sam said gently.

Jessie shrugged him off. 'If you were so sure, why didn't you arrest him?'

'There was an element of doubt.'

'I knew it,' Jessie said triumphantly. 'So you could be wrong?'

'I could be but I'm not,' Watkins responded coolly. 'A chap by the name of Thomas Richards ran a flower stall in a small town in the West Midlands. He became romantically involved with a wealthy widow. He told her that he planned to buy a run-down garden centre. A month before completion his sister, who was due to invest in the garden centre, died in an accident abroad. The widow stepped in and gave him thirty thousand pounds to enable the purchase to go ahead. Thomas Richards left on the day the purchase was due to complete, taking the money with him. The interesting part of this story, from our point of view, is that the name of the sister was Stella.'

Jessie sat down heavily on the window seat.

'We have a handwriting expert who can link samples of Thomas Richards' handwriting to samples of handwriting by Matthew Harrison, someone who committed a similar offence, and there appears to be a direct link between Harrison and Owen Phillips. We had witnesses travelling to Abbeyleigh to carry out an ID. Unfortunately, Phillips absconded before they arrived.'

Jessie could hear the sound of Owen's voice in her head: *Sometimes I feel like I've spent my whole life running*. 'Is that why he left?' she asked bleakly.

'We had him under surveillance. I think it's more likely someone got sloppy and spooked him.'

Jessie looked out of the window. It couldn't be true. Could it? She pictured Owen as he had been in the park, huddled into his coat, complaining of feeling unwell. As he had made his apologies to Anne and Phil and wished them all goodnight he had caught hold of Jessie's hand and, gripping it, had said, 'I love you, Jessie. Whatever happens, remember that.' Had he been saying goodbye?

Sam touched Jessie's shoulder. 'We'll need you to come down to the station, Jessie. Give a statement.'

Jessie looked up at him. 'He wouldn't take my money, Sam. He cared for me. I know he did.' Only after she had spoken did she realise she'd lapsed into the past tense.

'He's an accomplished liar.' Watkins said. Anyone could twist words but could you deceive with your kisses? Jessie felt sick. When he'd devoured her body, telling her she was beautiful and that there had never been anyone like her, had it all been a carefully prepared script?

'There could be an innocent explanation,' Jessie said, before adding beseechingly, 'couldn't there?'

'I don't think so, Jessie,' Sam said gently. 'Is there someone we can call? Someone who could come over? Anne, perhaps?'

It was the kindness in his voice, the sympathy spilling out of his eyes that caused the anger to spike in Jessie. She wouldn't be someone to be pitied. Not again.

'It doesn't make any sense,' Jessie said, beginning to pace. 'If all Owen wanted was cash, why didn't he take the money William offered him?' Jessie halted abruptly. 'Unless he did.' She bit her lip.

'What money?' Watkins asked sharply.

Suddenly cold, Jessie wrapped her arms round herself. 'William's not himself. Owen thought he was having a breakdown. He's never come to terms with the fact we weren't reconciled. He held Owen responsible.'

'Tell me about the money,' Watkins pressed.

'I came home the other day to find William and Owen arguing. Before they realised I was there I heard William offer Owen twenty-five thousand pounds to leave Abbeyleigh.'

'You're sure that's what you heard?' Sam asked sternly.

Jessie nodded.

'Did William know you were investing in Blackcurrant Farm?'

'I didn't think anyone knew except Owen, my daughter and Anne Jacobs,' Jessie said ruefully.

'You've been very helpful, Miss Martin.'

Jessie nodded, glassy-eyed with confusion.

Watkins turned to Miller. 'We need to have a chat with William Goode.'

Chapter Thirty-Four

William had just finished one case before the magistrates and was about to begin another when Watkins and Miller drew him to one side.

'We'd like you to accompany us to the station,' Watkins said.

'Why?' William asked in surprise.

'We want to question you about the disappearance of Owen Phillips.'

'Owen's disappeared?' William repeated, looking from one man to the other. 'But what's that got to do with me?'

'Are you going to come voluntarily or do we have to arrest you?' Watkins asked testily.

'I'm in the middle of something here. I can't walk out. My clients need me.'

'Find someone to cover. You have five minutes,' Watkins said tersely.

'This is outrageous! Sam?' William turned to Miller.

'I'm sorry, William. You'd better do as he says.'

*

'Jessie? Are you okay?' Anne asked as she opened her front door.

'I really need a friend,' Jessie said.

'And a drink judging by the look on your face. You're as white as a sheet. Come in.'

Settled by the roaring fire in Anne's snug, a brandy in her hands, Jessie told Anne what had happened.

'And Owen's gone?' Anne asked.

Jessie nodded. 'I keep coming up with explanations but it doesn't look good. Does it?' Jessie met Anne's gaze. 'Innocent people don't run.'

Anne shook her head.

'I just find it so hard to believe. I keep going over our conversations in my head. People can play with words but his kisses felt so real . . .' Agitated, Jessie stood the brandy glass on the hearth. 'When I think of all those nights, the things we've done together . . .' Nausea rising, she put a hand over her mouth.

Anne moved swiftly to sit on the arm of Jessie's chair and hugged her.

Raising her tear-stained face to look at her friend, Jessie asked, 'Do you think I was a fool?'

'Far from it. Only a fool could have resisted. If Owen had made a play for me, I wouldn't have said no,' Anne admitted.

Jessie stared into the fire, lost in thought, already wanting to forget, knowing she never would. 'I gave him my heart, Anne. Was he really going to break it for twenty thousand pounds? Did I mean so little to him?

He was my world and what was I to him? A business deal? A scam?' Her face hardened. 'An easy ride?'

Anne bent to retrieve the brandy glass and pressed it into Jessie's hands.

'They say there's one born every minute, don't they? I never thought I'd be one of them,' Jessie said.

'You're not. You're a good, kind person. You just trusted the wrong man and if I ever see that little shit again, it'll be his last day on this earth,' Anne vowed.

*

It was funny how William had never noticed how rough interview room one at Abbeyleigh Police Station was. Given time to sit and take it in, he saw the scuffed and dirty skirting boards for the first time. The walls, chipped and marked, were painted an ice blue. A coffee stain decorated the wall to his right; he wondered if it had been the work of one of his clients.

William had been expecting the police to call but not quite so publicly or so quickly. Clients, criminals, solicitors and court ushers alike had watched, open-mouthed, as Watkins had practically frogmarched William from the court building. The rumour mill would be doing overtime today.

Now, the door opened and the two officers came in.

'Sorry about this, William,' Sam began. 'It shouldn't take long.'

William parked his face in neutral. 'That's all right. I'm happy to help,' he said. 'Although I'm not sure how much help I can be.'

He felt naked without the counsel's notebook balanced on his knee and his favourite pen, a present from Hannah, in his hand, poised to take notes: a civilian.

'You understand that, presently, you're not under arrest,' Watkins said.

'I know the drill,' William said with a smile.

'Where were you between seven and eleven last night?'

'I was working at the office until seven thirty and then I left to see a client. I was with the client until ten and then I drove home.'

'What's the client's name?'

'I can't tell you that. Client confidentiality prevents it, I'm afraid.'

'Where does he live?'

'Assuming that it is a he,' William said. 'Stebbingsford.'

Watkins and Miller exchanged glances. 'You drove to Stebbingsford last night?'

'Yes.'

'What time did you get there?'

'Eight o'clock.'

'Do you normally see clients in the evening?'

'Sometimes, when I've got a lot of work on.'

'Is your car at the office?'

'No. It's at the garage having a service. It's been playing up but the diagnostics couldn't find a fault so they're giving it a tune-up.'

'Did you use your car last night?'

'No, I used my secretary's.'

'We'll want to inspect it.'

'You'll need Lynn's permission for that.'

'I'm sure your secretary will cooperate.'

'Why do you want to look at her car?'

'It's my belief you didn't travel to Stebbingsford alone, Mr Goode. I think you had Owen Phillips with you.'

William looked at Sam and grinned. 'Do you seriously believe I would do that? Why would I do that?'

Watkins walked to the door.

'You won't find her car at the office,' William said casually as Watkins reached for the door handle.

'Where is it?'

'I had it picked up this morning for a professional valeting. I thought it would be a nice way of saying thank you to Lynn for letting me borrow her car.'

'Which company?' Watkins asked through gritted teeth.

'Abbeyleigh Wash and Go. I asked them to be particularly thorough with the interior. Lynn's got two young boys and those crisps get everywhere. She's always complaining about it.'

Watkins slammed his way out of the room.

'Why did you go and wind him up like that, Will?' Sam asked.

'I don't like what he's implying. I take it I was right about Phillips?'

Sam nodded. 'Owen Phillips caught a train from Stebbingsford last night.'

William raised his eyebrows in surprise. 'Hell of a coincidence, I admit. But that's all it is.'

Watkins returned looking flushed. He sat down and glared at William. 'You're a criminal lawyer.'

'Yes, I am.'

'Some might say you spend your working life assisting offenders.'

'Everyone's entitled to their opinion.'

'I want the name of the scumbag you went to see last night.'

'As I said before, client confidentiality prevents me –'

'I want a name,' Watkins snarled.

'Perhaps you could approach your client, seek his permission?' Sam suggested.

'Perhaps.'

'You were seen at Phillips's stall at approximately four thirty yesterday afternoon. What were you doing there?'

'Discussing my retainer.'

'I wouldn't put it past you.'

'I was buying flowers for my secretary.'

'Flowers from Phillips?!' Watkins' tone was incredulous.

'I'm a busy man and his stall's handy.'

'What's wrong with your car?'

'I'm a lawyer, not a mechanic.'

'I'll want to examine it.'

'Be my guest.' William took out a bunch of keys, lifted one off the ring and threw it across the table. 'That's my spare.'

'Phillips bought a ticket for the eight fifteen train from Stebbingsford to London last night. You were also in Stebbingsford, supposedly to see some mystery client. You could have driven Phillips from Abbeyleigh to Stebbingsford.'

'I could have but why would I?'

'My colleague here tells me you're a smart man, Mr Goode. You had your suspicions about Phillips for a long time, didn't you?'

William shrugged and, feigning boredom, tilted his chair back.

'You follow up on a newspaper cutting and get information that, on the face of it, seems to confirm your suspicions. Why didn't you come to us? Your best friend's a police officer. He says you never mentioned it.'

'Jack's a good officer. One of the best. But I didn't have any proof. I didn't want to waste anyone's time. Anyway –' William's tone became more strident – 'I can't go around accusing people of committing felonies. I could get done for slander.'

'You could get done for a lot worse,' Watkins rejoined. 'The other jobs aside, if we catch him, we've got enough to charge Phillips with attempting to obtain money by deception. If we can prove you helped him to escape, we can charge you with assisting an offender. You'll be looking at a maximum of five years inside. Five years,' Watkins repeated slowly. 'Banged up with all those cons who have grudges against their lawyers. I wonder who they're going to take out their frustrations on? Did you think about that when you offered him a ride?'

William brought down his chair with a thump. 'Where's your proof?'

'To travel from Abbeyleigh to Stebbingsford in the time that he did, Phillips had to be travelling by car. His van is still here. Miss Martin didn't drive him and we can't find a taxi firm who picked up anyone answering Phillips's description. That leaves you.'

'Except I was travelling to Stebbingsford to see a client.'

'I want to speak to your accountant, Mr Goode, and I want details of all your bank and building society accounts.'

'Why?'

'Sam tells me you're an equity partner at Smith Mathers. I want to see the business accounts insofar as they relate to you, personal drawings, that kind of thing.'

'No way,' William replied. 'What have my finances got to do with anything?'

'You offered Phillips twenty-five thousand pounds to leave Abbeyleigh. I want to know if you paid him.'

'Excuse me?'

'You were heard to offer Owen money to leave.'

'By whom?'

'Your ex-wife.'

William feigned amazement. 'That's preposterous.'

'Are you calling her a liar?'

'I'm saying she must have misheard.'

'She seemed very sure. What were you doing at The Lodge that day?'

'I'd gone there to pick up some law books. I'd borrowed my daughter's key. Phillips turned up and went ballistic because I had let myself in. We got into a fight. Then Jessie arrived.'

'Are you denying you offered Phillips money?'

'Absolutely. I wouldn't give that prick a penny. I might have told him I wanted him to leave but that's it.'

'You knew of course that Miss Martin was investing twenty thousand pounds in Blackcurrant Farm?'

William's mouth dropped open. 'No! I didn't know that,' he said, looking shocked.

'Come, come, Mr Goode,' Watkins chastised him. 'Do you honestly expect us to believe that you didn't know?'

'I didn't,' William repeated. 'If I had, I would have gone to Jack.'

Watkins settled back, folding his arms. 'I know you helped him.'

William met Watkins' gaze. 'Why would I?'

'I think you regretted the affair with the hairdresser. I think you bitterly regretted the pain you caused your ex-wife. You were a prominent couple in a small town. I bet everybody had a field day when your dirty laundry got aired.'

'Is there a point to this?' William asked.

'My point is I think you felt guilty, guilty enough to risk everything to save your ex-wife from further humiliation. Phillips's arrest and subsequent trial would have had tongues wagging for years, wouldn't it?

'You wanted him out of the way so you could be reconciled with Miss Martin. You thought you'd dig around in Phillips's past and find something you could use as a lever against him to make him leave. Only you got more than you bargained for. I think you knew Miss Martin was going to invest in the farm. That's why you offered Phillips money. And then we arrived. You knew it was only a matter of time until we tied Phillips to the other jobs. I think you told him we were on to him and then you helped him get away. You had the means and the motive.'

'It's all circumstantial. Hell, my daughter could rip that to shreds and she's not even qualified yet.'

'I want the name of the client in Stebbingsford. I want details of every account you've ever opened and I'm going to check out your car and that of your secretary. If I find one piece of evidence that says you drove Phillips to Stebbingsford or that you paid him off, I will charge you with assisting an offender.'

'Owen Phillips is a lowlife and I'm glad he's gone but I didn't pay him a penny . . .'

Watkins leaned forward. 'I think you did and if I can prove it, I'll not only have you struck off so you can no longer practise law, Mr Goode, I'll have your liberty too.'

DECEMBER

Chapter Thirty-Five

Jessie had seen the penthouse flat at the Old Mill countless times via Phil Blunkett's sale particulars and on a personal tour with Phil himself, but never with her ex-husband's belongings scattered about. It felt odd, as if two parts of her existence that should be kept separate had collided.

The living room was large with glass down one side. A curved breakfast bar divided it from the stainless-steel kitchen. William was standing, with his back to her, looking out of the window as the last of the daylight faded away.

'You'd better not let Watkins catch you here.'

'He's leaving. They're not pressing charges.'

William wheeled round. He looked gaunt.

'Leaving?'

Jessie watched the relief flood into his face.

'Thank God.' He poured himself a large scotch and drank it quickly. 'How do you know?'

'He's just been to see me. The attempt at deception will be added to the other charges to be brought against Owen when they eventually track him down. As for you, he was confident Owen would corroborate his suspicions but, until then, he's got no proof.' Jessie paused. 'You did help him get away, didn't you?'

'Not wearing a wire, are you, Jess?'

Jessie laughed.

William stood his empty glass on the breakfast bar. 'Yes, I helped him to get away.'

Feeling for the arm of the leather sofa, Jessie sat down abruptly, her temples suddenly tight with fear. 'My God, Will! You could have gone to prison.'

There was a trace of a smile on his face. 'If Watkins is leaving, I'm in the clear.'

'For now,' Jessie cautioned.

William sobered. 'Yes, for now.'

'Why did you do it?'

'Owen said the whole town was pissing themselves about what happened with Chelsea. I couldn't let you be humiliated by him the way I was by her. I didn't want the police to arrest him either because I didn't want there to be a trial. I know what goes on, how rough it can be.' He met her gaze. 'I meant what I said in August. I was prepared to do whatever it took to win back your trust.'

Words failed her. William had risked everything to protect her: reputation, livelihood, liberty even, and he had done so without any indication that she would feel any differently towards him at the end of it. Jessie's head swam with the enormity of what he'd done.

'Thanks for not telling Hannah that the police were after me,' William said.

'I've had the devil's own job keeping her in Devon,' Jessie admitted.

'What did you tell everyone about Owen?'

'That we'd rowed and he'd left. Nothing else. Gossip is rife of course. The juiciest snippet I've heard is that you've been questioned over Owen's disappearance.'

'They think I bumped him off?!' William's expression betrayed a certain amount of pride that people thought he had the bottle.

Jessie nodded. 'How did you find out about him?'

Sitting down, William recounted his suspicions and where they'd led him.

Jessie listened, wide-eyed.

'When Hannah told me you were investing in the farm I guessed that was Owen's endgame.'

'So you offered him the money instead?'

'Yes.'

'Why couldn't the police trace the payment?'

'Because I never made it.'

Jessie looked at him in surprise. 'Then why did Owen leave?'

'Jack tipped me off that one of Owen's previous victims was coming to ID him. I offered Owen a way out.'

Jessie turned this over in her mind. 'So Owen knew he was going to get caught if he stayed?'

'Yes.'

Jessie frowned. 'If they find him, Owen will say you helped him.'

'Probably.' William was stoical.

Jessie let the pieces of the jigsaw fall into place. All this intrigue because she had refused to listen to a man she had known intimately for over half her life. Jessie felt ashamed. Ashamed that she had let herself be hoodwinked by Owen, ashamed that her former husband had felt the need to go to such extraordinary lengths to save her from herself: ashamed and touched. What more proof did she need of the depth of William's love for her?

Standing, she went to him. 'I don't know what to say.'

He stood. 'You don't have to say anything.'

'I was so mean to you,' she said.

'You were paying me back.'

'Not any more,' she whispered and opened her arms to him. 'I should have listened to you.'

Gratefully, William accepted her embrace. 'You loved him,' he said.

'I loved you first. When I think of what you did, the chances you took.' Pulling back, she touched his cheek. 'Jack said you could have got five years.'

'As a first offence, it wouldn't have been that much.'

'He said they'd have made an example of you. When I think of what might have happened.' She took a step back. 'You idiot!' She slapped his chest. 'What use would winning back my trust have been if you were locked up?'

'I didn't plan on getting caught,' he said cockily.

'They were close though?'

William nodded. 'A bit too close for comfort, if I'm honest.'

Suddenly cold at the thought of what could have happened, Jessie shivered.

'Hey!' William put his arms round her and held her close, stroking her back. 'Watkins is leaving. I'm safe.'

It felt good to be back in William's arms, Jessie decided. They were such strong arms: capable, safe.

A trial would have been hideous. Jessie cringed at the thought. William had known how the humiliation would crush her. While a part of her wanted Owen to pay for his crimes, the less noble part of her hoped that, should it happen, it would be a long way from Abbeyleigh.

A picture formed in her mind of William in prison garb. He might have assured her he didn't plan on getting caught but he couldn't tell her that he hadn't thought about it. William never did anything without thinking through the consequences. That he'd risked it all regardless was such an enormous gesture of love and yet no one could ever know of it.

She pressed a kiss to his cheek and then her lips found their way to his mouth. The kiss was passionate as he kissed her back. Breathless and a little shocked by its intensity, they backed away from one another. Neither spoke. Instead, they communicated with their eyes.

Can it be true?

Just the two of us.

We can have the future. You just have to believe. You do believe, don't you?

Yes.

Jessie threw herself back into William's arms, allowing his kisses to consume her, their heat blistering, and as Jessie returned fire with fire, she had never felt more alive. Finally, there was no guilt in admitting the truth to herself. She loved this man. And, after so long, the questions were gone. The moment of reckoning was here and Jessie had her answer. Their love was big enough to survive all that had happened to them.

As one, they edged towards the master bedroom, shedding their clothes as they went.

'Are you sure?'

'I've never been more sure of anything in my life.' She possessed his mouth, trying to convey the depth of her feelings through her kiss.

William fumbled with the zip of Jessie's dress and they both laughed at his ineptitude. Eventually, the dress was lost, his shirt and trousers too.

For a moment, as they stood by the bed semi-naked, the look they exchanged was one of shyness. It had been a long time since they'd last made love, longer still since they had belonged exclusively to one another. Had being with Chelsea changed him? Jessie wondered. Had being with Owen changed her?

'You're so beautiful, Jess,' William said as he reached out to brush Jessie's hair from her face. He let the back of his fingers drift along her collarbone, first one way and then the other as his gaze drank in the sight of her. 'I hardly dared hope,' he admitted as he took her in his arms.

He worked to unhook her bra. It was an art he had deftly mastered with one hand but today he used two, nerves making him clumsy.

Jessie was touched that he was nervous. He had doubted she would ever come back to him. The arrogant William of old who had often assumed too much was gone. In his place was the young man she had first fallen in love with: cocky, yes, but with an equal measure of humility. Over years of so much success so quickly that humility had been lost. Jessie rejoiced at its return. And yet it wasn't enough that they recapture the past. The past had been imperfect. She wanted the future, a new future, with the William of old.

Her bra was cast away and his fingers danced over her back as he pressed kisses to the rise of her breasts. Jessie sighed. There were no ghosts in this room. No former lovers to prey on their minds. Her body throbbed for William. 'I want you so much,' she said.

He broke away, his hands dropping from her hips. 'Say that again.'

'I want you so much.'

He smiled. 'I've yearned to hear you say that.'

He pulled her back into his arms, swinging her round, laughing into her hair before easing her back on to the bed. Knickers and boxer shorts were ripped off. The time for tenderness and patience was gone as desire took over. Together they rode the waves of passion fiercely, reclaiming each other, remembering, rejoicing.

Afterwards, exhausted but sated, they smiled at one another. William sought Jessie's hand. 'Now, that's what I call a scrape-me-off-the-ceiling orgasm.' He grinned.

Settling into his arms, Jessie gave a blissful sigh.

'I didn't intend for it to be so quick. I wanted to make love to you, to take my time, to know every inch of your body again.' He spoke with regret as he stroked her hair.

'We've got the rest of our lives to make love,' Jessie said, stroking his arm affectionately.

'Do you mean that?'

'I let you go once without a fight. I'm never going to do that again.'

'I'll never give you a reason to.'

Their kiss was gentle, their eyes full of tender promises and as contentment stole upon them they slept.

It was William who teased Jessie from sleep later by stroking the inside of her forearm. She gave him a dreamy smile.

'I had to wake you to make sure you weren't a figment of my imagination,' he admitted.

Laughing, Jessie nibbled his ear.

'Ow!'

Hooking her arm under her head, Jessie rolled on to her side. 'I want you to come home.' She watched the delight settle in his eyes.

'Are you sure?'

She nodded.

Trying and failing to curb his emotions, William pulled her to him. Jessie felt his tears fall against her temple. 'I've prayed, you'll never know how hard I've prayed,' he confessed. 'And I'm not even a believer.' He laughed. 'Well, maybe I am now my prayers have been answered.'

'We should ring Hannah. Tell her our news.'

'No, we should drive down and tell her in person,' William suggested. 'It'll be the best Christmas present we could give her. And why don't we treat ourselves too, after all we've been through this year? We could go back to Harbour Island in the Bahamas, spend Christmas there. Hannah could join us. What do you think?'

'It sounds perfect.' Jessie smiled.

'Being reunited with you in a borrowed flat doesn't seem quite right somehow. Being reunited in the Bahamas, with paradise just outside the door, sounds much more like it.'

She kissed him deeply, lingering in his embrace, the promise of all their tomorrows encapsulated in that one heady moment.

Easing back, she stroked his chest. 'I wanted to come and see you sooner.'

'After Walt suspended me, he banned you all from contacting me. Lynn told me.'

'Don't be too hard on Walt. The police were accusing you of all sorts, stealing from the partners, stealing from the clients. Walt didn't know who to believe. But that isn't why I stayed away. When I realised what a fool I'd been over Owen, I told Watkins I must have been mistaken about the money. He thought you'd threatened me to make me retract. I figured if I saw you again then I'd just make matters worse for you. It's been hell to stay away. I thought about ringing but what could I say until the investigation was over? Plus I was worried the police might be bugging your phone.'

'You don't have to explain yourself.'

'We'll go and see Walt together tomorrow and straighten everything out.'

'You think he'll reinstate me?'

Jessie kissed William's lips. 'We won't give him a choice. We'll get through this,' she assured him. 'And in twelve months' time this will all seem like a bad dream.'

William nodded. 'I love you, Jessie. I've never loved you more.'

'I love you too, darling.' She smiled. 'It's such a relief to admit it and not feel guilty.'

Later, after William had made good on his promise to make love to her, Jessie watched him sleep. *I want to matter to someone again*, she'd told Anne. By his selfless actions William had made it plain that Jessie could scarcely matter more. Her heart sang. She was in love again, with William, and the pearls looked every bit as beautiful as they had the first time around.

*

The following day William was reinstated, the holiday to the Bahamas was booked and, on Saturday, Jessie and William travelled down to Exeter to see Hannah.

'Daddy! Mum? What are you doing here? Is everything okay?'

'Everything's fine, sweetheart,' William said, hugging his daughter. 'Can we come in?'

Hannah led them through to the living room of the house she rented with three others. As she did so, William clasped Jessie's hand in his, giving it a squeeze. 'Your mother and I have something to tell you.' He watched Hannah's eyes widen. 'We've decided to give things another go.'

'You're getting back together?!' Hannah cried, looking from one to the other in astonishment.

'Yes, we are,' William said proudly. Jessie smiled and nodded.

'What about Owen?'

'Owen is out of my life,' Jessie said tersely. 'There are some things about Owen you don't know, things that I didn't know myself until a few weeks ago. Your father has saved me from making a dreadful mistake.' Jessie touched William's cheek. 'He's made me realise just how much I love him and how lucky I am that he loves me.'

'No,' William interjected quickly. 'I'm the lucky one.' He kissed Jessie's lips.

'Oh my God!' Hannah shrieked. 'You're really serious?! You're actually getting back together?!'

'Yes, darling,' William said.

'That's the best news ever,' Hannah exclaimed, bringing her hands up to her mouth in shock as she burst into tears.

'You're not supposed to cry,' William admonished, tears welling in his own eyes.

'I'm just so happy,' Hannah said. 'I always hoped you'd get back together but I didn't really believe it would happen.'

'Come here.' William beckoned Hannah and Jessie into his open arms. 'I want to hug the two most precious women in my life.' He pressed a kiss first to Hannah's head and then to Jessie's as he offered up a silent prayer of thanks. 'We've booked a holiday to the Bahamas to celebrate our reconciliation. We fly out on the seventeenth of December to Nassau and we'd like you to join us as soon as you can. Once you get there we'll travel on to Harbour Island and spend Christmas there.'

'It sounds wonderful,' Hannah said with a sob.

Humbled by her reaction, William eased Hannah back and took her face in his hands before gently wiping away her tears. 'I'm sorry for all the pain I've caused you. I will never do anything to hurt you or Mum again; you have my word.' He kissed her forehead. Then, stepping back, he clapped his hands together. 'Now then, why don't I treat my two favourite ladies to a champagne lunch to celebrate the fact we're a family again?'

*

The following Thursday morning, Hannah telephoned.

'Hello, Mum.'

'Hi, sweetheart.'

'Have you got the details of my flight to Nassau?'

'No, sorry. Your dad booked it.'

'He said he was going to email me the confirmation but I haven't received anything.'

'He's at court at the moment but I'll have a look in his inbox. If I see it, I'll forward it to you.'

'Thanks, Mum. I've got to go. I've got a lecture starting in a minute.'

Jessie hung up and went along to William's office. She quickly found the email confirming Hannah's flight and forwarded it on. It was only as Jessie was about to click out of William's inbox that she spotted the email from Chelsea. It had been received the previous afternoon. The envelope symbol was open, denoting William had read it.

With shaking fingers, Jessie called it up.

Darling,
Thank you for meeting me in Stebbingsford today. I could hardly wait for the day to arrive. I thought I would BURST. It was wonderful to see you again. You've been so generous. I know it's Marika's best interests you have at heart but money only takes us so far. Marika needs YOU and so do I. Is it so impossible? Think about it, sweetheart, please. Call me, we can talk things over. We were always so good together.
I LOVE U.
Chelsea

Stunned, Jessie searched for signs of a reply but found none. Had he rung her, instead? She reached for his diary. *Lunch with C at the White Hart, Stebbingsford, one o'clock*. Jessie slammed the diary shut.

They had made love in the shower on Wednesday morning and a few hours later he'd had lunch with Chelsea. She swallowed. My God, was it going to happen all over again? Had he already gone from her to Chelsea and back again?

Feeling sick, Jessie stumbled back to her own office. A quick scan through the database revealed that William had requested a cheque for three-quarters of the sale proceeds of the house in North Street. The cheque had been made payable to Miss C. Palmer. Jessie stared at the figures in amazement. Three-quarters of the proceeds. Why would he do that?

The telephone shook her from her thoughts. 'Yes?'

'There's a Mr Smith on the phone. He wants a conveyancing quote.'

'Okay.'

'Hello, Jessie.'

Jessie's world spun off its axis. Thinking she was going to faint, Jessie thrust her hand against the desk: cold, hard reality in a tilting universe. 'Owen?'

'Don't hang up, Jessie. Please don't hang up. Will you meet me? Now that I've finally plucked up the courage to ring you, I can hardly wait to see you.'

I could hardly wait for the day to arrive. I thought I would BURST.

Still reeling, Jessie simply said, 'Where?'

Chapter Thirty-Six

Jessie stared at the man who opened the door. His hair was short and blond. That threw her but his eyes were the stunning blue she remembered. Jessie had no doubt this man was Owen and yet at the same time he was a stranger.

'Thanks for coming.'

Drawing back her hand, Jessie slapped him across the face with all her might.

Owen rubbed his cheek, a rueful look on his face. 'I guess I deserved that.' He held the door open.

Jessie entered directly into an open-plan living room. The flat was spacious, all leather and chrome. In front of her was a picture window. She moved forward for a closer look, her heels clicking on the wooden floor.

Her eye was drawn to the balcony with its bold red railing and the river beyond, glittering in the pale winter sunshine. Tower Bridge stood proudly in view. She swiftly calculated the price of square footage in such a premium London location. The owner was a wealthy man.

'Is this yours?'

'Yes.'

She turned her gaze away from the mesmerising view and forced herself to look at him. 'Why did you call me?' she asked coldly.

'Because I wanted to explain.' He held his hands knotted in front of him. 'I didn't want to leave the way I did.'

'No, you were twenty grand short.'

'I wasn't going to take your money.'

'Easy to say now.'

'It must have been rough for you.' He looked contrite.

Jessie remained silent. Owen was the first to break eye contact.

'I'm sorry things worked out the way they did. It was unnecessary.' He stressed the last word, his tone sharp. 'If your bastard of an ex-husband hadn't interfered –'

'Thank goodness he did.'

'You don't understand,' Owen chided. 'I was going to stay.'

Jessie laughed. 'And you expect me to believe that?' Her tone was scathing.

Owen bent his head. 'I bet William's been pouring poison in your ear about me.'

'The police told me all I needed to know,' Jessie said sharply. 'If they catch you, I want you to tell them that you left because you thought you were being watched and that you drove yourself to the station.'

Owen's face hardened. 'You want me to leave William's name out of it? Why should I?'

'Because I'm asking you to.'

'Why do you care?'

'Because he's Hannah's father.'

Now it was Owen's turn to be scathing. 'We both know that's not the only reason. You're back with him, aren't you?'

Jessie lifted her chin, resolute in the face of Owen's contempt. 'William and I are flying to the Bahamas on the seventeenth of December for a second honeymoon.' At least they had been, but that was before she'd discovered he'd met Chelsea for lunch. Who knew where she stood now? Jessie forcefully pushed the tart from her mind. She would have to process the implications of what William had done when she was back in Abbeyleigh. She had more than enough to deal with right now.

Owen looked crushed. 'Because you want him or because you thought he'd be a safe pair of arms after me? Don't answer that,' he said quickly. 'I don't think I could bear to hear you say yes to either one.'

Jessie applauded him slowly. 'Very smooth, Owen, or whatever your name is.'

'I'll always be Owen with you.'

'Trouble is, I've had enough of your bullshit. If all you're going to do is lie to me some more . . .'

Agitated, Owen pushed his hands through his hair. 'It's not a lie. Christ, Jessie! I've missed you so much.'

He reached out for her but Jessie quickly backed away.

'I love you,' Owen continued. 'I've been in love with you from the first night we met. I didn't want to admit it to myself then and I don't now. But I haven't got a choice.' He sighed. 'I'd forgotten how love does that to you, narrows your options.' He poured himself a glass of red wine from an open bottle on the coffee table. 'Do you want a drink?'

'I haven't come to have a bloody drink with you.' Defiant, Jessie folded her arms. 'How have you got the gall to say you love me after what you tried to do?' She looked at him in disgust. 'I feel physically sick when I think of the things we did together. My skin crawls.'

'Oh Jessie, don't say that!' Owen begged. He slammed his glass down with such force the wine slopped on to the table. 'You have to listen to me,' he said sternly, catching hold of her arm. 'It's not a lie. I loved you. I still love you.' She tried to pull away but he tightened his grip, forcing her closer to him. 'You have to believe me, Jessie,' he begged. 'Why else would I risk this? I had to see you.'

Crushing her to him, Owen forced his mouth on to hers, effectively silencing her shocked cry. Then, wrapping his arms round her so that she could not escape his embrace, he continued to grind away at her mouth. When, at last, she let him inside, the violence ended and he was tender.

'Did that feel like a lie to you?' he asked, breathless when at last his mouth left hers.

'Let go of me, you bastard!' Jessie shouted, pummelling his chest as she wrenched herself free. Dragging the back of her hand across her mouth, she took a moment to regroup before slapping him again.

Owen turned away, hands locked behind his head in frustration. 'I didn't want it to be like this.'

Jessie laughed bitterly. 'How did you expect it to be?' she demanded. 'You targeted me at that wedding, didn't you? You already knew that I was separated from William, that I was comfortably off, that I lived in a fancy house on the edge of town. You groomed me.' Feeling the bile rise in her throat, Jessie brought her hand up to her mouth, fighting to keep her composure. 'I couldn't believe how lucky I'd been to find someone who was so in tune with me. Now I know luck didn't come into it. You moulded yourself into everything I needed you to be and, like a sucker, I fell for it.'

Cowed under her gaze, Owen drained his glass of wine and poured himself another. His voice was tearful as he said, 'You've got it all wrong. I can't bear that you think everything between us was a lie. It wasn't even meant to be you.'

'What?'

He waved the bottle at her. 'When I came to Abbeyleigh, you weren't the mark. Lydia Coates was. When I met you at the Sturridge wedding, I knew I had to see you again. I was in Abbeyleigh to do a job, but all that became secondary to finding ways to spend time with you.' He began to pace the room.

'How can I believe anything you say?' Jessie asked quietly, unnerved by how much she desperately wanted to believe him.

'Why would I ask you here, risk you bringing the police with you, if all I was going to do was lie to you some more?'

'Why tell the truth now?' Jessie rejoined. 'Where does it get you?' Drained, she sank on to one of the cream leather armchairs.

'It gets me a clear conscience,' he replied. 'You see, I need you to know how it was. I thought I could walk away from you like I have the others.' Owen met her gaze. 'I was wrong. A year ago I didn't even have a conscience, let alone a desire for it to be clear. Look what you've done to me!'

Jessie found the directness of Owen's stare unsettling and turned instead to look at the river. 'So it was only after the wedding I became your "mark"?'

'I didn't know what I was doing . . .'

Jessie threw him a withering look. 'From what I've been told, Owen, you knew exactly what you were doing.'

'I know it looks bad but you have to understand I'd never let anyone divert me from a job before. I didn't know what to do.' He took a slug of wine. 'I thought about leaving but I couldn't.

'In my head, I reached a compromise; my time in Abbeyleigh wouldn't be wasted because I'd set the job up with you instead of Lydia. It was a sort of dare to myself. Would I go through with it? Even while I was putting all the pieces in place, I wasn't sure how things would turn out.'

'But now you know for certain you wouldn't have stolen my money. Funny that.'

Owen scowled. 'Part of me wanted to take your money and pretend you were no different to the rest,' he said harshly. He took another drink. 'The prospect of staying terrified me. People like me . . . I've never led a normal life, but what I had with you was as close as I've ever come and I loved you, Jessie. I didn't want to leave. When I saw how upset you were after William offered me money to go, that's when I made up my mind to stay. I'd been bouncing back and forth between the two options but suddenly I knew I had to stay. I was going to let the deal go through and then a few months later I was going to say the boys had relented and pay you back in full with interest.'

'You'd have continued to run Blackcurrant Farm?'

'Absolutely.'

'As Owen Phillips?'

'Yes.'

'And all the time you'd have had this place and Christ knows how much money tucked away.'

'I planned to tell you I'd come up on the lottery.'

'I guess one more lie wouldn't have made much difference,' she said coldly.

'The last lie.'

'Was there any of the real you in Owen?'

'God, yes.' He stood his glass and the bottle on the dining table, and moved to kneel in front of her. 'When I was with you, *I* wanted to be with you; for the first time ever I wanted to be myself.' Tentatively, he placed his hands on Jessie's knees. 'It was important that you liked me for me.'

'I didn't know the first thing about you,' Jessie said dismissively, batting his hands away and crossing her legs.

'And I hated that.' He sat back on his haunches. 'I'd lie awake trying to figure out how I could tell you the truth and not disgust you. I came close a couple of times but I always lost my nerve. I couldn't bear to have you look at me the way you're looking at me now.' He gestured to her face and stood.

Jessie also stood. 'You ran because you were about to get caught and we'll never know, if it had been a few days later, if my money would have gone with you,' she said brusquely.

Owen's face hardened and he swiped his wine glass off the table, sending it crashing to the floor, before grabbing her shoulders. 'How many times do I have to say it? I was pretending with the others. I was a bastard with the others. It wasn't like that with you.' He lifted a hand to her cheek. 'I don't think you realise what it took for me to ring you today. How desperate I was!'

'What do you want from me, Owen, sympathy?' Jessie asked, bewildered. 'You sobbed in my arms at the death of an aunt who didn't exist. I felt your pain so keenly I cried with you. God, how you must have been laughing inside.'

'You felt my pain because I was projecting pain. A lifetime ago, I lost someone who meant everything to me. I was crying for her.' He hung his head.

'Your mother?'

'My mother?' He spat the words, his face contorting with hatred.

'Then who?' Jessie demanded.

'Stella was my sister.' He turned away and began to pace once more.

'And you can use her death like that?' Jessie asked, incredulous.

'I'm not proud of myself,' he snapped. 'All my life I've been a shit. Living down to expectations. My mother's son.' He pulled a face and took a swig straight from the bottle of wine.

Jessie's brow furrowed as she watched him. She recognised flashes of the Owen she had known. But where did this anger, this hatred, come from? 'What happened to you?'

'I don't want to talk about it.' He took the bottle with him as he walked to the window.

'Tough,' Jessie replied. 'I want to talk about it. You told me the person I was with was the real you. But I don't know what makes you tick. I thought I did. I thought: young boy, lost his mother early in life, working hard to make something of himself, striving to make her proud of him.'

Owen's laugh was bitter. 'You couldn't have been more wrong.'

'Then put me right.'

'Why?' He turned to her. 'I didn't ask you here to give you my life story. I just wanted you to know that what we had wasn't a lie.'

'But words are easy for you, Owen,' Jessie retaliated. 'You've been lying to me ever since we met. Give me something real. Give me your story.'

He glowered. 'I don't talk about that with anyone.'

'Then isn't it time you did? You didn't tell me the truth before because you didn't know how to. Well, I know the worst now. I know you were on the brink of swindling me. Give me the rest. Give me the reasons. What turns an intelligent, handsome young man into a lying, cheating bastard? I want to know.'

'I was born that way.'

'Is your mother really dead?'

'I hope so.'

'Why do you hate her so much?'

'I don't want her to become a part of us,' Owen said quietly, nursing the bottle in his arms.

Jessie looked at him in amazement. 'There is no us, not any more.'

'But there could be,' Owen said eagerly. Standing the bottle down on the floor, he strode across to her, taking her hands in his. 'We could start over, somewhere new. You and me, Jessie. Think about it. We could leave all this shit behind.'

Jessie pulled her hands away. 'Nice try, Owen, but you don't get to change the subject that easily. Tell me about your mother.'

'No.'

'What did she do to you that was so terrible?'

'Please, Jessie. Leave it!'

'Your father then, does he run a restaurant?'

Owen shook his head.

'What does he do?'

'I don't know.' Owen sounded exasperated. Then, throwing her a baleful stare, he said, 'You want it? You want all of it? My sordid tale?'

'Yes,' Jessie said.

'My mother was an addict. Practically a child herself when she gave birth to me. She turned tricks to fund her habit. My father was probably one of her punters. I never knew him, neither did she. Satisfied?

'We don't all get to have perfect childhoods with a family that loves us. You were incredibly lucky. Hannah was incredibly lucky. There are more people like me out there than there are like you. It's why I've never wanted to have kids. Why perpetuate the cycle?' Taking up the bottle of wine once more, Owen threw himself into an armchair and, scowling, hooked his leg over the arm.

'I can understand how your mother's lifestyle could have scarred you –' Jessie began.

'Lifestyle?' Owen repeated. 'You make it sound like a bloody option she chose at school. You can't know what it's like.' He pointed the bottle at her. 'You can't get inside my head. You wouldn't want to.' He strode back to the window. Several minutes passed as he stared out, occasionally swigging from the bottle.

'My sister, Stella, was two years younger than me. Same mother, different fathers. Our schooling was sporadic, and there was never enough food in the house so we were always hungry. Stella and I shared a bedroom. There wasn't much in it except a mattress on the floor. Mum didn't really believe in toys and games. Why waste her precious money on things like that when she could feed her habit instead? She should never have been allowed to have kids. She couldn't look after herself, let alone anyone else.

'She took the handle off the inside of our bedroom door so that when we got on her nerves she could shove us inside. We couldn't get out again until she remembered to open the door. Sometimes she didn't remember for days.'

Shocked, Jessie said, 'What happened if one of you needed the toilet?'

Owen turned to face her. 'There was a cat litter tray in the corner.'

Jessie felt sick.

Closing her eyes, she brought her hand up to her mouth. It was all too awful to contemplate.

'What's the matter, Jessie? Have you heard enough? Haven't got the stomach for it? Are you wishing you'd never asked me? Would you rather not know about the shithole I grew up in or how Stella and me were sent to every bloody school in the district and how we were bullied in every fucking one of them? Don't you want to know about all the times I wished I was dead?'

Jessie met his gaze. Not so long ago she wouldn't have believed a word Owen said but now she had only to look into his eyes to know all that he was telling her was true. Stripped bare and lacking in artifice, those eyes were now a window into his tortured soul. At last, the real man was revealed to her.

Distraught, Jessie imagined Hannah in Owen's shoes and wanted to weep for everything this traumatised little boy and his sister had gone through.

'I'm so sorry,' Jessie said, softly.

'I didn't want you to know,' he said wretchedly. 'I only wanted you to see the image, the nice guy. I needed you to love me so much.'

'And I did.' She went to put her arms round him, tears swimming in her eyes, but Owen backed away.

'You should go,' he said coldly. 'I shouldn't have rung you.'

Jessie stood her ground. 'I'm not going to pretend that any of this is easy to listen to,' she said earnestly. 'But I'm not going anywhere until you tell me the rest.'

He turned back to look at the river. Several minutes passed before he started to speak once more. 'Men came and went. I was thirteen when I noticed the latest taking an interest in Stella. She was growing up fast, starting to change, you know?' He looked over his shoulder.

Jessie nodded.

'I had always known that we had to get out. I'd been stealing money whenever I had the chance. Stella and I hid it under our mattress. It wasn't much and I knew it wouldn't get us far but when I saw him looking at Stella like that I knew we couldn't wait any longer.' He moved to sit on the arm of the sofa. 'We didn't own many clothes but we put on as many as we could, stuffed the cash I'd stolen into our pockets and when the chance came we scarpered.

'We slept rough for a few nights but I hadn't really thought it through. It was November and it was so cold. Stella got a hacking cough and I remember thinking I'd saved her from him only to kill her myself on the streets.

'Things were pretty desperate when I met Mrs Simmons at a soup kitchen. She arranged for us to be taken in by a Christian charity. We refused to tell them our real names because we didn't want to risk getting sent home again. They couldn't process us properly without that information so we ended up staying in their hostel and Mr and Mrs Simmons took us under their wing. Mrs Simmons was a librarian and she started giving us extra lessons after school to help us catch up. Mr Simmons ran a restaurant and on Saturdays he'd let us help out in exchange for pocket money.' Owen smiled. 'They were good people. We settled into a routine. It was unconventional but then our whole lives had been unconventional. Eventually, when we were both old enough to leave school, Mr Simmons offered us jobs in his restaurant. He agreed to train me as a chef and Stella worked as a waitress. We'd moved out of the hostel by then and Mr and Mrs Simmons were letting us stay in the flat above the restaurant.

'Tessa was a waitress. She was the first girl I'd ever fallen in love with. You were the second by the way.' He threw Jessie a look. 'We started seeing one another and it quickly got serious. For me, anyway.' He gave a hollow laugh. 'You'd have thought I'd have been smarter after all we'd been through but I was so naïve. Tessa used to laugh when I'd tell her how much I loved her. She'd laugh, too, when I'd tell her about my plans to own my own restaurant one day. She said I should have bigger dreams.

'Deep down I knew she didn't care for me the way I did about her. But I was so scared of losing her that it made me possessive, edgy and jealous. She accused me of making her feel claustrophobic. I didn't even know what that meant. I had to look it up in a dictionary. It took forever because I thought it started with "c-l-o".' Owen laughed at himself. 'I couldn't have done a better job of pushing Tessa into another man's arms if I'd tried.

'I was devastated though when it happened. What made it worse was that I walked in on them together in my flat. Tessa and Mr Simmons. A week later, Stella was killed in a hit-and-run accident and life lost all meaning for me.' He pulled back a chair and sat at the table.

'I was in a world of pain and I needed to escape. I'd seen Mum lose herself in oblivion a million times so I scored some coke and tried it. Mrs Simmons quickly realised what was happening. She told her husband. He was so petrified that I was going to tell his wife his dirty little secret that he threw me out. I didn't care about anything or anyone by that stage. I told the pair of them to go to hell. They'd saved Stella and me, took us in, fed us, educated us, set us up with jobs and that was how I repaid them.'

The look of self-hatred on Owen's face pulled at Jessie's heart.

'I already knew drugs weren't the answer. I decided to get clean and start over. The guy I used to score from knew a guy who could get hold of forged papers so I went to him. Pretty soon I had a new name. Then I stuck my finger down on a map and found a new town.'

Jessie joined Owen at the table.

'The first woman, a widow, owned a restaurant. I introduced myself as Mitch Johnson. There was no plan. I just didn't want to be me any more. Mitch was free from the baggage. I could make him whatever I wanted him to be. Nobody could hurt Mitch.'

'That man in Wales,' Jessie recalled. 'He called you that.'

Owen nodded. 'He wasn't mistaken. We did work together for a while.' Owen stroked the wine bottle. 'I took over in the kitchen and helped with the books. Eventually the widow and I became lovers. I suggested we open another restaurant in a neighbouring town. She agreed. I've tried to remember when it first occurred to me to take her money.' He shrugged. 'The opportunity was there and bam.' Owen banged his hand down on the table, making Jessie jump. 'I took it. She'd left me in charge of the second restaurant and we needed some building work done. She gave me a bundle of cash so I could pay the builders and I left the same night. And that's how it started.'

'Were you in love with her?' Jessie asked.

'Love? No. I told you, it was only you and Tessa that I've ever loved. I did care about her though.'

Jessie raised her eyebrows.

'I hurt her. I don't dispute that. But, in time, the second restaurant would easily have covered the money I took and, without me, she would never have had the nerve to open it.'

'That's no excuse for her pain.'

'There was no excuse for my pain,' Owen said coldly.

'How many have there been?'

'Too many.'

It was a glib answer and they both knew it.

'In order to be able to afford a place like this, you must have been swindling far bigger sums than the twenty thousand you were going to take from me, or not, as the case may be,' Jessie said.

'I took the money from the jobs and I invested it in property that I did up and sold on. This flat is the culmination of those property developments.'

'Did you feel guilty?'

Owen swallowed and picked at the label on the wine bottle. 'The first time. After that, leaving was easy. I didn't see the woman I'd been with. I saw my mother. I saw Tessa. I didn't think I'd ever fall in love again and that made me capable of doing the things I did without fear. I had choices. I accept that. I loved the life. You may find that repugnant, but there it is. Jealousy, fear, shame. Those emotions had ruled my life for so long. Now those words ceased to be in my vocabulary. I was insulated from them. I was . . .' He paused. 'Untouchable.' He smiled ruefully. 'And then I met you.' His voice became gentle. 'And you blew me away. You were smart and beautiful but, more than that, I found your capacity to trust, after what the dickhead had done to you, incredible. You inspired me.

'You didn't want revenge on the world. You just wanted to start over and find love with someone new. You believed in a right to happiness that I gave up on when I was a kid.' He laced his fingers together over the top of the wine bottle and rested his chin on them. 'I started to think about settling down. I'd never questioned my life before. It was what I did and I was fine with it. But all of a sudden it didn't seem that great any more. And then I'd lose my nerve. I'd think that me and happiness were never meant to go together and I'd go back to Plan A and hate myself for being weak. I'd change my mind a hundred times a day. She means nothing, I could leave tomorrow. She means everything, I can never leave. In the end, it wasn't my choice.'

Jessie realised that in the gloom of the winter's afternoon she could barely make out Owen's face. Rain or sleet was being blown against the glass and the river looked angry.

He was a criminal who had hurt and used countless women. Then she remembered the man she had held sobbing in her arms. Stella had been real. Tessa had been real. The restaurant had been real. He had changed the context but the people and the places had been real, a parallel universe.

Owen lit a lamp on the nearby bookcase and their reflections were thrown eerily back at them. He moved to stand in front of her.

'With you I felt fear for the first time in a long time; that was how much you meant to me. I felt fear every time you walked out the door and went to work with him. You made me care again and sometimes I hated you for it.

'I began to think you could save me from myself. I guess, in a way, you did.' He cupped her face in his hand. 'I'm giving it all up, you see. Going straight. Without you, that probably wouldn't have happened. But I couldn't leave without seeing you again.' There was a catch in his voice. 'You'll never know how much I've missed you. How many tears I've shed thinking about what I've put you through. You worked your magic better than either of us could ever have imagined.' He stroked her cheek. 'You turned me into a blasted pearl diver, Jessie, and the truth is, I'm drowning without you.'

Jessie watched the hurt pour from his eyes.

'You truly loved me?' she whispered, standing.

He nodded. 'I never lied to you about that.'

'I kept remembering the way you held me, the things you said. I found it so hard to believe that when you made love to me it meant nothing to you.' Jessie's voice cracked.

'It meant everything to me, darling.' Owen's own voice was ragged with emotion as he swept Jessie into his arms, his embrace suffocatingly tight. 'I love you. I always have.' He paused. 'I always will.'

Afraid to let go and confront the feelings that were threatening to swamp her, Jessie clung to him. 'I wanted so much to believe,' she admitted.

Edging back, Owen lifted her face so that he could look into her eyes. 'When I touched you, when I kissed you, when I held you and made love to you, it was me doing those things. For real.'

He moved closer, as if to kiss her, but Jessie backed away.

'I can't take this in.'

'You need time to think about what I've said.'

Jessie's eyes narrowed. 'Why didn't you just go?'

'Because I want you to start over with me.'

'What?' Jessie exclaimed. 'Are you mad?'

'I've never been more serious.'

'I couldn't possibly.'

'Why not?'

'Because my life is in Abbeyleigh.'

'With him,' Owen said bitterly. 'He lied to you before. What makes you think it would be different this time?'

'The words "glass houses" and "stones" come to mind,' Jessie said tartly. Then she remembered Chelsea's email.

'Let's not make this about him,' Owen pleaded. 'Let it be about us. You loved me, Jessie. A part of you still does. I can see it in your eyes. So, be with me. Do you think I'd have told you everything if I didn't want us to spend the rest of our lives together?' he asked beseechingly. 'I tried to forget you. I tried to convince myself I could walk away but you kept tugging at my heart. I'm a selfish man. I want it all and I want you to share it with me in Canada.'

'Canada?'

'I have French-Canadian citizenship. I set it up years ago. An escape route, in case I ever needed it. I'm going to make a new life for myself in Quebec City. The plan is to buy a restaurant on the Grande Allée, French Canada's very own Champs-Élysées. I've got a room booked at Le Château Frontenac. I'm going to stay there for a couple of weeks and then find a place to rent until the right restaurant comes on the market.

'Come with me. Quebec City was made for lovers and you'll be seeing it at a magical time of year. With its cobbled streets and city walls, it's one of the most stunning cities in North America. They have a lot of snow in the winter but they also have a wonderful spring, a hot summer and the most magnificent autumn you'll ever see. It's a different world, Jessie. It could be our world.'

Jessie could feel Owen's enthusiasm engulfing her.

He clutched her hand. 'If you want to practise law, you can, or you can be an equal partner with me in the business. Whatever you want to do is fine by me. Just say you'll come with me.' Owen's eyes shone with passion.

Her heart in free fall, Jessie knew she had to put some space between them.

'You can't do this to me,' she said, pulling her hand away. 'It's not fair. I've spent the past few weeks hating you.'

'And now?'

'And now, I don't know how to feel.'

Owen levelled his gaze at her. 'I'm the same man you loved.' He gripped her shoulders. 'The same man,' he implored. 'Except now there are no secrets between us. I've told you the truth and that's all I'll ever give you from now on. I swear, on my life. Look into your heart, Jessie. You love me, too. Admit it. You love me, too. I know you do. Say it, please!'

'Maybe I do,' she responded. 'But you're asking me to throw my whole life up in the air.'

'Take that leap in the dark, Jessie.' Owen's voice was cajoling. 'Just think of the alternative, life with the dickhead. How long do you think it will be before you and William slip back into the same old routines? Death by boredom before you're fifty. That's if he doesn't cheat on you again. Don't short-change yourself. Don't settle for the little life with William when you could have everything with me.' He put his arms round her, his lips crushing hers.

The kiss made Jessie's heart leap and then hang between beats. She was going to do something she'd regret if she stayed much longer. 'I have to go,' she said, pulling free.

Owen held fast to her hand. 'Before you do, tell me you love me.'

Jessie hesitated. The little life Owen had described with William beckoned. It had been everything she'd desired that morning. But that was before the re-emergence of Chelsea, before the reappearance of Owen.

He squeezed her hand. 'Tell me.'

'I love you,' she whispered.

It was true. Knowing he hadn't lied about his feelings, knowing she hadn't been wrong to love him back left Jessie feeling vindicated. Clean. Her heart soared as Owen held her tightly once more, bending his head to hers.

'But . . .' she said, backing away.

Nodding, Owen pressed his fingers first to his lips and then to hers. 'You need time. I understand. I'll contact you again before I leave, I promise. All I ask is that you think about what I've said.' He stroked her cheek with the back of his hand. 'Don't close your heart to me, Jessie. Not yet.'

*

He hadn't even tried to hide it. As the train hurtled through the darkness back to Abbeyleigh, Jessie thought about William and Chelsea. He had risked everything to win Jessie back and yet he seemed prepared to throw it all away again. He had even given Hannah his word he would never hurt either of them. So why was this happening now?

She looked at her reflection in the train window. Unless there had been a mistake and Marika *was* his. It made perfect sense. The lunch date, the email, the cheque. And, if William had fathered a child, Jessie knew he'd want an active part in its upbringing. And with the child would come the mother. William and Chelsea reunited would leave Jessie free to go to Canada. Jessie's heart beat a little faster. It was possible. It was more than possible.

With a growing excitement, Jessie pictured herself helping Owen set up the restaurant while she practised her schoolgirl French. Then, once she felt confident in the language, she could apply to whatever the French-Canadian version of the Law Society was to find out what qualifications she would need to practise law in Quebec. Thank goodness she had been made a partner at Smith Mathers. That would look good on her CV.

She thought about the people in her life she could admit the truth to: her father; Hannah and Anne, definitely; William, possibly; Jack and Sue, absolutely not. Hannah. Jessie sobered. Her daughter had been so excited about the prospect of the reconciliation she would be devastated to discover it was off again. But, if William was planning on building a new life for himself with Chelsea and Marika, surely Hannah couldn't begrudge Jessie a new life too?

As the train pulled into Abbeyleigh station, Jessie's mind whirled. Get a divorce, get a promotion, get a life. They had been her three New Year's resolutions. Well, she'd got the divorce and the promotion. Who would have guessed the new life might mean a move to Canada?

Chapter Thirty-Seven

William was singing along to an Ed Sheeran CD in the kitchen when he heard Jessie's key in the lock. Slinging a tea towel over his shoulder, he went to greet her.

'Hi, sweetheart. I called but your mobile was off.' He tried to kiss her lips but she turned her head. He grazed her cheek instead. 'Everything okay?'

'Long day,' Jessie muttered, head down as she took off her boots. 'I've got a splitting headache.'

'You look a bit pale. New client, wasn't it? London?'

'That's right.' She followed him into the kitchen. 'You cooking?'

He nodded. 'Nothing special. I'll set it going now you're home and I'll get you some pills for your head.'

Jessie gave him a wan smile. 'I think I'll have a bath.'

*

William poured two mugs of tea and carried them upstairs. He knocked on the door with his elbow before entering. To his disappointment, Jessie was already immersed in foamy water.

'I thought this might help.' He stood the mug on the corner of the bath.

'Thanks.' She sank down as if to shield herself from his eyes.

William sat on the closed seat of the toilet, frowning as he sipped his tea. Perhaps she just didn't want to give him the wrong idea. She had a headache after all.

'What happened to your mobile?'

'Battery's dead.' She didn't meet his eyes.

'Are you sure everything's okay?'

She swallowed a mouthful of tea and put the mug down. Waves erupted across the bath. The water, rising and falling, lapped at her breasts. William steadfastly averted his eyes, concentrating on her face instead.

'I know you met Chelsea for lunch. I found her email so don't bother denying it. Hannah wanted details of her flight to Nassau. I went to look it up.'

Christ almighty! He put his mug down and quickly knelt beside the bath, feeling sick as he reached for her arm. Instantly she withdrew it, sinking it into the water. 'It isn't what you think. I would never do that to you again.'

'You gave her a cheque for a small fortune. She wants to start over.'

'That may be what she wants but it isn't what I want,' William said. 'And it's not going to happen.'

'When were you going to tell me the baby's yours?'

'What?'

'You heard me.'

She rose majestically from the bath, water streaming down her lithe body, bubbles clinging to her arms, her breasts, the rise of her stomach. She snatched a towel from over his shoulder and swaddled herself in it before stepping from the bath. Watery footprints led back to the bedroom.

'She isn't mine.'

'You gave Chelsea three-quarters of the proceeds.' Jessie threw the words over her shoulder.

Taking hold of her arm, William halted her progress, turning her to face him. 'Marika isn't mine,' he said firmly. 'I felt sorry for Chelsea. She's had it rough since I left her.'

'My heart bleeds.' Jessie snatched her arm away.

'She made a dreadful mistake and it's something she's going to have to live with for the rest of her life. I know how that feels and I'm not going to punish her for it any more. The money will buy her a fresh start.'

'Did you sleep with her?'

'No.'

'Did you want to?'

'What do you expect me to say, Jessie?' William asked, exasperated. 'Yes, I found her attractive. Yes, it would have been easy to go to bed with her. Did I? No. I didn't tell you about the meeting because I was worried you'd misinterpret it. I wanted to pay her the money and now I've done that and she's gone.'

Jessie looked sceptical.

William caught hold of her hand. 'I told Chelsea I didn't want to build a life with her. I told her the only woman I wanted was you. She's out of our lives for good, I swear.'

As he looked at her, William was shocked to see something akin to anger burning in Jessie's eyes. It was almost as though she had wanted him to tell her something different. But that was madness. She'd had a long day, she wasn't feeling well and to top it all she'd been carrying around a thousand questions about their future without being able to press him for answers. He needed to cut her some slack.

'It's going to be okay, darling,' he whispered as he tenderly kissed her temple. 'We love each other. Nothing can spoil that.'

*

Jessie watched the clouds play hide-and-seek with the moon. She'd managed to eat a little of the meal William had cooked. Then they'd watched television: some documentary about space she hadn't even tried to follow. As soon as she could, she'd gone to bed, pleading her headache. Hours later he had tiptoed into the room and crawled into bed beside her while she pretended to sleep.

It had been that easy. Like the lie about her mobile. One lie begets another lie and another. She could see how Owen and even William had succumbed: a lie to get them what they wanted, another to smooth over a problem, a lie to cover a lie. What harm could they do? But it was as though the lies were building blocks and put together they became a wall, imprisoning the liar inside.

And so we've come full circle, Jessie thought. *It's as though William and I are married but this time I'm the one who's being unfaithful, in my mind at least.* Sighing, Jessie rubbed her temples. The fake headache had become real.

Was this how William felt, torn? Wanting and loving both Chelsea and me. Jessie tried to remind herself that Owen was a criminal and, as such, there could be no future with him. Equally, she made herself relive the fact that William had taken another woman into her bed and then welcomed her home a few hours later as if nothing had happened. It made no difference. Owen was not all bad and her marriage to William had been suffocating long before he'd even kissed the tart.

Jessie turned on her side. William looked so at peace lying there. She put her hand on his chest, felt his heart beating. He had told her the truth about Chelsea, of that she had no doubt. William loved her. However much at that moment Jessie might wish he didn't; however much she had wanted him to be Marika's father, if only for a moment. Anything to save her from the agonising decision she now had to make.

Chapter Thirty-Eight

On Monday afternoon Jessie received a text from Owen.

'Can you meet me outside the Northey?'

Hastily rearranging her commitments, Jessie ran towards the high street. A red Vauxhall sat outside the Northey Hotel. It flashed its lights as she approached. Opening the door, Jessie threw herself into the passenger seat. 'Are you mad?' she exclaimed, her heart beating wildly. 'What the hell are you doing here? Do you want to get caught?'

'I'm being careful,' Owen replied, tugging down the peak of his baseball cap. 'We need to talk. Can we go to The Lodge?'

Jessie hesitated. William had a case in Stebbingsford Crown Court. He was unlikely to be home much before five o'clock. She checked her watch. It was only two.

'Okay.'

*

Taking her by the hand, Owen led Jessie into the sitting room. 'You've had time now to think about what I said to you. I need to know if you can find it in your heart to forgive me, Jessie, to trust me again.'

'I believe you when you say you loved me.'

'Love,' he corrected quickly. He took her hands in his. 'If you let me into your life again, I swear I will never let you down.' From his jacket he drew out an envelope. 'An early Christmas present,' he said.

Inside the envelope was an Air Canada ticket to Quebec City. The departure date was the seventeenth of December. The same day she was due to fly to Nassau with William.

'I'm flying out tonight,' Owen said. He laid his hands on her shoulders. 'I know what I'm asking of you. I do. But follow your heart, Jessie. I'm not going to push you,' he added quickly. 'If you decide to use the ticket, we can plan our future from there. If you don't, then I'll know you chose him and I won't contact you again.'

It was a thought Jessie could hardly bear. 'I wish it didn't have to be this way.'

She had walked around in a fog of confusion since her meeting with Owen. William had feared she was sickening for something.

'I wish someone didn't have to get hurt. I love you both. I want to be with you both.'

Owen's kisses halted her flow of words. His hands were suddenly everywhere. Under his touch, her heart spun like a top.

'Owen,' she protested, backing away. 'We can't.'

He grabbed her to him. 'This may be the last chance we get. Please, let me show you how I really feel about you,' he begged.

Weakened by desire, Jessie nodded. She wanted him so much: the real Owen. Why fight it?

They kissed their way from the sitting room to the bedroom. But, on the threshold of the bedroom, her ardour cooled. Memories of the room, of the lies, seemed to come at her from all sides. Moreover, this was now the room she shared, once more, with William.

Owen's lips were on her neck, his hands working their way inside her jumper. 'I love you, Jessie,' he whispered.

She felt her pulse quicken. Her hands traced a path across Owen's strong shoulders. She imagined herself naked in his arms: his lips on her skin, hot kisses teasing and arousing her, his hands bunching in her hair as her own hands moved lower.

The bed was reaching out to embrace them and welcome them back. She imagined Owen taking her there, touching the very core of her being. At its height their lovemaking would become a thing of beauty. They would both feel it, revel in it and be humbled by it.

Owen's mouth closed over hers, then he stepped back, tugging his shirt over his head and casting it aside. He looked every bit as good as Jessie remembered. Her heart leapt with desire.

Grabbing her hand, Owen ventured further into the room. Jessie glanced at the bed with its confection of pillows. William had had Chelsea in this room. It was only right that she should take Owen here and close the circle of deceit once and for all, whatever the outcome.

Will William know, just by looking at me, that I've been unfaithful? she wondered. *Should I tell him the truth straight away or mislead him as he once misled me? Do I join the merry-go-round of deceit?* And then she checked herself, realising she was already on it.

She dropped her gaze to the floor. Could the circle of deceit ever be closed? By taking Owen here wasn't she guilty of perpetuating that deceit? He did it so I did it so he'll do it again and so will I. Were they condemned to dance this dance forever? Concentric circles holding them captive for the rest of their lives?

'Owen . . .' She backed away, already bereft as his hands fell away from her.

'Jessie –' He reached for her again, more roughly this time.

'No!'

'Because it's here?'

'Not just because it's here,' she said quietly.

'You've chosen him,' Owen said, eyes downcast.

'No.'

She watched the hope leap in his eyes. 'Then come away with me tonight. Let's not wait!'

'I won't be rushed, Owen. This is too important.'

He leaned in to kiss her neck. 'Let me show you what you mean to me . . .'

She moved away and pressed her fingers to his eager lips. 'If we are ever to get beyond what you did, if we are ever to have a future together, I need to know the real you and I yearn for that. But if I choose you then I have to finish with William first. If I sleep with you here behind his back, I'm behaving no better than he did with her. You must see that?'

Owen shook his head as he cupped her face in his hand.

Jessie turned her head to kiss his palm. 'I love you,' she whispered. 'And I want you more than I can say.' Jessie felt as if she were drowning in the ocean of his eyes. 'But someone has to break the cycle. Someone has to be the better person.'

'Why does that person have to be you?' Owen asked, his voice cracking with emotion.

'Because I have to be true to myself. You once told me that's all you'd ever want from me.'

'I did say that, didn't I?' he admitted ruefully. 'Can a guy change his mind?'

It was dark when Jessie woke. She knew instinctively that Owen had gone. His envelope stood on the dressing table. Through her tears she read the words he'd written on the back.

> *I hate goodbyes, Jessie. 'I love you' doesn't say enough. You mean the world to me. Don't settle for the little life with him. Take that leap in the dark with me. Use the ticket, please . . .*
> *Until Quebec.*
> *Love Owen*

Jessie stowed the envelope in the top drawer of her dressing table before jumping into the shower just as William's voice floated up the stairs. Encased in steam, Jessie shouted a greeting as she scrubbed herself, dreading that some trace of Owen might remain.

William opened the shower door. Water sprayed his blue shirt, darkening it to navy. He laughed and kissed her soapy shoulder. 'Case dismissed,' he said with a chuckle. 'You are looking at a very happy man. I got you a present for the holiday.' He waved a gaily wrapped package in the air. 'It'll be waiting for you when you get out. Of course I could always join you.' He tugged at his tie.

Jessie kissed his lips but in a perfunctory rather than inviting way. 'I'm finished,' she said. 'Sorry.'

He accepted the knock-back good-naturedly and handed her a towel. 'I'm going to hide your present,' he told her with a mischievous grin.

Five minutes later, Jessie tied the belt on her silk robe. The bedroom was deserted. Her eyes were drawn to the dressing table. The top drawer was open. The present wedged amongst her make-up. Owen's envelope was gone.

She found William sitting in the kitchen, a bottle of scotch on the table, an empty glass beside it. He flipped the envelope back and forth in his fingers.

'When were you going to tell me the bastard was back?' he asked calmly.

'I-I . . .' Jessie stammered.

'Maybe you weren't going to tell me at all,' he pondered, pouring himself another drink. 'Maybe you were just going to fuck off to Canada with him.' He tossed the scotch back. 'Nah, you wouldn't do that, would you? The man's a criminal. He lied to you. He used you. You wouldn't give him the time of day, would you?' He made as if to rip the envelope in two.

'Don't!' Her anguished cry startled them both.

'Jessie?' Bewildered, William stood, the chair crashing to the floor behind him.

'He told me the truth about himself.'

'The man wouldn't know the truth if he fell over it,' William said contemptuously. 'He knows about the reconciliation, doesn't he?' William's shoulders hunched. 'You told him.' He made it sound like a betrayal.

Maybe it was.

'Yes.' She swallowed nervously.

'That's why the ticket is for the same date.'

Jessie nodded.

'He wants you to choose between us.'

'Yes.'

'And you told him to go to hell, didn't you?' William's eyes bored into hers. 'Didn't you?' he repeated menacingly.

'No. I . . .' Words failed her. How could she go on without hurting him? But how could she stop? He had to know it all now, the possibility that there would be no reconciliation. Everything.

'When did you hear from him?' William asked suspiciously.

Jessie could see the muscle in his cheek working. Frantically, she searched for an answer that wouldn't ignite his fury. 'A few days ago. I went to see him. I needed to talk to him,' Jessie said. 'To find out why.'

'Was talk all you did?' William's face was full of questioning concern but there was hope in his eyes. Hope that she was about to dispel the fear that had begun to gnaw away at him.

Jessie tried to park her face in neutral but one look at him told her it was already too late. She couldn't hide her guilt.

Leaping forward, William grabbed her shoulders and shook her. 'How could you?'

The disgust was plain in his voice. His fingers bit into her arms but Jessie didn't complain. What right had she to complain? He'd told her about Chelsea in this room. She wondered if she'd looked as he did now: desolate, destroyed.

'I'm sorry,' she said ineffectually.

'By Christ, I wish I had slept with Chelsea now!' he raged.

'I didn't sleep with him,' she said quietly.

'Then why do you look so guilty?' he demanded.

'Because I wanted Owen to make love to me and isn't that as bad? I love him, you see.' Jessie saw William flinch. 'I love you both.'

'Love? You don't know the meaning of the word.'

She smarted under his gaze, his contempt almost too much for her to bear.

'When were you planning on telling me?' he asked coldly. 'At the airport? Is that what you were going to do, Jess? Were you going to let me believe I had everything and then snatch it away at the last minute? I know I hurt you but, Christ, I didn't think you had it in you to be so cruel.'

'You make it sound planned. It wasn't,' Jessie said, beginning to cry. 'I only got the ticket this . . .' Her voice trailed away but the damage was already done.

'He was here.' The words fell, cold and hard, from William's compressed lips. He flung the envelope across the kitchen. 'This morning or this afternoon?' His stare was icy and then he blinked. A terrible realisation dawning. 'How far did it go before you stopped it? Did he have his tongue down your throat and his hand up your top or had you already undressed for him?' William shook his head. 'Were you down here or upstairs?' His face hardened. 'You were in our bedroom with him, weren't you?'

Jessie began to sob. 'I'm sorry.'

William folded his arms, unmoved by her tears. 'Is that why you were in the shower? Were you washing the smell of him off your skin? Hoping I wouldn't notice?' He began to pace. '"The little life with him"?' William said coldly. 'Is that what you think we have? It was enough for me. Why couldn't it have been enough for you? How could you let me dream the way I have? How could you kiss me and tell me you loved me? How could you deceive me like that?'

Horribly familiar, the words were daggers to her heart. She'd asked herself the same things, night after sleepless night, when he'd told her about Chelsea. She had thrown similar questions at Owen about his lies and now here was William throwing them back at her.

'I did it because I shared the dream, because I do love you,' she said desperately. 'The last thing I wanted was to hurt you.' The words sounded hollow even to her.

That's what they'd all said. Maybe they'd all meant it but it hadn't stopped any of them doing the things that had caused the hurt in the first place, had it? They had all willingly climbed aboard that merry-go-round.

'Are you sure about that?' he asked. 'You let me carry on believing, Jess, and that was cruel. However much I hurt you before, I didn't deserve that.'

Seeing the tears in his eyes, she reached out to him but he knocked her hand away.

'I didn't want it to be like this.'

'How did you think it was going to be?' he asked tersely. 'Breaking hearts is a messy business.'

'I don't even know yet what I'm going to do,' she said. 'I need time to think. I don't want to make a mistake I'm going to regret for the rest of my life. I don't want to choose between you, but I must.'

'Well, maybe I can make the choice a little easier for you by telling you to go to hell.'

'You don't mean that,' she said.

'Don't I?' He pushed past her.

'Where are you going?'

'To pack a bag and catch an earlier flight to Nassau. I don't even want to be in the same country as you right now.'

Chapter Thirty-Nine

Three days later, swaddled in her thickest winter coat, Jessie walked briskly through Abbey Wood.

Look into your heart, Owen had said.

And she had. Endlessly. But how could anyone choose between two men they loved? Jessie stamped her feet against the cold. She could be happy with either man. But could she be more happy with one? She would never know. She had loved and hated them both in the past year. How could she trust her feelings now? Yet somehow she knew she must.

A pearl diver to the end, Jessie knew she had to have it all. She wouldn't be satisfied with anything less. But, in order to hold those pearls again, she first had to find the courage to dive into the water.

She listened to the rooks calling to one another, their harsh cries rending the icy air. It was true: the answer had been in her heart all along. She had just been too afraid to admit it. For it would take a rare courage to make the relationship with him work. Their life together wouldn't be easy, but then whose life was? There would be times when she would stop and wonder what would have happened if she had chosen a different path. But if she was lucky those times would be few and he would grant her the space to come to terms with them. There would be changes to be embraced, compromises to be made, but the one thing she was certain of was that the good times with him would eclipse the bad.

Her mind was alive with plans as she made her way with renewed vigour back to The Lodge. Released from the paralysis of indecision, Jessie felt happy for the first time in days.

As she walked back down the lane, however, her thoughts turned to the heart she would be breaking and she moderated her stride. He would live in her heart forever and she knew a piece of her would die without his love but it had to be this way. Would he understand? She doubted it. Would he forgive her? She hoped so, in time. To be with him would mean letting the best thing that had ever happened to her slip through her fingers and she wasn't prepared to let that happen. Some pearls carried too high a price.

Once inside, Jessie poured her feelings on to paper. Then, once the envelopes were sealed, she allowed her tears to fall for the end of her life with one man before her heart leapt with joy at the beginning of her life with the other.

'I've got two letters,' she told the FedEx representative later. 'One to go to Quebec City in Canada, one to go to Nassau in the Bahamas.'

Chapter Forty

In Nassau the temperature was a comfortable twenty-two degrees centigrade.

As William approached, the Bahamian receptionist fingered one of her colourful braids and smiled. 'Did you enjoy your diving trip?'

'It was fantastic,' William replied.

She handed him his key. 'A letter arrived for you by courier this morning.'

'Thanks.' William glanced at the handwriting and his heart sank.

Once in his room, he threw down his key. His hair was still wet from the sea and his body ached. He didn't know what he wanted more: a cool shower or something to eat and drink. What he certainly didn't want to do was read her letter. Why spoil a good day? He let the envelope fall on to the table.

It was late by the time he returned to his room. A warm flower-scented breeze greeted him as he stepped on to the balcony. He sat in one of the loungers and took a swig from his bottle of beer. *This is paradise*, he thought.

Beneath him, lost in the velvety blackness, he could hear the surf. It was paradise indeed and he was alone. He retrieved the envelope and let it rest on the lounger in front of him while he drained his beer, figuring it would be better to be slightly drunk when he read what she had to say.

There was just enough light coming from his room to make out her writing. He read the letter through twice and then closed his eyes against the tears that were threatening to fall.

Chapter Forty-One

In Quebec City it was snowing again but nothing could dampen Owen's enthusiasm. He had just finished viewing a building he had seen a hundred times or more in his dreams: Stella's.

The realtor had taken refuge in his car but Owen remained on the terrace staring up at the majestic building that had started its life as home to a wealthy timber merchant and his family. Over time it had evolved into a restaurant with bed-and-breakfast accommodation on the upper storeys but it nevertheless retained the grandeur of its early years. There was a dignity in the way the windows, large and bold, stared out at the street. Equal in number, they surrounded the substantial front door with elegant symmetry, like so many well-turned-out children hanging on to the skirts of their mother.

A narrow path had been cleared across the terrace. On either side, several days' snowfall had been heaped. Owen kicked out at the latest covering with his booted foot. A large flagstone glistened wet beneath. He calculated there was space for three tables on either side of the path. It was perfect.

Returning to the street, he studied the five curved stone steps that led up from the Grande Allée to the terrace. The centre of the bottom two steps had been worn away over time and now dipped like a lady curtseying.

He turned and saw the realtor click his seat belt into place, eager to return to his centrally heated office. Owen waved in acknowledgement.

Back at the hotel, Owen brushed himself off before collecting his key. It had been a great day. He'd found a gem of a place and the owner wanted a quick sale. He ached to tell Jessie the good news.

'Monsieur.' He turned at the receptionist's voice. 'There's a letter for you.'

Owen recognised Jessie's handwriting immediately but steeled himself against ripping the envelope open until he got to his room. Once there, he set the envelope on the table while he poured himself a drink. He smiled as he read her letter.

Chapter Forty-Two

A thousand thoughts collided within her as Jessie waited for the door to open. She wondered how she looked. It had been a long journey. She'd done her best with hair and make-up, but was it enough? She wanted to look beautiful for him.

As the door opened, she gave him a shy smile, uncertain how she would be received. But before she had the chance to deliver the speech she had been rehearsing all the way across the Atlantic, William swept her into his arms, hugging her and swinging her round, laughing as he did so.

'I can't believe you're really here.'

'Didn't you get my letter?' Jessie asked, dismayed.

William set her down. 'I got your letter. I just didn't dare believe it, not until you were standing in front of me and now you're here and I still don't believe it.' He grinned.

Jessie was humbled by his smile. She'd been so scared by his parting words in the kitchen. Fearful that, despite her resolving that he was the one, he might not want her any more. She could imagine the torment her indecision had put him through and her heart swelled with love. William was everything and she had so nearly let him go.

Her carefully planned speech had flown from her mind but what did words matter when they could say so much more with their eyes and their lips? As he took her in his arms, Jessie rejoiced at the nearness of him.

Holding each other tightly, they let the fears they had harboured slowly dissolve. And when they kissed it was as though they had never been parted. As William bent his head to kiss her neck, Jessie's hand sailed into his hair, anchoring him against her.

'You're the most precious thing in the world to me,' William whispered. 'I love you so much.'

'I love you too.' Was it possible to only know the true depth of love after pain? Jessie wondered. She edged back. 'There's . . . there's something I need to say,' she stammered as bits of the speech returned to her. 'I asked Walt to get me an assistant and he agreed. The money I'm generating from Phil's developments will more than cover it. What I'm trying to say is, it won't be like it was before. I know, in the past, at uni and working towards my partnership, I let myself get blinkered. I lost sight of the fact that I needed a life. I won't let that happen again. With the help I'll be getting and with Marie to help you, we should be able to work fewer hours. I thought we could both go down to a four-day week and buy that weekend place in Devon you always wanted.'

William bent his head to Jessie's. 'We'll look for a place as soon as we get back.'

Their kisses had an edge to them now. Jessie craved him and one look told her William felt the same. His fingers teased their way beneath her top, stroking her belly and a dozen butterflies took flight inside her. Seeking his mouth, Jessie melted into him, the heat of their passion fusing them together.

Suddenly, he removed his body from hers and a cool hand gripped Jessie's heart.

'What about Owen?' William asked.

'It's over.'

'You've told him that?'

'Yes.'

'Will he accept it?'

'Yes.'

'How can you be sure?'

'I made it plain that there's no going back. He'll respect that.'

Jessie pictured her letter to Owen.

> *Dear Owen,*
> *This is the hardest letter I have ever had to write. I won't be coming to Canada to start a new life with you. I've thought long and hard about what I should do. I'm a wreck who hasn't eaten for days or slept for nights.*
>
> *Know that I love you and that I always will. There is a special place in my heart that belongs to you but when all is said and done,*

it's not enough. I am honoured that you opened up to me. I know how hard it was for you to do that. Please know that nothing you told me that day has led me to the decision I am making now. It's simply that when I looked into my heart, as you told me to do, it was William I found there.

My love for him isn't a better love, a deeper or stronger love. But it has a durability built upon the years we have spent together, the problems we have endured, the sacrifices we have made for each other. You called my life with him a little life. You may be right but it's a life I am content with.

You offered me excitement, a brand new country, a different way of living and I was sorely tempted. I hate that you gave me back my heart only for me to turn round and break yours. It was never my intention to hurt you. If you asked me how I reached this decision, I would simply say: a love has to stand strong against all the world can throw at it. When everything was falling apart, William stood resolute, while your first instinct was to run. I understand why, of course I do, and I know you came back for me but it's not enough. Canada is a big country. Embrace it and all the opportunities your life there will bring you. Know that you are the man you've always wanted to be. You don't need artifice or deceit. Be yourself. When life comes knocking meet it head on, the good and the bad. And when that little boy inside you tells you to run and hide, don't listen to him.

You needed him once to survive but you don't need him anymore. You're strong enough to cope. The love we shared you'll feel again with someone new, however impossible that might seem to you right now. One day someone will come bouncing into your life full of energy and promise and you'll want nothing more than to spend all of your tomorrows with her.

I will think of you often under Canada's big skies and I shall smile when I remember you. I hope you smile when you remember me too. Love is finding a home for your heart. Find yours and be happy.

Love, Jessie

Jessie turned as William stroked her cheek.

'I hope you're right because I won't share you. So help me, I can't share you. I've done that for too long.'

'You don't have to be afraid,' Jessie said as she covered his hands with her own. 'When I looked into my heart, darling, it was you I found there, no one else. I'm so sorry for what I put you through but I had to be sure. For all our sakes, I had to be sure.'

He nodded then turned away as if the intensity of the moment was too much for him. Jessie trailed her fingers down his arm until their hands met.

'I ordered champagne,' William said. 'In anticipation of your arrival. We should drink a toast.'

As he opened the champagne and poured it, Jessie took in the splendour of the suite for the first time. An overflowing fruit basket stood on a table by the window. The pages of her letter were scattered around it as if he had only recently put them down.

Her hand lingered on his as she took the crystal flute from him. 'To us,' she said.

'To us,' he echoed.

She took a sip, giggling at the exuberant bubbles and he laughed with her. Setting her glass down, she nestled against him with a sigh.

His face lit up as he smiled at her.

Jessie knew then, without a shadow of a doubt, that she had made the right decision. William's smile alone was worth the trip. She had never been more in love. He was every bit as intoxicating to her as the champagne and it was a glorious feeling. She might be a long way from all that was familiar but, in every way that mattered, Jessie had come home.

'Why me and not him?'

'I told you in the letter.'

'I need to hear you say the words.'

Jessie held his gaze. 'While I had feelings for you both, I realised that, for me at least, love is synonymous with trust. I can't give myself fully to a person unless I know their commitment is as strong as mine. You betrayed me but I made it possible. If our relationship had been all it should have been you wouldn't have strayed. I know that. And by your actions since, you've more than proved your love for me.

'When things got tight for Owen, he ran. He came back and wanted to make a life with me. And I believed him and was dazzled by him. But his first instinct was to run. When things got rough for you, you stayed to fight against everything and everyone that was conspiring against you, even though I made it almost impossible for you.

'You risked everything to save me from further heartache. It was reckless and foolhardy and quite possibly the nicest thing you've ever done because you did it without looking for the kickback. I'm here and I will love you forever because you never ran away.'

William handed her back her champagne flute. A diamond ring sparkled at the bottom of the glass: his grandmother's ring. Jessie looked up at him through misty eyes.

'Will you marry me . . . again?' William asked earnestly.

'Yes, darling. I will.'

William's kiss was fierce and Jessie's heart soared. Soon they would make love, with paradise just outside the door and tomorrow they would start over, embracing their new life together: pearl divers reunited.

Reviews are crucial to all novelists whether they be established stars or just starting out.

If you would like to, you may leave an honest, short review of *The Flower Seller* on Amazon or Goodreads.

If you would like to find out more about me and my books:

Please visit my website at www.ellieholmesauthor.co.uk or follow me on:

Pinterest: https://uk.pinterest.com/EllieHWriter/

Twitter: @EllieHWriter

Facebook: http://www.facebook.com/EllieHWriter

If you would like to be among the first to hear about my latest releases I invite you to join Ellie's Readers' Group by signing up to my mailing list using the link below. If you sign up via this link I will send you a bonus chapter *The Flower Seller Six Months On* for you to enjoy as a thank you.

http://www.ellieholmesauthor.com/sixmonthson

Love, Ellie x

Acknowledgements

To my family for always believing in me. To my best friend, Simon and to Vicky, Sheila and John for keeping the faith.

To my beta readers: Mel, Angela, Lesley C, Lesley K and Janet – your insightful comments were invaluable.

To everyone at Frinton Writers' Group and The Third Thursday Group – your support and encouragement has been greatly appreciated.

To the wonderful Broo Doherty of DHH Literary Agency – thank you for making me a better writer.

To my writing friends – thank you for your kind words and sage advice over the years. In particular Liz Harris, Fenella Miller, Nicola Cornick, Maria McCarthy, Maureen Lee, Jackie Marchant and Phillipa Ashley.

To everyone at the Romantic Novelists' Association.

Finally to everyone who has made this book a reality including the incomparable Tim Inman, the wonderful George Edgeller, my fabulous cover designer Berni Stevens and my fantastic editor Jennie Roman.

Lightning Source UK Ltd.
Milton Keynes UK
UKOW02f1145020616

275453UK00002B/11/P